Choosing THE BEST

Victor J. Ratzlaff

CHOOSING THE BEST

ISBN: 978-1-4866-0472-2

Word Alive Press
131 Cordite Road, Winnipeg, MB R3W 1S1
www.wordalivepress.ca

Library and Archives Canada Cataloguing in Publication

Ratzlaff, Victor J. (Victor James), 1935-, author
Choosing the Best / Victor J. Ratzlaff.

Issued in print and electronic formats.
ISBN 978-1-4866-0472-2 (pbk.).--ISBN 978-1-4866-0473-9 (pdf).--
ISBN 978-1-4866-0474-6 (html).--ISBN 978-1-4866-0475-3 (epub)

I. Title.

PS8635.A898U55 2014 C813'.6 C2014-901402-3
C2014-901403-1

I would like to dedicate this book to my wife.
Thank you for all your support and help with editing.

Chapter One

September 1956

ONLY TWO WEEKS INTO HER SECOND YEAR AT THE UNIVERSITY OF Alberta, Iris Marten's faith was being rocked like never before. She knew from last year's students that Professor Blake Grimshaw was tough on students with religious faith. Some called him the Grim Reaper. Iris felt he took almost sadistic delight in demolishing students' belief systems. If he were more overtly harsh on students, he could just be overlooked. But he came across as a caring, considerate man. He displayed a kind of logic that was hard to fight. He used very subtle sarcasm laced with humour. Iris found that before she could mount some kind of internal defense to what he was saying, he had her arguing against herself. He'd stealthily sowed the seeds of doubt and the seeds had taken root before she knew what had happened.

She remembered one of Grimshaw's lectures in the first week when he began by talking about how similar the basic learning and emotions of chimpanzees and other primates were to humans. He also talked of early human development and the study of artifacts, including tools of these early hominids living a million years ago, and how they weren't any more advanced than present-day apes and other primates. Iris had wondered where, in all this, Adam and Eve lived and breathed.

Walking to her Psychology 20 class, Iris's mind slid back in time to high school in Badger Creek, Saskatchewan. Her father Peter, a science teacher, had become the principal of the Christian School. That was in spite of nearly being kicked out of the community because his scientific views of creation differed from the school's. Now he and his second wife, Trish, were living happily in that small prairie town and the issues of creation had receded somewhat.

Peter had been concerned that the university experience would be a big challenge to Iris's faith. Back in September 1955, she felt confident her belief in Christianity would remain solid. A year and a half later, she wasn't so sure.

Maybe she'd have done better had she followed her father's suggestion and gone to the University of Saskatoon, but she doubted their psychology faculty would be any more sparing on Christian beliefs. She had wanted to attend university in Alberta, as she'd heard the medical school had a very good reputation. She hoped that was still the case.

Iris had settled into her seat several minutes before Professor Grimshaw strolled into the classroom. He had an intelligent face with a benign smile but sharp, piercing eyes. He started out talking about some of Freud's ideas on personality structures. He spoke of *ego* and *superego* as concepts accepted by the whole scientific community.

"Thanks to great luminaries like Sigmund Freud, we can better understand the effect religion plays in our society. You see, the natural drives in human life like hunger and sex need some control so we can all get along. We call this control *superego*. But, as most of you've noticed, religion has utilized this superego for its own purposes. Religion has done this by using guilt and fear. When humans are exposed to an overactive superego, guilt results."

He hurried on with breathless enthusiasm. "Now if there were just human-to-human relationships at stake, the pressure to comply to ruling forces wouldn't be too bad, but religionists developed the bright idea that if there were a higher authority like some invisible supreme being, religious leaders could get greater compliance and so achieve better control of the populace. They needed to fashion a god. So they did."

Some young girl stuck up her hand. "Is guilt such a bad thing? It makes us feel badly about doing stupid or selfish things."

The Professor smiled. "True, but when we're stuck with too heavy a load of guilt, as when we have a god saying it's wrong, then we have the basis of most psychological illnesses like depression, chronic anxiety, obsessive-compulsive disorder, and so on."

A young fellow who Iris thought was a Christian asked, "Why do you so easily rule out a real god just because you developed some psychological theories?"

"I'm just saying that we might now understand how the god idea got started," Grimshaw said. "These days, we know a lot more about how the universe came to be and how life evolved and we don't need to have a god to explain nature. In the pre-science period, the mysteries of life became too hard to understand without a supreme being who made it all happen. So they fashioned a god to meet their needs. Now you see, maybe God didn't make man; man made God."

Iris's mind was in a jumble and her stomach felt tight as she left the classroom, finished school for the day. She headed back to Mrs. Malloch's home, where she boarded, and flopped on her bed with a groan. What was she to think about the Bible and its teachings? Was it written by a bunch of guilt-driven religious freaks beguiled by their mentors and using guile to control readers with guilt and fear? Whenever she tried to read her Bible now, she found herself thinking that, maybe, man made God.

✦ ✦ ✦

The sun was setting behind some dark clouds as Iris stepped onto the city bus that had just screeched to a stop in front of her. The stench of diesel smoke assaulted her senses as she tossed her coins into the receptacle. There were some things about a city she could do without. The day she'd own a car couldn't come soon enough. As she settled into a seat by herself, she thought about the party she was going to. It was billed as a welcome party for Varsity Christian Fellowship. She'd attended quite a few of the organization's meetings last year. Some of the speakers were encouraging and even inspiring, but on many occasions, she had gone away empty. Many of the speakers seemed to be from a very different world than the one she faced. She felt many of the students at VCF were in education, engineering, or arts faculties where faith wasn't pummeled as much. Her discussions with these Christian students made her feel they were quite comfortable with their faith and they weren't being jarred by their educational experience.

As the bus droned on toward the campus, Iris reflected on her first year. She'd taken Psychology 10. It was quite basic, nothing too challenging or controversial from the female professor. Botany 10 was a delight, taught by a very kind man who obviously loved plants. An organic evolution zealot taught Zoology 10. His main mission on earth, it seemed, was to dissuade all students from any religious view of creation and to preach the gospel of Darwin with the same vehemence as the Apostle Paul preached the Christian gospel. She knew that this prof's teaching seriously troubled many of the Christian students. Since she already had it figured that God could've used evolution to bring about all life forms, she wasn't too much bothered. Still, she had to admit that the heavy emphasis on all life developing through pure chance mechanisms did depress her. Couldn't these professors at least recognize the possible existence of a supernatural being? No, to do that would be unscientific!

The bus stopped near St. Stephen's College. She had to hike another couple of blocks to the Students Union building. She looked down at her slacks and sweater as she entered the room for the party. Her clothes were casual, nothing to draw too much attention. She wasn't interested in making an impression with male students—not like many of the other girls there, Iris noted. She was attending university to become a doctor, not marry one.

The room was filling up rapidly. She didn't spot anyone she knew. Seeing an empty table, she took a seat, surveying the crowd for anyone who might join her. A moment later, a group of guys and a girl approached. A tall, nice-looking guy with blond hair and blue eyes smiled and asked if it would be okay to join her. Iris invited them to sit.

"I'm Tim Branton, and these are my fellow theology students, Jane Hilton, George Black, and Bill Trealov," the tall guy said smoothly.

Iris nodded and smiled. "I'm Iris Marten."

When they all got settled, Iris asked, "Have you been to these meetings before? It's the first time I've seen theology students here."

"No," Jane said. "We've never been here before. We thought we should see what happens at these meetings since we're studying church history this year—investigate all branches of Christendom, you know."

Tim laughed. "We haven't been to any campus Christian-based group before. Since some of us will be going into some aspect of church ministry, we thought we should acquaint ourselves with all kinds of Christian groups to round off our experience."

Iris didn't know if she liked being in one of these groups that rounded off their experience. The singing began. She noticed that the theology students didn't join the singing, she assumed because the choruses and hymns were unfamiliar. After announcements about the coming season, a speaker stepped up to give a talk. He was a fourth-year education student who spoke humourously about campus life and ended up exhorting the students to maintain a disciplined life of prayer and Bible reading. Iris noticed that the theology students were looking bored and rolling their eyes at one another.

Several more songs were sung and, following a flute and piano duet, the meeting ended. Tim came around to Iris and asked where she was attending church. Iris said, "I haven't really made up my mind. Last year, I attended a Baptist church down town, but as a student my needs weren't being met."

"Why don't you come to a small coffee party our faculty is having next Thursday? Eight pm in the Dean's office of St. Stephen's College. It's for theology students and their friends. I'm sure you'd like it."

"That sounds interesting. I'll let you know if you give me a phone number I can call."

"Here's mine," Tim said, his blue eyes flashing. He scribbled his number on a piece of paper and gave it to her. Iris could feel her heart speed up as he did so. He was certainly handsome—and charming.

Chapter Two

When the city bus dropped her off and left a noxious diesel cloud in its wake, Iris noticed it was nearly 10 o'clock. She ran up the steps of her boarding house, unlocked the door, and stepped inside. She could hear some rock music coming from Lucy's room. She must be studying—a bit unusual for Lucy, she thought. She knocked on the door to wish her goodnight.

"Come in."

When Iris poked her head in, Lucy raised her eyebrows and said sarcastically, "Well, it's a relief to find my socialite friend safely back, when I've slaved over my courses as usual."

"Ah, baloney, Lucy. That's the greatest distortion of the truth I've heard since my last Grimshaw class."

Lucy giggled. "Just sit down and tell me how it went tonight."

Iris kicked off her loafers and plopped on Lucy's cot, pulling her feet under her. "Well, it was a bit different than I expected. There was the usual singing, games, and speeches, but what I found interesting was the people who ended up at my table. They were a bunch of theology students."

"What's so odd about that?"

"It's unusual for theologs to show up at VCF. They seem to think our group is too conservative and simple-minded."

"Were there any nice-looking guys in the group?"

"You would have to be interested in that! As a matter of fact, there was a neat-looking fellow. He even invited me to attend a coffee party of his faculty next week." Iris blushed.

"You *are* going to attend, aren't you?"

"I suppose I might. It would give me a chance to get a different view of Christianity. I think I need a fresh look." Iris gazed up at the ceiling as if she could discern what to do from the paint flaws and cracks.

"Why bother looking for another view?" Lucy swiveled on her chair and tossed her lovely blond hair out of her eyes. "You're way too serious about religion and philosophy. Just charm that handsome guy like I know you can, and have some fun. Get some colour into your life."

"You mean like you do?" Iris smirked.

"Well, not quite like I did last year. I almost lost a year of education. Way too much social life! But you know me. I just have to have my social fixes to keep me going. I just need to keep my head and not get snarled up with any more guys. You'd better take a lesson from my failures." Lucy laughed as she proffered the advice, but Iris could see she was quite serious.

"Lucy, I am not about to lose my virginity or my chances of getting into medicine just for a little fun with a guy. You needn't worry your pretty head about that."

✦ ✦ ✦

Tim Branton drove his new red VW onto his quiet Edmonton street. The car was a gift from his father when Tim got his bachelor's degree. Stopping in front of his house, he got out, opened the heavy wooden gate, and then drove up near their garage. He whistled a happy tune while running up the steps, one of the songs sung from the VCF party. He couldn't get that experience out of his head. The image of that pre-med girl was the main reason. She was sharp and a real looker. He couldn't wait to see her again at the faculty welcome event.

The Brantons lived in an older but elegant home near the university. A six-foot-high stone wall breeched by a huge wooden gate with a stone arch lent some privacy. Huge elm trees snugged up to the house on either side gave the home a very comfortable and picturesque appearance.

As Tim walked through the door, he could smell fresh baking. Briefcase still in his hand, he walked into the kitchen where his mother was unloading another tray of cinnamon rolls.

"Who are all these for? Dad and I have large appetites for cinnamon rolls, but that's a bit much."

"For sure. You don't need all those calories. If you're real nice to me today, I'll give you three. The rest go to Women's Aid at our church. Hopefully some hungry street people will get to enjoy cinnamon buns."

"Mom, you are so kind and generous. I hope some of those virtues rub off on me."

"I think they already have. The profession you have chosen means you're heading in the right direction."

"I hope so. I've got to make some phone calls before supper." Tim grabbed one of the cinnamon rolls and took a huge bite as he headed to his room.

Yanking the curtains back, he looked out of his window as he chewed. Tim focused a moment on the familiar back yard with the mature vegetable garden. He thought of his mother. She was still pretty, although he could see some greying of her light brown hair and quite a few lines showed around her eyes and mouth. She was compassionate, always thinking of the poor and disadvantaged. She was a good organizer, too. Her leadership in her church's Women's Aid was impressive. Tim could see that his talents and interests followed more that of his mother than his father.

Tim wiped his mouth with his hand and flopped down on his bed. He traced a ceiling crack with his eyes. His dad was a whole other matter! He knew he wasn't as close to his father as he was to his mother. Dad was just too busy with his all-important life! Yet he admired him in many ways. He was a very successful banker and he was the chair of many important committees at the bank. He also had amazing social skills. Their home was often the centre of committee meetings tied in with some drinks and lunches. His father loved organizing parties. At all of these events, he was the catalyst for social interactions. Tim had noticed that his father particularly loved to chat with women. His ability to engage women in energetic, titillating conversation was truly a gift. In Tim's mind, his father's interactions skirted all too closely to being flirtatious. Tim wondered how many husbands felt uncomfortable with his father's brand of socializing. Somehow, his father seemed to get away with it. Tim envied him.

A more important consideration for Tim was the question whether his mother was disturbed by her husband's social life. Tim thought so. He had watched his mother during some of these parties and noticed that her eyes would look stressed and her smile contrived. He could sense she wasn't happy when Dad really got going.

"Supper!" His mother's call jolted him out of his reverie. He'd forgotten to do his phoning to organize the students' portion of the coming Theology Faculty Club social. Well, he'd have to do it after supper. He could hear his father's voice. He'd come home on time. His other last-minute chats with clients or staff usually got everyone home late.

"Hi Tim," his father, Frank Branton, said as Tim entered the dining room. "How did things go with your courses? Are you getting what you hoped for?"

"Yeah, I think so. I'm enjoying the course on church history. The one on church governance is practical, I guess, but not very exciting."

"It's not too late to switch to economics or commerce. Someday you'll have a family and a need to find a house. If I'm not mistaken, most clergy struggle all their lives trying to find decent accommodation for their families. They're always at the mercy of whatever money their chintzy church members think they want to toss toward their pastor."

"Dad, you're so sure I've made the wrong choice. I think that if we're generous with our lives, we'll not be in need."

"Sounds like your mother's philosophy. Nice guys don't always win, you know."

"Let's get this meal underway, guys." Alice, Tim's mother, sighed deeply wishing she could clear this problem away for good. "We've been over this issue too many times before."

After the food was passed around, Tim's father cleared his throat. "You know I'm not against generosity. Just because I don't attend church too often doesn't mean I don't buy into Jesus' idea of being kind to your neighbour. I think I'm just as good a citizen as most of the folk who regularly attend our church. One way of being a good citizen is to provide well for your family."

Tim rolled his eyes. "Please pass the butter."

✦ ✦ ✦

Once again, Iris was riding in the smelly bus, this time heading for St. Stephen's College for the theology faculty's coffee party. She hoped she hadn't offended Tim Branton too much. He'd offered to give her a ride, but she'd refused since she didn't like the idea of getting too tight with him at this point. She needed to keep her focus on getting into medicine. She wondered about her motives for getting involved with the theologs at all. She supposed it was to explore another take on Christianity than the one she'd grown up with. Her dad and Trish would worry if they knew what she was doing. Well, that was just too bad. She needed to carve out her own path in life.

As Iris made her way to St. Stephen's, she glanced at her skirt and sweater. Nothing very fancy; in fact, fairly plain. But that was okay. Keeping with the plan! The weather was great for the time of year—first part of October. The leaves were mostly yellow and many had fallen. There was a delightful musty odour of decomposing leaves. As she walked up the steps into the old, venerable building, she sensed the thousands of other students who had preceded her. The sound of loud chatting and robust laughter greeted her as she stepped through the door of the Dean's office.

"There you are. I sure hoped you could make it." Tim walked quickly toward her with a big smile. He took her hand and drew her toward a small group of senior-looking ladies and gentlemen. "Let me introduce you to some of the faculty." Tim politely did the introduction and after some light chatting about Iris's university studies, Tim said, "Come, let me get you something to drink and then I want to introduce you to some of the students."

Tim guided her toward the juice table. She chose some tomato juice and then they headed to a table of noisy students. Tim yelled out that he wanted to introduce Iris to them. They quieted some and introductions were made. There were two girls and five guys. Tim and Iris sat down and soon Iris was in superficial conversation with two students near her. One was a girl named Pat who seemed vivacious and witty. When Iris asked her what courses she was taking, she said, "Mainly theology courses. I have my BA, so I wanted to focus on theology and religious studies."

"What do you intend to do when you finish your studies?" Iris asked.

"I hope to get a position as a minister in a large church—an associate pastor to begin with, I suppose."

"Not too many women in those positions, are there?"

"That's starting to change," Pat said. "Big churches want a woman's perspective. These days, women parishioners are demanding that they're understood and appreciated and that they've a voice."

"You certainly have ambitious plans. I'm almost envious of you," Iris said with a laugh.

"What are your educational goals, Iris?" a guy named Blake asked. He was sitting next to Tim, fussing with his pipe to keep it lit.

"I hope to start medicine next year. I think I would like to specialize. Not sure in what, though."

"It seems you're also encroaching on what's typically a man's domain," Pat said.

"You're right, Pat." Iris looked back to Blake. "What do you intend to do when you're finished theology?"

"I'd like to research early church history and the origins of New Testament documents."

"That's fascinating," Iris said. "Blake, I'd like to ask you what you think of our current New Testament Scriptures like the King James Version. Do you think they give a reliable record of what actually happened?"

"There could well be parts that are historical, but there's lots of stuff that's a fabrication of the early church trying to impress a skeptical populace," Blake said. "That's the point of my investigation—to try to understand more of what really happened."

"What do you think of the biblical account of Jesus?" Iris felt she might embarrass some people with this question, but somehow she didn't care.

Blake blew out a great plume of smoke. "He likely was historical. I think we can get a faint picture of who he was through Mark's gospel, but even there, much of it is contrived by the second-century church, when the idea of the resurrection began to take hold."

Iris's eyes widened and her mouth dropped open. "Oh! I see! Well, I wasn't quite expecting that."

"Iris, you have to understand that there's a great diversity of understanding re: the Christian religion in our faculty," Tim said. "I think most of us agree that Jesus was the greatest moral teacher in history and if we take nothing more from the New Testament, we'd be wise to follow Jesus' great moral imperatives, like doing for others that which you would want for yourselves."

"I'm with you on that one," Blake said with a grin.

Iris decided to push these students into declaring their beliefs a little more. "I'd like to know what some of you think the most important teaching of Jesus was, and what he's asking of us today?"

All were quiet, looking around at one another as they tried to collect their thoughts. Tim shoved his coffee cup around on the table and said, "Well, for me, it's to love our neighbours as ourselves. That's his most important teaching and it's good for today just as it was for his time. The most important thing I can do is to become aware of those in need, whatever that may look like, and do something to help them."

Everyone remained quiet for another few moments. Finally, Jill, the other girl, spoke up. "I think Jesus once said that the work of God is to believe in the one who was sent."

Iris nodded to Jill with a smile. "I think you're right. John's Gospel quoted him as saying that."

Blake pulled his pipe out long enough to say, "You must understand that the Gospel of John was written seventy to a hundred years after Jesus presumably made that statement. I think this is another case where the church was thinking very creatively about what would make a good story for the faithful."

"Do you all believe that?" Iris looked quite astonished.

Everyone started to talk at once. Then all stopped and Jill said, "I think John is more reliable than Blake makes it out to be."

Another embarrassing pause. Then Tim said, "Well, Iris, a lot of us take a more liberal view of the Bible than some of the more evangelical wing of Christians. Most of us buy into the higher criticism that developed in Europe in the last century. For me, I just read a lot between the lines and try to understand my moral responsibility for mankind and then do the best I can."

Most of the group grunted their agreement. Iris rounded her lips and just nodded. Tim seemed so sincere in his passion to help the poor and disadvantaged. And he was so very handsome! His words were also compelling—she needed to be careful with what she was accepting as fact here. She certainly would have to give this liberal point of view a lot of thought.

Chapter Three

IT WAS THE MID-TERM BREAK AND IRIS WAS READY FOR A CHANGE. Besides, she longed to have a good visit with her family. Her dad and she had always been close. Then in the last years of high school, she had found a new friend in Trish, who became her father's second wife. She was even excited to catch up with her younger brother, Ralph.

Iris had taken the city bus to the Greyhound terminal and now she lined up, waiting to be processed for the bus home. Fortunately, the fresh breeze was taking most of the diesel smoke away from the line-up. She wondered if everyone found diesel fumes as loathsome as she did. Eventually she mounted the steps and found a seat near the back. She wanted to think about her life, especially about the liberal take on Scriptures. As the bus moved along the streets of Edmonton, she could see people in cars, people walking the streets, and even people inside their homes and she wondered what their lives were like. Did they have ideological conflicts like she had? Probably not. But maybe they had to deal with even more serious problems, like alcoholism or incurable cancer.

Soon, the bus was in the open country and humming along eastward at highway speeds. She needed to sort out what the theologs had talked about. She hated the idea that the New Testament Scriptures might not be reliable. Were her theology friends more honest and realistic, basing their views on historical evidence? She'd have to do some research on her own. That seemed far beyond what she could accomplish, short of dropping the idea of medicine and going fully into religious studies. She wasn't going to do that.

Iris looked over the passing scenery and noticed that most of the trees were devoid of leaves now. The bare branches stretched sturdily out in the breeze. The trees stood solidly and boldly, anchored by a system of roots.

She wondered if the Bible was like that. Some of the details of Scripture were not necessarily historical and, like leaves, would fly away in the wind of criticism. What was left was solid truth and was anchored in God. She thought about putting herself in God's position. If he created the universe and all life including mankind—and she could accept nothing else—then would he not want to leave a revelation of himself, especially if it would do mankind a lot of good? Yes, it would seem so. Would he not want to leave something that was reliable—even though he chose to give his revelation through fallible mankind? Again, it would seem so.

The wind was picking up. Clouds of dust swirled over the stubble of grain fields. She could feel the bus being buffeted at times. She was glad she was in a large, loaded bus well able to defy the wind. She thought about her life. Would she be blown off course? Tim came to mind. Though she had determined to keep herself free of distractions, she knew Tim was a threat. She couldn't help being attracted to him. His words seemed so well thought out and his speaking voice so mellow, and he was so handsome. His blond, curly hair and bushy eyebrows perfectly crowned his expressive face. He was tall and had the build of an athlete. His smile really did something to her insides. Then she thought of what he said and she found that unsettling. He said most of them (probably including himself) had bought into higher criticism of the New Testament documents. What could that mean other than he was somewhere down the road toward a liberal view of the Scriptures? She supposed some of that might be okay, provided he had his head on right regarding Jesus and the work he came to earth to accomplish. She'd have to talk to him sometime about his personal views.

✦ ✦ ✦

The Greyhound slowed to a crawl as it approached the bus depot of Badger Creek. Iris couldn't recognize any vehicles, so she wondered if her dad had been delayed. Then she spotted him emerging from an unfamiliar vehicle. She felt her heart pounding as she watched him searching for her. She bounded out of the bus and flew into his arms. It was so good to be home and feel those wonderful arms around her again. She pulled away and just looked into her dad's eyes. Both had tears welling up.

Finally, Peter said, "It's so nice to have you home again. All at home are dying to see you. Come, let's get your bag and get on our way."

"What's with this car, Dad? I don't recognize it. Don't tell me you ditched the old one."

"You guessed right, I traded it in on this one. The old one had multiple organ failure and was pronounced dead."

Iris threw her bag into the back and crawled into the seat next to her dad. "I like it. It's a Dodge, isn't it? I thought you didn't like Dodges."

"I think most of the brands are good. However, some are lemons—just like humans."

"Present company excluded, Dad?" Iris asked with a smirk on her face.

Peter chuckled. "I may be biased, but I think so."

Iris loved this comfortable banter with her family, especially her dad. She looked out the window and saw the familiar bushes guarding the dry creek bed. Some of the bushes still hung tenaciously to their leaves as though too embarrassed to be stripped naked. She recalled a recent dream where she found herself in public stark naked and reaching for anything that might cover her shame.

"You seem quiet, Iris. What's going on in the wonderful brain of yours?"

"You wouldn't want to know. My brain often goes on rabbit trails that make little sense. How is life at your school? Are you still quite busy teaching and being principal?"

"Yes, of course. Teaching is still my joy, but the principal part is going well, although not as much fun."

"Are you still experiencing opposition because of your view of creation and the timing of the origin of life?" Iris asked.

"Very little, now. I've no doubt that some parents and even some of my students aren't happy with my being principal because of my views on the creation issue, but most are giving me good support. For that, I'm very grateful."

Iris worried about her brother, Ralph. He was so determined to stand up to his mother's beliefs about creation. She wondered if he was in for an ideological crash when he entered university. "How are things going between you and Ralph, Dad?"

"We seem to have an unspoken agreement. We don't bring up this issue in order to argue our views. We respect each other's right to think differently about it and, thankfully, we get along quite well. He's thinking of going into church ministry in some way and talks of going to a Bible school or seminary. He mentioned Briercrest at one point."

"Sounds like a good choice to me."

"Yeah, I'm settled about that, too. Well, we're home, daughter," Peter said as he stopped the car outside their garage. "You go greet Trish and Ralph and I'll get your bags."

✦ ✦ ✦

The door burst open and out rushed Ralph with his arms held out. "Iris, you're home!" Ralph and Iris threw their arms around each other and hugged and danced around in a circle.

Iris then pushed herself back and really looked at Ralph. "You've grown another two inches and now you're taller than me. Your voice is different."

"They tell me it's natural, so don't worry about it."

Iris's eye caught sight of Trish and she called out her name in great excitement and enveloped her in a big hug. Everyone was in tears by this time.

"Supper is ready," Trish said. "Put your stuff in your room, Iris, use the facilities and get yourself to the table. We can talk there."

Around the table, there was a lot of banter and light talk of what was going on at Ralph's private Christian school, of which Peter was principal. Iris was eager to catch up on Trish's work at the library. Then the whole family cleaned up and washed the dishes.

"How about brewing some tea and we can sit in the living room and talk more. I've lots of questions I want answered," Peter said. "Is that okay with you?"

Soon all four were seated comfortably, teacups in hand.

Iris looked around, raised her eyebrows, and said, "Am I the object of an inquisition?"

"Of course not," Peter said, chuckling. "We all have questions, including you, I'm sure. But since the biggest changes are probably in your world, I would like to ask how you like your courses so far."

"I love organic chemistry, physics, botany, and zoology. I always liked the sciences. I'm also taking another psychology course this year. I must say I'm quite ambivalent about it."

"Why's that?" Trish asked.

"The prof is so critical of Christianity. His basic philosophy is that man created god rather than God created man. Man did so in order to better explain the difficulties or unexplainable things of his confusing life, and to control the populous."

Peter could see the pain in his daughter's eyes. "Did you find your faith buffeted by those kind of remarks?"

"Sure. He always seems so utterly convincing. Of course, my brain tells me that he's accepted the concept of a universe devoid of a higher being, one that is totally naturalistic, but I can't help feeling my spirit's in a bloody mess by the time he's finished each class." Iris was laughing by the time she finished but the pain was still in her eyes.

Peter took a deep breath. "You know, Iris, your professor is right when he suggests we humans look for an explanation, even a supreme spirit being when life gets very difficult and perplexing. Maybe God made us that way because he wanted us to seek and depend on him. The view we decide to take is a matter of faith, I think. We've been given a remarkable revelation of the God in the Old and New Testaments. When I read the Bible, I find it very difficult to believe that that revelation was a total fabrication by man. It comes down to faith."

"I wish God didn't make it so bloody hard to be sure about his existence. Why is he always hiding himself?" Iris had discarded laughter for tears.

"It's all about understanding and trust, Iris," Ralph said, stretching his arms above his head. "People not born of God can't discern the things of the Spirit. They're going to get it wrong every time no matter how learned and clever they seem to be. So you shouldn't be surprised."

"Ralph, you are very right there," Trish said with an appreciative grin, "but I think God made life hard to understand for us humans and he left finding him not all that easy. If his existence were overwhelmingly obvious, where would the joy be for God and us when we found each other?"

"Trish, you nailed it." Peter sat up straighter in his chair. "It's like God wanted our search for him to be an act of humble repenting of our failures and trusting him for his forgiveness and his power to renew our lives. For those without those motives, God wants them to easily find some godless explanation for the mysteries of life."

"That sounds like God isn't really interested in saving the lost," Iris said.

"Oh, he cares enough to have died for us," Trish said. "I think Peter is just saying that God is absolutely committed to giving mankind a free choice to choose him or to choose man's own way."

Everyone was quiet for a while. Then Iris, with shiny eyes and a wobbly voice said, "I think you guys have helped me understand things better from God's point of view. Thank you for being a loving and wise family for me."

"Not a day goes by, Iris, when we don't pray for you and ask God to give you wisdom and understanding. Yet I doubt you'll be saved from struggling through this and many other difficult issues. God's not only calling you to be a doctor, but a real human being so you can help others."

Iris closed her eyes and various emotions played on her face. Finally, she said, "Well then, you've all got to keep praying for me."

Chapter Four

IRIS WALKED BRISKLY ALONG WHYTE AVENUE TOWARD A SMALL CAFÉ. She wore slacks and a warm fall coat, enough for the typical of fall weather with night frosts and daytime thawing conditions. Winter was threatening. A few short snowstorms had already occurred. As far as Iris was concerned, the weather was just fine—little to distract her from studying. She felt she had made good progress since the mid-term break. But today, she had received a phone call from Tim, inviting her to a small cafe on Whyte Avenue. Part of her had felt quite reluctant to accept, as she would lose a whole night of studying. Another part of her was drawn to him. He had told her he wanted to get to know her better. Besides, they both needed a break from all their studying. It was to be just a small meal—mainly so they could do lots of talking. It was almost six and she was nearing the café. Tim had offered to pick her up in his car, but Iris had told him that would be unnecessary as she lived nearby. Was she getting herself into a mess from which she would have trouble extricating herself in the future? She sure hoped not. Tim had a soft heart for poor and unfortunate people and he was a bright leader type.

She spotted him waiting outside the café. He wore a warm jacket and gloves, and a big smile. "I'm so glad you could come, Iris. You look great."

"You look good, too. Did you walk all the way from your home?"

"Sure. It only took me about thirty-five minutes. I needed the exercise. Come on, let's go in and see if we can find a table where we can talk."

A waitress seated them and left menus. They both decided to go with the special—fish and chips. While they waited, they caught each other up on their courses and how they'd fared with mid-terms.

Iris wanted to keep the discussion light during the meal. Maybe they could talk about both their histories after they ate. She did not intend to get emotionally involved with Tim. There was a lot about Tim that was unknown to her. She wasn't at all sure what philosophy or religion guided his life; furthermore, she needed to keep her eye on the academic goal she had set for herself. She wasn't going to be sidetracked. As they were eating their meal, she caught Tim's eyes and they held their gaze for a few seconds. She smiled briefly and broke off her gaze. *I need to keep myself under control. That's not going to be easy. He's so handsome.*

After the dishes had been cleared and each had a cup of coffee, Tim said, "Well, Iris, I'd love to hear about your life, starting from your birth."

"I don't remember much about my birth; I was quite young then." Iris's eyes twinkled.

"I'll accept historical evidence." Tim grinned and waited.

Iris looked up to the ceiling and drew in a deep breath. Where was she to start and how much should she say? Iris then summarized her life in about fifteen minutes. She included the struggle with her faith during high school. She also told him how she came to have a new understanding of Jesus through her father and Trish's studies on the life of Jesus. She noticed that Tim kept nodding for her to continue. She couldn't read his face. She felt she'd said enough without specific questions inviting her to say more. "Well, that's mostly it. Now I would like to hear your story. First of all, I would like to hear about your family."

Tim said he was an only child. He told her about his father's aspirations for him to eventually join him in the financial world, but that he'd been more drawn to the values of his mother, such as caring for the needs of the oppressed and poor. He'd been greatly influenced by some of the mission efforts of his church. He wanted to be a part of making a social difference, especially among the disadvantaged.

"Tim, I think that's wonderful! I've met so many students who are only focused on their careers and how it's going to make them wealthy. It's good to hear someone who cares for the good of others—someone who wants to give rather than just get."

"Thank you. You're very kind to say that."

"You mentioned that your mother's actions inspired you. Who or what else influenced you?"

"I can see you'd make a good news reporter. Okay, let me see. Our minister once preached a sermon I've never forgotten. It was on Matthew 25. You'll remember this was Jesus' parable about the sheep and the goats. The king (God) commends his subjects. When he was hungry, they gave him something to eat. When he was thirsty, they gave him drink. When he was a stranger, they invited him in, and when he was in prison, they visited him. Of course, the subjects were surprised and asked him when these things had happened. The king replied that when they did those things for the least of the brothers, they'd done it for him. I've never forgotten that parable. It drives my life. When I die, I want God to say, 'Well done, thou good and faithful servant.'"

"I'm impressed." Iris paused, looking up to gather her thoughts. "Would you see yourself becoming a missionary—preaching the gospel and so on?"

"Not in the way you suggest. You see I think our mission is to give our lives and our talents toward the betterment of mankind. I hope I'm not offending you when I say that some parts of the church of Christ have focused on converting people to Christianity and then leaving them, thinking that's all they have to do. Even James, in the New Testament, says that faith unaccompanied by action is dead. We need to be sensitive about people's suffering and willing to help these people with whatever their physical or social problems are."

"So, you're saying that your responsibility is in helping people with their social and physical needs, but not to teach people how to become believers in Christ?" Iris knew she was being confrontational, but she had to really see where Tim was coming from.

"Yes, it's something like that. I think that people should have the right to choose what they want to believe. It's not my job to pressure them into believing my way. If they're interested in what I believe, they can ask and I can tell them how I've chosen to believe. I need to be respectful of whatever religious view they've chosen." Tim's eyes sparkled with confidence.

Iris's eyes opened wide in response to that last statement. Should she push further? She really needed to know. "What you're saying then is that, so far as God is concerned, as long as their social problems are being met, their religion is of little consequence."

Tim laughed a little, flushing. "No, I wouldn't say it quite that way. I think there are many ways to God. Some are better than others, but that's for God to judge. I personally have chosen Christianity since I see in Jesus' life the best example of a worthy and selfless life given for others, but I need to respect others in their unique journey to find God. I think that God accepts people in other religions if they sincerely seek him."

Iris looked at her watch and said she felt she needed to get home. She needed to get a few things done before bedtime. She felt somewhat muddled inside and needed to process what Tim had said before discussing this topic further. "Thanks, Tim, for being so honest and forthright. You have given me lots to think about." She chuckled, but didn't feel all that happy.

Tim walked her home. They chatted about the houses and yards they passed. No further deeper matters were discussed. When they reached Iris's house, Tim took her hands and said a warm goodbye. She was glad he didn't try to do more. Tim had probably read her mood and realized she needed time.

⬩ ⬩ ⬩

While Iris studied hard to prepare for the Christmas exams, Tim had notified her about a fundraiser for the Biafra crisis in Africa. He was helping to organize it and he had asked her to play her oboe during a silent auction. She was excited about the idea and wanted to help. After her last exams, she'd gone to bed early to get a good sleep. Now it was Saturday morning and she was finishing practicing for the performance. She was to meet the pianist from Tim's church and practice together an hour prior to the fundraiser that evening. She had also been invited to Tim's church for the Sunday morning service.

She was quite willing to go with him, since she had wanted to get a better idea what this church really believed. She had to admit many features of liberal Christianity were attractive. They took Jesus' call for serving the poor and disadvantaged very seriously. They didn't just talk about social problems, like some of the more evangelical churches she knew. Tim's church took action. The other thing she found attractive was that churches like Tim's were more respected in the academic circles. Their moral values and teaching was more in line with non-religious community-minded citizens. Still, something about accepting the theological and philosophical underpinnings of Tim's church niggled at her conscience. She would need to keep her eyes and ears open during the service.

At the fundraiser, it was fun to help serve a light meal and pour tea and coffee. The oboe performance had gone well. At least, she received many compliments. The presentation about the huge humanitarian disaster and its need was done well—all too well, in her mind. It left her a little depressed.

She was glad they would have a small part in doing something for the good of that sad region. The carols they sang at the end helped lighten her mood.

She met with Tim at the end of the fundraiser. After a little hesitation, she agreed to be picked up at her place Sunday morning for the church service. Going in and sitting with him definitely would carry a message she wasn't quite ready for. They weren't really dating already, were they? Maybe Tim thought so. She still wanted a little distance between them.

✦ ✦ ✦

As Tim drove his VW up to the church, Iris was impressed by the building's pleasing architecture. It wasn't pretentious at all, but rather tastefully refined. The inside matched. The windows were stained glass portraying scenes from the Bible. The high arched ceiling and windows gave her the feeling of reverence toward God. Though there were quite a few people already in their pews, there was a remarkable silence, as if these people were already in a worshipful mood.

Soon after they got seated, powerful and wonderfully played pipe-organ music flowed over her, leaving her with goose bumps. The well-organized and carefully chosen liturgy and prayers all blended flawlessly with the polished sermon that followed. Not a word was misplaced or stumbled over. Each sentence was spoken with a strong impact.

The minister's main theme was the sharing of our resources with others in need. He used the story of Jesus feeding the five thousand. He said that he believed the miracle was seen in the sharing of every one's lunches. He was sure many if not most families would have brought small baskets of food along, some having more than needed. He pointed out that the miraculous effect Jesus had on that crowd was to give that crowd a spirit of generosity so they could share with each other. He said, "I really doubt Jesus fabricated new food. Today's need isn't for more food being produced, but to take from our plenty and give to those who have none. We also need to share from our plenty in education with those who have none. This might mean leaving our comfortable lives and moving to a third-world country." He then pointed out a number of humanitarian ventures their church was already involved in. He also suggested new ventures that might be considered to help the poor and uneducated even in this country.

"Some of our evangelical friends, in their mission endeavors, place special emphasis on getting lost people saved," he went on. "But if these lost people's stomachs are growling from hunger or they're unemployed and they are anxious about their next dollar, they aren't going to concentrate on the gospel tract pushed into their hands."

The pastor let that sink in, and then he said, "Let me tell you a modern parable. Some Christian folk were sitting by a river when they became aware of someone floating down the river. They could see he was in serious trouble, so one of them jumped in and was able to pull the severely injured and half-drowned person to safety. To their astonishment, other similarly injured and drowning people were seen floating down the river. Valiantly, the small group tried to save them also, some were successfully recovered but others were not. After dozens more came floating and continued efforts were made to save as many as possible, one of the rescuers had an idea. Maybe, some of them should go up the river and see if anything could be done to stop these people from being injured and falling into the river. So, some went up stream and they finally saw the cause of this disaster. Thugs were sneaking into vegetable crop fields and stealing from the farmers. Any farmer who didn't give the thugs produce was beaten and thrown in the river. The Christian group notified the appropriate authorities and soon the carnage was stopped.

"The lesson here is obviously that sometimes we need to do more than try to feed the hungry, bind up the wounded, or even to give people the right way to believe. We may need to find out what leads to the problems people are facing and try to do something about that. We may need to get into politics or at least vote for leaders who have a humanitarian view of life. We also may need to become water engineers or agronomists and go to third-world countries to help correct the root issues behind poverty and disease."

The service ended with a challenging call to humanitarian action using the various talents God had given to all. In the foyer, Tim introduced Iris to many of his friends. Most seemed very friendly and polished in their social manners. She also noticed nearly all were successful business people, well educated. They wore fine clothes. Obviously, these people enjoyed life in a fairly high income bracket.

As she and Tim left the church, the minister's sermon was still resonating in her. Iris was moved to do more, much more, for the poor and needy. What form would that take? Did she have the resources to do anything significant? She wondered and remained unsettled.

✦ ✦ ✦

It was Monday and Iris was eastbound on a Greyhound bus to be home with her family for Christmas. She was glad the bus ride gave her the opportunity to sort out some of the issues raised by Tim, his theology friends, and Tim's church. She wondered if the evangelicals like her church in Badger Creek had gotten it wrong. Were they so focused on Jesus' prayers in the Gospel of John and the gospel message of St. Paul in his New Testament letters that they had lost the notion of meeting the social needs of people? The evangelicals had become quite smug in thinking they had the only right take on the gospel of Christ. In fact, they had it down to Four Spiritual Laws that were being distributed as small booklets on campus. Just present these laws to the unsaved, have them say a prayer, and that was it. End of mission! Nothing was being done to help the poor be more successful in their small businesses. Nothing was being done to help farmers become more efficient and productive. Nothing was being done for those living under oppressive political systems. She could see why people like Tim had become social activists. They were doing tangible things—not just building idealistic theological structures and then hiding behind them in self-righteous complacency.

Chapter Five

December 1956

Milton Saunders settled into his Greyhound Bus seat with a book. It was about human sexuality. It would be helpful for his psychology course, but he knew he had a particular interest in the subject that went beyond the necessities of his course. His aim was to do well in all his courses, but reading this book wouldn't make a lot of difference, he supposed. He was just interested in the book. The bus was now making its ponderous way through the streets of Edmonton and would soon be heading south on Highway 2 to Calgary, his home, and Christmas.

He watched the passing service stations, cafes and motels along 104th Street. The sun was just rising and it seemed to be successful in waking up these tired businesses. It was just after eight—time for the business to get started, he thought.

As the bus began humming its way down the highway, Milton's thoughts went to his educational pursuits. He was now half through his third year at the University of Alberta. He'd been in the Arts and Science program the last two years. In his first year, he was in the Arts program, majoring in painting, both oils and watercolour. He loved to paint, but he'd always known he wanted to be a doctor even more. He still painted, mainly for relaxation. Some of his professors had told him he had real talent in painting. He was quite proud of some of his works. But, no, medicine was his goal now, and he'd just been accepted into the Faculty of Medicine for the following year.

For a time, Milton just watched the passing scenery. The landscape was essentially white, marred only by lonely poplars and a few fence lines.

The highway was busy, shouldering the increased load of Christmas traffic. He looked around the bus and noticed that many passengers were dozing, not surprising after an unusually short night necessitated by the bus's early morning start.

Milton's mind drifted to his parents. His father was a hard worker and a high achiever and proud of it. He had been rewarded with a good income. The real-estate firm he established was doing well, thanks not only to some talented agents but also to his efficient management. He knew his father had been disappointed in Milton's choice of education. His father would have preferred Milton to join him in his business. His father had been greatly dismayed when Milton had gone into an Arts program. His father saw no value in those studies. He was somewhat relieved when Milton changed to pre-med, but Milton suspected his father was still disappointed.

His mother was a very different person. She cared little for money or the power it brought. She was a tenderhearted woman, showing compassion to anyone in need. She was also artsy, developing designs used by companies making cross-stitching patterns. Another feature he found interesting about his mother was her enthusiastic pursuit of atheism. She even regularly attended an atheist club. He'd never understood why she had that passion. His father's parents had been devout Anglicans and his father occasionally attended the nearby Anglican Church. He probably would have gone more often were it not for his wife's scornful comments about anything religious.

The bus stopped in Red Deer to take on passengers, and one of them took a seat next to him. A woman in her forties, he thought. She nodded toward him and then opened a novel and began reading, signaling she wasn't interested in conversation. Well, he wasn't either. He felt he needed to process some serious stuff before he met his family in Calgary. As the bus made its way back to Highway 2, Milton gazed at the various businesses along Gaetz Avenue and wondered what it would be like to live in that small city. When the bus finally regained highway speed, Milton's mind drifted back to an earlier time in his life.

✦ ✦ ✦

The year was 1948 and Milton was thirteen. He was growing rapidly and he noticed with some pride the bulging of his muscles. He was astonished at the changes in his genitalia. His emotions were on a rollercoaster. One day he wanted to be in charge of everything to do with himself and the next he wanted to be an obedient child again.

One thing that disturbed him was his fantasy life. He found himself dreaming about touching other males. Lately, he noticed he was fantasizing about even kissing other males. He instinctively thought there was something wrong with that. Maybe it was more than instinct. He remembered his paternal grandmother had taken him to her church about a year ago. The preacher had told the story of Sodom and Gomorrah, where men wanted to have sex with men who were staying at Lot's house. He could remember the preacher saying, "Homosexuality is sinful. God judged Sodom for this and burned it to a crisp." So, Milton was troubled and tried not to allow his fantasies to go in that direction.

It wasn't that he disliked girls. In fact, he always had felt safer with girls than with boys. Part of it was that he liked doing things girls usually did, like dressing in nice clothes, reading, drawing pictures, and making bouquets of flowers. He loved music. He hated shooting gophers, playing war games, and hockey. In the presence of boys, he somehow felt inadequate and not accepted. All too vividly he recalled an incident at school. At recess, he'd walked out to the playground with a couple of girls and noticed a group of boys preparing to play scrub softball. One of the boys yelled to Milton to join them because they needed another fielder. Another boy shouted back, "Milton won't come. He's a fag." The rest of the boys laughed. One of the girls told Milton to just ignore them. But something very painful had lodged deep inside Milton.

Actually, the person with whom he felt most inadequate was his older brother, Brett. He was a tall, handsome guy built just like his father. Just like his father, Brett was good at sports. Milton felt too much like a klutz so he avoided athletics, especially team sports. He actually did fairly well in skiing for some reason. Brett was always the star in any team sports like hockey and baseball. He and Brett had drifted apart and they had little to do with each other.

One day his father, Fred Saunders, had come home early from his work, just after he and Brett arrived home from school. His father had picked up the sack containing ball gloves, bats, and baseballs and yelled, "Come on boys. Let's play a little scrub baseball."

"Hey, yeah!" Brett had shouted. "Let's go, Milt."

"Ah, I don't know, I've got some homework I'd like to do before supper." Milton had been glad he'd found an excuse.

"Oh no, you won't," his father had said. "If you don't practice, how are you ever going to get good at playing ball?"

Milton had seen the determination in his father's eyes and had thought he'd better at least try. He'd been sure he would make a fool of himself and, once again, disappoint his father.

They moved out to their back yard and his father suggested they start with just playing catch. His father fired the ball at Brett, who caught it smoothly and threw it back, right into his dad's glove. His father then threw to Milton, who missed catching it and had to fetch it out of the bushes.

"Hey, Milt, that was a perfectly thrown ball. You should've had it." His father's chiding further decreased his sense of confidence. Milton then threw to Brett, but Brett had to pick it up after a bounce.

"Let's try some batting practice," his father said. "Pick up a bat, Milt. Better take that light bat. It's the one girls usually use."

Milton awkwardly held the bat and stood about five feet from the garage door backstop. "Brett, you do the pitching and I'll do the fielding," his father yelled.

Brett fired perfect pitches into the garage door, with Milton ineffectively flailing the bat each time. His dad rushed in from his spot on the lawn, grabbed the bat from Milton and said, faced flushed with frustration, "Milt, you look like a girl with that bat. What's with you, anyway? Here, I'll show you how to hold the bat and swing. Throw me a pitch, Brett. I'm going to stand like this with my bat up here and I am going to keep my eye on the ball all the way in. Okay, Brett."

Brett wound up and fired a perfect strike and his father smoothly swung, sending the ball far over the fence and into the neighbour's yard, fortunately missing their house. "See how I swung the bat, Milt? Now try again. Brett, throw nice, easy pitches." Milton saw his father's impatience rising. He just wanted to get away.

Once again, he stood, trying to hold the bat the way his father told him. When Brett lobbed the ball slowly toward Milton, he swung his bat, missing by an inch or two. Brett repeated the throw, but Milton missed again. On the third try, Milt managed to make contact but the ball bounced off the bat and struck him on his jaw.

Fred Saunders yelled, "Oh for heaven's sake, Milt. I don't know how you managed to be in our family. You don't look anything like a Saunders. Let's go in for supper."

Milton had never really connected with his father. He could not remember a time when his father seemed to be proud of Milton or his accomplishments. Now, more than ever, he felt he was a total misfit and a disappointment to the whole family.

✦ ✦ ✦

The bus driver's announcement that they'd be at the Calgary station in fifteen minutes nudged Milton back to the present. He needed to somehow live with his family during the next two weeks. Hopefully his dad and Brett wouldn't press painful buttons. He knew he'd have good visits with his mother. The question of Milton's homosexual tendencies had never been discussed in his family and, if he could help it, it would not be broached during the Christmas break. He suspected his grandmother was more aware of Milton's inner makeup than anyone else in the family. He wanted to visit her, maybe even the next day. Somehow, he felt more accepted by her than by those of his own home.

The bus pulled to a smooth stop in front of the terminal. He spotted the Saunders' sedan with his mother waiting inside. When he got off the bus, he enveloped his mother in a big hug. The thought came to him that he would never have hugged his father had he come to pick him up. He threw his bag in the trunk and was about to go to the passenger side. His mother quickly motioned for him to drive and handed him the keys. Milton grinned.

Little was said on the drive home, other than talking about the weather and the trip from Edmonton. When they arrived, he met Brett and his father. Brett had flown home the previous day from Vancouver. Talk was cordial and superficial during the lunch his father had prepared. Brett said he had taken a few days off to be with his family. After his mother had cleared the table, Milton offered to help wash the dishes, so he could have a little better chat with his mother. His father and Brett went to the living room to visit.

Milton began putting plates into the soapy water to soak. He then turned to his mother. "So what are you planning for Christmas Eve? Do you think you and Dad might go to a church service this year?"

His mother grabbed a tea towel and said with raised eyebrows and a crooked smile, "Milt, you know I wouldn't do a hypocritical thing like that. Your dad said he wanted to go and take whoever wanted to go with him. He usually attends at Christmas and Easter. I really don't see why. If he truly believed, he should go every week, I would think."

"Mom, I've often wanted to know why you have such strong views about anything religious. Did your parents think the same way?"

"Yeah, they did. The Strubbels were atheists or agnostics for generations. There was a time when I thought there might be something to Christianity. I was a child, and I had a good friend from a Christian family. Then her father abused her. That did it for me. I think I'm a better citizen than most of that crowd of hypocrites." Gladys Saunders took a deep breath. "Let's talk about something else. How goes it with your courses?"

Milton filled her in on how he was doing. He was glad to say that his marks were very good and he told her that he'd been admitted to medicine. "I'm still painting, but I don't get a lot of time to do that, particularly in the last two weeks when I was cramming for exams. I'm also still singing in the mixed chorus. I can't get enough of that. I wonder if I'll have time to do that when I'm in medicine."

"I hope you do. You should never deny your artistic side. It will give you the balance you need when you're in that hectic business of being a doctor." Milton could see the passion in his mother's eyes.

"Yes, I think you're right." Milton nodded. "I know how much you've valued your piano ability and your design business."

When they finished the dishes, they joined the others in the living room. The rest of the evening was mainly about Brett. Fred was very interested in Brett's achievements, activities and goals. Milton was all too aware of the lack of interest his father showed for his own achievements. Milton was quite amazed at all Brett was doing besides his studies in economics. He was a student's union leader and attended many social events. He had several close female friends, but none of the relationships had matured into a possible marriage.

Fred threw his head back and chuckled. "I think the reason your marks haven't been exactly stellar is because of your too ambitious social life."

"Not to worry, Dad," Brett said, laughing. "I'm passing all the courses that are important and I'll do you proud one day. But life can't be all work and sweat. There has to be some fun too, you know."

Milton could see in his father's eyes that he delighted in his son, Brett. In all likelihood, if his father were in Brett's shoes, he would be doing the same things.

* * *

It was December 24 and Milton was determined to spend some time with his grandmother. He knew she'd be joining the Saunders family on Christmas Day, as that was a family tradition, but he wanted some time with Grandmother alone. He felt considerable inner turmoil and needed to somehow unburden himself. His grandmother might be of help. He recalled many times when he shared his deepest concerns with his grandmother—concerns he didn't feel free to share with his parents.

Milton borrowed his mother's car to drive to his grandmother. What should he share with her? He wanted to talk to her about his medical aspirations and what he wanted to do after he became a doctor. He hadn't decided if he wanted to go into a specialty or become a general practitioner. He liked to talk to her about these kinds of decisions, even if she didn't have the answers. Her questions seemed to help his decision-making. Should he divulge his biggest worry? No, probably not. She might not understand and, even worse, she might reject him if she understood his real situation.

When she opened the door, his grandmother gave him a big smile, took his hands, and looked squarely into his face. "It's so good to see you again, Milt. Come, let's sit down with a cup of tea. I want to hear how you are doing."

"I want to hear about you, too, Grandma. I think of you often when I'm studying. I always sense that you're aware of me. I feel a connection with you even when I'm away."

"When you sense me, it's probably my prayers for you. I pray for you a lot, you know."

"Thanks, Grandma. You always make God seem so real."

His grandmother chuckled. "That effect is just the Holy Spirit operating through me, I guess."

"Well, I don't know much about that, but keep it up. It's working." Milton laughed. He felt so relaxed and warm inside when he was with his grandmother.

His grandmother's eyes grew serious. "Milton, how's your year going—in terms of your courses, I mean?"

Milton filled her in. He also told her about being accepted into medicine next fall. Her eyes sparkled with pride. When he finished, she said,

"I'm so proud of you, Milton. You'll make a fabulous doctor. You're bright, sensitive, and compassionate—the main attributes of a good doctor."

"That's so kind of you to say." Milton thought that was the most encouraging thing anyone had ever said about his goal of becoming a doctor.

"Now, Milton," Grandmother started with a glint in her eyes, "what about your love life? Have you spotted a girl you might be interested in?"

Milton's smile faded. What was he going to say? Should he confide in his grandmother regarding some of his fears? If he told her, his secret would soon be all over the community. "Well, no. Not yet. I've been so busy with studies, you know, Grandma."

His grandmother tilted her head, pursed her lips and stared at Milton for a moment. "You seemed to hesitate on that one. I want to assure you that what we share here stays with me. No one is going to know what we say unless you tell them."

Milton felt reassured and with that came an overwhelming desire to unload on his grandmother all that he feared. With a flushed face he began, "Well, okay. I would ask that you keep this confidential, at least for the time being." He saw his grandmother nodding. "I fear that I, well, ah, that I might be homosexual. There you have it." Milton's eyes were wide with pupils fully dilated.

His grandmother smiled slightly and nodded. "Actually, I'm not surprised. I've been around the block a few times, as the saying goes. I want you to know that what you said does not in the least change our relationship. I love you just as much now as I did when you walked in here."

"How can that be, Grandma? You know that homosexuality is a horrible sin. How can you say you love me?" Tears were glistening in Milton's eyes.

"Who says homosexuality is a sin? I don't. And the Bible doesn't say that, at least the way I read it. If you ask me if having sex with another male is sin, I'd have to say that it is, according to what St. Paul says in the New Testament. Let me ask you, Milton, have you had sex with another male?"

"I've never had sex with anybody. I've never even kissed anyone except you and my mother. Even though I don't know much about God, I've always thought acting out my homosexual fantasies was bad or evil."

"I'm glad to hear that. You know, I'm a praying woman, and I'm going to pray that you're going to be cured from this homosexuality. And until that happens, I'm going to pray that you remain sexually pure."

"I can't help my fantasies about wanting contact with other men. When I see certain men, I instantly desire to be close to them, to touch them and them me. I have to admit, sometimes the thought of having sex with them comes unbidden." Milton looked rather hopeless.

"You can't be responsible for those thoughts coming from time to time. What you do with them is what's important. If you don't act on them, you're not sinning. But listen, I am going to pray that you will meet people in Edmonton who can help you with these fantasies, as you call them. Another thing, I am going to pray that you will find Jesus becoming real in your life, not just knowing about him, but also experiencing the reality of his life. Without God's help, you'll not be able to overcome your desires."

"Oh, Grandma, I'm not very religious and I don't know anyone in Edmonton who is a Christian or anyone who could help me with my problem."

"Just keep on the lookout for someone to help you and I will pray that you will find someone who will help." His grandmother smiled, and a bit of hope sprang into Milton's heart.

"Okay, Grandma, I promise I'll do that."

"Good, now let's have some lunch. I don't know about you, but I'm starved. I've baked some of those buns you always like. We can stuff them with salmon filling. Some green tea will go good with that. Come, you can help me get it ready." Grandmother hustled to the kitchen as she waved Milton to follow.

Milton felt relief and hope inside him. And, he realized, he was hungry too.

Chapter Six

Christmas in Badger Creek, 1956

Iris walked into the Badger Creek Christian Church with her family. It was the Christmas Eve service. What a difference between this church and Tim's church! Inside and out, Badger Creek was built for practical use, not aesthetics. This place was utterly casual and there seemed to be even an accepted small degree of disorder. It was noisy.

In the service, singing was loud and boisterous. Musical renditions were a bit ragged, far from perfect. But the contributors were enthusiastically applauded. The pastor then delivered a short message that was loosely organized, punctuated by a clear, almost blatant declaration of the gospel—how people could find a new life through Jesus, whose birth they were now celebrating. The service ended with a rousing rendition of *Joy to the World* and a final prayer. In the prayer, the pastor said, "Now I pray that all of us will find for ourselves, each in our own unique way, the true meaning of Jesus born in the flesh, not just to save us once but to keep on saving us."

The other huge difference she'd noticed between this church and Tim's was the literalistic view this church took on Scripture. She realized she was drifting closer to the view that the Bible was just a history of how man or a specific group of people understood God.

Iris knew she had become much more critical. She found the theological and philosophical foundation of this church was light-years away from Tim's church. What was she to think about that? She would have a talk with her dad and Trish, and even Ralph about these differences. Then she thought about the pastor's last prayer. That was different. What did he mean by not just saving us once, but to keep on saving us? She would have to talk about that as well.

* * *

Iris sat in a chair across from the Christmas tree. She'd helped Trish decorate it the night before and she thought they had done a nice job of it. She sipped her coffee and looked fondly at her family. How fortunate she was to have been raised in a home like this! She loved how each of them was so interested in each other's lives. She loved how they thought. Ah, but she had to admit there had developed a divergence in their theological views. That brought a twinge of sadness.

"Iris," Peter said, interrupting her thoughts, "you have given us a superficial report on your courses and your life on campus. But I'm curious about what's happening to you spiritually?"

"I knew you'd get to that sooner or later, but now you've cut to the quick and I've to come clean." Iris gave her dad a crooked smile.

"I'm not demanding anything. I'm just inviting you talk about it, *if* you wish."

Iris took a deep breath. "I don't know how to start. I have to admit there have been some changes. I seem to still be in a state of flux in my spiritual thinking. When I was home at fall break, I told you about some theology students I got to know. One guy, Tim, I've gotten to know more than the others. I've even attended his church a few times. I tell you, that church is hugely different from ours."

"Tell us how it's different," Trish said. "Is it as different as my Catholic Church is from the Christian Church?"

"Oh, yes, and then some." Iris looked up to the ceiling to collect her thoughts. "The architecture, the music, and the reverence in the service are comparable to Catholic churches, I would think. The theology is probably more divergent from Badger Creek Christian than even Catholic services, at least the ones I've been to in Badger Creek."

"How so?" Trish asked.

"Well, basically, Tim's church is really quite liberal. Most of the theology students and Tim's church take a view that the Bible is merely a collection of manuscripts recording the history of people's attempts to find and understand God. They don't believe that God gave man a perfect revelation of himself. Their view of Jesus is also different. They see him as a remarkable leader, way ahead of his time, and one who continues to be a moral luminary. They would see him as a wonderful moral compass for our society. If I have understood them correctly, they don't really think of him as God but, rather, as a good reflection of God. The idea that Jesus somehow atones for our sin and makes us perfect doesn't fly very well in their church. They see atonement as a construct of the first century church looking for a way to overcome the powerful religious influence of pagan Rome." Iris could see that all had incredulous looks on their faces. She was afraid that she'd overwhelmed them.

"Okay," Peter began, "what do you see as the attraction to Tim's church and their way of believing?"

"Yeah, that's been a question that's often come to me, Dad. I think I am most attracted because of their strong social conscience. They really care about people who are poor and deprived of the economic and social amenities that the rest of us enjoy. They not only talk about it but make substantial efforts to help these people."

Ralph's face was flushed with emotion. "Why is it that you are always the one in our family to veer off the path of plain Christianity?"

"I didn't say I believe just like they do. I have to say, though, that some of the ways they think are appealing. I'm just trying to sort it all out." Iris almost looked apologetic.

"Do those guys think they've a corner on the truth?" Ralph asked.

Iris vigorously shook her head. "No, to the contrary, they don't claim anything of the sort. In fact, they think Christians don't have a unique claim on ultimate truth. They accept all religions that are attempting to find God. They don't claim Christians necessarily have it right. They would see many ways to God, Jesus being one of the ways. They do believe theirs is the best way, but they respect the Hindu's, Buddhist's, and Muslim's ways as being just as valid."

"I can see your faith is sliding down the tube. If you find that garbage appealing, you're in big trouble." Ralph got up and began pacing. "I really doubt any of those guys in that church are Christians. They're just a bunch of pagan philosophers."

Peter took a ragged breath and said, "Ralph, you could be a bit more diplomatic and sensitive. But I do think you might have something in your final assessment."

"So you're going to just toss out that church's views as being irrelevant and without a shred of truth?" Iris looked hurt.

Trish, who had been quiet for a while, straightened up and said, "We need to keep from getting too emotional here. We need to respect the intellectual and philosophical struggles Iris is going through. We all have to sort out for ourselves what the truth is. What we now need is for us to prayerfully exercise patience with Iris until she herself comes to the truth about these issues, hopefully with the guidance of the Holy Spirit."

"You're right." Peter stood. "We aren't going to solve this tonight. Let's just let it go for now. I have great confidence in my children that they'll come to a godly way of thinking about the ultimate truths of life. It just needs some time. Let's get to bed. Tomorrow's Christmas.

Chapter Seven

February 1957

EVER SINCE LAST SEPTEMBER, MILTON HAD BEEN IMPRESSED WITH HIS biochemistry professor, Dr. Sandoski. He was highly recognized for his research work, but much more than that, he was an excellent teacher. He possessed an instinct regarding what was truly important to know. He seemed to realize his students were going to forget a lot of the details in the course, but knew they needed to know overarching principles in the future. These he taught with infectious enthusiasm that kept his students on the edge of their seats. His sense of humour was rarely critical of others, but usually directed at his own weaknesses. His humility was a rare and beautiful feature. Dr. Sandoski often invited students who were having any difficulties with their courses to drop in to his office or lab for help. The most unique feature of Dr. Sandoski was that he would, from time to time, drop hints about his faith. He viewed the incredible complexity and beauty of the universe to be convincing evidence of a wonderful creator.

After Milton's visit with his grandmother, he had become more sensitive to religious issues. Comments about spirituality by Dr. Sandoski had increasingly piqued his curiosity of late. Something about the lives of his grandmother and Dr. Sandoski smacked of something real and attractive. He wanted to talk to Dr. Sandoski—share with him some of his concerns about his life. Mostly, he wanted whatever Dr. Sandoski had. He lived by some principle that made him shine like a light in a dark place. Milton wanted it too.

After class, Milton quickly moved to the front and approached Dr. Sandoski. He was busy for a moment with another student. When he looked up, he smiled at Milton. "Can I help you?"

"Dr. Sandoski, would it be possible to meet you sometime and talk about the course and, ah, well, talk about some other concerns as well?"

"Why of course. You're Saunders, aren't you? Do you want to meet in my lab this afternoon, say after four?"

"Sure, um, that would be great for me!"

Milton picked up his lunch from his locker and headed for the library to work on a physics project. When he had finished eating, he tried to concentrate but found his mind shifting back to Dr. Sandoski. What was he going to ask Dr. Sandoski? Milton didn't know. He hadn't quite understood how glucose molecules could be broken down by enzymes to release energy necessary for cell function. But he knew that wasn't the only thing to ask. Well, he would just have to wing it when he got there.

✦ ✦ ✦

Milton knocked nervously on the lab door. Dr. Sandoski opened the door and, with a big smile, invited him in. Milton noticed the distinct smell of organic chemicals. For some reason, he loved these smells.

"Your last name is Saunders, but I'd like to know your first name, if you don't mind," Dr. Sandoski said.

"Milton. It's Milton Saunders."

"Come on in, Milton. Have a seat. I've got some tea. Care for some?"

"Sure. I'll just take it black." Milton took a seat near Dr. Sandoski.

"Milton, you didn't come here just to smell my stinky lab. What's on your mind?" Dr. Sandoski looked relaxed and accepting as he poured the tea for Milton.

"Well, first, I wanted you to help me understand how energy is released from glucose molecules when they're acted on by enzymes in the body. I'm interested because I'm going into medicine."

Dr. Sandoski drew some diagrams on the blackboard and soon was able to get Milton to understand the process. Then Dr. Sandoski paused. "Now, Milton, you look like that wasn't the main reason you came. What else is on your mind?"

Milton didn't respond immediately. "I noticed that you often refer to God as though there actually was one. How come you believe that when so many other professors mock religion?"

Dr. Sandoski laughed gently as if he weren't surprised at the question. "Belief in a creator is a very individual thing for everyone. We all have to answer to that one, whether we're a secretary, farmer, or a teacher, even a scientist. It's not something we can decide on the basis of scientific evidence. Each one has to decide on the basis of the light that person receives."

"How does one get that light?"

Dr. Sandoski smiled. "It comes from God. Actually, from the Holy Spirit, the third one of the trinity. I've the feeling he's already given you some light, or you wouldn't be here."

Milton's eyes opened wider. "Maybe that's so. I've certainly been thinking of it often of late. My grandmother is a Christian and she said much the same thing."

"Good for her. You're very fortunate to have a grandmother like that."

"But what about the idea that scientists have found there's no need to consider a God since science, and particularly evolution, sort of destroy the old story of God creating the universe as recorded in the Bible?"

"There's no real conflict between the biblical story of creation and modern science—at least to my way of thinking. I suppose some of the skeptics would think that the Bible should have a story that reflects modern science in every way. If God had his writers do that, no one in the pre-science period would've understood it. No, God had it written in a poetic way so that people of all ages could get the idea that God created the universe and was lovingly behind all life and existence. He wasn't concerned about the details of exactly how it was done. Neither should we."

"Are you saying then that the earth is very old, like the scientists say?"

"I see no difficulty with that view of the age of the universe. If one understands the Genesis story as poetry, then the days can become long ages and then there isn't any conflict. The order of the creative events actually fit quite nicely with current ideas of evolutionary development."

"That's such a refreshing way of seeing the creation question. Thank you very much for that." Milton was already feeling better.

"I want you to feel free to come here any time to talk about chemistry or about anything else you've on your mind. I have the feeling you'll be here again soon."

"Thank you so much, Dr. Sandoski. This means so much to me." Milton got up and walked toward the door.

"You will make a very good doctor, Milton. I can tell you have the gift for it."

Milton felt so relaxed with this man. Milton smiled and asked, "How can you tell?"

"You have the sensitivity and humility that's needed."

Milton laughed. "That's what Grandma said."

"Tell your grandmother that she's so bright, I'd like to employ her in my research lab." Dr. Sandoski chortled as he waved Milton a goodbye.

✦ ✦ ✦

The strong smell of carbolic acid hit Milton's nostrils as he approached the specimen he was to dissect. It was a shark brain. A few minutes later, he heard some quick steps and then a greeting. It was his zoology lab partner, Bill Street.

"I think I'm going to develop a migraine with that awful smell," Bill said.

The zoology teaching fellow called the students to order and sketched on the blackboard the main features of the shark brain. Then he went through the procedure for dissecting the brain. The lab became quiet except for low mumbling as the students tried to identify the structures. Working together, one reading the anatomical description in the notes and the other following the structural features on the brain, Milton and Bill made good progress. They finished the exercise well ahead of others in the lab. Milton enjoyed working with Bill. He had a good sense of humour and was warm and friendly.

Milton had once heard a rumour that Bill was gay. He couldn't help but feel there was something to it. Since the noise level in the lab began to increase considerably, Milton knew any discussion between him and Bill wouldn't be overheard. He took the opportunity to ask, "Bill, I was told by someone, I won't say by whom, that you were gay. Is there any truth to that?"

Bill flushed a bit. "Yes, that's true. Why is that important to you?"

Now it was Milton's turn to flush around his neck. "Well, I wanted to just say that I understand some of the feelings you have."

"Are you saying that you're gay, too?"

Milton moved a little closer to Bill and said in a soft and low voice, "I'm not really sure, but I know I've some features of homosexuality. I often daydream about… encounters. So, I guess that makes me gay."

"Have you actually had sex with another man, Milt?"

Milton shook his head. "No, I've never had sex with anyone. What about you, Bill?"

"I had a male friend for a while and we had sex from time to time, but we had a falling out and I don't have any partner at the moment."

Both stopped talking and just looked at each other. Milton found himself attracted to Bill, more as a friend than anything sexually. He wondered about Bill. He didn't feel comfortable to ask what Bill's feelings were. So Milton just said, "You must understand that there're a lot of things about myself I don't understand in this area. For now, I want to stay free of any sexual encounters."

"Why? Do you think that it's sinful or something like that?"

"I'm not religious, if that's what you're thinking. I've a grandmother who definitely thinks it's wrong. I haven't figured out what I am yet."

"You don't want to burn any bridges, you mean. You're wanting to keep your options open," Bill said with a grin.

"Yeah, that's about it, I guess. Thanks for being so honest with me." Milton smiled.

With that, time was up. The class was given next week's lab project so they could read up on the subject.

✦ ✦ ✦

Milton usually took the bus to campus. This morning was unusually nice for February. The sun was shining with only a few clouds lazily moving east. It was still frosty, but the day promised thawing temperatures. He'd gotten up early and eaten a cold cereal breakfast left by the boarding house owner. Briefcase in hand, Milton was on his way to campus on foot. The main reason for this walk was to do some serious thinking. After his previous talk with Bill at the lab, he'd met him briefly after one of their classes and Bill had suggested they have coffee at the SUB café. Obviously, Bill had wanted to talk some more about what they'd discussed.

Milton more frequently thought about his last visit with his grandmother. He couldn't get away from the fact that his grandmother was praying for him. He knew she wanted him to find some Christians friends, or at least a church to attend. He knew churches would have no patience with his homosexual tendency. He would have to keep that secret if he attended.

Milton knew Bill wasn't sympathetic to Christianity. In fact, he wondered what he was doing, befriending him. Bill wasn't going to be good for his plan to stay uninvolved with any sexual activity. Bill was a nice guy, however, and he sure was handsome. Milton would need to keep the boundaries clear.

Soon, Milton found himself on campus. He needed to shut off his daydreaming. When he entered the med building, he caught sight of Bill. Milton nodded and Bill smiled back. *Keep up the boundaries.*

✦ ✦ ✦

The zoology lab had been quite hectic and there had been no opportunity to talk with Bill. Now they were sitting in a booth in the café with cups of steaming coffee.

"So, what have you on your mind?" Milton asked, raising his eyebrows.

"Oh, nothing special. I just wanted to know more of why you've made some of your choices."

"So you think I'm confused, illogical, or worse?" Milton said with a crooked grin.

"No, not at all. I just got the feeling that you felt that giving in to your homosexual impulses was somehow immoral. Is that the case? If so, why?"

Milton's mind was flitting about, looking for a logical and, hopefully, acceptable answer. He didn't know if he could come up with one. He finally said, "I told you I am not a religious guy, but I have to admit I've some feelings about what I should or shouldn't do. Maybe it's my grandmother's values I'm dealing with. I don't feel comfortable with acting on my fantasies."

"I take it your grandmother is a Christian and attends a church. Do you think you'd find answers in a church?"

Milton took a sip of his coffee while he tried to formulate his answer. "I have to admit I've thought about that. But I know some churches don't like homosexuals."

"You're so right about that. I'd stay clear of churches. They're homo-haters. If you wanted to attend, you'd have to keep your orientation secret. Living like that is being hypocritical. Worse, actually. It would be pure hell, to my way of thinking."

Milton paused for a long moment. "I suppose you're right. I'm not exactly rushing to find a church. I just wonder if some of the churches have it wrong. Maybe the Bible isn't so tough on gays as we think. Maybe I'll have to do some reading to find out."

"Don't even bother. I can tell you that the main guy who wrote in the New Testament is Paul. Well, he made it clear that homosexuality is an ugly sin. So how's that going to help?"

"Well, I still want to read it for myself. I'd especially want to see what Jesus said on the topic."

"The surprising thing is that Jesus didn't say much of anything about it," Bill said. "Maybe it was just his apostles that had hang-ups about it. More likely, it was the first-century church fathers who put words in Paul's mouth."

Milton felt somewhat confused and discouraged. He looked at his watch. "Listen, thank you for this discussion. You've given me a lot to think about. I think I need to get back to my boarding house for the dinner they've prepared."

✦ ✦ ✦

Once again, Milton walked to campus rather than taking the bus. He needed to think. He was on his way to meet Dr. Sandoski. He'd caught him just before he left the classroom. He seemed quite willing to meet briefly with Milton at four. Milton wasn't quite sure what he wanted to talk about. There was no science issue this time. He just needed Dr. Sandoski's take on Christianity versus homosexuality. He was nervous about how disclosing his sexual orientation would affect Dr. Sandoski. Somehow, he felt he would be more open to issues like that than many other Christians.

When Milton knocked, the door opened quickly. Dr. Sandoski smiled a greeting and invited Milton to take a seat on a lab stool.

"Good to see you again, Milton. What have you on your mind today? I've the feeling it's not about chemistry."

"You're right. I'm still pondering the place of Christianity in my life."

"I'm glad you're still thinking about it. That means God is answering your grandmother's prayers," Dr. Sandoski said, chuckling.

"Well, there's a hitch in my consideration of Christianity."

"Oh, what could that be?"

Milton felt fear rise within him. But he had to speak. "You see, I think I might be gay. You know, homosexual."

"What makes you think so?" Dr. Sandoski didn't appear too surprised.

"I have fantasies of close encounters with other males, like sexual encounters, you know." Now was the moment he feared. Would Dr. Sandoski reject him?

"Have you acted on them, Milton?" Dr. Sandoski's face was warm and accepting.

"No, I haven't. I somehow always felt it was wrong." Milton focused on his hands, avoiding Dr. Sandoski's gaze.

"That's good. That makes things less complicated."

"Do you think my situation precludes my becoming a Christian?" Milton's mouth was very dry.

"Certainly not! There's absolutely nothing that bars any person from becoming a Christian if they desire to do so." Milton finally looked at Dr. Sandoski and saw that he was smiling, but there was fire in his eyes.

"Well, I've heard that the Bible teaches that homosexuals are sinners and can't be accepted into the church."

"Not the church I go to. You need to meet the Jesus I know. Do this before thinking about what the church will think of you. Jesus will tell you what to do next."

Milt looked a bit perplexed. "Do you think I should read some of the Bible on what Jesus thinks?"

"That's a great idea. Read the Gospel of John first. Then there are three other gospels in the New Testament you can read."

"Okay, I'll find a Bible."

"Now don't spend all your time reading the Bible. You're my star chemistry student, and I'd hate to see you fall from that position." Dr. Sandoski laughed heartily.

"Thank you again for your help. Could I ask you to keep the information about my sexual orientation confidential?"

"Of course I will, Milton."

"And, may I come to see you again if I need to?"

"You sure may, Milton. My door is always proverbially open. Especially to you," Dr. Sandoski said with an accepting twinkle in his eyes.

Chapter Eight

April 1957

Iris worked tenaciously on her second-year courses. She'd easily qualified to enter the Faculty of Medicine, but she knew she had to set a pace that would carry her through medicine and, perhaps, into a specialty. In order to achieve her goals, she'd limited her social life. That included Tim. He'd called her from time to time and they had nice talks on the telephone, but she refused to go out on dates.

The one exception to her rigorous study schedule was attending Tim's church. She attended nearly every Sunday. She continued to be impressed by the church's willingness to help homeless people and work at food banks and soup kitchens. Iris became a regular volunteer to help make up the food parcels in the church kitchen. She enjoyed doing this job, since it gave her a sense of doing something worthwhile for the poor people of Edmonton. She also valued getting to know other volunteers, like Brenda, a friendly and talkative elementary teacher. The two often talked about the service component of their church. Brenda also talked endlessly about her work, politics, music, and even sports. One day, Iris asked her what she thought about the previous Sunday's Easter message.

Brenda stopped what she was doing and just looked vacant. "I really don't remember it very much." She flushed and added, "Reverend Smith must have said something about the resurrection, I suppose."

"Yes, he did," Iris said. "He said that many people believed Jesus rose from the dead. He also said some believed Jesus swooned and looked like he died but was actually still alive when taken down from the cross. He then said, 'Whatever you believe about this, the important message for this

Easter is that Jesus was an incredibly selfless person. He helped people to think positively about themselves so that their emotional illnesses and misconceptions of themselves were healed and their bodies responded positively both in physical and emotional ways. He taught people how to give rather than take. Most of all, he taught people to forgive. Even on the cross, he forgave people who were trying to kill him. So, the lesson for us this Easter is to be more like Jesus.' At least, that was mostly what he said, I think."

"Wow, I'm impressed how you remembered just what he said. How do you do that?"

"Well, I was quite curious as to what he would say about Jesus on Easter. That helped me to remember, I guess." Iris put down the package she'd just made and looked at Brenda. "What do you think of that message? Do you think what he said is the real message of Easter?"

Brenda looked flustered. "I don't know. I have my own thoughts about those things. I'm a private person about my faith and don't feel comfortable talking to other people about it."

Iris realized she had overstepped a line here. Brenda was so talkative, Iris thought she would be glad to discuss this issue. She had been wrong. "I'm so sorry to have embarrassed you. I should have been more sensitive."

"That's okay. I guess I talk a lot, but not about my personal faith. That's off limits."

"Advice taken," said Iris. "Now let's finish these parcels or I'll start eating the contents. I'm getting very hungry."

Were other people in this church like Brenda? She thought so. She had never heard anyone talk of their personal beliefs. Curious.

◆ ◆ ◆

Milton was once again heading back to Calgary and his home. On gazing out the bus window, he was impressed by the beauty of the Alberta landscape. Everything below the horizon was some shade of green. Leaves were just emerging from swollen buds. He loved the light shades of fresh poplar leaves against the dark green bristling branches of spruce. Crows scouted out potential nesting sites. It was the latter part of May, and spring seeding was pretty well done. In fact, young grain had begun to sprout in every field.

Going home brought a sense of relief—his year of hard studying was over and he could now have a break for the summer. There were some negatives, however. He would have to re-engage with his family, and that wasn't going to be easy. He almost laughed at the thought of how different he was from each member of his family. His personality was similar to his mother, but she was an atheist and he was attracted to Christianity. Milton had none of the athletic and social gifts of his father and brother. What did Milton have? Well, he'd made good marks in pre-med—better than Brett had done in his courses. He could paint and sing better than the others, he guessed. He was also gay. That surely was different!

Milton noticed that the bus was just passing through Airdrie. They would soon be arriving in Calgary. He needed to decide a few things. Should he tell his parents about his interest in Christianity? That would trigger a sharp reaction, he was sure. Then he wondered when he would tell his family about his being gay. Milton felt fear spreading through his abdomen. He wasn't ready for that—not yet, at least.

✦ ✦ ✦

The first day at home passed without incident. On the second day, Milton went out in search of a job. He hated being dependent on his father for his tuition—especially since his father didn't approve of his choice of vocation. Within hours of his starting to search, he landed a job with a restaurant as a server. Since most of the employees were women, he felt comfortable. Working closely with men made him feel tense, like he wasn't going to measure up.

A week later, it was Milton's twenty-second birthday. His mother organized a party with his parents, his brother and Rachel, his grandmother. Gladys worked hard to make the party pleasant and enjoyable for her second son, and Milton hugged her several times in thanks. Brett had made a special effort to get home in time for the party. Milton suspected his mother had put considerable pressure on Brett. Still, Milton was happy Brett had made the effort.

When his grandmother arrived, she shouted her greeting to Milton and waved for him to sit beside her on the living room sofa and tell her all that had transpired since they last visited. "Tell me about your examinations. Were they tough? How do you think you did?"

"They were challenging all right, but I think I did okay. I sure studied enough for them." Milton enjoyed his grandmother's intense interest in him. The fact that she knew he was gay and still really cared about him filled him with gratitude and love.

"But you are already accepted into medicine, even before your marks are back?"

"Yes, that's true. The faculty based their acceptance on my performance up to that point."

"Well, all they needed to do was to ask me. I would have told them you were one of their best prospects."

"Thank you, Grandma. You are always so encouraging."

Gladys was hustling about moving food from the range to the table. Fred was helping the best he could, though he required many prompts. Milton, aware of the dinner preparations, was tempted to jump up and help, but he also knew the tradition in this home—the birthday person was to have no part in food preparation or cleanup. He turned his attention to the conversation that had started between Brett and his grandmother.

"Okay, everyone, come and sit," called Gladys.

When all were seated, Gladys said, "Rachel, you usually ask the blessing before your meals. If you wish you may do so now."

"Thank you," Rachel said with a relieved smile. "I would be happy to. Our Father, we thank you for being able to enjoy this special meal together. We ask a special blessing on Milton on his birthday. In Christ's name we pray, Amen."

"Thank you, Mother," Fred said. "I like to have a prayer before meals. I suppose it's because I grew up with it. I wouldn't mind starting up with it again if it wouldn't annoy Gladys so much."

"You'd be doing it just to satisfy a ritual you learned in childhood," Gladys said with a smirk.

"No, I really feel grateful to God for many things, including food."

Brett decided to weigh in. "Maybe before we decide if it's a good idea to pray before meals, we should decide if there's a God to hear us?"

"Look, I spent a lot of effort to get a nice hot meal on the table. Maybe we should leave the philosophy for later and get on with the meal," Gladys said, holding up her hand.

"You're right," Rachel said, "but I can't wait to get on with this interesting discussion." Gladys groaned but Milton nodded.

All were silent while the food was being spooned out. When everyone was eating, Milton said, "Mom, you did a great job with this meal. You prepared all my favourite dishes."

"Thank you. I'm very happy to do this for you, but also for everyone else here. We don't get to do this very often anymore."

All nodded and grunted their agreement. Then all were quiet again. Milton remembered he had been planning to sound out the family about his intention to explore Christianity. This seemed to be a good time. He looked across the table to Brett. "You seem to doubt that there's a God. How did you come to that conclusion, Brett?"

Brett looked up and almost choked in surprise. "Well now, that is a big question." He paused to think. "First of all, I've never thought much about a God growing up. I suppose I was affected by Mom's idea of a god being something fabricated by primitive man so they could explain the unknowns of life. Since we've come to a more scientific understanding of life, we don't need such explanations."

"So what's your other point? You said, 'first of all'?" Milton asked.

"The other thing is that I've taken some biology courses at my university and I think the Bible is totally wrong on how and when life began. The Bible says all life was created in a literal six-day period some ten thousand years ago. Science is now very clear on life evolving over many millions of years. Radiometric dating of rocks has repeatedly shown that the earth is well over four billion years old. So, I have no faith in some religious writings that are so unscientific. And, I haven't been very impressed that the ridiculous nonsense put out by other religions on life's origins make any more sense."

"Amen to that," muttered Gladys.

No one spoke for a few moments while Milton swallowed some water and cleared his throat. "That's more or less what I thought too, at least until I took an organic chemistry class. Our prof is considered a brilliant scientist and a researcher as well as a fine teacher. He believes in a God. In fact, he is a Christian. I went to him once and asked him about how he could be a Christian, believing the Bible, while also being a scientist. I brought up the issue about the biblical account of creation as being completely out of step with science. He said he viewed the Genesis story as poetic, where there was no attempt to be scientific. He said if God had inspired his writers to put down facts about life's origin as we now know them, the readers over the last two or three thousand years would have been totally confused. My prof thinks the poetic account nicely gives a picture of creation that would be understood over thousands of years. He says the point made by Genesis is that God created the universe, the earth, and life on it. Genesis doesn't say *how* he did it."

Rachel clapped her hands and smiled broadly. "I've always said that the Bible isn't a science text. It was never meant to be."

"That is an impressive argument," Brett said. "But it would take more than that to convince me."

"So, Milton," Gladys asked, "are you interested in becoming a Christian like your professor?"

Now Milton felt he was being put in an awkward spot. He had to say something. "No, I'm not there yet. I have to say I'm leaning toward the idea that there's a creator behind the universe. The complexity and the beauty of the universe and life on earth is so great, I cannot imagine there not being massive intelligence behind all this. But as far as believing anything else, like Jesus rising from the dead and so forth, I'm not there yet."

"So you're leaving it open for possibly doing that in the future?" Fred hadn't said a word in the discussion to this point, so it was a surprise to Milton that he was this interested.

"Yeah, I suppose I am. I need to do a lot of research and thinking on the life of Jesus before I make any move in that direction."

"That's wise," Fred said.

Rachel leaned toward Milton. "Just keep your mind and heart open to the truth when it presents itself."

"I'm planning on doing just that, Grandma." Milton smiled and nodded.

✦ ✦ ✦

Her exams were finished! Iris walked out of the gym where the examinations had been held and felt an enormous sense of relief. She was convinced she had done well—after all, she had studied hard enough. She saw groups of students obviously talking about how they answered the various questions. She hated rehashing the answers. That just made her doubt. So, she headed for her boarding house where she could relax. Maybe she could read a novel to get herself in a different space. Then she'd need to decide when to go home. She wanted to get a little shopping done before that. She wouldn't mind doing a few other things she never allowed herself before, like going to a museum and an art gallery. There was a life outside of zoology, botany, and physics, after all.

Then there was the question of Tim. He had made her promise to have a meal at some restaurant to celebrate the completion of their university courses for the summer. She would be finished her pre-med studies and Tim would be finished his second year of theology. She still really liked him. She doubted she'd fallen in love with him, but she couldn't be sure. A few concerns still made her hesitate to let herself go into a lifelong commitment. She worried about the sincerity of his love for her. He seemed content to have so many other female friends. Then there was the question of his theology. Although she'd become more liberal in her thinking, she wondered about how pleased God was with this trend. If she were on her own, she could make adjustments as light came to her. But if she were hooked up to Tim, that might be much less likely.

When Iris got back to her room, she was notified that she had gotten a call from Tim, so she called him. He sounded excited to be talking to her. His voice was such a smooth baritone. He suggested a nice restaurant on Jasper Avenue. He could pick her up. She happily agreed.

On the way to the restaurant, they chatted about their examinations. Tim said he had a good feeling about them—at least he wasn't worried.

After they got their food served and began eating, Tim said tentatively, "Are you still planning to take a specialty after obtaining your medical degree?"

"Yes, I think I am. I've not made up my mind as to what yet. I need to experience the different disciplines first." Iris cut a juicy piece from her steak and savored the flavors before proceeding. "I want to be a consultant in some way. I don't want to slog away at being a family doctor all my life."

"Have you ever thought about going to another country where they really need a general practitioner? That should be challenging and interesting enough to satisfy you."

"Are you interested in doing something like that?" Iris could guess where this was going.

"I've often thought about doing some mission work, say in Africa or India. If we were to get married, we could start planning something where you could be serving as a physician and I in an administrative capacity in the mission as well as functioning as a minister."

"So you've got my life all planned out already?" Iris grinned with her mouth but not her eyes.

"I can dream, can't I? We would make a good team, helping out where there is such a huge need. The sense of accomplishment in one of these places would be very rewarding for you, I'm sure. Come on, Iris, admit it."

Iris felt the pull of this challenging life. She also had a heart to serve in some meaningful way. But was this to be accomplished at Tim's side? She just felt confused. "I'm sorry, I'm not quite with you in your vision. Maybe I will be in time. I need to get my feet wet in medicine first."

Tim took another forkful of mashed potatoes, chewed awhile, drank some water and finally asked, "Is your hesitation having anything to do with not being altogether happy about us getting married?"

Iris had hoped it wouldn't get to this. It was a fair question and she needed to be honest for his sake as well as for herself. "Okay, I need to be honest and let you know where I'm at. I have been so focused on my courses and planning my future studies that I haven't allowed myself to think about our lives together. I really like you, and I respect your goals and aspirations, but I'm just not ready for a permanent relationship. Do you understand?"

"May I be so bold as to ask you if you have some other relationship that I'm competing against?"

Iris reached over and put her hand on Tim's. "No, I have no other guy I'm interested in. I can't say that no one else has approached me for a date. I've just let them know I'm not interested or I tell them I already have a relationship. I'm just asking you to be patient with me. I need more time."

"I'm glad you were honest with me. I suppose I can wait, but that's not going to be easy."

"Thank you so much, Tim." Iris smiled sweetly and squeezed his hand.

✦ ✦ ✦

Iris had endured the long bus trip from Edmonton to her home in Badger Creek, Saskatchewan. She'd arrived home around two in afternoon after being picked up at the bus station by Trish. They had a good visit on the way home. Ralph, now fifteen, was still in school, where her dad was principal. Iris had taken a small snack along to tide her over on the bus, but now she was starving. Trish soon had a sandwich made along with some coffee. After they were comfortably seated around the kitchen table, and Iris was enjoying her sandwich, Trish asked with a twinkle in her eyes, "So, have you found a guy you want to share the rest of your life with? Is this Tim still in the picture?"

"There is nothing very subtle about your questions," Iris said with a laugh. "I'll be equally direct with my answer. No, I haven't a promising partner yet. I must admit that Tim would like to make it so. But I'm just not ready yet. I'm still too young, I guess."

"Well, I doubt it's just your age. You're twenty-one, aren't you? Lots of girls that age are getting married. I think your passion for developing your career keeps you from romantic ventures."

"Yes, that's about it. I sometimes wonder if I'm wired up correctly—sexually, I mean."

"Oh don't worry about that, my dear. When the right time and the right guy come along, your hormones will flow in abundance," Trish said with an enthusiastic nod.

"Yeah, I guess that's true. Tim still might be the guy for me. It's just that I'm so unsettled as to where my career's going. I don't even know what I'll do regarding specializing."

"You shouldn't feel rushed into any decision about a life partner. Your dad and I have been praying every day that God will bring the right guy into your life. When it's God's time, it will be the right man for you."

"I hope so. Just keep on praying." Iris's eyes glistened with tears.

✦ ✦ ✦

After the evening meal was almost over, Iris could see Ralph had something churning in his mind. "You look like you've something you need to get out, Ralph. I've never known you to be hesitant about speaking your mind."

"Well, I didn't want to offend you too much just after you returned home. That wouldn't be very nice!"

"My, haven't you become sensitive about my needs. This is new. Now out with it, brother!"

"Okay, here goes. I've been thinking about your liberal leanings on Scripture quite a bit. Have you figured out how to put the brakes on your slide down the slippery path toward unbelief? My idea is that you have to make up your mind what beliefs you're not going to give up. If you don't, you'll keep on compromising until you haven't got any beliefs to hang on to. The most important beliefs are about Jesus. Have you decided what you're not going to compromise on, Iris?"

Peter, Trish, and Iris looked at each other in wonder. Then Iris said, "Ralph, you should either become a theologian or a lawyer."

Peter nodded. "I agree. I couldn't have said that better. I think all of us need to deeply consider what Ralph said."

Iris just sat there with her mouth open for a while, trying to formulate her thoughts. "Ralph, you obviously did some deep thinking about this. I appreciate that about you. Yes, I know I've become more liberal in that I don't take the Scriptures nearly as literally as you do. I know there are some positions Tim's church takes that I cannot agree with. Mostly that has to do with our understanding of Jesus. Is he the Messiah? Did he die and rise again to life? Is he God? I still think he is all of those things, but Tim's church isn't quite sure."

"I'm happy to hear what you still hold to be true. You had me really worried after you were here last Christmas," Ralph said. "Let me ask you what you think of Paul's teaching in the New Testament. Do you think we can take his writings as authoritative, like they are a true reflection of God's thinking?"

"Where did you find all these questions? Have you been taking apologetics courses?" Iris said, puzzled.

"I didn't go to a course, but I'm reading a book on the dangers of liberalism in the Christian Church. I got some of these ideas from there," Ralph said with a slight look of embarrassment for being found out.

"I wondered why you were asking about our church's views on certain issues the other day, Ralph," Trish said.

"Well, you deserve to have an answer to your question, no matter where you got the question," Iris said. "Currently I'm leaning toward the notion that Paul's writings should be taken for the wisdom he obviously possessed, much like any other church father writing in the first or second century after the birth of Christianity. Some of the things he said may have had good application when he wrote, but are irrelevant now—like the advice for women to wear head coverings and his advice to not allow women to teach men in the church. Yeah, I believe Paul said a lot of good stuff, but I wouldn't take every word as the true words of God, if that's what you mean."

"I get that queasy feeling you're sliding down that greasy slope again," Ralph said. "For me, I feel I need to plant a flag on Paul's letters. I believe God gave him the words for the New Testament that God wants us to take as truth for our lives. I doubt God would've allowed Paul to write stuff that was untrue or misleading."

"Who gave the leaders of the church's first few centuries the right to include Paul's writing as the true words of God, while other writers, like Clement, Ignatius, Polycarp, and even Augustine, weren't given that authority? Who had the right to say the true revelation of God had come to an end with writers like apostles Paul and John?"

Ralph shifted forward in his seat. "I'm sure Paul and John had little idea their letters were going to become Scripture and later writers not. We just have to believe that the Holy Spirit led the early church fathers in their councils to accept what would eventually make up the New Testament. It comes down to trusting God that he would leave the church with a true revelation concerning the new covenant of Christ."

Before Iris could respond, Peter interrupted. "Okay, you two, stop! You both would do well on debating teams, without a doubt. You can continue your discussion tomorrow, after you've given your minds a rest. Right now, I'd suggest we all go to our rooms and, hopefully, get some good sleep. I know I'm ready for it."

Chapter Nine

September 1959

THE FALL WEATHER WAS GORGEOUS AND IRIS'S HEART ALMOST ACHED with the anticipation of taking a nice walk in the North Saskatchewan River valley. She had just finished a few days of rushing about getting the books she needed, finding where her third-year medical classes were to be held and what groups she'd be placed in for clinical experience. Iris had found she would be working with a group of five, whose names she'd written down. She knew the four others to some extent, but very little of their personal lives.

Their class was to have an introductory lecture in the morning. She supposed they'd be told what kind of attitude they should have about this wonderful profession, and how they should conduct themselves on the wards with patients. After that, they were to go into their groups and a preceptor would take them to see some patients. She couldn't wait. They'd finally be able to meet and examine patients with some real diseases and disorders they had studied about in the last two years. But now she wanted to grab a bite to eat and go for a long walk. She wanted to plan her approach to this year of studies as well as decide some things about her social life. She had notified her landlady that she wouldn't be around for the evening meal.

Iris stuffed a sandwich from the SUB café into a bag with her jacket and headed down behind the campus toward the river valley. There were well-used paths, so she didn't have to concentrate on her feet. She could just take in the scenery and think.

As she walked, Iris reviewed her last two years. She had worked as hard in medicine as in her pre-med years. Her marks had been good. In fact, she was always in the top two or three of her class. She wondered why she worked so hard. It was just in her nature, she suspected.

Maybe part of it was running away from Tim and the marriage he was still hoping for. He sure was tenacious in chasing her! He graduated this past summer and was now working for his church doing administrative work. He still wanted to go to a third-world country to build a vocation in that setting. Maybe she was running away from working overseas. But, no, mostly she still wasn't sure she wanted to live with Tim the rest of her life. She was still attending his church and getting involved with projects when time would allow. She liked that work and enjoyed the people.

Through the summer months, she'd found clinical jobs in Edmonton, one in the school for the deaf and another with the tuberculosis sanatorium. They'd been easy work, and she'd had plenty of time for trips to Badger Creek to see her family. They were all concerned with the liberal bent she'd taken in her view of the Bible and Christianity. She also sensed they didn't think Tim was good for her. Well, she'd decide, not her family.

Iris's mind went back to her medical class. It was mostly men. She was one of five women. Most of these women weren't particularly feminine in their behaviour and attitudes, she thought. She doubted many would ever marry. She wondered why she hadn't found some of the men attractive. Some, she found, were nice. A guy named Milton seemed very kind, sensitive, and friendly. He was quite nice looking as well. Actually, he was in her group this year. That was good.'

She'd been taking oboe lessons on and off since she was eleven, and she thought she'd keep up with them to better deal with the stress of being a doctor.

✦ ✦ ✦

Milton was up early. He wanted to have an early breakfast at his boarding house. That could be easily arranged if he was satisfied with cold cereal and toast. A long walk was what he really needed. He wanted to enjoy the fall leaves with their rich reds and yellows, before they fell to winter. He wanted to walk along Saskatchewan drive to have a better look at the river and the north escarpment, across the river. From there he'd head into the campus. He took off at a brisk walk. He noticed the fallen leaves of varied sizes and shapes on the path. The carpet of leaves ranged from green to yellow and through to bronze—even punctuated with a few brilliant reds.

He looked over to the north escarpment of the river valley and noticed the vibrantly coloured banks of trees, the dark green spruce contrasting with the predominant yellow poplars and birch. Cresting the escarpment were the majestic parliament buildings with their gleaming limestone. The striking buildings reminded him of a gigantic upside-down bell. The view made him proud to be an Albertan. He remembered the first time he saw them and how impressed he was then.

Milton's mind swept back to his pre-med years. He was glad he'd gotten his Bachelor of Science degree. He would never regret taking any of the many courses in that program. When he thought about the past two years in medicine, a sense of deep certainty enveloped him—he had gone into the right profession. He felt he was made for it.

His pace slowed as he recalled the hard work he'd put into his medical courses. He almost laughed aloud at how he'd developed his own rigorous study habits. He'd planned a tight schedule for every day of the week. One good side effect was that he'd had less time to fantasize about other guys. The more he focused on his studies, the less he was interested in sex, and that was good, he knew.

Milton had become convinced he was gay. He hated himself. He felt dirty, like a freak. He longed for some relief from his condition. Now that he had come to believe there was a God, he feared God hated him and was blaming him. Nature seemed so beautiful and if God was nature's creator, then God must be beautiful and wonderful too. He wondered what it would feel like to be accepted by God. He doubted that would ever be possible, at least the way he was.

He looked at his watch and thought he'd better be picking up his pace. His mind went ahead to the beginning of his third year of medicine. Today, they'd find out what clinical groups they'd be in. He always felt insecure relating to other guys. He hoped there'd be some women in his group. He felt more comfortable with them.

♦ ♦ ♦

November 1959

The morning had been tough for Iris. She'd been assigned a patient on the paediatric ward of the University of Alberta Hospital. Her job was to take the history on a girl who had developed leukemia. The long-term outlook was grim. Few if any survived longer than a few years. The parents were overcome with grief. They were trying to put up a brave front, but Iris knew their spirits were crushed. After she finished, she headed to the cafeteria. She didn't feel hungry, but she needed to eat to keep up her energy. She also had the sense that she needed to talk to someone, and she spotted Milton sitting alone. She quickly picked up a few items and some coffee and walked to his table.

"Hi, Milt. Mind if I join you?"

"Sure, Iris. I'm glad to have your company."

"Thanks. You might not want my company today. I just went through a very traumatic interview with the parents of a newly discovered case of childhood leukemia."

Milton reached over, touched her forearm, and said, "I'm so sorry—both for you and the family. Those are such sad cases. I wish there was some wonder drug that could kill just the cancerous cells and leave the other cells intact. Do you mind telling me about the interview? How did it go?"

Iris felt tears fill her eyes. It was so good to have someone else really care about how she felt. "I'm sorry, I didn't think I'd get choked up about this. I need to toughen up, I guess."

"No, don't do that. Your sensitivity and compassion is exactly what people with terrible diseases need."

Iris smiled and choked out, "Yeah, I agree." She drew a tissue from her pocket and blew her nose. "This girl is only eight years old and the only child they have. The girl is the sweetest thing I've seen in a long time. She has a very close relationship with her parents, especially with her father. He's trying to be brave, but I could see how torn up he is. He had to excuse himself from time to time so he could cry away from the girl's presence. The mother is better controlled, but she looks so sad. The girl, Cheryl, seems the strongest of the three. I'm surprised how strong she is considering her degree of pallor."

"How were you dealing with your emotions?" Milton asked as he stuffed a plum into his mouth.

Iris took a drink of water. "I wasn't much better than the father. Several times my vision blurred so much I couldn't write notes. I had to blow my nose several times. I suppose they must've wondered what kind of doctor I am that I had so little control of my emotions."

"They'll remember you all their lives. They saw you really cared. That's so important, I think. Did you find out if they had any family or other support?"

"Yes, I did try to explore that a little. Both of the couple's parents are living and probably will help where they can. The trouble is, one set lives near Grimshaw and the others in Saskatchewan. I asked if they belonged to any church or other religious organization. They said they didn't. So I didn't know where else to go with that."

"Do you belong to a church? I ask because you brought it up with the parents."

"Well, I attend a church in Edmonton most Sundays. I have to say I used to be more connected when I was at home in Badger Creek, Saskatchewan. Do you attend a church?"

"No, but I've begun exploring Christianity, recently."

"How did that come about?" Iris was a little surprised at how free she felt talking to Milton. He was such a good listener and his kind brown eyes seemed to invite her to share her feelings.

"I had an organic chemistry prof names Sandoski who's had a profound influence on me," Milton said.

"Oh, I've heard about him. You were very lucky to have had him. I had a different organic chem. prof who was okay, but certainly didn't have charisma like Sandoski. I'm curious what you learned."

Milton filled her in on many of his off-handed comments in class as well as the nature of their private meetings. "I found him such a brilliant man but with a disarming humility. He was so caring and accepting. I asked him about his faith since he often referred to it in his classes. He told me about Jesus and what he came to earth to do. I haven't made the plunge into Christianity yet, but I've come to believe in a god. That's surprising, since my mom is a card-carrying atheist."

Iris looked at her watch. "I'd love to hear more of your life, but I think we need to be going to our class."

"Right. This has been a very enjoyable conversation. Thanks again for joining me at lunch." They smiled warmly at each other and then hurried off.

✦ ✦ ✦

Later that afternoon, Milton walked with an easy gait toward his boarding house. He felt a bit weary after a heavy day. Most of it was seeing patients and discussing the findings with their preceptor. There were some classes thrown in as well. Although the clinical work was tiring, he was excited about seeing the conditions they'd studied in class come to life in real patients on the ward. He enjoyed the enthusiasm the preceptors showed when they talked about the physical findings of patients presented to the students. He knew he was in the right profession.

His mind turned again to his lunch with Iris. He felt a little embarrassed about how personal they'd gotten, but he also felt good about it. He knew he'd done Iris a favour by encouraging her to talk about the interview that had obviously distressed her. He felt surprised at how comfortable he felt with her. He'd always thought of her as very bright and far above him. He'd been afraid to interact with her because she seemed so determined and focused in her approach to medicine. But he found her very easy to talk to and she was willing to be honest and vulnerable. Milton visualized her face in his mind. Yes, she had very nice eyes. Actually, she was a very pretty girl. He realized he had a pleasant feeling about her.

Milton recalled their discussion of churches. *She must be a Christian,* he thought. Maybe, they could have some more discussions about Christianity in the future. He'd love to find out what she felt about Jesus.

✦ ✦ ✦

After supper, Iris settled into her routine of reviewing her notes from her day at the hospital and deciding what reading she needed to do to make the most of her clinical experiences. Her mind, however, kept bringing her back to the lunch with Milton. He'd been exactly what she needed after that painful interview with that leukemia patient and her parents. She saw Milton's face again with those sensitive brown eyes. He somehow saw into her need and opened himself to it as if he really cared.

Then she saw a picture of Tim. He was a bit taller and maybe more handsome in the way people usually see it. But Milton had broad shoulders and a strong, lean torso—just not as athletic as Tim.

Iris tore herself away from these daydreams and made a herculean effort to focus on her studies. She was only partially successful that evening and, later, as she crawled into her bed and pulled her blankets over her head, she again saw Milton's face with his curly dark brown hair.

Chapter Ten

Spring, 1960

Ever since Christmas break, Iris had become increasingly interested in specializing after qualifying in medicine. She was also drawn to research and felt the need to do a year or so of that. Ultimately, though, she wanted to be a clinician where she would see patients. She never forgot that eight-year-old girl with leukemia. She was still alive, but had experienced several brushes with death. She remembered what Milton had said about her sensitivity to patients and knew she had the talent to work with patients.

Around mid-January, Iris heard through one of the residents that the virology lab was looking for a researcher and that the offer was open to one of the third- or fourth-year medical students. She was instantly excited. It was her chance to get her foot into the door of research. Iris applied and, within two weeks, she had the job.

The job, she was told when she applied, was to work with Dr. Pinsky on Tuesday afternoons every week, typing out results of his research. She was also asked to learn about the process of virology research. If she developed into someone of obvious value in this area, she would be given more responsibility—and more pay. She hoped her studies wouldn't suffer, but even if they did a little, the eventual payoff in research experience would be worth it.

After Iris had been working in the lab for about a month, Dr. Pinsky asked her to see him in his office. She wondered whether he'd found some problem in the way she had handled the transcription of his work. She knocked and when he opened his door, he greeted her with a big smile. "Come in, Iris, take a seat."

"You wanted to see me?" Iris asked hesitantly.

"Yes. I've been very pleased with your work so far. I've noticed you're getting the hang of the research routine we're up to here. As you know, we've started to do some research on the poliovirus, how it spreads and how commonly we find the virus in those without clinical disease. We'd like you to join our research team. You'll still have things to learn about research, but you've demonstrated talent in this area. I've high hopes for you."

"Why, thank you, Dr. Pinsky." Iris was overwhelmed by his words of encouragement and by the incredible offer. She never dreamed an opportunity would turn up this soon. "I hardly know what to say. I know that I'll work very hard to deserve the trust you're placing in me."

"I'm sure you will. Now let's go over to the lab and I'll point out where you should start."

Dr. Pinsky and his chief lab assistant filled Iris in on what they had been doing so far and their plans for future investigation. Initially, most of her work would be to look for the virus in laboratory animals bred to be susceptible to the poliovirus. She would be checking their stools, mainly, and tabulating the results. Eventually, she would be testing stools of humans contracting the disease.

When Iris left the lab, she practically floated along the street with glee. She was going to do actual research. This meant she'd have to be even more disciplined in her study and work habits. No time for socializing!

As she approached her boarding house, she thought of Tim. He'd wanted to take her out to a dinner again soon. She decided a phone call was going to have to do. At this rate, she thought Tim was going to lose interest in her. She wondered why that hadn't happened already. If that happened, so be it. Right now, her career came first. Surely, Tim would understand that.

✦ ✦ ✦

Iris dialed Tim's number. It was suppertime and he'd most likely be home. When he came to the phone, he sounded excited to hear from Iris.

"Hey, Iris, it's been entirely too long since I heard from you. I hope you've got good news for me regarding a meal we can enjoy together."

"Tim, I'm so busy now with that research job, I'm finding it hard to squeeze time for a meal together. Dr. Pinsky wants me to join his research team on their work with poliovirus. Now, I don't know where I will find the time to study as I should."

"Why was it necessary to load yourself down with this research work while you're studying medicine? Could you not have done that after obtaining your degree?"

"Well, there are many reasons."

"I'm just finishing my supper. Why can't we have coffee in that café near your place? I promise I won't keep you more than an hour. Surely you can spare that."

Iris paused a moment. "Okay, I'll meet you there at 9:30—that's if you drive me home after that. I don't want to walk at that time of night."

Later, when both had settled into a booth and given their orders, Iris began. "The reason I took this job now was that I saw it as an opportunity to get a head start on doing research. It'll mean that when I'm finished fourth-year medicine, I can go right into serious research and maybe achieve something before I go into clinical work. I know it's going to be a challenge, but I think I can do it if I work hard and efficiently. Please try to understand, Tim."

"I'm trying to. I'd hoped you and I could build our lives together. I think we could support each other as we develop our careers."

Iris looked into Tim's piercing blue eyes and wondered if he was reaching the end of his patience. "I can understand your impatience. I know myself well enough that I'm sure I couldn't do what I plan to do these next few years and be married at the same time. I wouldn't be any good as a wife. Eventually, I want to slow down some and then I can see a marriage and even children, but I'm just not ready for it now."

Tim took a long breath and looked up as he was trying to formulate a response. "I'm very busy with my new work with church missions. I need to plan what I'm going to do about serving in a third-world country for a time. I'd hoped we could work on those plans together, but I see I'll have to make some plans for myself only." Tim looked into Iris's eyes. "That's going to be hard for me to do."

Iris felt tears well up. "Tim, I want you to feel free to find someone else—someone who could share your work and vision for service better than I would. I'm not saying that I don't want to marry you. I am just saying that I feel it isn't fair for me to ask you to wait until I'm finished my specialty training before we get married."

Tim reached for the tab that had been placed near his coffee cup. "Thank you, for coming out and being honest with me. I'm not giving up on you yet." He smiled a crooked smile with sad eyes as he helped Iris with her coat.

✦ ✦ ✦

A teaching session given by a dermatologist was the last class of the day. Iris got up to walk back to her boarding house. As she left the medical building, she breathed in the unusually warm air of spring. She noticed that the leaf buds were swelling and a few blades of green grass were emerging from the brownish thatch. She even noticed two crows flying over her. She thought of them mating soon and building a nest. That brought her to thinking about herself. She had begun to feel a deep visceral desire to satisfy her sexual and reproductive needs. She knew these desires would have to wait, perhaps never to be fulfilled.

As she slowly walked along the sidewalk leading to the street, she thought of Milton. They had met for lunch a number of times, and she continued to find him easy to talk to. She loved discussing difficult issues arising from her research work as well as her clinical work in third-year medicine. Milton also asked her for her opinion on his educational experiences. Iris realized that their growing friendship was non-sexual. She felt little if any sexual attraction coming from Milton. That was okay, since she had no time for a new relationship. She had enough trouble trying to figure out what to do about Tim.

Just before leaving campus, Iris noticed her classmate Myra Sometka. They soon joined and walked together, their boarding houses in the same direction. They chatted for a few minutes about what they had just learned. Myra then abruptly changed the subject and said in a lower tone, "I've noticed you often have lunch with Milton. What do you think of him?"

Iris was a little surprised at this question. "I find him quite nice and he's very easy to talk to. Why do you ask?"

"I just asked because I wondered if you're attracted to him, like in a sexual way?"

"No, but why are you concerned about that? Are you interested in having a relationship with him?" Iris felt bringing up this issue was none of her business.

Myra chuckled. "No, not at all. I was more concerned about you. I didn't want you to get hurt. Do you know that Milton is gay? At least, he seems to have many of the characteristics of a homosexual."

Iris stopped walking. She felt a wave of electricity wash through her. She quickly tried to recover and asked, "So you and who else made that judgment, and on what basis?"

"I have some experience with homosexuality, and I think I have a good sense of who might have that condition. I'm not saying he definitely is one, since I'm only making a judgment by his personality."

"Are you saying you have the skill to judge Milton because you know someone who is homosexual?"

"Okay, Iris, I'll tell you why. You see, I'm lesbian and I know quite a few others who are gays or lesbians. So I have some experience." Myra had gone pale around her mouth.

Iris opened her mouth, unable to speak for a moment. "I see. Thank you for sharing that with me. I can assure you what you said will remain between you and me."

"I would appreciate that. I just wanted you to be aware of Milton for your sake."

"I don't know if I'm grateful you told me or not. I just feel overwhelmed right now." Iris paused, took a deep breath and started walking again. "I guess some things fit with Milton. He's very sensitive and artsy. He prefers to have female friends. Also, I've never felt anything sexual coming from him. However, I would think we would need to have to have more evidence than that to make such a judgment, wouldn't you think?"

"I agree," conceded Myra. "I think a lot of you, Iris, and I wanted you to be aware."

Iris turned to Myra. "Thank you for sharing that with me. I'll need to take some time to process all of this. Certainly, I will not say anything of this to anyone."

"I know I can trust you on that, Iris."

◆ ◆ ◆

That evening, Iris had difficulty focusing on her studies. Was Myra a homosexual? Obviously so or she wouldn't have admitted it. Could Myra be right about Milton? Myra admitted to be only guessing. Maybe she was wrong.

But then she thought about Milton and his behaviour. Did he act like he was gay? She definitely needed to research the subject of homosexuality.

Then she asked herself a question she knew she had to answer, and soon. How was she going to relate to Milton from now on, given the new knowledge she had? She knew what she decided to do was extremely important. She found herself praying for wisdom. She hadn't prayed for a long time. *I haven't been very faithful in my prayers, God, but I need to have your answer about what kind of attitude I need to have toward Milton. Please help me to know how to relate to him.*

Iris settled enough to get several hours of effective studying done. As she prepared to rest for the night, her mind went to Milton again. As she began praying again, she had a thought. *Why not treat him as Jesus would? Okay, but how would Jesus relate to him?* Immediately, she knew that he would show him understanding and compassion. *Okay, so that's the way I'll treat him.* She wondered if she should approach him about her suspicions. That could bring up Iris's discussion with Myra and she couldn't implicate her. No, she would wait for him to bring the issue up, even if it took years.

Then she thought about the words understanding and compassion. She felt these words were given to her as an answer to her prayer. She needed to take them seriously. Understanding could come with her reading about homosexuality. She realized she had only a vague idea about this disorder. As far as the compassion was concerned, she felt she needed to keep on caring for him even though he was gay. A little regular prayer to ask God to help her accomplish that would be a good plan, she thought.

The next thing she knew, it was morning.

✦ ✦ ✦

During the month of May, Iris ignored all appeals of spring to lure her into nature's beauty. With Spartan determination, she poured herself into long hours of study. Her written exams and orals went by in a blur. Soon she was at the other end of them, facing the freedom of summer. This year, the holidays would be short—only two weeks. Then she would be back in the lab, this time working full-time—at least until her fourth-year medical studies started again in September.

Besides working in the lab this summer, she had another project in mind. She planned to study about homosexuality. She would read the various psychiatry books on the subject and check out current literature about any research being done in the area. By fall, she hoped for a good understanding of this disorder.

During the last few weeks, Iris had met Milton several times and had lunch with him once. She tried to treat him the same as always, but found herself trying to read more into his words, actions, and even his physical movements. Whenever she prayed for God to help her, she just got the message, *"Don't judge him. Just love him as I do."*

Now it was time to unwind in Badger Creek country. She needed to reconnect with her family. But the homosexual issue would have to remain her secret, at least for now.

Chapter Eleven

Fall, 1960

THROUGH THE SUMMER, MILTON WORKED FOR THE TUBERCULOSIS Sanatorium in Calgary. The work was interesting but easy, leaving him lots of time to read. He went to the City Library and read most of the books dealing with homosexuality. He also read medical journals in the General Hospital dealing with this subject. By the end of summer, he was aware of many of the theories regarding causation and had a good idea of the treatments available. He was left confused, since so many ideas of causation and treatment were different and conflicting. Most of the writers seemed to be thinking that the cause was an overbearing mother. He didn't feel his mother was that way. Many other writers felt there eventually would be a genetic or hormonal cause found to explain the condition, but nothing in these areas had turned up.

With the more relaxed work schedule at the sanatorium, Milton found himself plagued by sexual fantasies. He fantasized about some of the male workers at the sanatorium. Despite all his efforts to prevent it, he found himself imagining what it would be like to kiss and do much more with them. His grandmother's image repeatedly came to him at these times. He imagined her praying for him to not act on his fantasy life.

The days of September flew by rapidly for Milton. There were so many new patients with exciting diseases. Fourth year was comprised mainly of working up patients on the wards and presenting them to residents or preceptors. He loved these experiences.

One of the patients he interviewed and examined caused him do a lot of thinking. He was a man in his fifties who had colon cancer. The cancer had spread to many parts of his body and it was just a question of time. He was a Christian. It was the way he and his family handled his grim outlook that moved Milton to think more deeply of his own faith, or lack of it.

Milton had been assigned this patient. He'd talked to him several times after the initial interview and physical examination. Jake was often in pain, requiring narcotics. What amazed Milton were Jake's positive attitude and his constant state of peace. Milton was also surprised to see that same sense of peace and acceptance in the wife. Milton saw a deep affection between the two. Granted, there were often tears shed by both. There seemed to be a sense of hope, not that he would be miraculously healed, but that their futures, whatever that would be, would be secure and safe. Milton saw a similar response when Jake's two children came to visit. Milton could see that they dearly loved their father, but there was an amazing calmness about them.

Around ten days after Jake had been admitted, Milton decided to see him again. Milton timed the visit for after Jake had been given some narcotic. Jake was clearly losing ground, but his mind was still bright and alert. They chatted for a while about the weather and the activities of the ward.

Then Milton asked, "Jake, could I ask you something about your attitude and the way you think about life?"

"Sure, anything you want to ask."

"I've noticed that you, and also your wife and children, are so calm. You seem to be facing death with a peace that I don't understand. Would you mind telling why?"

Jake shifted about to try to find a measure of comfort. "Yes, I can tell you." Jake looked Milton squarely in the face. "You see, I'm a member of the Kingdom of God. I've given my life totally over to God. I know he's accepted me because he promised that whoever believes in his son, Jesus, and believes his death pays for all our sins and makes us perfect in God's sight, will become his children. Not only that, Milton, but God has promised me that because I believe in his resurrection, this old body will be raised to life and be with him always. So, even though there's sadness in my family because we will be separated for a time, our futures are bright and full of hope."

Milton paused for a while, trying to process Jake's words. Then he asked, "So, it's your hope for another life after this one that keeps you positive?"

"Sure, that's part of it. There's still this life. I sense Jesus being with me all the time. I'm always talking with him. It's also that way with my wife and children. They're always telling me how Jesus has spoken to them, especially in this period when I've become so ill. Jesus speaks to them in their prayers, while reading the Bible, their thoughts and even in what their Christian friends say to them."

Milton was stunned into silence. Was this really possible? It seemed so. How he longed for that kind of living. Finally, Milton managed to speak. "Jake...you've given me a lot to think about. I'm really so glad for you, and also for your family. Thank you for what you said." Milton smiled and excused himself, promising he'd be back the next day.

✦ ✦ ✦

For the rest of that day, Milton pondered what Jake had said. Milton felt an urgency to do something about it. But what, exactly, was he to do? Then Dr. Sandoski came to mind. He hadn't talked to him since his pre-med years. Would he still want to talk to him? He recalled the professor usually had time around 4:00 p.m., when Milton had visited him so many times in the past. It was past four now—it would have to wait until tomorrow.

The next afternoon, Milton knocked on Dr. Sandoski's lab door. He could feel his heart racing.

"Come in."

He walked in and found Dr. Sandoski pouring some light yellow fluid from a beaker into a large glass cylinder in a boiling bath.

"Just a second, I'll be with you as soon as I finish."

When he had completed his task, Dr. Sandoski turned to Milton. "Milton! It's been entirely too long since you've come to visit. What's happening in your life, my boy?" He hugged Milton, surprising him, especially since Dr. Sandoski knew he was gay. "Well, go on. Tell me why you came today."

Milton again had that wonderful feeling of being accepted by this kind man. "Well, I've frequently thought about what you told me."

"You do take your time to think over these issues." Dr. Sandoski laughed.

"Well, I guess I do," admitted Milton with a grin. "Lots of things have happened to me, but I won't bore you with that. I was assigned a patient the other day. He is dying of cancer, but he and his family have a most remarkable peace about their situation. I finally asked him the reason. He told me it was because they were Christians. He said he was forgiven of all his sins because of his belief in Jesus. He also said that because he believed God raised Jesus to life, he would be raised to life, too, and live forever with Jesus. So, even though he would die, he would see his family again in another life. Well, that really impressed me."

Dr. Sandoski chuckled for a bit, stroked his chin, and said in a soft voice, "So, what are you waiting for? Do you want me to tell you what you already know to do?"

"You mean, I should just believe like Jake does? Is there something I need to say or do?"

"You can talk to God any time. You can just say to him what you want."

"When?"

"Right now. I'll be a witness." Dr. Sandoski nodded and smiled with an accepting twinkle in his eyes.

Milton took a deep breath. "Okay, here goes. God, I want what Dr. Sandoski and Jake have. I believe that Jesus died for all my sins. Come and take over my life. I want to be with you, Jesus, forever."

Milt looked up. He could see that Dr. Sandoski still had his eyes shut, but tears were dribbling down his cheek. A thought occurred to him just then. Dr. Sandoski was Jesus to him for this moment. He sensed relief and thankfulness for what had just occurred. Now, he too was a child of God.

Dr. Sandoski found some tissue on the lab counter and blew his nose. "I have two recommendations for you now. Don't take as long to do them." Dr. Sandoski laughed. "The first thing is to tell a few people what you just did. Do it today. It's important for your faith. The second thing is to find a good church so you can grow spiritually. Do you know where you would choose to attend?"

"No, I have no idea."

"Well, I have a suggestion. Come to the church my wife and I attend. After you've attended once and think you could continue, join a home study group. I have a group in mind that I think would be very helpful. It's led by a man named Patrick Benson. You're going to be tempted *not* to do all this. But you need to say, 'To hell with my fears. I'm going to do what is right.' The Holy Spirit will give you the courage to go." Dr. Sandoski chuckled again but had that very kind twinkle in his eyes.

Dr. Sandoski then gave Milton the church's location and the way to get there. Milton walked out of the room with a sense of peace and hope he'd not had for a long time, maybe never before.

✦ ✦ ✦

Milton was determined to attend Sandoski's church, but he was afraid. The closer he got to Sunday, the more fearful he became. Where was this Holy Spirit Sandoski talked about? He needed help. He wondered if he should phone Sandoski. Maybe he could give Milton a ride? Milton knew the way and he knew what busses to take. So what was the problem? He realized he was fearful of what the church would do if they found out that he was gay.

Milton remembered what Bill Street, his old zoology lab partner, had said about Christians. He had been quite critical about them because of their being so judgmental. According to Bill, most churches considered having a homosexual orientation a sin. He told Milton once that most churches considered being gay a choice. Milton had trouble with that. How could it be a choice when same-sex fantasizing started in early childhood? Certainly, he didn't choose to be gay.

That Sunday, Milton put on his only suit and best shirt and tie. He made sure his shoes were polished to a high shine. Once off the bus, he had to walk a block or so. The church was large, capable of holding probably five hundred people. There was nothing fancy about the church, just modest architecture. He had come a bit early so only about fifty people were present. They were mainly in the foyer, standing around in small groups, obviously enjoying themselves. A fellow around forty spotted him and immediately came over and introduced himself as Gerald and asked him if he was new there. Milton admitted he was and Gerald led him into the sanctuary and asked him where he would like to sit. Milton pointed to the back row. Gerald smiled. "Milton, I hope you enjoy the service." Milton thanked him and sat down near the aisle. The church began to fill quickly and soon the sanctuary was about three-quarters full. He was surprised by how many people his age were present. Obviously, this church appealed to students in high school, college, and even university.

The hymns were unfamiliar. Not surprising, since Milton had virtually never been in a church other than for weddings and funerals. However, he loved the lyrics. They were so rich with meaning. The pipe organ and the gorgeous harmony from the people moved him to tears. The choir sang and his skin felt covered by goose bumps. He longed to be a part of that choir.

Then the pastor delivered his message. He spoke on Jesus' encounter with Simon the Pharisee, who invited Jesus for a meal. Their meal was interrupted by a prostitute. Milton was deeply moved by the love and acceptance of Jesus. He couldn't help but see a parallel between this despised outcast and himself as a homosexual.

When the service ended, Milton's eyes roved over the congregation to see if he could spot the Sandoskis. He felt a tap on his shoulder, turned, and found the smiling face of Dr. Sandoski, who then introduced his wife. The three of them briefly discussed his church experience. Then Dr. Sandoski asked,"Milton, would you be interested in meeting the head of a small home group? You remember I advised you to consider becoming a member of such a group."

Milton hesitated a moment."I suppose so, since you feel quite strongly about it. I sure don't know what to expect."

"You're going to have to trust me on this. I'm quite sure you will come to really appreciate this group."

"Sure, I can meet him or her."

Dr. Sandoski said,"Him," and walked briskly to another part of the foyer, Milton in tow. Soon he found the man he was looking for and greeted him enthusiastically."Patrick, I'd like you to meet Milton Saunders. Milton, this is Patrick Benson and his wife, Linda. Milton is a fourth-year medical student. He has shown great promise. He has also become a close friend of mine. Milton has recently come to faith in Jesus and I advised him to get into a home study group. Of course, yours is the best group going, so I'm recommending he join. He might feel he can't take the time from his studies, but that's his choice. I'll leave you, since I need to find my wife, who's arranging lunch."

As Dr. Sandoski left, Milton noticed Patrick was taller than average with a sturdy frame. He had light brown hair. The most impressive thing about him was his warm brown eyes and very accepting smile.

Patrick gripped Milton's hand."Milton, we are happy to meet you."

"Is this your first time in our church?" Linda asked.

"Yes," Milton said."I very much enjoyed the service. It's all very new to me, actually. I've never been to a regular church service before."

"Milton, would you be free to join us for lunch?" As Patrick asked, he glanced to his wife who was nodding.

"I have no other plans. Sure I could. I hope I'm not a disruption."

"No, not really. We have three growing children to feed. So if you're willing to compete with them for the available food, you're welcome," Linda said, laughing.

Milton noticed that Linda, who was average height and fairly slight, was full of energy with a bright, cheery smile.

The Bensons collected their children and moved to their car. Milton felt accepted by this couple. He wondered what they would think if or when he divulged the truth of his being gay. He doubted Dr. Sandoski had told them anything about his problem. Should he confide his secret to these people?

The noon lunch at the Bensons was simple, but just fine as far as Milton was concerned. There was lots of lighthearted banter between all the members of the family. Milton learned their oldest was Jennifer, age fifteen, the next was Trent, thirteen, and the youngest was Nathan, age eleven. Milton also found out that Patrick ran a plumbing and heating business. Linda worked as an investment adviser in a bank.

As soon as lunch was over, the three children excused themselves to go play with some friends. Patrick began clearing the table. Milton quickly got up and helped.

"Just stack them up on the counter, guys," Linda said, "and then we can go to the living room and do some visiting. I'm very curious about the kinds of courses medical students take."

When all three were comfortably settled, Linda asked, "Milton, would you mind telling me in a simple way what a fourth-year medical student's life is like?"

Milton gladly summarized what his clinical experiences were like and the nature of his study program to prepare for his examinations in May.

Patrick asked, "I'm very interested in how you became a Christian, Milton. Are your parents Christians?"

"My father came from an Anglican background and attends church once in a while." Milton noticed both the Bensons watching him intently with kind, accepting expressions. "My dad's mother is a Christian and has had the greatest early influence on my coming to faith. My mother is an avowed atheist, so she was of little help. Probably the most important recent influence came from Dr. Sandoski. I was very impressed with his scientific achievements and equally impressed that he also had a deep faith in Christ. After a lot of foot-dragging on my part, Dr. Sandoski helped me to put my trust in Jesus, just last week."

The Bensons expressed their amazement and delight. "What a godly man that Sandoski is!" Patrick said. "I would like to tell you about our home group, in case you're interested. I know you've got heavy time constraints, but if you think you can afford the time, I know you would enjoy the group and find it helpful in your spiritual growth. We meet here each Friday at seven p.m. We sing a little, pray a little, talk a little and study a book of the Bible. Our study stays fairly simple, not too esoteric. We keep the study on a level where new believers, like yourself, will feel comfortable."

Milton felt attracted to such a group. He knew he needed and wanted to read and understand the Bible. Then he felt a wave of fear. Would there be people there that he would find intimidating, especially men? What if they should find out he was gay?

Patrick said, "I sense you have some concerns about being in our group. Feel free to ask any questions you may have."

Milton again wondered if he should tell the Bensons his secret. It would be a lot easier to tell them than to tell the group. What did he have to lose, except the friendship of these very nice people? Milton surprised himself when he found himself blurting out, "You need to know something before I agree to go to this group. You see, I'm gay, or at least I think I am." Milton's cheeks were blotched red.

There was a moment's pause and then Patrick said, "Milton, I wasn't aware of that." Patrick looked over to his wife before saying more. She gave a very slight nod. "We don't feel we have a right to judge in these kinds of situations. We all suffer from physical, emotional, and spiritual defects. God's love and mercy is open to all. We as forgiven sinners have one main job, and that's to love each other and leave the judging to God. You are no different than any of us when God looks at us as his children. We still accept you, Milton. And I'm quite confident that the group will accept you also."

Milton smiled with relief. "Thank you so much for what you just said. That makes me feel a lot better. I've been told by many people that Christians hate homosexuals."

"You're right," Linda said. "Many Christians have that attitude, partly because they don't understand how it comes about in people and partly because they think it's their job to judge. We feel we should just leave the judging to God and love people in whatever state they're in."

Milton realized the Bensons were not only informed about homosexuality, but they were non-judgmental and accepting. He recognized the same acceptance that he felt with Dr. Sandoski.

"Milton," Patrick said, "would you mind telling us if you have a male partner? Knowing that would help us to understand your situation better."

"I presume you're meaning a sexual partner." Milton's eyebrows raised. "No, I don't have one. I've never had sexual relations with anyone, let alone another man."

"One more question, then." Patrick screwed up his face. "Why do you think you're gay?"

"Well, right from about ten years old, I knew I was a bit different. I felt insecure playing with other boys and safer playing with girls. Then in my teen years, I began having fantasies." Milton's cheeks became blotchy again.

"I'll ask another question, if you don't mind." Linda repositioned herself in her chair as if she were trying to formulate a difficult question. "Do you ever blame others, like your parents, or bad experiences with other children, for your being gay?"

"No, I don't think so. Like lots of other people, my childhood wasn't perfect. I never connected too well with my father. I often felt he wasn't very proud of me. My mother was always caring, maybe too doting at times. I've a brother whom I always look up to. He seems to have everything I didn't have."

"You mean your brother was more accepted by your father?" Linda asked.

"Yeah, I guess that's so," Milton said in a glum voice. Milton had slumped down into the couch.

"Well," Patrick said, sitting forward in his chair, "you've been very brave, trusting relatively strange people the way you have. You've helped us a lot to get to know you. We want you to know two things. One, we will not think any less of you. Two, we will promise to keep what you said confidential. We've the same rules in our group and we abide by them strictly."

Milton took a deep breath and straightened in his seat. "Thank you for that. I find it hard to talk about these things and yet I'm glad I did. I appreciate your accepting me the way I am. Yes, I would appreciate you keeping this information to yourselves."

"Have you decided if you'll come to our group?" Linda asked. "You won't offend us if, for any reason, you can't see doing that now."

"Yes, I want to come. I'm a bit scared, but I know I need to be a part of this group. There may be some days I can't come because of school, but I think I can make it most times."

As Milton got up to leave, Patrick walked over to him and enveloped him in a warm hug. Patrick then looked into his eyes and said, "We're glad to have gotten to know a little about you, Milton. We hope to get to know you even better in the future. You are very important to us."

Milton went home that evening with a deep sense of hope for the first time in a long while.

Chapter Twelve

Early March, 1961

Like a hawk diving for its prey, Iris was focused on her final examinations that would earn her the cherished medical degree. Written exams would start in the first week in May and oral exams would follow. The amount of time she could devote to her research in Dr. Pinsky's virology lab was considerably reduced in the last few weeks. Dr. Pinsky understood. Other priorities, like playing oboe, had to yield to the push for exam preparation. Even her Sundays were taken up by studying. She would have to put a hold on her mission projects at Tim's church.

It was Saturday evening and she was in her boarding house room sitting in front of her desk piled high with medical books. She had spent most of the day at the library and felt worn out. She was tempted to turn in, but knew she'd need to stick with the plan she'd set for herself or she'd be sorry. She felt so full of worries and concerns for the future. She felt the need to unload on someone, but whom? She could call Tim. He'd be glad to talk to her, but deep down she knew he wasn't the one she wanted. She needed to talk to Milton. He understood what she was going through. And he cared—at least in a different way to Tim. She imagined Milton was right there with his warm, caring eyes fixed on her. On impulse, she reached for the phone and in a few seconds was talking to Milton.

"What are you up to, Iris? Let me guess, you're sitting in your room trying to study, but you've hit the wall. You're stalling out."

"You are so right. You must possess extra-sensory perception."

"No, I just took a guess on the basis of how I felt. Would you be interested in coffee? I've got an old pickup now. I could meet you at your door in ten minutes."

"You're a lifesaver. See you in a few minutes."

Iris quickly pulled on her coat and gloves and headed to the front door. She found the landlady and told her she was going out for coffee.

"Dress warm. There's a cool breeze out there," came from somewhere in the kitchen.

Iris peered out the window, looking for Milton. Why did she feel so comfortable with him? Maybe it was that he was gay. She didn't have to worry about his having any romantic feelings. They could just be friends. Yeah, she guessed, that was it. She chuckled at this thought.

Milton drove up in his vintage pickup. He jumped out and held the door open for Iris. His cheery smile almost overwhelmed her. "You needn't have opened the door for me. We're just friends, you know."

"Oh, I don't know why I want to do it. I just respect you so much, I guess."

Iris flushed and thought, *he may be gay, but he sure knows how to charm a girl.*

Once they were seated in a Whyte Avenue café and had ordered their cups of coffee, Iris said, "Thank you for caring enough about me to be willing to do this. I needed to talk to someone." Iris looked into Milton's expectant face and continued, "Actually, I really wanted to talk to you since I knew you would understand some of the pressures we're under these days. And, you're just fun to talk with."

"You honour me. You know, I find talking to you not only helpful academically, but also energizing. You are a very interesting person." Milton paused. "Why don't you tell me how things are going for you? Are you still happy with your research project?"

"I've had to shelve that work for now, at least until I'm through these exams." Iris sipped some coffee. "The work I'm doing with Dr. Pinsky is quite exciting and I hope I can get most of the data collected by the end of the summer."

"Just what are you working on in the lab, Iris?"

"Well, I've been checking urine and feces of laboratory mice for the presence of poliovirus. We're trying to determine the main way the virus spreads and how it's transmitted from one animal to the other. Once we're finished with that project, we're moving to human polio patients. After that, we're going to do the same thing on animals and humans who have been treated with the new oral vaccine. That's when things really get exciting."

"Some of that research sounds dangerous. Is there a risk you might become infected with the wild poliovirus?"

"There's always that chance. We're taking lots of precautions when handling potentially infected stool. Dr. Pinsky isn't too worried."

Milton looked a little concerned. "I hope he isn't putting his workers at risk. I'd be really careful."

"I will. Thanks for your concern."

"What about your oboe playing? Are you still taking lessons?"

"No, I stopped the lessons about three weeks ago. I hope to get back to that in the summer. I've also stopped playing in our little ensemble. I don't know if I told you I started up a group last Christmas."

Milton looked very interested. "No, I didn't hear about that. Who's in it?"

"There's a violinist, Sandra Miller, an education student. Then there's a pianist, Myra Sometka, from our class, and me on the oboe. We have a lot of fun. Unfortunately, we could only practice about two hours a week because of our busy schedules."

✦ ✦ ✦

Milton took a drink of his coffee. The mention of Myra brought a wave of concern to him. He suspected she was a lesbian. He'd overheard some girls talking about Myra when he was in pre-med. He wondered if Iris knew this about Myra.

He wondered if she suspected he was gay. He knew he should tell her some time. The way Iris looked at him, he thought she might have feelings for him. He needed to be fair with her. Not yet, though. Besides, she was Tim's girl, wasn't she? He decided he would find out. "How's it going with Tim these days?"

"That's a stop-and-go situation. I think he'd like to get on with it—get married, I mean. I just don't feel right about it. I'm so focused on my studies and research, I'm afraid I wouldn't make much of a marriage partner. I suppose these are just excuses. The truth of it is that I'm not sure how deep our friendship is. You know, Milt, I enjoy our friendship more than I do Tim's and mine." Iris looked into Milton's eyes and held them for a moment.

Milton had a feeling he needed to do something, and now. "Iris, I need to tell you something about myself." Milton shifted about and flushed around his neck.

"I'm listening," Iris said calmly.

"I believe that I am gay. You need to know that."

"I've heard something to that effect." Iris kept her gaze on Milton.

"How did you know? I suppose Myra might have suspected and talked to you. The other day she asked me, out of the blue, if I was gay. So I know she's aware of my situation."

"Milton, may I be so bold as to ask you if you have been active? I mean, have you had sexual partners?" Iris thought they had to be brutally honest with each other if their friendship were to continue.

"No, I'll admit I have been plagued by sexual fantasies, but I've not acted on them. I hope I never will."

"Why's that?"

"I've got a grandmother who, I think, suspected a long time ago and told me repeatedly what the Bible says about homosexuality. And then, recently, I've become a Christian and am going to a helpful home study group. They've been very accepting of me. Somehow, it seems, when I attend that group regularly, I'm not bothered by these fantasies. Keeping my nose in medical textbooks also helps," Milton said with a grin.

Iris straightened and her eyes widened. "So, you're a Christian. I sure didn't know that. How did that happen? I'd love to hear about it."

"Well, my grandmother had an important influence on me during my early years, but in recent times, the most important influence on my life was Dr. Sandoski, my organic chemistry professor. I think I've spoken of him to you before. Last fall, he showed me how to put my faith in Jesus. Actually, the home group I'm going to is part of Dr. Sandoski's church."

"That's wonderful." Iris had tears in her eyes. "I've heard about Dr. Sandoski and his faith. Unfortunately, I never had him as a professor."

For several moments, Milton looked out the window and followed car lights. Then he turned back to face Iris. "Now that you know I'm homosexual, I would understand if we didn't see much of each other." Milton looked very sad. "You need to focus on someone who has a future. You're wasting your time with me."

"Oh Milt," Iris said, placing her hand on his, "knowing that you're gay doesn't change my friendship with you at all. I've been reading quite a bit about homosexuality. I can't say I'm very impressed about the various treatments to cure this situation, but I'm still hopeful there's going to be something out there to help you. That is, if you want help."

"Well, I didn't choose this condition and I would go for anything that offers a cure. Actually, I'm trusting God to show me what he wants me to do about it."

"I will add my prayers to yours in this regard."

"I'd appreciate that. You're very generous and accepting."

"Thank you." Iris smiled warmly.

They sat for a while, neither speaking. Finally, Milton looked at his watch. He sighed. "I guess we'd better be going back to the war zone."

Milton paid for the coffee and they stepped out of the café and headed for his pickup. When they got to the vehicle, Milton put his hand on her arm. "Iris, I hope we can continue being friends, but I don't want our friendship to keep you from finding a compatible mate. I'll understand if we see a little less of each other for now."

Tears filled Iris's eyes. "I care a lot for you. If you're okay with continuing to see each other as before, I'm happy."

"Well, we'd better get going before I start crying too."

They both gave a tearful chuckle and got into the pickup.

✦ ✦ ✦

It was Friday night again. Milton wondered if he should miss the home group in favour of studying. But then he thought that the benefit from this group greatly outweighed the value of a few hours of school work. He began getting himself ready. Since he'd got the pickup, he could get to the Bensons much quicker. En route, he reviewed his experiences in the group. They just seemed to have oceans of love. He felt such acceptance when he sat with them, in spite of his sharing with the group that he thought he was gay.

The men in the group continued to shake his hand and many even hugged him. The other men seemed to catch the idea from Patrick. He knew deep down that he needed these touching contacts that weren't sexual in nature. He also found the group's friendship inwardly fulfilling, bringing him hope.

In terms of Scripture study, they first studied the Gospel of John. He suspected the group did that mainly for his benefit. He'd found the Gospel of John quite foundational. It gave him a good idea of what being a Christ follower was. In the last few months, the group had been studying the book of Romans. On a recent Friday night meeting, Patrick talked about the meaning of Jesus' death. He pointed out that Jesus hadn't only died *for* our sins, he had died *to* sin. He referred to Romans 6:10: "The death he died he died to sin, once for all, but the life he lives he lives to God."

Patrick had said, "Jesus was tempted just like we are before he died, but after he died, he was dead to sin. It no longer held any temptation for him."

Then he had read the next verse: "So you must also consider yourselves dead to sin and alive to God in Christ Jesus."

"So," he had said, "by faith, we can identify with Christ's death and consider ourselves dead to sin. Sin no longer has power over us and we can legally claim victory over sin." Milton knew he had needed this message.

Milton had often pondered these ideas. He surely needed victory over his imagination and the temptation to experience sexual intimacy with other guys. Recently, he'd bumped into his old zoology friend, Bill Street. They had talked about their sexual fantasies. Bill told Milton that he would be a lot happier if he actually had sex with guys from time to time. Milton had to admit he was still tempted, especially when he hadn't been in touch with his group for a while. He really needed his home group.

When Milton entered the Benson house, Patrick rose and embraced Milton. "I'm so glad you could make it out. I know the pressure to study is high these days."

Milton smiled broadly and thanked Patrick. Milton felt that he needed those hugs much like a severely dehydrated hiker in a desert needed water. The hugs and handshakes met some deep need within him.

When the group had settled, and an opening prayer had been offered, Patrick asked the group if anyone wanted to share anything important that had occurred in their lives the previous week. Several in the group talked about their experiences. Milton felt he should share what Bill had told him. He did so and then added, "Bill made me feel as though I were missing out on something I deserved to have. I just told him I had made a choice to not participate in something I didn't feel right about doing. Of course, he told me I was stunting my enjoyment of life for the sake of my restrictive religion. I told him how important the group was in making me feel more comfortable with people, especially males. I don't know if he understood me, but I'm telling you I feel myself changing inside. I find this group very encouraging. I find that for several days after group meetings, I virtually have no homosexual fantasies."

Several made appreciative comments and Patrick voiced what everyone was feeling. "Thank you, Milton, for having the courage to say what you did." Patrick turned to the rest of the group. "I also want to thank you as a group. You have opened your heart to Milton. You have been praying for him and you have been loving him like Jesus would and does. What we're seeing here is what a group is supposed to do—love and care for each other without judgment."

The group then went on in their study of Romans. Patrick asked the group to take turns reading through chapter eight. When verses ten and eleven were read, Milton felt the words sink into him, warming him deep inside. He read the words again, this time to himself.

But if Christ is in you, although your bodies are dead because of sin, your spirits are alive because of righteousness. If the Spirit of him who raised Jesus from the dead dwells in you, he who raised Christ Jesus from the dead will give life to your mortal bodies also through his Spirit which dwells in you.

Milton heard Patrick tell the group that the power to live this new life comes by the Holy Spirit and is a gift to all believers who ask for it. "God never pushes this gift on Christians. We need to ask for what is ours by inheritance."

The group became quiet and thoughtful. Milton knew he would have to read the whole section again on his own. He was hopeful that God would give him the power to live a life that pleased him. Maybe that included doing something about his sexual orientation.

✦ ✦ ✦

Iris had spent the last two hours in Rutherford Library searching for a better understanding of kidney function. Her notes and the text she'd been using didn't do justice to the subject. She'd found a recent renal function review in one of the journals that was quite helpful. She now had a much better understanding of how the kidney tubules concentrated urine. She looked at her watch and noticed it was after twelve. No wonder she felt hungry.

She stuffed her notes into her briefcase, pulled on her coat, and headed for the exit. Her eye caught site of another student leaving the library. *That's Myra Sometka,* she thought. She had an idea. Why not see if Myra would have lunch with her? She'd been studying about homosexuality whenever she could slip that in between all her other work.

"Hey, Myra," Iris called. "Hold up. I want to talk to you."

Myra stopped and waited for Iris to catch up.

"Myra, have you eaten lunch yet?"

"No, I was just going to do that now."

"Why don't we have lunch together, maybe at the SUB? I have some things I'd like to ask your opinion on," Iris said with a smile.

"Sure that's fine by me. The only thing is, I doubt my opinion is worth much, I'm so confused about so many medical issues." Myra laughed.

"I know exactly what you mean." Iris joined her in laughing.

As both walked briskly toward the Students Union Building, Myra said, "Let's agree that we won't talk about medical stuff, okay?"

"Well, what I wanted your opinion on could be construed as medical, but I'm hoping you won't mind giving me your personal opinion, not text-book stuff."

"So this is about homosexuality, I suppose. You said you were going to do some reading on this subject. Now you have some questions for me to see if I fit the bill?"

"You guessed right. Would you give me your opinion?"

"Sure. Hopefully we can find a quiet spot. I don't like people listening in on this kind of conversation. People just don't understand and many are very biased, you know. I just don't want to promote trouble."

"I understand," said Iris. "We can find a decent place to talk, I'm quite sure."

When they got to the lunchroom, there were a few students eating their lunch but they were all grouped around the television watching a show featuring Elvis Presley. The two headed for the back of the room, away from the TV and settled down to eat.

"Okay, Iris, shoot."

"Well, I was interested in knowing when you first suspected you might be a lesbian?"

Myra thought a moment while she chewed on a sandwich. "I think I was six when I realized I was different than other girls. They were all into dolls, dressing up like ladies, playing house and so on. I was interested in doing what boys were doing like playing in the mud, climbing trees, and playing cops and robbers. Most of my friends were boys. People just called me a Tom girl."

"You wouldn't have known anything about homosexuality then."

"No, of course not." Myra took a sip of water. "It wasn't until I was entering adolescence, maybe around thirteen, when I didn't have the same interest in boys as other girls did. That was a time of great confusion. I found myself seeking a close relationship with certain girls I admired. I wanted these special friends to like me more than anything else."

"What attracted you?" Iris asked.

"Well, they had features I admired—features I didn't have but desired for myself, I suppose. I just wanted them to accept me as their special friend."

"Do you mind me asking when you actually found friends like you desired?" Iris knew Myra might not like to talk about this.

"When I was about seventeen. I found another girl who had similar feelings as I did. She was twenty-five. It was at a YWCA camp and she was one of the leaders. We didn't do anything sexual other than some touching, you know. We became quite close. I realized then that I got more pleasure out of special girls than boys. I just had no interest in doing anything intimate with boys."

"Do you have a special friend now?" Iris wondered if she was pushing too far.

"Yeah, I do, several actually, but mainly one. We room together." Myra didn't elaborate and Iris didn't feel she could delve any deeper into Myra's private life.

After stuffing her lunch bag into her briefcase, Iris asked, "Do you mind me asking what your family was like?"

"So you want to psychoanalyze me." Myra laughed. "I don't mind. There were three of us children in the family. I had two older sisters. Both are straight. My parents always favoured my two sisters. They were very social and had lots of friends. They were very feminine and loved clothes and played with dolls until they were in junior high."

"Did you feel you couldn't compete with them for your parents' affection?"

"Yeah, that's about it. I knew I could never be a nice girl like they were. So I didn't even try."

"What was your father like?" Iris had heard that fathers were weak in lesbian situations.

"Oh, he was okay, I guess. He was quite busy in his real estate business and didn't spend a lot of time with us, certainly not with me. When he was around, he was friendly enough."

"And your mother?"

"She and I never connected. Her head was always in space somewhere. She loved her social group. She was forever attending her ladies' meetings. She was into the lives of my sisters, but I didn't rate. She was always annoyed at my going out to play with boys. I think she just gave up on me. I still have no relationship with her. We just tolerate each other when we meet, and that's not often."

"Do your parents know? About your orientation, I mean."

"I think Dad knows, but he doesn't talk about it with my mother. I doubt if she knows."

"Have you ever come across Christians who have expressed opinions about homosexuality?" Iris knew this was a loaded question.

"Oh, sure." Myra chuckled. "My uncle is a Christian and he has pronounced his views on homosexuality many times in my presence. I think he suspects. He tells everyone who'll listen that homosexuality is sin and homosexuals are all going to burn in hell. He loves to say that homosexuality is a sinful choice. 'They need to repent,' he says, 'and ask God to forgive them and God will straighten them out if they're willing.'"

"What do you think?"

"Well, he's well meaning, I suppose, but he's just ignorant about the whole issue. I had no choice in this orientation. I would be only too happy to be straight. If God sees me as a sinner because of this orientation when I had no choice, then he isn't fair. How can I believe in a God like that?"

Iris didn't believe God was like that, but she knew she wouldn't help by arguing. "You've had some tough things happen to you in your childhood."

Myra chewed on an apple and said, "Yeah, well, thanks for caring. Say, do you still meet with Milton?"

"Yes, we still have visits. We have had discussions about his orientation. So we're facing it."

"Do you have feelings for him?"

Now Iris felt under the microscope. "Yes, sometimes. He's such a nice guy. I find it so difficult to see him live his life out as a gay. I know he loves children and would be very happy if, somehow, he could have his own family. But I have to be realistic, I guess. Barring a miracle, this relationship can't go anywhere." Iris was on the verge of tears.

"I'm sorry, I know what you're facing. You'd be a fool to hold out any hope he might change to being straight, in spite of what Christians sometimes claim."

"You know, Milton's become a Christian and he regularly goes to a Christian home study group."

"Don't build up your hopes. 'Once a gay, always a gay.' I just don't want you to get hurt more than you already are," Myra said with deep concern in her eyes.

As if both knew it was time to go to their class at the University of Alberta Hospital, they dusted the crumbs off their clothes, put on their coats, grabbed their cases and headed out. Both were in deep thought.

Just before entering the conference room for class, Iris reached out and gently grabbed Myra's forearm, bringing them to a halt. "I want to say how much I appreciate you. You were very open and honest with me, even though we talked about things usually kept private. Thank you, Myra."

Myra's eyes glistened with tears. "You are the sort of person people can trust, so it's easy for me to share. You always surprise me with your acceptance and care, even though I am a lesbian. You are a special person."

"Oh, thank you. If you don't stop this, both of us will be crying in class. No one will believe that we are becoming professionals."

✦ ✦ ✦

Iris walked out of her preceptor's room, where she had experienced a trial oral examination. Dr. Sorgan had agreed to do it for several of the students in his group. Iris spotted Milton sitting in the waiting room.

Milton gave Iris a big smile. "Well, how did it go?"

Iris slumped down next to him and groaned. "I think I should've done better. He shot questions at me about topics I've never heard about. Sometimes, he questioned me like a prosecuting lawyer—trying to pick holes in my arguments. He's usually nice, but not today."

"I experienced the same thing. He had me rattled enough that I doubt if I could have given him the name of my mother if he asked."

They laughed, enjoying each other's friendship and relief that the practice orals were over. Milton stood and pulled Iris up with him. "Come on, let's go get some coffee before sweating it out with our books again."

"Good idea. I, for one, will be glad to have all the exams behind us."

After settling down in the cafeteria with steaming coffee cups in hand, Milton asked Iris, "Have you heard where you'll be interning?"

"Yes I have. As I've told you, I applied here in the University Hospital so I could be closer to where I do research with Dr. Pinsky. I was told three days ago that I'd be interning here. How about you?"

"I requested the Royal Alexander Hospital and was accepted. I wanted to get out of this place for a while. Getting to know other doctors would be a benefit, I think."

Iris sipped at her coffee and nodded. "Yes, I can see that advantage in getting a broader experience. I don't think I have much of a choice, though."

Milton glanced around the cafeteria while collecting his thoughts and then looked back to Iris. "I'll miss having these chats with you. I hope we can still keep in touch this next year. Maybe we could give each other our call schedules so that we can tell when we're both off. We could at least telephone each other."

Iris smiled and held Milton's eyes for a moment. "I'll miss you just as much." Iris's eyes began to glisten with tears. "It has been so nice to talk to you about clinical problems or anything, for that matter. You're such a good listener and I like your thinking."

"Well, thank you. You know, you are the best friend I've got. So I would really love for us to see each other often in spite of where we're interning."

They both got up and walked over to where the dirty dishes were stacked and then separated, Milton heading for his boarding house and Iris to the hospital library. Both were in deep thought about their relationship and all the questions that it held.

Chapter Thirteen

May 24, 1961

MILTON HAD DECIDED TO STAY AROUND EDMONTON FOR A WEEK AFTER his final written and oral examinations. He wanted to connect with his church before heading back home to Calgary. Patrick had phoned him the day before informing him of a work weekend at their church's retreat centre. The men of their small group would be involved. It would take place Friday night and all day Saturday. Patrick, for one, would be doing some plumbing. There would be all kinds of jobs for unskilled people to do, he reassured volunteers. Milton's first inclination was to excuse himself, because he was nervous about how he would function socially with men. An inner voice said to go. He gulped down his fears and agreed to join the group. In his mind's eye, he could see the faces of those fun-loving and friendly men. He was so pleased to have this caring group of men in his life.

The day was warm and clear, so the evening was expected to be perfect. Milton had on his hiking boots, denims, and an old sweater. He'd brought leather work gloves, too. At four-thirty, Patrick pulled up to his boarding house with his station wagon. There were three other men inside. Fear again clutched Milton's heart, but he breathed a prayer for strength and crawled inside. He was greeted cheerfully.

When they arrived at the camp, Patrick met with Pete, the manager, and went over the list of jobs he had for them. After a few minutes of planning, Patrick, pointing to Milton and Blake, said, "Why don't you two inspect the cabins and make a list of repairs that could be done today. Then we'll meet with the manager and we'll decide what is reasonable to do today. Milton, here's a sheet of paper and a pencil."

Milton and Blake nodded and headed for the first cabin. When they got there, they looked at the roof and saw missing shingles. Inside, they noted bunks that were rickety and some cracked windows. They found similar problems in two other cabins. The other cabins were in good shape.

The two men returned to the main building to report their findings. When they got there, coffee and doughnuts were being served so they could get some nutrition while they talked. They were told that there would be a wiener roast after it would be too dark to work. Soon the men were ready to go back to do their assigned jobs. Milton and Blake headed out to look for supplies.

"Pete said he has some replacement shingles and some lumber in the storage shed. We can get the stuff we need and get started," said Blake, who had some experience doing renovations.

"I'm with you," Milton said. "You just have to be patient with me as I have very little experience with this sort of thing."

"Don't worry, I'm happy to give you a few pointers as we go along."

Pete did indeed have most of the supplies that were needed. Blake showed Milton how to remove damaged shingles and replace them with new cedar shingles. When Milton had finished his project and climbed down from the roof, he went inside the cabin. "I've finished that job. What could I help you with in here?"

"Good, you're just in time to help me put this new brace on this bunk," Blake said. "Just hold that end on to the upright there while I whack some nails in here."

They were given a sheet of glass that needed cutting to size for the cracked windows. The two worked together measuring, scoring, breaking glass along score lines, and puttying them in place. Milton had never done this kind of work before, and he found the whole operation fascinating. The two men focused on their work with minimal talk. As each helped the other, work progressed quickly. Over the course of the next two hours, all the repairs were completed. The sun had already set by then and work had to stop.

"Well, that was fun," Blake said with a chuckle. "We got a lot more done than I expected in the time we had."

"I hope I wasn't too much of an encumbrance. I've never done anything like this before, so you had to show me how to do everything the first time. You might have been better off alone."

"No, not at all. You caught on quickly and, really, you were a big help. I liked working with you."

Milton realized how good he felt working with Blake. They hadn't talked much more than what was needed to get the work done. Yet, there was something very fulfilling about working together doing an important project and then enjoying the finished work together.

As they walked to the main building, Milton thought he would express some of his feelings. "That was about the most enjoyable thing I've done in years. You made me feel so comfortable working with you, even though I knew nothing about building and renovating. You're a great teacher. Thank you, Blake."

"Well, thank you for those kind words. It's easy to be a good teacher when you've a good student."

They laughed and clapped each other on their backs. By that time, they'd arrived at the building to report what they'd done. All seemed to have gotten a lot done and were in good spirits. Patrick suggested they wash up and head over to the fire pit for the wiener roast.

When they got there, the manager and his wife had the fire blazing. Roasting sticks, wieners, buns, and condiments were laid out on a table. Patrick asked one of the men to ask the blessing and soon everyone was roasting their wieners and chatting about their work. There was a lot of light-hearted joking and laughter. Everyone seemed to be enjoying each other.

Milton sensed there was something different about the fun these men were experiencing when compared to other, non-Christian groups he'd been with in the past. These men were pulling for each other with encouraging remarks, always respecting each person's gifts and uniqueness. It was the first time he'd ever really felt relaxed with a group of men.

The next day, they teamed up to clean up the beachfront of the small lake. The dock had to be rebuilt to some extent. Also, hiking paths were improved and some even built from scratch. Milton worked with a man named Mark on cleaning up the beachfront, raking up trash and smoothing the sand. Milton was glad for his sturdy gloves. They then helped with the dock repairs.

At noon, Pete and his wife brought out some sandwiches, coffee, and watermelon. All were ravenously hungry. Everyone sat in the shade of some poplars to enjoy their lunch. Pete was elated about how much had been accomplished. When the men had nearly finished eating, Pete said that the only thing he would like done before they left was some painting of the main building where the sun had caused a lot of peeling. He said he had lots of paint, brushes, and ladders.

While Milton and Mark were heading to the work shed to get their supplies, Mark asked, "How do you like our small home group, Milt? Do you find yourself growing spiritually?"

"Oh, I can't tell you enough how much I appreciate our group. Actually, only about half of it is because of the teaching of the Bible. Mind you, I love the teaching and becoming more acquainted with Scripture. What I really love are all you people. I find the love of Jesus coming through you. Your acceptance of me as a gay person was totally a surprise to me. As a result, I've noticed changes taking place in me that wouldn't have happened with only a mental knowledge of the Bible and Christianity."

When they reached the work shed, they picked paint and brushes and headed back to the main building. Mark finally asked, "So, what are some of the changes you have noticed?"

"Well, I'm not totally sure yet what's happening, but I've noticed that when I've had enjoyable, warm, accepting interactions with the group, especially with the men, I've much fewer fantasies and desires."

"I would've thought it would work just the opposite way," Mark said as he stopped walking and looked at Milton. "You know, I would've thought associating with men would increase your desires. I would've thought it would be better for you to associate more with women."

Milton started walking again. "I don't think it works that way. Not for me, anyway."

"I'll admit I'm surprised."

This time Milton stopped walking and faced Mark. "With you thinking that way, Mark, why would you have accepted me and have been willing to work with me? I don't get it."

"Actually, it wasn't easy for me. I had to get lots of reassurance from Patrick and Linda. They told me they felt God was telling them to love and treat you just like a straight guy. He pointed to the way Jesus treated prostitutes and tax collectors as examples of how to treat those different from us. Well, my wife Janette and I decided we'd do just that. And I'm glad we did. I've really come to care a lot for you."

They decided to start walking again, but remained deep in thought. Milt felt tears filling his eyes as he thought about how much he appreciated these men.

That night, as Milton crawled into bed in the boarding house, he thought about the last two days. He realized he'd experienced more genuine fun and enjoyment than at any time in his life. He felt pure health had seeped into his being. He truly felt fulfilled as a result of living and working with the men of his group. His mind went to the spiritual source of these men's lives and realized that it was Jesus. His eyes filled with tears and his chest filled with gratitude for the love that God poured into him through these men. Soon he fell into a deep and restful sleep.

✦ ✦ ✦

The year of rotating internship had just barely begun when Iris got a call from Dr. Pinsky's office wanting her to drop by to discuss her research plans. The new crop of interns had already had their initial briefing and had been issued uniforms and locker keys. The next day, they'd start out at 7:00 a.m. on the paediatric floor to meet with the house staff. For now, she'd planned to go to the suite she'd been assigned, arrange her furniture, and unpack all her stuff. All her boxes were sitting in the middle of the floor. The last thing she needed was a lengthy discussion of her research project. But then, she was very interested in the research, so she had better visit Pinsky to keep him happy.

When Iris got to his office, Dr. Pinsky's secretary knocked on his door. Soon Dr. Pinsky appeared and pointed her to a seat in front of his large desk. "Well, I see you've survived the LMCC exams and will be starting medical slavery tomorrow. I thought I'd better salvage you before you're too sleep-deprived to think rationally."

"I hope interning won't be that arduous. That might be the case in some hospitals, but here, we're mainly looking over the shoulders of senior house staff. I think I can still spend some time on my research project."

"Well, we can only hope. Where are you at with your project, Iris?" Dr. Pinsky leaned back in his chair, tapping his fingers together.

"I'm still collecting stool from laboratory animals, checking for poliovirus. We want to see how many mice shed the virus after being fed virus-contaminated food. Then we want to see if the mice that have positive stools can infect other mice that have been bred to become infected with polio."

"That sounds good. What do you hope to accomplish this next year while you're interning?"

"Well, I hope to spend at least one afternoon a week in the lab to finish up with these animal studies. I'd also like to write it up so it can be part of a publication. Then, if I've time, I'd like to plan studies to be done on recently diagnosed polio patients, checking for poliovirus in stool, urine, and saliva. Maybe, I can even get started on that project."

Dr. Pinsky nodded, rounded his lips and then said, "I suppose you'd like the help of some of my lab assistants."

"Oh, that would certainly be a big help, Dr. Pinsky. I can do all the planning, but I won't have the time to do all the organizing such as finding the patients, arranging interviews, and all the tabulating that will be necessary."

"I'll look into that." Dr. Pinsky sat up straight. "So where do you see all this research going? How are you going to test out the new oral poliovirus vaccine once we get our hands on some?"

"Well, my plan would be to try to find out how poliovirus is transmitted best in humans. We'd give the new oral poliovirus vaccine to people who want to be immunized. Then we would test their stools, urine, and saliva for oral polio vaccine, or OPV, just like we did for polio patients. Then maybe we can find out if stools from immunized patients will infect our special lab animals. We'd then need to look for OPV in the animals' stool."

"That sounds like a good plan, Iris, but I doubt you'll get too far in the human studies during your intern year."

"Well, at least that's where I would like to eventually go."

Dr. Pinsky remained thoughtful for a minute. Iris wondered if he was going to nix the project. He took a deep breath and said, "Go ahead, Iris. Keep me informed and I'd like a copy of all your data. If there's any change of plans or any new ideas you have related to this research, I want to know. Iris, I want you and those who work under you to keep your work confidential. If you have any questions or ideas you want to discuss, talk to me. Don't even discuss too much with the lab assistants. Do you understand?"

"Yes, sure, Dr. Pinsky, I understand." Iris wondered why this research was so important to him and why he was so possessive of this project. It almost seemed he didn't trust her to use the information properly.

Dr. Pinsky got up, smiled briefly, and held the door open for her. She grabbed her file folder and headed for the lab with a kind of empty feeling. She wondered how much support she was going to get from Pinsky. Well, she wasn't going to let his attitude bother her. She'd just do her job the best way she knew.

* * *

Milton had received a wedding invitation from his brother, Brett. He was getting married to a girl he met at the university. She'd just graduated from an educational program and had gotten a job in a school district in North Vancouver. Brett had finished his degree in economics and had gone on to become a chartered accountant. He liked the weather in Vancouver and so was happy to find a job somewhere in North Vancouver.

After getting the invitation, Milton hadn't known what to do. He'd been well into his rotating internship and hadn't known if he could get away. He'd phoned his parents to get their advice. They had felt he should make every effort to go to the wedding or Brett would be greatly offended. Milton hadn't been so sure about that since Brett and he were not close. He had thought the pressure for him to go had been coming mainly from his mother. She'd even offered to pay for the flight to Vancouver.

The next day, Milton had made inquiries and, to his surprise, he'd been given leave to go. Since it involved a weekend he wasn't on call, he would be missing only three days of work.

Now, Milton was on a Trans Canadian Airline flight to Vancouver. He'd be there in an hour or so. He had an aisle seat next to a couple that were chatting with each other. He shut his eyes since he wanted to prepare himself for the meeting with his family. That wasn't always pleasant, he knew. At best, he'd have a chance to visit with his grandmother who was also going to the wedding. Having a successful and meaningful conversation with his parents was never certain. He thought he'd have a better chance in a one-on-one conversation with his mother, but not with his father. His father and he had so little in common.

The one thought that weighed heavily in his mind was whether he should tell them about his homosexuality. It was high time that they knew, if they weren't aware already. While he was at it, he wanted to tell them about his newfound faith, about the church and small group he was attending. He doubted they would be very happy about any of this, but he felt he shouldn't be keeping secrets from them. After all, they were his parents. He hoped there'd be an opportunity where just the three of them could be together, perhaps at a restaurant.

He wondered what his father would think about his going to a church. He knew his father had grown up in the Anglican Church. Would there still be a soft spot for a spiritual dimension of some kind—something they could build on?

Milton was looking forward to talking to his grandmother. She was flying out with his parents and would be staying at the same hotel. He hoped to arrange a separate meeting with her to allow for better sharing.

✦ ✦ ✦

A hotel shuttle brought Milton to the hotel. He soon found his parents' room. After briefly catching up on each other's lives, they told Milton that his grandmother would be visiting Brett and his bride early the next morning before the couple's flight to Hawaii. Milton suggested that he could have a visit with his grandmother before the wedding. He also hoped to visit with his parents the following morning over brunch. Fred and Gladys agreed readily with this plan.

Milton knocked on the door of his grandmother's room. The door opened and Milton looked into the smiling face of his beloved grandmother.

"Milton, I hoped you'd come. How is my boy?"

"Fine, Grandma." Milton could see that his grandmother had aged and seemed more physically fragile, but she seemed as bright as ever. "I've thought of you a lot over the last few years. I've felt your prayers and want to thank you for all of them."

Rachel pointed Milton to a cushioned chair, and she sat on the couch. "Well now, if you appreciated my prayers, then you should be willing to give me a report on what God has been doing in your life. Have you thought any more about becoming a Christian?"

"I sure have, Grandma, and I have accepted Jesus into my life."

"Well, glory be! You've brought joy to my old heart." Rachel's brown eyes shone with excitement. "How'd that come about?"

Milton talked about his meetings with Dr. Sandoski and the long period of evaluating Christianity before finally making the decision. He then told her about his church and the small group meetings. "My time with the group, especially associating with the men, has really helped curb my desires."

"So, have you had any fantasies about girls?"

"Well, not really. I like to be with another girl in my class, but I can't say I have a sexual attraction to her."

"Oh, that may come in time, Milton. Just stick with that group and keep trusting God for your emotional health."

"I'm trying to do that, Grandma. Keep praying for me."

"Have you told your parents about your homosexual tendencies, Milton?"

"Not yet. I've decided to do that tomorrow morning at brunch."

"I'll be praying for you while I'm visiting with the newlyweds."

The two chatted for another fifteen minutes, and then it was time to get ready for the wedding.

✦ ✦ ✦

Milton thought the wedding was a glitzy affair with four best men, four bridesmaids, a ring bearer, and a flower girl. Brett's wife came from a wealthy family, so nothing was spared in making it a very memorable time. Milton thought that in the unlikely event of his ever getting married, he would like it plain and simple. It could feature some nice hymns, a message from a pastor, a simple exchange of vows, and then a potluck meal. Even if he ever did consider marriage, no one would ask him for his opinion, he supposed.

He was disappointed in the music performed at the wedding ceremony and at the reception. It was mainly popular, modern music that carried little meaning and actually bored him silly. At his own speculative wedding, he would have lovely baroque music. He would be happy, but everyone else would be bored, he imagined!

A minister officiated and a vague reference was made to God. Jesus was mentioned once at the end of a prayer. At his ideal wedding, the minister would preach a sermon about the couple needing to make Jesus the head of their marriage. Maybe then the couple would get their marriage started on the right foot.

Milton was glad when the wedding dance was well underway and he, his parents, and his grandmother could leave. He was bored and tired. Milton drove their rented car to the hotel. Rachel was escorted to her room since she was quite tired. Milton's parents wanted him to visit for a short time before retiring. Milton was tired, but agreed.

Milton's mother wanted to talk about the whole wedding. Finally, Fred's yawns became too distracting for Gladys to continue. Milton suggested they all go to bed and have the brunch that was advertised by the hotel. Milton's dad quickly agreed and they moved to their respective bedrooms.

Milton slept well. After a leisurely shower, he read the newspaper until it was time for the brunch. As he waited for his parents, he prayed that he would be helped with courage and wisdom in saying what needed to be said.

Milton noticed the pleasant aroma of coffee and cinnamon when he and his parents entered the brunch area. Milton asked a cook for an omelet with all the fixings. As the three chatted about their hotel experiences, Milton savoured the omelet. Milton was surprised by how well the visiting went, with his father actually asking quite a few questions about his hospital experiences and his plans for the future. It seemed his father was much more accepting of the profession Milton had chosen. His mother, of course, had always supported him in his vocation and was eager to know his plans.

The plates and uneaten food had been taken away and they were left with their coffee. Now was the time, Milton thought. "Mom and Dad, I want to make sure you know all about me. I don't want to keep any secrets." Milton noticed that both their eyebrows were raised as they stared at Milton.

"I want to tell you that I'm gay. I am homosexual." Milton paused a moment for that to sink in. "I don't know if you had suspected that, but I wanted to make sure you knew."

His parents sat there with their eyes wide and their mouths hanging open as though trying to cope with the shock of what Milton had said.

Eventually, his father said in a husky voice, "Well, your mom and I have speculated on that possibility several times, but it does come as a shock when you tell us right out like that."

"Are you sure, Milton?" his mother asked. "Have you seen a psychiatrist about that?"

"No, I haven't. I don't need to, mother. I studied this condition a lot and I know. I've known since I was about thirteen. I was just too scared to tell anyone."

"Do you live with a guy?" His dad's face had gone a bit pale.

"No, and I'm a virgin. I don't live with a guy like in a marriage, if that's what you mean."

His parents breathed out a sigh of relief. His mother fidgeted with her coffee mug. "Have you looked for some help?"

"Well, yes, but maybe not in the way you're thinking. That brings me to another matter. I've become a Christian and I now regularly attend a church in Edmonton."

"When did *that* happen?" asked his mother as she stiffened in her chair.

"I did it last year. A biochemistry professor I had in pre-med showed me the way. I've never regretted doing that. Life makes much more sense now."

"I know your dad's mother had a hand in that decision." Milton's mother looked accusingly at her husband. "She was always going on about her beliefs about God and Jesus. So you swallowed her bait, did you, Milton?"

"Well, she did nudge me to consider the existence of God, but it was the professor who helped me really think through the scientific issues that kept blocking my progress."

"Why are you so quiet, Fred? I suppose you think he did the right thing?"

"You say a chemistry professor in the university is a Christian?" Fred finally asked. "And he talked you into it?"

"No, not like that. He'd say things about his belief in God from time to time in class. I approached him to get some answers, especially regarding how he believed in a God considering all the scientific knowledge he had."

"You were convinced that he made good sense." Milton could see his father was very interested in their discussion.

"Yeah, Dad, it made very good sense. It has made me see such a wonderful world, full of marvelous beauty and complexity that could only be explained by an incredible creator."

Milton could see that his father was quite moved. He saw tears glistening in his eyes.

Fred finally took a deep breath and said, "You know, what you said reminds me of when I was in my teens in a confirmation class at our old Anglican church. One of the ministers taught the class. He said much of what you said and I can remember being very affected. I said to myself then that I wanted to always believe like that." Fred looked up to the ceiling. "Well, somehow, I got going on selling houses and lost my youthful ideals."

"You're not going religious on me, Fred, are you?" Gladys looked worried. "At least think this thing through. Life isn't about believing something you can't see and can't measure. It's not about believing something you imagine but can't prove that it exists. Get real, you guys. Life is what you see, touch, feel, smell, and taste—nothing more."

"Alright, Gladys, you've made your point. I happen to think there is something to what our son has found. I'm going to give what he said some serious thought."

Milton's mother sighed in frustration and resignation, as if to say she was giving up trying to talk sense into her husband, or her son, for that matter.

✦ ✦ ✦

Walking back to her suite from the cafeteria, Iris noticed the mainly clear sky with the August sun still high in the west. What a perfect day for a walk. She desperately needed a break from her work in the virology lab. The microscopic work had left her eyes, neck, and shoulder muscles aching. Once in her suite, she changed out of her work clothes—a plain dress covered by a white lab coat. She pulled on a bright blue sweater and her slacks. She laced up her runners, put on sunglasses, grabbed a water bottle, and trotted out of her suite. Her goal was to walk toward the Saskatchewan River valley. She needed some exercise, and even more importantly, time to think.

As she walked, she thought about the last month. The internship experience on the paediatric ward was exciting. She had seen lots of new diseases that she had never heard of before! Some of it was scary, especially when she was asked to assess a sick infant. They seemed so small and she felt so helpless, trying to understand why they were ill. They couldn't tell her anything. She found she could only guess by what the infant's parents said. She was often amazed at the paediatricians, how they could tell what was wrong. They seemed to be better guessers than anyone else.

She missed Milton. So often, she felt the need to discuss a difficult case with him or just to let off some steam when she was frustrated with medical politics. She had talked to him by telephone about once a week. Those conversations were nice, but not as good as face-to-face encounters. Maybe it was good that she was more separated from him. She could feel herself becoming infatuated with him. There was no future there. Oh, if he weren't gay, she'd go after him like a bulldog after a bone. She shook her head and began walking more swiftly, trying to shake off the feeling of losing something precious.

Iris thought of Milton's newfound faith in Christ. He seemed to be excited about it. She remembered the time she was involved in the "Jesus Studies" with her dad and Trish when she was attending high school. She was filled with joy and peace, then. That had certainly changed. Maybe it was just the realities of life making the difference. Still, whenever she visited her dad and Trish, she found their excitement in their Christian faith had not diminished. Something had changed in her. Maybe it wasn't for the best. If only she knew how to find her way back to something that had somehow slipped out of her grasp. For one thing, she should get back to more regular attendance at Tim's church and get more involved with the mission projects the church organized.

Chapter Fourteen

September 1961

For the last month, Iris had attended Tim's church every Sunday. She'd been informed of a weekend camp for handicapped children being organized at their retreat centre at Pigeon Lake. It was planned for near the end of September. She volunteered to help with the camp, since it aligned with one of her few free weekends. After she'd agreed to go, she discovered that Tim would also be there and this excited her. Perhaps something would come of their relationship after all. She had decided to open her heart to that possibility.

She was enjoying the interactions with the handicapped more than she expected. Many of them were children with Down syndrome. A few had cerebral palsy and some had mental retardation of unknown cause. Once she got over the initial fear of not knowing how to communicate, she began to appreciate their unique personalities and talking to them at their intellectual levels.

Iris was heading toward her cabin after helping with the dishes in the dining hall when she was stopped by a familiar voice. "So, how're you liking the work here, Iris?" It was Tim. She'd had brief words with him at the beginning of the camp, but had not really visited.

"Oh, it's such a nice time of the year with the leaves turning and the fall air so stimulating. The kids are fun once I started to understand them a little. Yeah, I'm glad I came. How goes it with you?"

"I agree with you. It's such gorgeous weather and it's fun to help with these kids. I always find doing this camp very fulfilling." Tim motioned for her to sit down on a log next to the main building. It gave them a nice view of the lake. Once they sat, Tim asked, "So, are you being overwhelmed by the internship and the research, like I suspected?"

Iris laughed. "I'll admit it is a challenge. I work on research one day a week. That means I have to squeeze in my on-calls during the rest of the week in order to do my share. But I'm surviving. I really like the research. Actually, it's getting quite exciting since we have been breaking some new ground with finding how poliovirus infects new patients. I'm not supposed to say anything more about it. I've been sworn to secrecy." Iris drew her index finger along her sealed lips.

"So, what you're saying is that you still haven't got time to indulge an old friend with a shared meal." Tim smiled, held Iris's gaze for a second and then looked back at the lake, waiting for an answer.

Iris found his tanned face so handsome. And those piercing blue eyes seemed to look right into her heart. He was so patient with her, always allowing her time and space to make up her mind. Why had she held off for so long? Iris lightly laid her hand on top of Tim's and spoke softly, "I think I'd *make* time to enjoy a nice meal with a handsome guy like you, Tim."

Tim grasped her hand. "Just name the time and I'll make the arrangements."

◆ ◆ ◆

Iris arrived in the foyer of the residence a bit early. This way she could better watch for Tim and meet him outside, where his coming wouldn't attract as much attention. Somehow, she still felt tentative about Tim and didn't want other resident staff talking about their relationship. As she sat there, she reviewed the last time Tim had taken her for dinner—about two weeks ago. She'd enjoyed the experience and she had felt Tim did, too. They'd done a lot of talking, much of it about the work Tim's church was into. Tim had been careful to allow some emotional space between them that Iris still needed. When he had dropped her off afterward, he had opened the car door for her, taken her hands while holding her gaze, and kissed her lightly before wishing her goodnight.

As Iris reflected on that last date with Tim, she thought about Milton. She'd kept up their weekly telephone visits. Some of them were quite lengthy. All of their discussions had stayed within the bounds of their agreement—no religious or sexual topics. A lot of their discussions were on a scientific basis. A significant part dealt with their feelings and past experiences that held deep emotional content. Iris was continually amazed that, while getting more involved with Tim, she could never share with him like she could with Milton. She had to face reality. Milton was never going to make a husband. She'd just have to work on slowly building something more between her and Tim.

She saw Tim's car coming into view and she dashed out of the door and walked briskly toward him.

Tim jumped out and opened the passenger door for Iris. "You look great, Iris. You could win this year's university beauty queen contest, hands down."

Iris blushed in spite of the obvious flattery, thanking Tim with her best smile. She had gone to extra trouble with her hair, make-up and selection of clothes. She wanted to look pretty for Tim. She hoped that the evening at the restaurant would help them move into a deeper, more trusting place in their lives. Mostly, she hoped her heart would co-operate. She needed to fall for Tim and allow Milton to fade into the background.

The drive to the restaurant took them through the river valley. The trees were showing off their fall colours to the fullest. The yellows of the poplars and birches gleamed brightly against the backdrop of the deep green blanket of spruce and lodge pole pine. As if the scenery could stand any more beauty, nature deftly dabbed in the brilliant reds of high bush cranberries and mountain ash. All of this was set against the breathtaking blue sky. Iris took in the scene and choked up with emotion. What a wonderful creator God was! She could only take Tim's hand and point with her other. Tim nodded. "Amazingly beautiful, isn't it?"

When they reached the restaurant, Iris realized she had never seen the place before. Tim seemed very familiar with the host who met them. In fact, he was on a first-name basis with the woman. She quickly showed them to their table. As Tim took Iris's coat, he greeted someone else at a nearby table. Before sitting down, he went over to that table and began an animated conversation with the two women seated there. Iris took note that they were both quite attractive and in their 20s. Iris heard him giving one of them a compliment at which she blushed noticeably. After coming back to his table, Tim explained that they had done some volunteer work at the church this past summer, before they went back to their university studies.

Iris recalled that Tim, on several previous occasions, had enjoyed flirting with attractive women. She wanted the evening to be one where they really found out about each other. How was she to proceed with this issue? Or was it an issue she should be concerned with? She felt she needed to find out.

Their meal proceeded without incident. It was nice, but nothing special, she thought. Their chatting was mainly about catching each other up on their vocations. When the main dishes had been removed and they were sipping their coffee, Iris asked, "Tim, what are your parents like? Are they very social people? I ask just to find out more about your family."

"Well, Mom has her own social circles that she feels comfortable in, but she really isn't too much of a social person. In a large group, she can often feel quite uncomfortable."

"What kinds of groups make her uncomfortable?"

"Oh, I suppose ones organized by my father. He's very social, and finds all kinds of excuses to have a party. Mostly it's with his bank and other business partners. He heads lots of community boards and often arranges lunch meetings with them."

"Do you think your dad is aware of how these meetings bother your mother?" Iris knew she was prying but she needed to find out what made Tim tick.

"You know, I really doubt it. He gets so cranked up at these meetings, he just isn't thinking about how others feel. So long as most people are laughing and having a good time, he's happy." Tim laughed at this as though he enjoyed this reflection of his dad.

"Is your dad's socializing better with men than with women? With whom is he most comfortable?" Iris hoped Tim would not see through her questioning.

Tim looked quizzically at Iris. "Well, he's good with both genders, I guess. But, come to think about it, he loves to engage women in conversation, just light-hearted stuff, you know."

"Do you think your mother interprets this as flirting?"

"Quite possibly. Yes, you guessed it. He does flirt with women, even married ones. I sometimes think he must make some of the women's spouses or boyfriends jealous. Dad's so smooth at it, they can't really complain too loudly. Furthermore, they wouldn't want to say much and risk their spouse's job security." Again Tim laughed at the humour he saw in that situation.

Iris thought she didn't dare inquire further. Actually, she had learned a lot about Tim, more than she liked. Maybe it was unfair to judge Tim based on his father, but he did demonstrate similar characteristics.

On the way back to her suite, Iris tried to stay upbeat, but she felt a touch of sadness had crept into her spirit. She felt she needed to learn much more about Tim before really committing to him.

Once the car came to a stop near the residence, Tim shifted about to face her and then reached over and took Iris's hand. "We've talked about a lot of serious stuff, Iris, and I think that's necessary for our relationship to keep developing. I'm hoping you feel as I do, that we're meant for each other."

Iris saw the longing in Tim's eyes and wished she were in the same place. "Tim, I want us to keep seeing each other. I may not be quite where you are, but I want us to keep discovering each other's lives."

"Okay, that's fair enough." Tim moved closer. "Is it okay if I kiss you goodnight?"

"Sure, Tim." Iris tilted her face up to his. He kissed her tenderly, and then pulled back. Iris saw passion smoldering in his eyes. Then Tim pulled her into a tight embrace and pressed a deep and prolonged kiss on her lips. After separating, they looked at each other for a few seconds. Iris felt startled with Tim's intensity. She realized she wasn't sharing his passion in their relationship. She just needed more time, she supposed.

Tim drew back and opened his door. "I'll walk you in."

In the foyer, Tim asked, "Could we meet again in a week or so? I'd like us to go to a movie and then eat out somewhere. Would that work?"

"Sure. When you phone me, I'll need to check on my on-call schedule first."

"Okay, 'til then." Tim nodded and walked out.

✦ ✦ ✦

Milton had just returned from the cafeteria after a heavy Friday on the paediatric floor. He walked to his suite window and looked out on the hospital complex. The work had been strenuous, with lots of patients to see and reading necessary to make the best diagnosis and treatment of each clinical case. He loved this rotation. Paediatrics was his future, he was certain. He loved children of all ages.

What a blessing it would be to have children of his own! Could this be possible? He knew he'd have to become heterosexual before that would happen. He'd heard of some homosexuals who had fathered children, some inside marriages and some outside. He'd never allow himself to father children while still having homosexual leanings.

Tears spilled out of his eyes as he looked up into the cloudy sky. He cried out, "Oh God, please do something to fix what is broken inside. I know that being gay was not your intention for me. Your intention was for me to be fully male and to be united for life with a woman who is fully female. Please make me whole." Milton slumped into his couch and sobbed for a few minutes. As he settled, he felt peace steal over him as he remembered the verses in the Gospel of John about living in Jesus and Jesus living in him. "Okay, Jesus, I'll trust that you'll do your work in me, whatever that is."

His phone rang. It was Kent, one of the men in his small group. "Milt, I wondered if you would be interested in joining a group of fellows from our church in a football scrimmage tomorrow afternoon at the park just below Saskatchewan Drive?"

Milton knew what he needed to do. Face up to his fears and do it. "Yeah, that would work. I'm free tomorrow. I could get my reading done in the morning and meet with you in the afternoon. What time?"

They agreed two o'clock would work. Milton began reflecting on what he had just agreed to. He was going to be with a group of men, and that still brought waves of terror to his gut. Furthermore, he didn't even know some of them. Even worse, he was a sports klutz. His father and brother had been careful to teach that truth to him from a young age. Then he remembered his prayer. Maybe this was part of the cure. He dearly hoped so.

✦ ✦ ✦

Milton felt a heavy stone in his gut as he emerged from his truck and saw a number of men tossing a football around. His hands were clammy and his mouth felt dry. His autonomic system was in overdrive. As he tentatively walked toward the group, he heard Kent yell to him, "Over here, Milt. I want you to meet some of the guys." There followed enthusiastic handshakes with broad grins and encouraging comments. A few more men arrived over the next ten minutes. During this time, Milton got a chance to catch and throw the football several times. He still felt a bit awkward, but was surprised that he hadn't forgotten the skills he'd learned from his older brother many years before.

Kent called out to everyone to organize a scrimmage. He pointed out the teams and outlined the basic rules. They'd be playing tag football with a red cloth halfway into each guy's back pocket. Yanking the cloth out would be equivalent to a tackle. He handed out the red cloths and each team huddled to pick roles. Kent, who was on Milton's team, suggested a guy named Tom be quarterback.

Milton's team won the toss and would start with the ball. Tom suggested a play. Milton was told to block for Tom while Tom looked for a receiver. When the play got started, Milton stepped in front of an opponent and sent the player flying. Tom got a good look and threw successfully to a receiver who was tackled almost immediately. Tom slapped Milton on the back. "Just keep doing that, Milt, and we'll be alright. That was great."

Milt felt something like courage replacing the knot in his gut. The game went back and forth with the two teams equally matched. At one point when his team had the ball and they were in a huddle, Tom told Milton to run out to receive the ball. When the play started, Milton raced forward and then out to the right, as he had been told. Tom threw a perfect pass and Milton caught it and raced for the end zone. No one laid a hand on him. Everyone on his team as well as most on the opposing team cheered wildly for Milton and clapped him on his back. Something happened inside Milton in those minutes after the play. It was a wonderful feeling. As he walked back to his side for the huddle, he realized that he felt good not only because he'd scored a touchdown, but that he was cheered on by these men. That male affirmation was a precious gift. On top of that, Milton realized he wasn't as klutzy as he'd always believed.

After the game, the group met up at a nearby A&W for refreshments. Milton thoroughly enjoyed the good-natured banter. He connected well with some of these new guys.

That night back in his suite, he stood at his window and reflected on the afternoon. This time, he looked up at the sky and said, "Well, God, you made that happen for me. Thank you."

He felt he had to tell someone about his experience. No, not just someone. Iris. He walked over to the phone and called her. She answered immediately. After a quick review of their interning experiences, Milton asked, "Have you eaten yet?"

"No. I was just waiting for you to call." They both laughed. How nice it was to talk to this wonderful woman, Milton thought.

"Would Kentucky Fried Chicken on Whyte work for you?" Milton asked.

"Sounds a lot better than the cafeteria. I get so tired of their menus."

"Okay, I'll pick you up in about thirty minutes."

✦ ✦ ✦

After they sat down with their meal packages and drinks, Iris looked at Milton's face. He appeared alive and happy. And he was so handsome she just wanted to lose herself in his eyes. "You look like the cat that ate the canary, Milt. What's happening in your life?"

Milton told her of his love for paediatrics and his desire to become a paediatrician. He then went on to talk about his experience with the men of his church that afternoon. "I don't quite understand what happened today, Iris. As you know, I often feel insecure with men, especially ones who seem to have their lives together and have good families. I've also always felt inept when it comes to sports. Well, both of these situations converged this afternoon and I was terrified."

"With all of that weighing on you, why did you choose to go?"

"I just knew that I needed to face those fears and get involved with normal male activities. I think it's what I need to make things right inside me. At least, that's the way I see it."

"What happened this afternoon?"

Milton told her about the game and described the feeling of affirmation he'd experienced. "It's like I'm getting something I was meant to have as a child. I don't know, but it seems there is something very health-giving in associating with these normal guys."

Iris paused and shook her head as she thought of how she should respond. "I don't know why it works that way. I'm so happy that you feel better for these experiences. From what you've told me about your family, I understand you didn't get too much affirmation from males. Maybe there's some benefit from getting that now. 'Better late than never,' they say."

"I'm thinking you're right. I know, the more I do these things with heterosexual men, the less I am obsessed with thoughts of homosexual encounters."

"I must say, I've never come across that thought in the literature I've read about homosexuality."

"Neither have I." Milton paused, and then added, "There's more to this than just associating with average men. There is a God factor here."

"What do you mean?"

"Well, I've come to think God's original intent for me was that I be whole—like other men. Something went wrong. My thought is that now that I'm a new creation in Christ, the Holy Spirit within me can right the wrong. My job is to trust that he'll remake me into what God's original intention was. Do you understand what I'm saying?"

"Oh my, that's kind of heavy. I suppose I could use some of that theology for my own many failures." Iris felt a bit overwhelmed, but, at the same time, hopeful for Milton.

"I'm not presuming to know what or how God is going to do something within me, but I know I need to trust that he loves me and will use my life for good if I give him freedom to do his work in me." Milton's eyes shone with passion and hope.

"Okay, I'm with you on that, and I'll keep praying that you won't miss anything God wants for your life." Iris was almost breathless at the strength of Milton's convictions. Her mind flitted over to Tim and she thought what a huge difference there was in the spiritual perspectives of these two men.

✦ ✦ ✦

The day after Milton met with Iris, he was called to see a child in the Emergency Department. The child and his mother had been referred to a staff paediatrician who, in turn, arranged for Milton to make the initial assessment. Milton examined the boy carefully and decided he had a viral infection and could safely be managed at home. He gave the boy's mother written guidelines as to what to do should his condition worsen and then informed his staff paediatrician.

Milton was about to leave the Emergency Department when he caught site of a familiar face. It was Bill Street, who was walking toward the exit door.

"Hey, Bill. Good to see you after so long. What brings you here?"

Bill didn't say anything, but just stood there, waiting for Milton to get close to him. He then said in a low voice, "I came in to have an infection taken care of."

"Oh, what kind of infection? Something serious?" Milton looked quite concerned.

"They think it's gonorrhea. They gave me some penicillin and I should be okay. My last partner must've had it. I need to be more careful, I guess."

"Are you okay to have a coffee with me? Or are you too uncomfortable?"

"Oh, I'm okay as long as I don't urinate," Bill said with a weak grin. "I've had my first dose of penicillin, so I'm not in a hurry."

"We can swing around to the cafeteria before you go home."

When they had picked up a snack and some coffee, they sat at a table with no one else near.

Milton took a sip of his coffee. "I heard you were working for a chemical firm here in town. Are you still there?"

"Yes. I'm still plugging away there. It's a bit boring, but it pays well."

"Just what does your work entail?"

"I'm just doing the quality assurance thing. I do chemical assays on the various products from the reactors, make sure they're meeting standards, that sort of thing."

"Well, that sounds exciting to me. But I guess there might not be enough variety to keep your interest." Milton took a bite of his doughnut and waited. Bill seemed depressed.

"That's just about it." Bill nodded grimly.

"How long have you been with your present partner?" Milton wasn't sure how much questioning Bill would feel comfortable with, but he had to try.

"Well, I just broke up with him when I found he gave me an STD. We weren't getting on too well anyway."

"Do you mind if I ask you how many partners you've had, say in the last two years?"

"Well, let me see." Bill looked up at the ceiling. "I must've had about three steadies, but then I've had plenty of one-time contacts."

"Stop me if I'm pushing you too much, Bill, but I'd like to know, approximately how many different people have you had sex with?"

"I'm not sure. I would guess maybe thirty to forty in the last two years."

"Wow," Milton gasped, shaking his head. "Bill, that's scary."

"Why? Because of the danger of STDs?"

"Yeah. Eventually you'll get Chlamydia, papilloma virus, or even syphilis."

"Oh, I've had warts burned off several times already."

"That's depressing. I thought you once told me that you believed in long-term relationships. What happened to that idea?"

"You're right. That was the plan. But life doesn't always work the way you want it to. I'm still looking for the right guy, someone who is compatible and less selfish than the guys I've been with so far."

Milton wiped the crumbs off his face and thought of how he could help his friend. "You seem a bit depressed, more so than just having this STD. Do you generally feel down?"

"You would, too, if you had this damn infection and lost an intimate friend." Bill flushed and Milton realized he'd offended him.

"I'm sorry, Bill. I should have been more sensitive. I just want to help you."

"Well you're right. I usually am depressed. It's not easy being gay, as you well know. No, wait, maybe you don't. I hear you're celibate. Well, that just doesn't work for me."

"I think I would be much like you, if it weren't for some very caring people I've met."

"What do you mean?" Bill looked up from his cup and stared at Milton.

Milton knew he had to tell Bill some of his story. He briefly sketched out his interactions with Dr. Sandoski, becoming a Christian, and being involved with the small group. "I've been helped by these Christians and, especially, the straight men in this group. I'm not saying I'm cured of being gay, but I'm finding strength to resist sexual activity with men. And I have hope, Bill. I had none before."

Bill looked stunned for a long moment. Then he shook his head and said in a low voice, "Milton, you're in for a big fall. When that happens, I hope I can be there to help you. You well know there's no cure for homosexuality. You're dreaming. You seem to think being gay is a disorder, a disease—something you can be cured from. It just isn't so. You of all people should know the difference between most men and us. I believe it's some kind of genetic difference, just like some people having type O blood and others type B. Someday they'll confirm that."

Bill was talking louder and with more animation. "We've got to start seeing being gay is no more a disorder than being straight. You talk about me being depressed. Well, I used to be much more so than now. I've found some courage to keep living by attending some gay-support meetings. The new thinking is that we gays need to get organized—become more militant. We gays need to shrug off this idea that we've a disorder and we need to push our culture to accept homosexuality as a normal minority in our society."

Milton noticed that Bill had become quite emotional and he knew that arguing with him would be fruitless. "Okay, Bill, I see what you're saying. I can see you're very passionate about this. I personally can't share your enthusiasm that these changes you're hoping for are going to bring the fulfillment you desire. But I don't want to try to fix you or judge you. I don't know what it's like to walk in your shoes. All I can say is where I am. I can't even predict my own future, whether God will cure me of being gay or not. I think I've been given some new light about God and life and I intend to follow that light."

Both were silent for a few moments, and then Bill said, "I need to be going. There's a lot to think about here and I need to do that in the quiet of my own flat."

While they took their cups to the belt for dirty dishes, Milton said, "Yeah, I need to make evening rounds on the children's ward before going to my suite."

As they walked toward the emergency entrance where Bill's car was parked, Bill said, "Thanks for being interested in me, Milton. We have our disagreements, but I hope we're still friends."

"That we are, Bill. I definitely want to keep in touch." Milton looked into Bill's eyes and shook his hand.

"If you become truly heterosexual, I might be knocking on your door for some instructions." Bill chuckled.

"That would be a great pleasure for me. Goodbye, Bill."

Both held each other's gaze for a moment before Bill turned and left.

Chapter Fifteen

October 1961

Iris had eaten a light meal in the cafeteria in anticipation of the snack Tim had promised after the movie. She presumed he was planning to find a restaurant. She hadn't been able to find anything to wear that suited the occasion. So the day before, she'd gone to a dress shop on Jasper and bought a few items. She'd been overly encouraged by the clerk to buy a sweater with a somewhat revealing neckline. Now that she tried it on at home, it seemed a bit risqué, but she admitted it did wonders to her appearance. Well, perhaps it was time to quit riding the fence in her male relationships.

She was a few minutes early for Tim, so she decided to just sit in the foyer and relax a bit. She thought of Tim and his motives. He certainly seemed to be ratcheting up his pursuit of her. She found herself excited by his attention. So what was holding her back? She thought again of his theological leanings. Well, she wasn't much more orthodox than he was, she realized. Maybe he could change in time. He certainly had a good heart for missions. That must count for something.

Not surprisingly, she thought of Milton. What an incredibly sad situation, not only for his own life, but also for a relationship that could have been—a relationship that had absolutely no future. She was glad for him that he had found some solace and hope in Christianity, but she feared for the time when he would need to face the fact that he was gay for life. She'd read the statistics and the story they told were not encouraging.

Tim was his usual charming self on the way to the movie theatre. She used to be suspicious of his flattery, but now she just soaked in his complimentary remarks. He certainly didn't miss telling her how pretty she looked in her sweater.

"You've become very much prettier in the last few years," Tim said as he again made an appreciative sweep of his eyes over her face and neckline.

"Thank you, Tim," Iris said with a sweet smile.

Tim pulled to a stop in the parking lot of the theatre, jumped out and held the door for Iris. Iris saw him make another sweep over her body. It was almost a hungry look. Perhaps she was exaggerating in her mind the effect her sweater had on him. Well, she just intended to relax and enjoy the evening.

The movie took her by surprise. The title seemed innocuous enough, but she soon realized it had a lot of explicit sexual scenes with even more sexually suggestive narrative. Some of the erotic scenes seemed downright pornographic and she wondered how it had escaped the censors. Admittedly, there was an overall theme of courage and caring, but the clear message was that sexual desire could safely be expressed outside marriage, provided it was done with care and love. Iris looked over at Tim quite a few times and noted that he was deeply absorbed in the movie.

On the way out of the theatre, Tim took Iris's hand and said excitedly, "Iris, I thought we could go to my apartment and have some lunch there. That way, we could watch something on television if we wanted to."

Iris stopped walking looked into Tim's face. "What's wrong with a restaurant?"

"Well, I'm getting a bit tired of that. Moreover, you haven't ever seen my pad. I'd like to show it to you."

Iris felt a red flag go up, but then she reasoned that she should be strong enough at her age to handle herself properly. There would be the matter of how it would look to others. "Tim, appearances are important. Have you thought of that?"

"Iris, where I live, no one knows me or cares about me. Are you worried there might be spies checking on you?" Tim said with a crooked grin.

Iris laughed nervously. "Well, no, Tim. That's not the point."

"So, what is the point? We're, after all, both mature people. If you'd rather we go to a restaurant, we can do that. I don't want you feeling uncomfortable."

Right then, Iris couldn't think of a good excuse to not go to Tim's place. "Okay, as long as you behave yourself," she said with a laugh.

When they got to Tim's apartment, he showed her through it and then went to the fridge and pulled out some snacks he'd prepared. They both laughed at the indelicate way Tim had set out the food. This helped to relieve some of the tension Iris felt inside her. Tim offered her a beer, but she refused, saying she couldn't stand the taste.

"Do you mind if I have some?" Tim asked.

"Not at all. Go ahead. I'll just have some water."

They loaded up on their snacks and drinks and Tim motioned for Iris to take a seat on the sofa.

"Mind if I turn on the radio for some music? There's some nice jazz on CKUA right now." Tim walked toward the radio.

"Sure, that would be nice." Iris smiled appreciatively at Tim.

Tim got the music going softly and then sat next to Iris with a comfortable space between them. "So what did you think of the movie?"

Iris thought she might as well be honest. "I thought there was a lot of sex in it and the movie seemed to underrate the institution of marriage."

"Yeah, it didn't leave too much to the imagination in terms of sex. But, you know, the main point of the movie was to show how people who have unconventional sexual values can still show generosity and deep caring. To my mind, it was one of the best movies I've seen in a long time."

Iris pushed her lips out and thought for a moment. "Well, I guess I'm still too much of the old school, with the idea that sex should stay inside marriage."

"Times are changing. I think that even many Christians are rethinking the old Jewish morality of confining sex to marriage. I think it was a male control issue for them. They wanted their women as their own property, including their sex. Early Christians just adopted the Jewish custom. In modern times, women have shrugged off male control and are now making their own choices regarding sex. Furthermore, these days, we have ways to prevent births of children when the social environment is not conducive to ideal childrearing. So, the moral landscape is totally different now. We can act responsibly while living with a very different set of sexual values."

Iris began to see how very different her upbringing was from Tim's. She agreed with Tim that moral responsibility was the important factor here. As long as one could prevent bringing children into the relationship, perhaps sex outside of marriage was still in the realm of good morality. Something in Iris still made her feel uncomfortable with pre-marital sex, yet something else in her was excited about doing it.

Tim got up, pulled Iris up to stand and said, "Iris, let's not get all philosophical and let's just enjoy the evening. Let's dance to this music. It's so lovely."

"Sure, but you might be sorry. I'm not too good at it."

"We don't need to do anything complicated, you know."

They began dancing and Iris was surprised how easy it seemed to be. Soon, Tim pulled her closer so they were cheek-to-cheek and their bodies were touching. Iris noticed Tim squeezing her even closer until she said with a little chuckle, "Oh Tim, I'm out of breath."

Tim pulled back and looked into her eyes. She noticed that hungry look again. She had the feeling he wanted more than to just chat and dance.

"Why don't we sit for a while, then." He pulled her down onto the couch while keeping his arm around her shoulders. Soon his lips were touching her neck. Alarm bells went off in Iris's head. Was he going to keep going until…? She needed to stop things. But did she want to? Part of her wanted to go all the way. *The moral landscape is totally different now.* Tim's hand stroked the skin just above her neckline. He was kissing just under her ear. She could feel something deep inside her wanting to yield to his touch. She felt herself sliding somewhere she wasn't sure she should be going.

A thought shot into her head. *Have I decided to marry him? If not, would this experience hurt a marriage to someone else?* She rationalized that everyone was having premarital affairs these days. Iris caught sight of the passion smoldering in Tim's eyes. Then another question broke into her jumbled thoughts. *Would God approve of this?* She felt herself begin to rationalize again, but then she realized she was being taken to a place she'd not chosen to go. Why was she submitting to Tim? Why was she submitting to that evil that was behind all this? With a mighty heave of her moral courage, she said just above a whisper, "No."

Tim didn't seem to hear, so she pushed him away and yelled, "No, Tim, I want this to stop right now."

Tim slowly pulled his hand from under her brassiere, sat up and stared at her with his mouth open. "What's the matter, Iris? Am I hurting you? Going too fast?"

"No, Tim. It's just that I'm not comfortable with what we're doing."

"What's the matter with what we're doing, Iris? We're two adults enjoying ourselves. We're not hurting anyone. So what's the issue here?"

"Well, I happen to still believe in God and the revelation he gave mankind. In that revelation, sex outside marriage is considered a sin."

"Oh, for crying out loud, Iris, that's a very old interpretation of the biblical discussions about sex and marriage. We're living in the twentieth century."

Iris felt a rush of courage. "Tim, you spoke of women these days being free to make up their own minds about sex. Well this woman has made up her mind. It's not going to happen today."

"What's the matter with you, Iris? You've had me on a string all these years, keeping me at arm's length, never really committing to a real relationship. Are you wired up wrong or something?" Tim's eyes were no longer hungry. They flashed with anger.

Something like an explosion went off in Iris's mind. "Okay, Tim, I didn't want to admit it to you, but I'm a lesbian!"

"You've got to be kidding me! Ah, I don't believe that. Are you serious?" Tim stood and his face was filled with confusion and shock.

Iris pulled herself together and stood up, still facing Tim. "I think you'd better just take me home."

Tim mumbled, "Yeah, okay."

Both pulled on their coats and, without a word, walked down to Tim's car. Nothing was said on the way back to Iris's suite.

Iris let herself out and said softly, "Thank you, Tim, for the movie and the snack. We're on different wavelengths. At least for now, we seem to think too differently to make it work together. Good night."

A weak "Good night, Iris," came from Tim and he slowly rolled away down the street.

✦ ✦ ✦

Iris awoke the next morning in a foul mood. Her life had come loose from its moorings, it seemed. She looked at the clock on her dresser. Six-thirty—a half-hour before she usually got going. And it was Saturday, a day she was going to get a lot of reading done in the library. Judging by the way she felt, she was never going to achieve that goal. She felt more like jumping into a hole and pulling the top over her. Her eye caught the portrait of Tim on the dresser. She fired her pillow at it and the photo went crashing to the floor. When she picked it up, she noticed a huge crack across the protective glass. "Well, that crack sure has rich symbolic significance!"

After a few rapid and careless strokes of her hairbrush, she was satisfied. She pulled on an old faded blouse and the oldest jeans she could find before going to the kitchen to make some strong coffee. Today she needed to re-evaluate her life. Lots of things needed to change.

Iris banged about the kitchen as if all the furniture, cupboards, dishes, and kitchen aids were her enemy. Bits and pieces of last night's debacle replayed themselves in her agitated mind. Each scene evoked a variety of emotions—anger, injustice, guilt, and remorse.

Her stomach was in a knot, but she thought she'd better eat something if she were going to get through the day. She grabbed a box of cornflakes and a jug of milk and headed for the table. After consuming a bowl of cereal and a couple of sips of coffee, she decided to plan her day. In order to clear her mind and think, she needed to walk. Yes, she'd clean up the place a bit and go for a long walk in the river valley.

Finishing her coffee and noisily setting the dirty dishes into the sink, she pulled on her runners and her down-filled coat. When she stepped outside, she saw her frost-covered car, a secondhand Ford bought with the help of a recent small loan from her dad.

Well, she'd leave it and just head in the direction of the river valley. Walking briskly for thirty minutes, she found a path that led off the street into the valley. The sun was just emerging to announce a new day. She noticed the crimson shades of the clouds in the east. The beauty of the clouds overwhelmed her and tears rushed into her eyes. Were there aspects of life still to be enjoyed? The sun seemed to think so. She stood for a few minutes, soaking in the glowing horizon. Then she resumed her walk. Her pace quickened as she again replayed the scenes of the night before.

Iris realized she needed to think logically if she were ever going to get anywhere. She laid out the facts. She might as well count her relationship with Tim finished. They had irreconcilable differences in their basic values and their views of life. Milton was a wonderful guy, a friend like no other. But he was gay and marriage was not only very unwise for themselves, it would be a disaster for their children—that is, if their marriage were ever consummated. No, a marital relationship was out of the question. She knew the sensible thing for her to do was to look around for another mate. After all, she had the looks going for her. She could maybe trap some unsuspecting guy and try to make something of her life. Deep down, she knew that couldn't happen. Milton had ruined her for anyone else. Maybe that had been at least part of the problem with her and Tim. She admitted she was in love with Milton. Her own emotions had betrayed her. With that thought, she kicked violently at a rock on the path, sending it flying into the bushes. Angry tears surged into her eyes. Iris impatiently swiped her hand over her face to clear her tears, shook her head and stared up to the tops of the trees while walking slowly. She needed to set her emotions aside and focus on the life before her.

Then a thought came to her. She needed to tell herself and everyone around her that she'd excluded marriage as an option in her life. What better way to do this than to maintain the idea she'd given Tim—that she was a lesbian. She knew she'd fit in well with many others of the females in medical classes who seemed bent on their career rather than marriage.

Then she thought of her clothes. With a bitter laugh, she visualized herself wearing clothes that would least attract potential male suitors. Her focus now would be exclusively on medicine. She'd even distance herself from Milton. She needed to train her emotions to focus on her vocational objectives. Iris began to feel a little better, now that she'd made some decisions. She held her chin up higher and headed back to her suite. When she got there, she took her revealing new sweater and stuffed it into a corner of the bottom drawer of her dresser. She then yanked a dozen other items of clothing from their hangers and unceremoniously pitched them into the same drawer. Then she caught a bus that went east on Whyte Avenue. She got off near the Army and Navy store. She marched in and, thirty minutes later, walked out with a bag full of drab looking slacks, skirts, and blouses, as well as a dark, army-green coat. With steel in her eyes, she headed for the bus stop.

✦ ✦ ✦

Milton had been called to the Emergency Department to see an eight-week-old baby that was sent in by a family doctor. Since the paediatric resident on call, Dr. Bryce Peterson, was quite busy, Milton was told to make the initial assessment. The referring doctor had suggested a diagnosis of either GER (gastro-esophageal reflux) or milk allergy.

Milton carefully questioned Mrs. Flint, the baby's mother. She told him, "When he pukes, he shoots it a long way. It's gotten steadily worse over the last week."

"How have the feedings been going?"

"Oh, he gobbles down the formula like he's quite hungry, but then, about ten minutes later, he'll puke several times with the milk ending up on the floor or on the wall."

Milton asked, "Does he cry as if in pain?"

"Not really, but I've noticed a funny thing. Before he vomits, he has a bulge in his tummy. As soon as he vomits, the bulge disappears."

"Would you mind feeding him some milk now so that I can see what happens?"

Sure enough, what the mom described occurred in front of Milton's eyes. Milton even noticed the bulge moving from left to right over the upper abdomen. As he had leaned closer to see the bulge move, the baby let fly with a projectile streak of vomit that hit him in the neck!

Milton looked a bit shaken. "Oops. His aim is pretty good. Don't worry, Mrs. Flint. Excuse me, I'll need to step out and check a medical text about these findings."

Milton went to the desk, sponged off the milk from his neck and white uniform, found a paediatric textbook, and looked up pyloric stenosis. He recalled a surgical resident talking about a case he'd seen. He was amazed how much this case fit the textbook description. He telephoned Dr. Peterson and waited for him to come.

Milton sat back in his chair and thought about his time so far at the Royal Alexandra Hospital. His first two months on the surgery rotation had been enjoyable, but he never felt drawn to that specialty. When he started his paediatric rotation, he soon felt he'd come home. Somehow he felt he was where he needed to be. He loved to deal with children. They were so forthright and honest. He also loved the challenge of guessing their symptoms from their behaviour, especially with infants and toddlers. Interviewing parents and discussing their children's diagnosis and treatment was usually fun. He admitted that dealing with mothers felt better than talking to fathers. That was just part of his disorder, he presumed.

Dr. Peterson swept around the corner. "Hi, Milt. Tell me about that vomiting baby Dr. Gordon sent in."

"Yeah, okay. The baby's eight weeks old and has been vomiting for at least a week. The vomiting has become progressively worse. His mother says the vomiting is projectile and tends to occur during or immediately after feeds. She's also noticed a bulge over the abdomen just prior to vomiting."

"Okay, what did you find?"

"Well, first of all, the baby looks quite scrawny as if he's lost weight. I didn't find anything else on physical. Then I had mom feed the baby some formula and I noticed after he'd taken half a bottle that he developed a bulge in his upper left abdomen. I saw it move over to the centre and then he vomited into my neck."

"Into your neck? What were you doing, holding the baby up?"

"No, the vomitus shot over three feet and hit me," Milton said, laughing.

"So, what is your best guess here?" Dr. Peterson asked with a grin.

"Pyloric stenosis."

"Sounds reasonable. Let me have a look."

They went to the room where mom was walking about, cradling her infant. Dr. Peterson's examined the child quickly but gently. He took more time after that to press more deeply into the baby's upper abdomen. "Ah, I think I feel it." He turned to Milton. "Here, put your two fingers right here and gently press in, making circular movements. See if you feel anything."

Milton did so and after a few seconds said, "Yes, I feel something like a marble."

"It's the thickened pylorus that's blocking the outlet of the stomach." Dr. Peterson looked over to the mother, speaking more to her than to Milton.

Dr. Peterson looked at Milton for a moment as if he were trying to decide something. Then he said, "Mrs. Flint, Dr. Saunders has done a good job in assessing your child. I agree with his diagnosis. I'd like to have him tell you what this condition is and where we go from here." Dr. Peterson nodded at Milton.

Milton felt excited and grateful to be able to do this job. He described the condition in layman's language, indicating that it was not too common but could become very serious if not operated on. He reassured the mother that the surgery was quite simple and almost always highly successful. "It will require a general anesthetic and an operation where the muscle fibres of the thickened area are cut across. That will relieve the obstruction. When the cut area heals, there's almost never a recurrence of obstruction." Milton drew some pictures on his clipboard to demonstrate the nature of the surgery.

"When can this be done?" Mrs. Flint asked with tears in her eyes. She hugged her infant even closer.

Dr. Peterson said, "I'll talk to the staff surgeon on call and he'll set things up. We'll let you know as soon as we have a time."

"Oh, I'm so scared. He's too small to have surgery, isn't he?" Mrs. Flint's tears were flowing.

Milton put a gentle hand on Mrs. Flint's shoulder and looked into her teary eyes. "Lots of babies even smaller than Trent have surgery, Mrs. Flint.

The outlook with this surgery is very good and you'll be feeding him again tomorrow if things go as they usually do."

"Maybe even tonight, actually," said Dr. Peterson. "And, I can tell you Dr. Sweldon is very good with surgery in infants, Mrs. Flint."

That evening, Milton assisted Dr. Sweldon. The paediatric resident would usually have done the assisting, but Dr. Peterson was still quite busy and Dr. Sweldon wanted Milton to assist since he had come up with the right diagnosis. Dr. Sweldon had also been quite impressed with Milton's work when he was on the surgical rotation. Milton enjoyed being able to be involved with the baby the whole way through, from admission to discharge. He was especially delighted to see how happy the baby's mother was that night when she was able to feed her baby, even if it was just glucose and water.

✦ ✦ ✦

The weekly medical rounds had just ended and Iris was eager to get back to her ward. She was in the psychiatry rotation, now, and needed to find out about the new admissions from the night before. She bumped into a psychiatry resident and took the opportunity to ask him how many admissions had come in overnight. There were none, so she realized there was no rush to get back. As she turned to head out of the conference room, she spotted Myra. She had been interning at the Edmonton General Hospital. Iris waved to her and soon they were greeting each other as long-lost friends.

"Myra, are you in a hurry to get back to the General?" Iris asked.

"Not too much. I'm on obstetrics now, and there aren't many cases in right now. The ward knows where I am if they really need me."

"How about joining me in the cafeteria for some coffee? I'm dying to catch up on your life."

"Sure, let's do that," Myra said, grinning.

On their way to the cafeteria, they caught each other up on their internship programs. Once they were seated with cookies and coffee, Myra leaned closer to Iris and said, "I heard you have come out of the closet."

"What? Where did you hear that? There must be something wrong with your information." Iris looked dumfounded.

"Well, I was told you thought you were lesbian. Is that true?" Myra raised her eyebrows.

Iris's mouth dropped open as a realization dawned on her. "Yes, I did tell someone that I was lesbian. I was very angry at the time and wanted to get clear of him. I'd no idea he'd believe me and, worse, spread the gossip." As Iris thought about what Tim had done, she grew angry. How could he be so naïve as to believe her, and so vindictive as to start these rumours?

"So, is this rumour going to jeopardize your chances to find a guy to marry? What about this Tim guy? Are you still thick with him?"

"No, I've kind of given up on him." Iris didn't want to malign him even though he deserved it.

"Say, I couldn't help but notice that you've bobbed your hair. You don't wear earrings or have any lipstick on. Any reason for that?"

"Okay, this guy who got me mad enough to tell him I'm lesbian is out of my life now, and I don't have anyone else around with any marriage potential. I'm going to just do medicine. So, to celebrate this new focus in my life, I thought I'd dress and act as if I had only that focus. No men in my life anymore, you understand?" Iris had become more animated than she had intended.

Myra laughed long and hard. "You should be glad this rumour about you being a lesbian is out. It'll assure potential suitors you're not available." Myra laughed until her face was quite red.

"I don't see that this whole situation is that funny," Iris said with a grimace. She was glad they had a table well separated from others in the cafeteria.

"Oh, by the way, was the guy who spread this rumour Tim, by any chance?" Myra said, controlling her laughter.

"Okay, yeah. It was Tim."

Myra took a sip of her coffee. "What's happening with Milton? Do you still keep in touch?"

Iris's heart rate sped up a notch. "We've kept in touch. I still have feelings for him, but my emotions are under strict discipline now. I'm training my feelings to wind down as far as Milton is concerned."

"Best of luck. Emotions are hard to quell. In the battle for predominance, emotion usually wins over willpower. I learned that in psychiatry," Myra said with a crooked smile.

Iris returned the smile, and then glanced at her watch. "Sorry, I must be going."

As the two walked out of the cafeteria, Myra said, "I'm sorry I laughed at you. I could have been more sensitive."

"Don't worry about that. I'd laugh at myself if I felt better about my life. It's in such a mess. I need to take whatever steps I can to keep me sane."

"Well, I wish you the best. You're still my best friend, Iris."

"Thanks." Iris couldn't say more or she'd start to cry.

* * *

Milton trudged through snow to the residence. It was mid-December and winter had set in. It was nearly 4:00 p.m. and he'd just come off the orthopaedic ward. He enjoyed the experiences on this ward, especially when it had to do with children. He was set on being a paediatrician. He'd applied for a position at the University Hospital, as he thought it had the best program. He realized he might have to finish his residency program in some other city, since none of the Edmonton hospitals had complete paediatric training programs.

Milton walked into his room and loneliness enveloped him. He needed to talk to someone. His mind went to Iris. It always went to her when he was in need of a heart-to-heart talk. He realized that for the last few months, she hadn't contacted him. That was a little unusual for her, he thought. Had she finally given up on him? Now that was a depressing thought.

Milton tried to get some medical reading done, but he threw the text down. He found a novel, but try as he might, he couldn't get into it. He reached for the phone and dialed a number he knew by heart.

"Hello, Dr. Marten here."

"This is Dr. Saunders. Might I have a word with you?"

"Oh, Dr. Saunders, I think that might be possible."

"Dr. Marten, would you be interested in seeing some Christmas lights on the way to an A&W?"

Milton heard nothing but silence for a moment.

"Are you still there, Dr. Marten?"

"Ah, yes. Dr. Saunders, I will be available in the foyer in twenty minutes."

"Excellent, Dr. Marten."

As Iris emerged from the residence, Milton noticed she looked very different. Her hair was bobbed and she wore dark slacks and a dark brown trench coat. When he held the door open for her, she smiled. He noticed she wasn't wearing lipstick. He also decided that for all the differences in her dress, hairstyle, and makeup, she still had a beautiful smile.

✦ ✦ ✦

Iris noticed the restaurant was nearly empty, so they would have good opportunity to talk without being overheard. When they settled into a booth with their snacks and drinks, Milton asked, "What's with the change in dress and makeup? Have you joined a cult?"

Iris laughed. "No, I decided I'd forget about marriage and focus on medicine."

"Oh, so you want to discourage male attention? You find that too distracting, I presume." Milton had a trace of a smile.

"That's just about it."

"Does this have anything to do with announcing that you're a lesbian?"

"So, you've heard that rumour too?" Iris rolled her eyes.

"I have, but don't believe it." Milton kept his eyes fixed on hers.

"Why not?"

"You're definitely heterosexual."

Iris grinned. "So my charade won't get past you. I'm not surprised. You know me too well. I should've been more careful in exposing my feelings to you."

"I feel honoured to know you as well as I do. There are still many things I don't know about you. I can understand if you don't want to share them. Let me try some questions, though. What about Tim? Is he still in your life?"

"Why would you care?" Iris wanted to tease out his true feelings for her.

"I wouldn't have asked if I didn't care. I care what's happening to you and how it's affecting you."

"And what about how that information would affect you?"

Milton thought for a moment before answering. "To be honest, I really don't know enough about myself to answer that properly. I know that I think of you a lot and I find Tim's interest in you challenging. Maybe, even more, I find your interest in him challenging. Does that answer your question?"

Iris felt something melt inside her. "Okay, Milt, thank you for being so honest with me. I can tell you that I've had a serious falling out with Tim. I can't see how we are or can ever be compatible. For now it's off."

"Don't answer if you're not comfortable, but does this have to do with his theology?" Milton picked up the remainder of his hamburger and took a bite.

"Oh, maybe indirectly, but it wasn't that issue that ended our relationship. It had more to do with how he disrespects my feelings. That's all I want to say about it, Milt."

"Fair enough. So, may I ask you about your poliovirus research? How is that going?"

Iris finished her root beer and looked up into Milton's face. He seemed more handsome than ever. "We're ahead of where we thought we would be when we laid out our plan last July. I'm already working with oral poliovirus vaccine and testing it out in mice as well as in human volunteers. Once I can start working full-time in July, we hope to move faster and have some publishable results in another month or two."

"Iris, I'm so proud of what you've achieved so far. I can easily see you might have a difficult choice between going into clinical work and continuing in research."

Iris appreciated the encouragement and smiled. "It's true, I love the research and I will miss it, but I know my future has to be in clinical work. I love helping sick people too much, I guess."

"That's the same for me. I know I want to become a paediatrician in clinical practice. It's where I belong," Milton said.

"I'm glad you've decided that. You're so good with children and their parents." Iris paused and then asked, "Milt, how are things going in your church, especially in your small group?"

Milton took another sip from his mug of root beer and then gazed into Iris's face. "Better than ever. I can't say enough about that group. They love unconditionally, without judging. I've experienced it coming from them in so many ways. The best way I can explain it is that they've shown me the love of Jesus. They all explain that their love *is* the love of Jesus being expressed through them. I hope I can give back as much as they've given me."

Iris felt herself longing for what Milton had. "Milton, you've done that already. You've shown me that love."

"Oh, thank you, I don't know in what way, but I'll accept your compliment."

Iris looked out the window for a second to collect her thoughts. "You mentioned before that you found relating to the men of your group helpful. Is that still the case?"

"Yes, it still is. I'm finding now that I have to take the initiative. I think the men know that's what I need to do. So, I look for ways to socialize with them, one-on-one, or in groups and get involved in work projects with them. I'm also working on relating to men outside the group. It seems when I take the initiative, the healing inside me proceeds faster."

"You mean the homosexual thing?"

"Yeah. All I can say is that my temptations have virtually dissipated. I dare not stop reading the Scriptures, talking to God, and meeting with my small group, or this could all go backward, I think."

Iris just looked at Milton for a minute. Then she took a deep breath. "You know, I'm starting to believe you're on to something. But I don't know how it all works. I'm really glad for you, though."

They headed out to the parking lot. Before opening the car door, Iris turned to Milton. "Milt, I was determined to gradually wean off of you. I failed miserably this evening, but I'm not sorry. Your friendship is far too important for me to ever let it go. Thank you so much for tonight."

Milton felt tears coming to his eyes. "Thank you for coming. Our friendship is very important to me as well. Please let's keep in closer touch with each other."

"Agreed." Iris smiled and then turned to go.

✦ ✦ ✦

Milton was finishing his meal in the cafeteria and pondering what he should do after getting to his room. Lots of reading needed to be done, he knew, but he wondered if he should follow up with Bill Street. He had thought of Bill several times that day. Maybe God was nudging him to make another contact as he'd promised. *Yes, it's high time to do just that.*

The weather was cold, even for January. His car objected to being disturbed on such a cold evening, but it eventually came to life. On the way to Bill's bachelor suite, he thought about his friend, picturing him in his mind. He was average height but slim with fine features. He had reddish blond hair and blue eyes. He had sounded pleased about Milton phoning him. In fact, he'd seemed quite upbeat.

Milton wondered what his goals should be in terms of this visit. Certainly, one goal was just to renew their friendship. Another goal would be to listen. He wondered if he should speak of his faith and his small group. Bill knew where Milton stood in terms of his faith. He sensed he should not speak of his beliefs unless invited.

The door of Bill's suite opened widely for Milton and Bill greeted him with a big welcoming smile. "Well it's about time you came. I haven't forgotten your promise that you would keep in touch."

"You could have contacted me, Bill. My number is still in the phone book."

"Ah, sure, but you docs are so busy. I didn't want to complicate your life more than it is. Don't just stand there. Get your coat off and come sit down."

Milton kicked off his shoes and hung up his coat. He looked around the suite with admiration. "You have a nice pad, Bill. I really like the décor."

"Thanks. Have a seat. Would you like some beer?"

"Sure. That would be nice." Milton really didn't like the taste of beer much, but he didn't want to offend Bill's kind hospitality. Milton settled into the sofa while Bill poured each of them a glass of beer.

Once Bill sat down, he turned to Milton and asked, "How goes your internship at the Alex?"

"Good. It's heavy work with long hours, but I'm loving it." Milton went on to describe the nature of his work and told him about several interesting cases.

Once there was a lull in the conversation, Milton asked, "How goes it with you? You seem chipper, a lot different than when I last saw you in the emergency department."

"Oh, I think I've finally got a handle on my life."

"Good. Tell me about it." Milton took another sip of beer and kept his eyes fixed on Bill's.

"Well, that last bout with gonorrhea scared me into some action. I decided to take careful precautions whenever I had sex. I now assume that all my contacts are infected with something and I regularly use a condom just like the ER doctor advised."

"Good plan, Bill. I was so scared for you. What else have you done?"

"Well, I attend a gay support group and that's really helping me to stick with the plan."

"You mean to use safety precautions?"

"Yeah, but also to find a guy who's going to be with me long term." Bill's eyes widened with excitement. "I think I've found a real neat guy who's in for the long haul. His name is Marvin. He's a big hunk, but he's unselfish, just the kind of guy I've always wanted."

"Bill, I'm so pleased you're living a safer kind of life. Will you be moving in together?"

"I'm hoping he'll move in with me, since my suite allows for the two of us to be together."

"You seem really pleased. I'm happy for that."

"What about you?" Bill asked. "Are you still doing the celibate thing?"

"Yes, I'm still celibate."

"You should have become a priest. Maybe you could still do that?" Milton could see the sarcasm in Bill's eyes.

"No, I don't think the Catholic Church needs any more guys who choose priesthood merely because they're gay." Milton laughed lightheartedly and then sobered. "Bill, I'm not in any great need to experience sex—not like I used to be tempted, anyways. As I told you, I believe God is changing me. Whether he will ever give me a wife, I have no idea. I just have to leave that up to God."

"You sound like a priest already. I'll recommend you for ordination."

"Thanks for being willing to put in a good word for me. They're sure to listen to you!" Milton offered a crooked grin.

They chatted amiably for another half hour. Milton sipped the last of his beer, and set his glass on the sleek coffee table. "Bill, I've so much enjoyed getting caught up with your life. You're free to call me any time, you know. Now it's your turn to initiate another visit."

As Milton opened the door to leave, Bill said, "Milton, you are one of a kind. You're definitely different than me, but I enjoy our friendship. I'll be glad to give you a shout sometime soon."

Chapter Sixteen

February 1962

It was Friday night again, and Milton was heading for the Bensons for the weekly small group study. The group had studied 1 Corinthians in the fall and now was well into 2 Corinthians. He had appreciated the study of Saint Paul's two letters to the Corinthian church, as they were written to a young church that was also young in the faith. He was young in the faith, too, so there was much to learn.

When Milton entered the Benson home, Blake said, "Hey, Milt. Glad you could come," and Patrick gave him a big hug. He shook hands or hugged most of the people that came through his door. Many present wanted to know how Milton's internship was progressing. He, in turn, caught up on their lives.

After some singing, Patrick asked for a report on their week. That was followed by a prayer time, mainly focusing on issues that arose from these reports.

The study was on 2 Corinthians 5. When they got to verse seventeen, Patrick asked Milton to read it. He read, "Therefore, if any one is in Christ, he is a new creation; the old has passed away, behold, the new has come."

"So, that's the new creation. What was the old creation?" Patrick asked.

Blake said, "Adam and all who followed."

"Right. So why do we need a new creation?" Patrick asked.

"Mankind became corrupt by choosing to do their own thing and so rebelled against God."

"Right again, Blake. So, what were the consequences of man's rebellion?"

"The relationship between God and man was broken."

"Blake, you should be teaching this course, you're so wise and have all the answers!" Everyone laughed.

Blake said, "Okay, I got the message: 'shut up and let someone else say something.'"

Patrick nodded with a laugh and then asked, "If we see something in our lives that's from the corruption of the first creation, what are we to do?"

This time, Mark's wife Brenda answered. "We don't have to accept that corruption. We can claim the new creation within us to really heal us and live there."

"Hey, you guys are brilliant. You don't need me to teach you!" Patrick laughed.

Milton felt a spark of hope ignite within him. He was convinced that the homosexual impulse within him was a corruption of what God had intended for him. If that were so, then he could deny the corruption of the old creation and accept God's original intention for him as part of the new creation. How was that to really happen? Milton surmised that, like anything else in Christianity, it would be by faith in God's promises.

Patrick carried on with the lesson, but Milton was only half listening. The other half of him was still pondering the new creation and the implications for himself.

✦ ✦ ✦

Time for another walk, Milton told himself the next morning. He wasn't on call, so he had the opportunity to walk in the morning after breakfast. In the afternoon, he needed to spend time in the library, doing reading around the cases he had seen in the previous week.

As he pulled on his runners and coat, he thought about the weather. It was quite warm for February. A chinook wind was blowing in southern Alberta, but there was only a light westerly breeze in Edmonton. He wouldn't need a tuque.

Milton had an urge to drive across the High-level Bridge and walk on the paths he had become familiar with during his medical training days. He always liked the views across the river. Once he got his truck parked next to Saskatchewan Drive, he quickly found his familiar route and set out in a brisk pace. He began thinking of the previous night's small group meeting. He couldn't get over the thought that he had stumbled upon a new idea. He could turn his back upon the corruption of the old nature, accepting only the new creation. That morning, Milton had recalled chapter twelve in Romans where Paul says, "Do not be conformed to this world, but be transformed by the renewal of your mind."

Yes, he thought, the renewal of the mind was part of the new creation. His previous craving for sexual contact with other men was part of the old nature's corruption. The homosexual thinking was a part of the old way of thinking. But now, he was going to accept by faith only the new creation with a renewed way of thinking.

As Milton looked across the Saskatchewan River valley to the parliament buildings, he was once again cheered by their gleaming white elegance. He turned again to the path in front of him and resumed pondering the topic upmost in his mind. His thoughts went to the Gospel of John where Jesus said, "If you ask anything in my name, I will do it." The promise was there. It was up to him to believe it and claim it as his own.

Milton recalled Kent saying at one of the small group meetings that he'd read a book about Christians tending to live too much without faith. The book cited the Scripture passage in Hebrews, "Without faith it is impossible to please God." So, the book stated, our goal should be to build up our faith so that our lives would be filled with the success and prosperity God desires for Christians. Kent told the group that the author urged Christians to say only words of faith and refuse to listen to or say words that spoke against faith.

Milton reasoned that his job was to believe for his healing from homosexuality for all he was worth and to never listen to anyone who spoke a contrary message.

✦ ✦ ✦

Iris always looked forward to the practice sessions with their little ensemble. They had been playing for well over a year now. They practiced once a week in the Education Building. They played a variety of music, mostly classical, but some jazz and even a little Celtic. These practices had allowed her friendship with Sandra, the violinist, and Myra, the pianist, to deepen. This was particularly so with Myra. The three often had coffee after practices. On this particular February day, Sandra had a date with her boyfriend after practice, so it was only Iris and Myra in the café.

Iris thought this was an opportunity to ask Myra a few more questions about her lesbian life. "Myra, do you meet regularly with other gays and lesbians?"

"Yeah, I do. There are quite a few gay groups in the city. Some meet regularly at bars. Our group meets once a month in one of our homes. All in our core group are female, although we often invite a few gay guys over."

"What do you do at these meetings?"

"Oh, mostly we talk and play games. We'll have a glass or two of wine with snacks. We all believe that we want to be relatively sober on our drive home."

"Are most in your group in long-term relationships?" Iris asked.

"About half are and they often come as couples." Myra took a sip of her coffee.

"What about you, Myra? Do you have a steady girlfriend?"

"No, Iris. I've had several sexual encounters in the past, but I've some quite close lesbian friends now with whom I've not had any sexual contact."

Iris played around with her napkin for a few seconds. "Your group seems quite a bit different than some of the gay bars I've been told about."

"Oh, yeah." Myra wiped her mouth. "Ours is probably a lot more tame. I think, in general, gay males are a lot more promiscuous than lesbians."

"It seems that way. Say, would I be able to visit your group sometimes?"

Myra raised her eyebrows. "For what purpose?"

"Oh, just to meet some of your friends and find out more about the way people in your group think, I guess."

"I'm sure it'd be okay, but I'd have to ask them. They might want to know your motives. They might be worried that you were gathering information in order to publish your findings about homosexual life in Edmonton."

"Oh no, Myra. You could reassure them that I'd maintain confidentiality. I only have an interest in homosexuality and how gay people think, for my own information. I don't want to just get the information from authors and speakers who are straight."

"Okay, Iris, I'll ask the group next time. You know, if the fact that you visited a gay group gets out, rumours will really grow legs."

"I know." Iris chuckled. "But I don't really care."

"You're still having boyfriend problems?"

"Yeah, it's true. Nothing's changed. I'm trying to put distance between the guy who wants me, and the guy I want is gay. So the more everyone thinks I'm a lesbian, the better. That way there are fewer distractions and I can get on with my primary objective, medicine." Iris spoke with her voice low and quiet, but her eyes blazed with deep determination.

"Sure. Have it your way. I'm not going to try and talk you out of the course you're taking. Actually, I'm doing the same thing, although for slightly different reasons."

Deep in thought, they slowly walked out of the café and headed for their cars.

✦ ✦ ✦

Iris was now on the paediatric rotation and she was enjoying it. No wonder Milton liked that rotation better than any other. In this age group, diseases progressed with lightning speed, it seemed. Then, when the child began improving, their recovery also seemed to occur over a period of hours instead of days as she was used to in adults.

On this particular day, Iris was on call with the junior paediatric resident. Around four in the afternoon, numerous urgent pages occurred, all calling for various physicians to go to the emergency department. Included were the staff paediatrician and the junior paediatric resident. Iris hurried to the emergency department to see if she could help or, at least, learn something. When she arrived, all the rooms were full and there were many stretchers in the halls. She asked a nurse what was going on. The nurse hurriedly explained that there had been an explosion and fire in a school.

Just after Iris got to the room where the junior resident was frantically making his assessments, he looked up and shouted for Iris to come near. "A ten-year-old boy is in room three. He was sent in for an assessment of acute anemia. The family doc is worried about leukemia. Would you assess him, make a list of tests you would like done, and then let me know? I don't know when I'll be free to talk to you, but you get started and do what you can, okay?"

"Sure, Dr. Ansco." Iris hurried off to the station to pick up the chart and then headed to room three.

The boy's name was Richard, Rich for short. His mother was with him and looked scared. "Are you a doctor?"

"Yes," Iris responded as evenly as she could. "I'm Dr. Marten, an intern, Mrs. Flanders. I'll be doing the initial assessment and then Dr. Ansco will see you as well. Usually, the staff paediatrician would see you, too, but tonight he's very busy with the fire victims and I'm not sure when he can see Rich."

"You go ahead, Dr. Marten. I'm just so scared about Rich. He's so pale."

Iris looked more carefully at the boy. He did look pale. His neck was swollen, as if his lymph nodes were enlarged. That wasn't good. Iris remembered the leukemia case she'd seen as a medical student.

Iris pulled up a chair to sit in front of Mrs. Flanders. Iris smiled and then asked, "When did Rich become ill?"

"Well, I noticed about ten days ago that he'd lost his appetite and was just moping around. A few days later, he started complaining of a stomach ache and he became a little feverish. About five or six days ago, he complained of a sore throat and in the last few days, he seems to have lumps in his neck." Mrs. Flanders spoke rapidly with a tremor in her voice. "Dr. Brown did a blood test and said his counts were low. What does that mean, doctor?"

"Let me get through taking this history on Rich and examine him before answering, Mrs. Flanders." Iris smiled again. "Do you know of anyone else who had similar symptoms, someone he might've been in contact with in the last few weeks?"

"No, I don't know anyone with a problem like Rich's. Everyone else in our family seems fine. Do you think this is something he caught from someone else?"

"I really don't know, but we need to think of infectious diseases. Let me examine Rich and see what I can find out." Iris rose and approached the bed. She looked at the chart and noticed that his temperature was slightly elevated. Rich looked at her with wary eyes. She smiled. "Where does it hurt, Rich?"

He pointed to his throat and abdomen.

"Open your mouth and I'll put a stick on your tongue, Rich." She looked at his throat and noticed huge tonsils. A few red spots were visible over his soft palate, along with a few red pinpoint spots on the inside of his lips. She felt his neck and the considerably enlarged lymph nodes. "I can see that your throat would feel sore, alright."

She checked his lungs and heart. Both seemed fine, except for the heart rate being up a bit. "Bend up your knees, Rich." She gently felt his abdomen. His liver seemed enlarged, nothing too remarkable in a boy with a fever. When she felt for his spleen, she was surprised how large it was. He groaned with pain when she tried to get an idea how far below the ribs it was. She also noticed a faint blotchy rash and a few more pinpoint red spots scattered over his chest and abdomen. There was not much else to find except that he did look pale.

Iris turned back to Mrs. Flanders. "Before I can say much about what's wrong with Rich, I need to get some blood tests done and talk to Dr. Ansco."

"How long will that take? We've already been here for nearly two hours."

"About an hour or so. We need to be careful and do the best we can, Mrs. Flanders." Iris smiled and nodded.

"May I have a word with you in the hall, Dr. Marten?" Mrs. Flanders stepped out ahead of Iris and motioned Iris to join her. Then she whispered to Iris, "Do you think this is leukemia?" Mrs. Flanders looked pale and frightened.

"Well, there are other considerations here," Iris started. "Please let us get these tests done and then we'll have something more to say about possible causes." Iris smiled patiently.

Iris grabbed her medical bag and the chart and hurried to the station where she wrote orders she thought were appropriate. Mainly, she wanted to get a hemoglobin, white blood count, and platelet count. She also wanted to look at the microscopic appearance of the white and red blood cells with a pathologist. She needed to be sure that this wasn't leukemia. She also ordered a throat swab for streptococcus.

Iris then found Dr. Ansco trying to establish an IV line in a child with extensive burns over her legs. He quickly looked over Iris's orders and said, "Sure, that looks okay. Let me know when the results come back."

While waiting for the lab work, Iris walked to the medical library to do some reading. Mainly she looked at Nelson's Textbook of Paediatrics. Most of what she found would fit with leukemia—especially considering the anemia and large lymph nodes, but his throat findings made her wonder about an infection, like streptococcus. While reading about a variety of infectious conditions, she stumbled onto infectious mononucleosis. To her surprise, a lot of the boy's history and physical findings fit with that condition. The only problem was, why was he anemic? Then she saw a sentence pointing out that occasionally, infectious mononucleosis cases develop pancytopenia, where all of the blood cells will be quite depressed for a time. She became excited. Maybe, this was what Rich had—not leukemia. Wouldn't that be wonderful!

Iris walked into the lab and found the lab tech who was just drying the slides with the blood smears. Iris knew the tech quite well. "Here you go, Dr. Marten. Do you want to take them to Dr. Harris? I think he's free."

Iris hurried to Dr. Harris, the pathologist, and gave him the tray of blood smear slides. Iris told him the story while he looked over the slides. He seemed to take a long time, studying them very carefully. "Well, that's very interesting. At first I thought this was going to be acute leukemia, but now I doubt that diagnosis. There is a pancytopenia picture here with all the cell types including platelets being markedly reduced. I'm not seeing any blasts that are typical of acute leukemia. What I am seeing are large numbers of enlarged atypical lymphocytes."

Dr. Harris turned to Iris. "So, Dr. Marten, besides leukemia, what other diagnoses should be considered?"

Iris felt her heart pounding in excitement. "I think infectious mononucleosis should be considered here, Dr. Harris."

Dr. Harris raised his eyebrows in appreciation. "Oh, Dr. Marten, you are sharp today! That's just what I'm thinking, but you know, we can't afford to ignore leukemia as a possible diagnosis. What is the next step?"

"Well, we must first rule out increased breakdown of red cells. We could do this by checking the level of new cells being formed. I already ordered a reticulocyte count. Also, we could check for hemoglobin in the urine. I've ordered that test as well. Then, I think we need to do a bone marrow aspiration." Iris's eyes were sparkling with excitement.

"That's exactly my thinking. So what would you expect to find in the bone marrow smear?" Dr. Harris obviously was enjoying this interaction just as much as Iris.

Iris took a deep breath. "Well, if this were leukemia, the bone marrow would be packed full of leukemia blasts with little of any normal cell series in evidence. If it were mono, one would likely see fairly normal cells, except there would be relatively few, because the bone marrow is essentially shut down on a temporary basis."

"Yes, you're right, Dr. Marten. One would probably see quite a few large lymphocytes, like the atypical lymphocytes we are seeing in the peripheral smear. Come have a look at them." Dr. Harris moved off from his stool and motioned for Iris to look through the microscope. She immediately saw what Dr. Harris had described.

"Thank you so much for being so kind and helpful," Iris said. "I'll talk to the junior resident and then likely the staff paediatrician on call. Likely one of them will do the bone marrow aspiration."

Dr. Harris nodded. "Dr. Marten, have you thought of going into pathology? You'd make an excellent pathologist."

"Oh, thank you." Iris's face flushed. "Actually, I would like to become a haematologist."

Dr. Harris smiled. "Go for it, Dr. Marten. You'll do well in it and you will enjoy it."

✦ ✦ ✦

That same evening, the staff paediatrician, Dr. Floden, confirmed Iris's suspicion that Rich had infectious mononucleosis. He told her that the bone marrow ruled out leukemia and was compatible with a case of infectious mononucleosis with acute aplastic anemia. Iris had already looked over the bone marrow smear with Dr. Harris, so she wasn't surprised. Dr. Floden had been very impressed with Iris's keen interest in the case, so he told her to break the news to Mrs. Flanders and her son. Iris was only too pleased to do so.

On entering the room, Iris could see the deep apprehension on Mrs. Flanders's face. Iris took Mrs. Flanders' shaking hands and said, "The news is good. It's not leukemia. He has infectious mononucleosis. He'll gradually get better in all likelihood."

"But what about the anemia?"

"We can't be absolutely sure about that, but in practically all of these cases, the bone marrow recovers its function in a week or so."

Pure joy flooded Mrs. Flanders's face and she hugged her son. Iris noticed the relief in Rich's face as well.

Iris's eyes filled with tears of joy to see how happy her message had made the Flanders. She told them that Dr. Floden would be in to see them in a few minutes and then she waved goodbye and left.

✦ ✦ ✦

As Iris walked home, she felt so full of joy she had to tell someone. Who better to phone than the one who'd care the most? Milton. Iris looked at the clock. It was nearly ten—he'd still be up. He answered on the first ring. Iris said, "Hi, you're sure eager to answer your phone. I suppose you were hoping for some call to action on the ward."

"Hey, Iris. What a pleasure to hear your voice. No, I was just sitting here waiting for your call."

"Oh, I didn't know you were a clairvoyant?"

"Well, my thoughts are never too far from you. Maybe I'm just getting good at guessing your thoughts and moods."

"Oh, so what kind of mood have you figured me to be in?" Iris laughed, twirling the phone cord around her finger.

"I'd divine that you are in a happy, buoyant mood. Am I too far off?"

"You're right as usual. Do you want me to tell you why?"

"I can hardly wait." Milton almost sounded breathless.

Iris giggled. "Okay. Here's what my day was like." Iris went on to tell Milton about the fire and the call to the emergency department. She also told him about Rich and his mother. Iris could sense keen interest as she described the course of investigation and the discussions with Dr. Harris.

When she finished, Milton said, "I'm so proud of you, Iris. I think God gave you that case so you could be sure you wanted to be a haematologist."

"Now, now, Milton, you were going to keep religion out of this."

"Oops, it just slipped out. I'll try to be more careful next time."

Iris giggled again. "You might be right. But I can't believe I could be worthy of the God of the universe stooping down to give me a sign like that."

"I can, Iris. He's like that. If I can get all excited about what happened to you, guess how he can. He loves you, Iris."

Iris began to cry. After a few seconds, she blubbered, "I'm sorry, I guess I'm quite emotional this evening. I realize that as much as I need the love of my family and people like you, I need God's love more than anything."

"You just spoke pure wisdom, Iris. I wish I could be with you now and give you a big hug."

"I would like that, too." Iris's voice began quivering again. "Thank you for always being there for me, Milt."

"When July first comes, we'll be working in the same hospital again, you in virology and me in paediatrics. The two disciplines often intersect."

"So you think we'll also intersect?"

"Yeah, that sounds lovely." Milton laughed.

"I guess we need to stop this conversation or we'll be crossing a line again."

"You're right. I want to say again that I'm so happy when you do well in medicine, and when you're happy, I'm happy."

When their phone lines disconnected, Iris thought, *we shouldn't be doing this, but I needed that visit so much.*

Chapter Seventeen

April 1962

SPRING HAD FINALLY ARRIVED. THE DAY HAD BEEN WARM AND SUNNY and most of the snow had melted. *Not bad for the last week in April,* Iris thought. She walked to the west-facing window of her apartment and noticed the sun low in the west bathing the clouds in a brilliant glow of pinks and oranges, even some greens. She wished she could luxuriate in the beautiful scenes of spring, but this was the evening she'd be visiting the lesbian group. Now she was having second thoughts. Her attendance would no doubt be awkward for others as well as for herself. She was doing it so that she could better understand homosexuality. She wanted to understand this condition in real people, not just as some kind of disorder she read about in a textbook.

As she gazed at the clouds, Iris thought about Myra's life. What an interesting girl she was! She was so talented in music. She could make a career out of music and teaching piano. Myra was also a very good doctor. She was finishing her rotating internship and was planning to start a residency in psychiatry at the University of Alberta Hospital in July. She would make an excellent psychiatrist. Iris doubted that Myra being lesbian would get in the way of being able to help her patients. Myra's deep caring for the needs of her patients would quickly overcome any awkwardness her sexual orientation might bring.

As she drove to Myra's rented suite, Iris wondered how she should conduct herself. The main thing would be to respect the group and be honest about why she was visiting. She wondered if she should speak about Milton, but knew it wouldn't be wise to break confidentiality.

Myra greeted Iris heartily. From the suite's entrance, Iris could see six women in Myra's living room. "Let me introduce you to the women who have come so far, Iris." Myra looked relaxed and in control. After introductions, Myra said, "As most of you know from our last meeting, Iris asked if she could visit our group. As I've mentioned, Iris is a classmate and dear friend of mine. Since Iris is straight, you might ask what her intentions are. Before I invited her, she told me she has a close friend who is gay and so has a great personal interest in learning about people with this orientation. She feels, as I do, that the information in the medical literature falls far short when it comes to understanding homosexuality. Is that a fair assessment, Iris?"

Iris could feel her neck flushing and her heart pounding. "Sure, Myra. I suppose you could say I'm a snoop." Most chuckled or at least smiled. Iris felt encouraged to carry on. "I care for and respect Myra very much. I guess I just wanted to meet up with some of her lesbian friends to see what I could learn from you. My main motive is to better understand my gay friend, but I also to understand this orientation better in general."

Myra greeted another couple just arriving and then invited Iris and others to have a seat. Iris chose a chair next to a couch. Myra took orders for drinks—red or white wine. A tray of cheeses, crackers, and olives circulated as most chattered light-heartedly. Iris realized a blonde, Sandy, was eying her and so she wasn't surprised when she asked, "Iris, is your gay friend also in the medical field?"

"Yes, he is."

"Has he come out?"

"I think certain groups know about his orientation, but he has not generally broadcast this information." Iris felt that she could be headed for troubled waters.

"I suppose not, or we would have heard of him." Sandra quickly glanced about the room. "Iris, you don't have to tell us, but I would be interested in what groups your friend has talked of his orientation."

Now Iris knew she was in trouble, but she had determined to be honest. "The main group where he's been open about it is his church, mostly with a small group of that church."

Everyone stopped talking. Most of the group looked to Sandra for her next question. Sandra didn't disappoint. "Does this church expect him to switch to become a heterosexual?"

Iris could feel the tension in the room rising. "I can't answer that for my friend. I know he holds some hope that such a switch could happen for him."

"What do you expect, Iris?" Sandra smiled, but her eyes were intense.

"Well, I've always thought that such a change isn't possible. He claims that since he's been involved with his group, fantasizing about same-gender sexual activity has dropped off considerably."

"So, is this group trying to give him some kind of therapy?" Iris felt Sandra was like a hungry dog chewing on a bone. Iris felt like the bone.

"No, no, nothing like that. As I understand it, the group just accepts him as he is and interacts with him as with anyone else. The group doesn't bring up the issue of orientation." Iris noticed that all the women were following the conversation with considerable interest.

"Hey, I think I'll join that group!" Myra said with a laugh. Everyone laughed with her, and the tension was relieved.

Iris glanced at Sandra, who looked thoughtful. Iris felt there were probably many other questions she'd like to have asked.

Myra passed the tray of snacks around again and then turned to Iris. "So far, Iris has been peppered with questions. I'm wondering if she has any questions she'd like to ask of the group." Myra looked expectantly at Iris.

"Well, sure." Iris felt shaky, but since the group seemed very open and honest, she might as well be, too. "Do you all feel that sexual orientation is a lifelong situation with which you are born?"

Several started to answer at once. Most seemed to take the view that it was lifelong, something one inherited.

Then a short, stocky woman with bobbed dark hair piped up. "I read recently that there is no scientific proof that homosexuality is inherited. I think being homosexual is mostly a matter of environment. I blame my lousy upbringing. My father was nice, but a weak man. My mom ran the show. She was and still is a battle-axe. I can remember her telling me I should have been a boy since I always acted like one. She told me many times that I'd never attract a man because I just wasn't sexy enough. She laughed at me whenever I tried to wear pretty, feminine clothes."

"You may be right about environment, Paula," Sandra said. "I suspect there is some genetic factor underlying sexual orientation, but it may not be expressed unless some environmental factors also come into play."

Iris thought Sandra talked like a science student. She'd have to ask Myra about that.

"What made you say that?" asked Paula.

"Well, I can't say my parents were very supportive of me. They weren't bad, just not there when I needed them. My dad was an alcoholic and was out of the picture a lot of the time. When he wasn't binging, he was at work trying to keep his business going. Mom was very proud of my older sister. She loved to buy fancy clothes for her and parade her before all of her doting friends. She also tried matching her with handsome boys in our area. With me, she just seemed uninterested. She'd often tell me that I was daddy's girl. Once when I was around eleven and the whole family was present, she said she was confident my sister would find a nice husband. She then looked at me and said I was probably not the marrying type. Well, I swallowed that as the truth for me. After that, I didn't even try to emulate my sister or other girls at school."

"Oh Sandra, I feel so badly for you," Iris said with deep concern. "We seem to all need affirmation from our parents at crucial times in our lives. What I've noticed is that both Paula and Sandra had mothers that didn't affirm their femininity. I wonder how common that is among lesbians?" Iris also recalled that Myra's mother also didn't support her very much, but didn't want to mention anything without Myra's permission.

Another woman who appeared to be around thirty offered her experience. "My mother was very caring in our family. She was very organized and made sure all our needs were met. She seemed to be close to my three brothers, but mother and I were always quite distant emotionally. I never felt comfortable to confide in her."

This same woman's partner cut in at that point. "I had very good parents. My mother was always warm and encouraging. So, Iris, your theory doesn't work out in my case."

Myra spoke up while looking at Iris. "Well, we've had quite an interesting discussion. I want to thank Iris for having the interest and courage to visit us. You handled yourself very well, Iris. I wondered, for a while, whether Sandra was going to scare you out of here." Everyone except Sandra laughed. "But I think we are all glad you asked those questions, Sandra. Now, if we don't switch gears, we won't have time for a round of Canasta. Let's move over to the kitchen table."

Iris hadn't played Canasta before, but she could learn. That would certainly be a lot easier than trying to answer all those penetrating questions.

Chapter Eighteen

June 1962

Iris was once again waiting in the foyer of the residence for Tim. She'd come down early to have some time to ponder her future. Tim had phoned her while she was working on the paediatric ward and asked her to join him at a café on Whyte Avenue. She was quite reticent, in view of their last meeting. On the telephone, he seemed very contrite and requested a very short visit to "clarify a few issues." She finally became willing when she realized she wanted to stay on good terms with him. Maybe she needed to see some aspect of Tim that she wasn't aware of. She wanted to give him another chance.

When Tim's drove up, she went out to meet him. On the way to the café, they chatted amiably about their work. Once they were seated with coffee and cookies, Tim looked into Iris's face and said, "Iris, I want to apologize for the way I acted the last time we were together. I guess I was responding more to my own feelings and I wasn't very sensitive to yours. I also want to say that I was not directly responsible for the rumours being spread about your being a lesbian. You see, I've a friend named Delmar. He noticed how down I was just after our time together. Well, I unwisely shared with him the fact that you called yourself a lesbian, not thinking at all that he would take me seriously. Well, he did. In fact, he blabbed it out in the Students' Union Building. I'm very sorry that this happened. I'm hoping you can forgive me and that we can become friends again."

Iris found the story incredulous. "Well, I don't know quite what to think. At least now I know that you didn't purposefully spread this rumour. As to whether I'll forgive you, I'll admit I was hurt by the way you seemed to not take my feelings into consideration that night. I suppose any couple, even in marriage, will do that to one another eventually. Yes, I'll forgive you Tim." Iris smiled at Tim in confirmation.

"I really appreciate that, Iris." Tim nodded with a hopeful smile. They nibbled on their cookies in silence for a time, and then Tim said, "I need to know if you've left any room in your heart for a possible renewal of our relationship."

Iris sat still, focusing on what was left of her cookie. After a few moments, she took in a long unsure breath and said in a soft voice, "I guess I'm not prepared to respond to that just now." Iris looked up, fixing her gaze on Tim's face. "I need to process this for a few days. Then, I'd like to meet with you again and see where our relationship will go. I know I'm always the one to stall, but I don't want to do something that could cause unnecessary hurt for either of us. How about I call you at your home next Tuesday evening and we can decide where and when to meet? Are you okay with that?"

Tim reached over and squeezed Iris's hand. "Sure, I understand that you need some space to think about this. Please don't feel rushed or pressured."

"Thank you, Tim," Iris said, smiling and placing her other hand over Tim's.

✦ ✦ ✦

Milton was glad he could finally escape the hospital wards. He'd been relentlessly pursued, it seemed, by the paging system. Supper at the cafeteria wasn't up to much, but it was nourishing, he conceded. His time on obstetrics had been very busy and, though he liked the work, he was very tired. A quiet evening alone would be nice.

As he walked into his suite, the phone was ringing. He hoped it was Iris. He heard the familiar voice of Bill Street as he picked up. "Hey Milt, glad I caught you. You're a hard guy to track down."

"Bill, it's been a while since I've heard from you. What's up?" Milton hoped it would be just a quick call. Would he be up to visiting Bill in person?

"Well, it's a bit too complicated to say over the phone. Would you be willing to drop by at my suite?"

There was something unusual about Bill's voice. He seemed emotional, upset even. *Okay, Milton. Do the right thing.* "Sure, Bill. Give me thirty minutes. I have to warn you that I need to get back by nine. I was up with deliveries most of the night and I need a good sleep." *Please, God, give me the strength.*

"Fair enough. What I've to tell you won't take long."

As Milton drove to Bill's place, he looked over the shrubs and trees along the street. The fresh beauty of the various shades of green, especially in June, always moved him. What a privilege it would be to have the time to paint those vivid colours. He could feel his insides relaxing and his weariness fading as he contemplated the hues he'd choose in painting such a picture. His mind flitted back to his friend's phone call. He was glad he'd made the decision to visit Bill. If he'd refused, their relationship might well be permanently fractured.

"Hello, Milton. Glad you could come." Milton noticed sadness in Bill's eyes.

"Bill, you're my friend. That's what friends do."

"Sit down, Milt. Let me get you a beer."

"Okay, but I only want one as I might fall asleep on you if I had more."

When Bill returned with two bottles, he set one next to Milton and sat down. "I guess I just needed someone who would listen to me for a bit."

"I'm your man, Bill. I can see you're torn up about something."

Bill took a gulp from his bottle, set it down and hesitated. Milton could see tears glistening in Bill's eyes. "You remember I told you about the guy I'd hoped could be a long-term partner?"

"Right, his name is Marvin, isn't it?"

"Yeah, well our relationship has fallen apart," he said in a soft unsteady voice.

"I'm sorry, Bill. When and how did that happen?"

Bill pulled out a handkerchief and blew his nose. He paused to regain control of his emotions and then said, "Things were going okay at first, but then I noticed him talking to people on the telephone a lot. One day last week, I answered a call and the guy wanted to speak to Marvin. When Marvin took the phone, I could hear that the conversation became quite intimate. Marvin then left the house and was away for over three hours. I asked him where he'd been and he just said he had coffee with an old friend. When I asked him who that was, he became defensive and told me it was none of my business. I told him we were partners now and there shouldn't be secrets between us. He just got angry and told me to get lost if I was going to be that selfish. We got into a yelling match and I told him to take his stuff and leave. Well, that's just what he did."

Milton slowly shook his head. "That would have been so painful. Do you regret telling him to leave?"

Bill's tears were flowing freely now. His voice quavered. "Sure I regret it. I loved him, after all. I've felt so torn up with rage and jealousy, but I still miss him. I feel so much self-loathing for not meeting all his needs. I wasn't good enough so he had to look for someone else."

Milton got up and put his hands on Bill's heaving shoulders and stood quietly until Bill's sobbing subsided. Milton resumed his seat and waited. Finally, Bill managed to speak again. "I've decided to do as you have, become a celibate."

Milton took a slow deep breath. "No, that won't work, Bill. You'll have to go through a period of grieving, but it will come to an end. When it does, the need to have sex will come back and you'll look for another guy to fulfill your needs."

Bill looked desperate. "If it works for you, why won't it work for me?"

Milton paused to collect his thoughts. He knew what he needed to say might not be accepted, but he would say it anyway. "I can see two reasons. One is that I have become a Christian and I receive strength through Christ. The second is that I'm receiving strength through the affirmation from heterosexual men."

"I'm not sure I know what you're talking about. You sound like a theologian."

Milton explained in simple words his faith history and also told Bill about the beneficial effects of his small group, especially the non-sexual hugging, handshaking, and camaraderie of the men.

"I can see you've got something I don't have. Maybe when I recover a little from this loss, I might have some more questions. Right now, I'm just not ready for that stuff."

Milton knew it was time to let Bill do some healing on his own. He finished his beer and got up to leave. "I've got to be going, Bill. You won't be far from my thoughts. Call me any time you want to talk again." Milton was going to shake Bill's hand, but then decided to hug him.

"You've learned that from your group, I suppose," Bill said with a lopsided grin.

They both laughed as Milton stepped out of the door.

✦ ✦ ✦

Iris thought the research was progressing well. Before she would go off on vacation for the last two weeks of June, she needed to meet with Dr. Pinsky to bring him up to date with her findings. She needed to keep him happy and closely informed, as he'd insisted. From where she was sitting in Dr. Pinsky's waiting room, she could see his closed office door. He always kept her waiting ten or fifteen minutes. *He's doing that just to let me know who's boss,* she thought with irritation.

Finally, the door opened and Dr. Pinsky emerged and nodded for her to enter and have a seat.

"So, you've served your year of hospital slavery? Have you learned anything other than how medical politics works?"

Iris grinned. "I enjoyed most of it. The experience helped me to decide what I wanted to do after I finish my internship."

"And what's that going to be?"

"I've decided to do haematology here in this hospital after my year in research."

"So you've decided to do clinical work instead of research? That's a pity." A flicker of disappointment crossed his face.

"Yes, I'm really excited about doing that."

"Well now, what about your progress here since our last update two months ago?"

"We've been collecting stool and saliva samples on experimental mice that have been exposed to poliovirus. We've also collected stool and saliva samples on new human polio patients. Furthermore, we've looked at the protective effect on mice and humans who've been given oral poliovirus or OPV. I believe I told you about the results of these studies on previous briefings. What's new is what we found on stool samples of mice and humans who've been given oral poliovirus immunization. We're finding that we recover OPV readily in stools of both mice and humans. We've started to feed uninfected mice with stools of mice given OPV, and our preliminary results show that these uninfected mice become immunized. Now we're doing the same in humans immunized with OPV."

Dr. Pinsky raised his eyebrows. "Are you planning to give human volunteers stool to eat from OPV immunized people? You might have trouble getting compliance!"

Iris laughed. "I may be strong-minded, but not that persuasive. No, we'd just test the stools of family members and other close contacts that weren't immunized with OPV to see if some of them became immunized by eating food that might have been contaminated by the immunized sibling. It isn't ideal, but if we can show that there is a significantly higher secondary immunization, we'll have shown that the same phenomenon occurs in humans as occurs in experimental mice."

"Okay, I think you'll have some publishable results if things pan out as you've predicted. Keep bringing me all your results, including all of your methodology. Do you have some details in print of what you told me just now?"

"Sure, Dr. Pinsky." Iris pulled out several pages of typewritten material and placed them on his desk.

"Good. Have a good vacation and we'll see you after the first of July. Iris, keep mum on all these findings. We don't want someone else scooping the results and publishing ahead of us, do we?"

"I'll keep the lid on our work, Dr. Pinsky."

◆ ◆ ◆

As agreed, Iris phoned Tim about another meeting. They'd made plans to meet again at the same café. Now Iris was waiting for Tim to arrive. After Tim's show of humility and understanding, Iris thought he seemed to have matured from when they first met. She wondered if he was still flirting with other women. She wondered also if his theology had changed. In the past, he'd seemed quite evasive when he talked of Jesus. She realized she'd shifted a bit toward a more liberal view of Scripture, but she couldn't get away from what she learned and experienced at the "Jesus Meetings" she'd had with Trish and her dad while she was in high school. For now, though, she felt herself willing to find grounds for a real relationship with Tim.

Iris thought again of Milton. Would she ever get him out of her heart? Maybe it would be better for her if he did find a male friend, she thought ruefully. Maybe that would help sort out her problems, though not so much for him.

On the way to the café, Iris learned that Tim was still heading up the missions board in their church. This involved both local initiatives and foreign missions. Tim still had an interest in living and working in a third-world country. His biggest hope was that he could live in one of the African countries where poverty and hunger were big concerns. They chatted about this on the way to the café and after settling at a table. Iris was again impressed by Tim's humanitarian passion. She wondered if and how she could ever fit into his world.

After they'd ordered food, Tim wanted to know what Iris's plans were for further medical training. Iris informed him of her plans to specialize in haematology once her year of research with Dr. Pinsky was finished. Iris chatted excitedly about her educational ambitions.

Their discussion was interrupted when the waitress came back with their pizza. Their food became the focus for a few minutes and then Tim asked, "I've asked you before but I'll ask it again. Would living in an African country and carrying on a medical practice appeal to you, Iris?"

Iris looked thoughtful as she chewed on a bite of her pizza. She could feel an impasse coming. She needed to be honest no matter the consequences. "Well, there are some problems that I can foresee. If we were in a poor country like you're describing, I'd be over-trained. At the most, they'd need public health personnel and general practitioners. I could see working in some university medical school in some of Africa's larger cities. It's doubtful you would find the work you would be looking for in these cities." Iris paused and looked out of the window. "If you were to go to some poor African country to carry out the service you envision for yourself, what would that look like?"

Tim shifted to a more comfortable position. "Well, I'd try to find out what the community felt their needs were. I'd ask what they needed to make their lives better. Then I'd go about trying to achieve that."

"How would you see doing that?"

"I'd see my job as bringing these needs to the attention of those who might have the resources to fund projects that met those needs." Tim's eyes were shining with enthusiasm.

"Tim, you probably have in mind some of the areas of need you'd attempt to address. What might these needs be?"

"Well, I can see there might be problems of unemployment, poverty, hunger, infectious diseases, and lack of education. Many of these problems can be met by our relatively affluent society."

Iris pressed on, as she really wanted to discover what Tim's vision was. "If you got the funds that you wanted and you got some projects going to help the needs you mentioned, would you also see a need to present the recipients with the knowledge of Christianity? You would be going out under the authority of your church, after all."

Tim raised an eyebrow and smiled. "You mean preach the gospel to them?"

"Yeah." Iris nodded while doodling with some table crumbs.

"You know, your suggestion, Iris, sounds like the old-style missions where the natives were offered food, employment, and education *if* they'd convert to Christianity. When missionaries offer this help, the natives probably feel pressured to give the missionaries what they want—conversion. I see this as coercion. The more modern way to do missions is to offer them the help they're asking for and allow them to choose whatever belief system they want. If they're impressed with the love they've been shown, they might even ask some questions about the missionary's beliefs. My job as a missionary is not to tie my help to my belief system. My help is given with no strings attached."

Iris nodded. "Okay, I get what you mean." Iris tipped her coffee cup up and drained it, signaling she'd had enough of that subject.

After a long pause, Tim asked, "Are you still firm on the idea of going into haematology?" Tim took another bite of his pizza but kept his eyes on Iris.

"Yes, I'm quite sure about that. I guess I could ask you a similar question. Are you firm about living in a third-world country?"

"Well, yeah. I just feel that in this country, social services are doing most of what missions used to do. Not so in Africa. There, the efforts we put into serving will really count. There are just no social safety nets there. I would love to be out there organizing relief."

Iris nodded and smiled. "I so much admire your desire to serve in this way. It seems, however, that our lives are going in two separate directions. I'll have to pray that God will give us direction. Do you pray about things like that?"

"Oh, in a general way, I guess. I don't get too specific. I always think that God gave us a brain to think and it's up to us to come up with plans to do humanitarian acts to help other humans when they're in need."

Iris decided she would do a little digging. "Do you ever think of God as someone who is interested in you personally and who has a specific plan for you?"

Tim drained the last of his coffee before answering. "Actually, no. I guess I see God as a force remote from the day-to-day activities of mankind. He has given us revelations of his purposes through various prophets in the past. God expects us to use our brains and resources for good. I never think of God having a specific plan for my life. What about you, Iris?"

Iris felt a wave of sadness invade her being. "For me, it's a little different. I'll admit my faith is not like it used to be when I was attending high school, but I still believe God is interested in my life and that he wants me to seek him for guidance."

Tim gazed into Iris's eyes for a moment. "Iris, the weather is nice and it's such a beautiful time in the year. Why don't we go to a park in the river valley where we can just walk and talk?"

"That sounds wonderful," Iris said with a big smile. They got up and walked to the till to pay for the food. Iris decided she'd talk about subjects that weren't as controversial and just have fun together.

As they walked through the park, they kept their conversation light, focusing on the wonders of nature. The setting sun flooded the sky with an incredible display of pinks and various hues of green and blue. They stood in awe at what they were privileged to observe. After a time, they resumed walking. They got onto the topic of family life.

"I'd love to meet your parents sometime, Tim," Iris said.

"Sure, we can arrange that. I'll need to phone them. They usually have a tight social schedule, but they'd be glad to slot us in at some point. I'd be happy to meet your parents, too. Would that be possible sometime, maybe when they come up to visit you?"

When they reached Tim's car, Tim took Iris's hand and said with a warm smile, "I've really enjoyed this time with you, Iris. Can we find a time to do this again soon?"

"Yes, that would be nice."

Chapter Nineteen

June 1962

It was the fifteenth of June and the clouds threatened rain. Iris awoke in good spirits. She felt the relief of being finished with her internship. She was also glad to have a break from her research project. She looked forward to the two weeks at her home near Badger Creek. She was glad she'd taken her Ford sedan for servicing. She'd needed some new tires and brake pads. Ever since she'd had an accident with her dad's car, she'd made sure to keep tires and brakes in good shape. Her mind went back to that time when a group of guys purposefully fixed her tire stems so they'd pop off while driving. She'd been lucky to come out the resulting accident alive.

Iris ate breakfast quickly and packed a few bags for her vacation. She pulled on some jeans and a sweater and was off. She headed east on Highway 16. Clouds were heavy and she noticed a few sprinkles of rain on the windshield. She didn't mind the weather. In fact, if it rained in Saskatchewan, it would be good. She'd heard the farmers there were worried about their crops drying up.

Iris thought about what Tim and she had talked about. There still seemed to be all too many unknowns when it came to Tim's theology. When she'd tried to find out what he thought about Jesus, Tim had praised the selflessness and generosity of Jesus and his willingness to sacrifice personal needs in order to help others. Tim had also been most impressed that Jesus was willing to die for something he believed. When it came to seeing Jesus atoning for mankind's sin through his death, Tim had been quite vague. She wasn't even sure he believed Jesus rose from the dead!

She thought again about the impasse they'd come to in their last meeting. Would she be willing to sacrifice her passion for haematology in favour of going to Africa and working as a sole GP in some remote village? She just couldn't get excited about that. Part of the problem was that she couldn't get excited about Tim's way of doing missions. She remembered that Jesus always told the crowds about the Kingdom of Heaven as well as healing the sick and even feeding them. Jesus was extremely concerned with how and what people believed. Jesus never suggested that the people he healed should choose whatever they wanted to believe.

Not surprisingly, the image of Milton came to mind. What a difference there was in the spiritual views of Milton and Tim! Although she hadn't queried Milton with the same questions, she was sure Milton would have a very different view of missions. She was sure Milton's take on the essentials of Christianity and his view of Jesus would be much like that of her dad and step-mom's. So, where was she in regards to her view of Jesus? She wondered if she'd lost ground somewhere in terms of her faith. She surely wasn't as simple and trusting anymore.

Iris admired the scenery as she continued east. Soon she'd be crossing the border into Saskatchewan, only an hour away from Badger Creek. A steady west wind was sending clouds skittering along. She could see waves in the grain fields like those of the sea. In spite of the clouds, no rain was falling. She suspected the farmers were looking hopefully at these clouds, but so far the clouds were failing to produce. Iris was reminded of a passage of Scripture in Jude, where false teachers were likened to rainless clouds. She could still hear her father quoting: "Waterless clouds, carried along by winds."

A wave of sadness overtook her as she thought about the Jude Scripture. Was her life promising much, but producing little of what God desired for her? Was her faith empty like those clouds? She prayed that this time at home would bring some new inspiration that would strengthen her faith. She thirsted for more reality in her trust in God. She prayed that she'd be a good listener with her father and Trish—even with Ralph. Ralph was attending seminary at Briercrest in Carenport, Saskatchewan. He'd likely be home, too. Ralph certainly would have strong opinions on the way her life of faith was going. She used to be threatened by his opinions. Strangely, she now felt she would like his take. A good conversation would be fun and, maybe, helpful.

* * *

As Iris guessed, Ralph was home. He'd just completed his first year at Briercrest, and he was employed at Badger Creek Christian Church as a youth pastor until his seminary courses started again in the fall. Reuniting with the family was fun and fulfilling for Iris. She enjoyed the small talk and generally catching up with the family as they prepared and ate dinner together. Her dad grilled hamburgers on the deck barbeque. While he did this, Iris caught up with his school situation. He told her of all the paperwork and marking that was necessary in the last two weeks of June. During the meal, Iris quizzed Ralph about the courses he'd taken and Ralph was delighted to tell her.

After the dishes were washed, the family settled in the dining room. Ralph started the conversation. "Okay, Iris, it's your turn. Tell us about your intern year. Did you discover what you wanted to specialize in?"

"Well, I found the year quite hard at times, especially with trying to combine it with the research project in virology. It was also fun and interesting. I'm sure I'll value all the experiences I had when I get into clinical practice." Iris loved to talk about her life with people who really cared. She went on, "As far as what I've decided to do after this next year of research, I'm going to specialize in haematology. I'll do the first few years in Edmonton, but then I'll have to complete my specialty training in some other city, maybe Toronto."

Ralph stretched out his long legs and tented his fingers. "What made you to choose haematology? Sounds kind of bloody, doesn't it?"

Iris chuckled. "True, we need to draw lots of samples of blood for tests. I just found the diseases we needed to investigate so fascinating. Some pretty sad cases come up in this discipline. In fact, it was a case of leukemia that helped me decide. The child died, but I felt I'd something to offer the grieving parents during the time I was involved with the case."

"I think you chose well," Peter said. "You chose for the right reasons: interest and seeing a way you could help others."

"I agree," Trish said. "How do you think this year of research on poliovirus is going to help you in the future?"

"I'm really not sure," Iris admitted with an embarrassed laugh. "I decided to do that before I settled on haematology as a specialty. I'm happy about doing it, actually. It gives me a sense of how research in any area is carried out. I've also learned lots about the scientific process and statistical analysis."

"It will teach you how to gather material for publication. That in turn could help in publishing interesting cases in haematology," Peter said.

"You're right, Dad. In fact, I'm very much involved in preparing for publication of the research results with Dr. Pinsky."

After Iris explained in general terms how the poliovirus research project was progressing, Trish asked with a soft smile, "What's happening with your love life, Iris?"

Iris knew that question would come eventually. She felt a little frustrated, because she didn't know how to answer it without giving away more than she wanted to. "Well, my love life is clearly the worst part of my life. In fact, it's in shambles most of the time."

Ralph pulled his legs in and straightened up in his chair. "We're listening, Iris."

"I'm hoping you'll understand as well," Iris said with a sad face.

"We promise we'll try," Trish said. "Just tell us what you're comfortable with sharing."

"Okay, I'll start with Milton. He's my closest friend outside of you guys. He's so sensitive and fun to be with. He understands me better than anyone outside my family. I love being around him. He has become a Christian and I really respect his maturity in the faith. But he's gay."

Ralph asked, "Is he active, that is, having partners?"

"From what he tells me and from what I hear on the grapevine, no, he's celibate."

"Does Milton hold out any desire or hope that he could change?" Peter asked. "I mean, to become a heterosexual?"

Iris thought awhile and then said, "You know, I'm not sure. Perhaps you should ask him." Iris gave a little chuckle, as that option seemed impossible.

"Actually," Peter said, "I would like to meet Milton sometime. Maybe when we make a trip to Edmonton to see you."

Iris nodded, then took a deep breath. "Now as far as Tim is concerned, we have a somewhat off-and-on relationship. Just now, we are on good terms."

"Is he interested in marrying you?" asked Trish.

"Yeah, he says he is. It's mostly me holding back."

Peter shifted in his chair and tapped his fingers together. Finally he asked, "Iris, would you mind telling us your biggest concern preventing you from going ahead with marrying Tim?"

"Dad, you always ask the most difficult questions. You're too much the teacher." Everyone waited with eyes fixed on her. Iris sighed. "Well, there are several issues. One is that he wants me to quit my training and head off with him to some poor and remote African community. He wants to organize and promote ventures that would improve the community's social wellbeing. And I guess I would operate a general practice."

"And you don't share that vision, I presume," Ralph said.

"Oh, I don't object to what he wants to do. I just don't see me doing that. I really want to do this research year and then go into haematology."

Trish got up and asked if anyone wanted some tea. Most did, so she went to the kitchen to prepare it. Conversation got sidelined with discussing Tim's current job. When Trish returned with a tray of tea and cups, she said, "Iris, you said there were several issues with Tim. Do you mind mentioning another one?"

"I'd hoped you'd forget about that." Iris gazed at the ceiling, trying to formulate her thoughts. "Well, to put it bluntly, I'm having trouble with his theology. He has a liberal view of the gospel. For him, the most important things we as Christians should be doing are to help people in their health, social, educational, and financial needs."

"That sounds laudable enough," said Ralph with raised eyebrows.

"Yes, I agree, but that's where it ends. He doesn't see that we also have a responsibility to teach them about Jesus. He sees attempts to do that as obligating the natives to accept the Gospel along with the food and other support."

"But that's what Jesus did," Ralph practically shouted.

"I know. I tried to tell him, but he just doesn't see it that way."

"Ah, he's into the social gospel way of thinking," Ralph added.

"The other thing that bothers me," Iris said, "is the way he thinks of Jesus. For him, Jesus is important mainly for his showing us a pattern of how we should live a selfless life of service for our fellow man. He doesn't make much of his atoning for our sins. At least he doesn't say much on that subject."

"He certainly sounds very liberal in his theology," Ralph said. "I wonder what he believes about Jesus' resurrection and ascension."

"I'm not really sure, Ralph."

"You need to ask him specific questions about his beliefs." Ralph looked deeply concerned. "You don't want to marry someone who has a distorted view of the Gospel. He may not even be a Christian. You wouldn't want to marry an unbeliever. You'd be unequally yoked."

"Oh, I just don't know. I'm so confused about where Tim is really at in his beliefs. When I'm with him, he soon has me convinced that he's a more caring Christian than I am."

"Wouldn't I give a lot if I could be a fly on the wall when he talks to his colleagues about theology and faith issues," Ralph said.

Iris's eyes widened. "Actually, he told me recently that he is participating in a comparative religion forum this fall. Maybe I could attend, if I could find the time."

"Ah, but if he knew you were there, he might couch his words. Maybe you could attend secretly," Ralph said.

Peter laughed, shaking his head. "No, that doesn't sound like a good idea. If he ever found out you went secretly, he might be deeply offended."

"I've got an idea." Ralph's eyes were snapping with excitement. "Iris, you find out exactly when that forum is. Maybe I can drive up to Edmonton and attend it. Tim wouldn't recognize me. Then I could swing by your place and we could discuss what I've learned. That would also give me a chance to see your place."

Iris tipped her head and her eyes narrowed. "Well, Ralph, I don't know how comfortable I'd be with you acting as my spy, but if you really want to do that, you could see for yourself. You'd have the theological training that would help frame better questions than I could."

"My time is quite flexible. I think I could make that work." Ralph looked positively gleeful.

Peter laughed and exclaimed, "Ralph, you made the wrong career choice. You should've become a detective for the RCMP!"

✦ ✦ ✦

The next morning, the family enjoyed a breakfast of waffles, Peter's specialty. Ralph excused himself as soon as he finished his third waffle. He said he had an early meeting at church and would be away for most of the day.

As soon as Ralph left, Trish poured coffee for the three of them. When she sat down, she looked at Peter and said, "Yesterday you mentioned you'd like to meet Milton. I couldn't get that idea out of my head before I finally fell asleep. I like the idea. For that matter, I wouldn't mind meeting Tim as well. I find it difficult to assess people without seeing them in person."

Iris slowly sipped her coffee before commenting. "Yes, maybe we could arrange that, if you were willing to drive to Edmonton." Then, Iris's eyes widened as she thought of another idea. "Hey, maybe we could invite the two guys here, during the next two weeks."

Peter began laughing. "Sure, but don't ask me to moderate the discussion."

"No, I didn't mean that," Iris said. "I thought of inviting them at different times, like one this next weekend and the other the following weekend. Then you'd get a good sense of what these two guys are like."

Trish glanced to Peter. "You know, I think we could manage that. Iris, you might have difficulty arranging their coming. They might have other plans."

"Maybe so, but I can always try. Even if I could get just one of them, it would be worthwhile, I think."

"I agree," Peter said, clapping his hands together. "Why don't you try phoning them this morning and we can start making plans."

Iris found a small pad with phone numbers in her purse and parked herself at the telephone desk. Soon Milton was on the line. Peter motioned for Trish to follow him to their den, where he quietly closed the door. Peter turned to Trish and said in a low tone, "I thought she should have some privacy making these calls."

Trish nodded. "Yes, I agree. Peter, if both come, we could be asked to be adjudicators of their characters. That might be very difficult."

"Ah, maybe so, but I think she needs all the help she can get in deciding what to do with these men. She's obviously asking for our help and we should do what we can."

Trish took Peter's hands in hers and said, "She knows we'll be praying for insight and wisdom. Why don't we do that right now?"

They both closed their eyes and each, in turn, prayed that God would bring one or both of these men to their home and that they'd receive God's discernment of their personalities and characters. When they finished, they sat and began planning the weekends, should Tim and Milton agree to come.

A knock on the door indicated Iris had finished her calls. When she came in, she looked very excited. "They're both coming! It's amazing that both were free. I invited them to drive out Saturday mornings and stay overnight. Tim said he'd be available this next weekend, but not the following. He's participating in this next Sunday morning service in his church, so he'll leave for Edmonton quite early Sunday morning. I told him I would make him an early breakfast. Milton can come the weekend after. He said he would be able to attend Sunday morning service at our church and then return to Edmonton after lunch." Iris clasped her hands together in excitement. "Oh, I hope this works out okay and I hope it doesn't place too much of a burden on you two."

Peter smiled. "It'll work out just fine. In fact, we prayed that God would help us, and I have a good feeling he'll do just that."

✦ ✦ ✦

Iris took another look at the kitchen clock. Ten minutes until Tim said he'd arrive. She felt herself becoming increasingly nervous. She couldn't predict how the interaction between Tim and her parents would go. She knew her dad would try to understand Tim's theology and she knew Trish would be trying to discern from speech and body language what the attraction was like between Tim and herself. She wondered what role she'd be playing during this visit. She prayed for calmness and sensitivity. She was glad Ralph wasn't going to be present. He was in charge of a boy's weekend camp. If he were here, he might ask embarrassing questions. She didn't need that.

Right on time, the doorbell rang, startling Iris. She opened the door to a broadly smiling Tim.

"Tim, do come in." She gave him a quick hug and then turned to Peter and Trish. "Tim, I want you to meet my mom and dad." Peter and Trish shook Tim's hand and invited him in to the living room.

Trish inquired about the trip from Edmonton. After a few comments regarding road conditions and weather, Trish excused herself to complete lunch preparations. Tim inquired about Peter's occupation and Peter briefed him on his work as principal.

"Does your school abide by the Saskatchewan Education's curriculum?" Tim asked.

"Oh, yes. We're closely monitored for that."

"What allowance do you have to teach religion in your school?"

"Well, we aren't given the same freedom as the Catholic schools, but we are able to express our Christian views of curriculum material."

Tim asked other questions about the school and seemed favourably impressed.

After Trish called them to lunch, she asked Peter to ask a blessing.

Iris felt a little tense while they ate. So far, Tim's visit had gone very smoothly. Tim was an excellent conversationalist, she realized, and she could see that her dad was impressed with him. Lunch conversation was light, mainly about university and hospital life.

As was the custom in the Marten home, coffee was served in the living room. Iris was not surprised when Peter started a discussion. "Tim, Iris has told us you're working for your church. Would you mind telling us what you do?"

"Sure," Tim responded with an enthusiastic smile. "I'm working on our church's mission board. I administer all the local mission activities and also co-ordinate our church's involvement in all the countries we have mission projects."

"In which countries does your church do most of their work?" Trish asked.

"Mostly in African countries like Nigeria. We have some projects in India as well."

Tim described several of these projects in Africa, where considerable aid had been given to promote better health and education. Most of the questions were coming from Trish. Iris could see Peter looking quite thoughtful. She knew he was trying to frame a question that would draw out Tim's thinking on spiritual matters. Then Peter asked, "In these mission projects in Nigeria, what emphasis does your church place on teaching Christianity?"

"We are happy to answer any questions the Nigerian people have concerning our faith," Tim said. "We also have regular church services there, just like here."

"Do your church's missionaries conduct regular Bible classes, say with children?" Peter asked.

"No, we don't. Our approach is to live out the life of Christ in making friendships, working alongside them, helping with developing better farming techniques and better public health. We show our Christian caring, love, and respect. We leave it up to them if they want to join us in our fellowship with Christ. We do it in Africa and India just like we do it here in Canada.

We don't pressure them by making them feel guilty about not accepting our take on Christianity."

"I understand, Tim." Peter nodded thoughtfully. "When we tie our Christian expectations to service we give to vulnerable people, they'll say they agree with those Christian expectations, but the sincerity in their faith may not be there."

"Well, that's exactly it." Tim smiled. "There used to be a saying that doing so made 'sugar Christians.' I think this came out of the West Indies mission work in the last century, where acceptance of Christianity was rewarded with jobs in the sugar cane industry."

"Your point is well made, but I would like to ask a potentially awkward question." Peter paused. "What for you is the most important message in Jesus' teaching?"

Iris almost choked and then glanced over at Tim. She could see that the question had momentarily stumped Tim. He recovered quickly and then, smiling somewhat artificially, said, "Jesus' teaching was mainly about love. He showed us how to do it and demonstrated how love can change people's hearts as well as change whole groups of people for good. He showed us how to change our selfishness through love." Iris could see Tim really coming alive as he continued. "Jesus showed us how to handle hate and rejection. He demonstrated the power of love. His love was so powerful that it took him to the cross. Now we can live in the strength and courage that he demonstrated." As Tim finished, his face was flushed with excitement.

Iris wasn't surprised by Tim's enthusiasm and confidence. She had seen this before. She also could see that her folks were impressed with his passion for missions.

"I agree that mission work in this country or abroad is doomed to fail if genuine love isn't expressed by the missionary," Trish said. "Love is the key to open hearts. The trouble is, love often involves hard work and sacrifice. In fact, it can only happen when we give our hearts to Jesus and allow his love to fill us."

"Ah, you're so right about that," Peter said.

"I think we're all capable of loving like that," Tim said with infectious delight in his eyes. "We just need to release our grasp of our selfish desires and allow Jesus' inspiration to release the love that's already there."

Once again, Iris was wowed by Tim's excitement about his faith. Why did she worry about his take on Jesus? Had she been taught the wrong way to think about Christ? Maybe the heavy emphasis on atonement by evangelical churches was misplaced and took away from Christ's humanity and lesson of love. She'd been reading the first three Gospels, and had found very little about atonement. She looked at her dad who was deep in thought. She wondered if he was also sorting out Tim's theology.

The conversation veered from theology to the part Tim would be taking his upcoming church service. Iris wondered what Ralph would've thought of Tim's views on his faith and missions. She now felt that his sitting in on Tim's comparative religions forum might be a good idea. He'd be able to sort out the wheat from the chaff, as her father used to say.

✦ ✦ ✦

Later that afternoon, Iris invited Tim for a walk. They took the path along the dry creek bordering the Marten home. They spent the next hour enjoying nature. The bushes were in their glorious best. Wild flowers were coming into bloom and Iris pointed out many of them, giving their Latin names. Tim asked, "Where did you get all this knowledge of plants?"

"Oh, a lot of it comes from growing up where there are lots of wild plants, but I did take botany in pre-med. Since then, I've read many nature books about plants, birds, and animals whenever I get sick and tired of studying human medicine." Iris laughed.

"You're a woman of many talents and interests."

"Thanks, Tim. You have many talents that I don't have—the gift of administration being one. Each of us was cut from a different cloth, I guess."

"True." Tim nodded and then took Iris's hand, slowing their pace. "Iris, I was impressed with your parents. They are very charming and interesting people. You've all made my visit very comfortable."

"Thank you again, Tim. I think they were quite impressed with you." Both had stopped and were gazing at each other.

"So, what about their daughter?" Tim asked with a little grin.

"Oh, I thought you performed well."

"Performed! You thought I just put on a performance to impress them?"

Iris realized she could have used better words. She looked up to the sky and focused on a cumulus cloud. "Well, I suspect that it was partly so. I'm sure you were also being genuine and truthful." Iris faced Tim again. "I'm not criticizing you. I think you've political talents and you know how to use them."

Tim was quiet as they resumed walking. After a few minutes, Tim mumbled, "I suppose you're right. Do you blame me for trying to impress your parents? I need them as allies in my effort to win you."

Iris glanced at Tim to make sure he was serious. He looked like he was. She didn't know what to say. She knew she had been dragging her feet for a long time when it came to her relationship with Tim. She had given him freedom to date other women. He just kept coming back. The truth was, she still wasn't ready to give Tim her heart. She wanted to get her parents' and Ralph's opinions. She also wanted Ralph's thoughts after he went to the comparative religion forum.

Finally, Iris began to formulate a response. "Tim, I know I must be a disappointment to you because of my inability to fit in with your life. I've given you the freedom to look elsewhere, you know. Part of my problem is that I'm finding it hard to get to know you. That's why I wanted you to come to visit my parents. It seems that just when I start understanding you, new questions arise."

"What questions, Iris?"

Iris hesitated. She didn't really care to get into a deep theological discussion. "Oh, like you never talk about having a close relationship with Jesus. For you, he seems more of a nice human who once lived and continues to be a good life model for you."

Tim stopped walking and faced Iris with an expression of surprise. "Iris, Jesus was the greatest prophet this world has ever seen. He is my energy, inspiration, and guide for my whole life. I feel shocked that you don't see that in me."

Iris resumed walking and Tim followed. "I do see those features in you, Tim, but I never hear you speaking of Jesus as being God."

"I suspected you and your family see Jesus in that way. I've taken the view that Jesus' life is a mystery in how he relates with God. There is very little in the first three Gospels that point to his deity, you know. What one sees is that the later the book was written, the more the idea of Jesus' deity is emphasized. This suggests that the early disciples didn't see his deity, but the later ones, including Paul, began seeing Jesus this way. Still later writers, including the writer of the Gospel of John, were strongly influenced by the first-century church thinkers who were eagerly promoting the concept of Jesus being God. What was influencing this change was the fact that the Roman Caesars were pushing the idea that they were divine. The first-century church needed something to give them more credibility and influence, so the idea of Jesus' deity was promoted. Now, I'm not saying I don't believe Jesus was divine. I just see it as a mystery we have to live with."

"I'm far from being a theologian, and I just don't know how to argue with you about these things. I have to think about what you've said." Iris looked at her watch. "I suppose we need to be making our way back. I should help Mom get supper on the table." They turned around and set a steady pace back to the Marten home. Little was said beyond comments about their lovely surroundings.

✦ ✦ ✦

Iris sat out on the deck waiting for her father and Trish to make their appearance for breakfast. She'd gotten up at five and made Tim a small breakfast. He'd needed to get away by six to make his service in Edmonton. Iris had eaten with him and then went with him to his car. He'd asked if a kiss would be okay with her. She'd pointed her face up to his and smiled sweetly. This kiss was brief but pleasant. The message in the kiss was that their relationship was alive, at least.

Noise was coming from the region of her parent's bedroom, so they'd be down soon. She was eager to hear how they felt about the visit and what they thought of Tim. She wasn't sure her relationship with Tim was becoming more defined. There were still many unknowns and uncertainties.

After her dad and Trish had finished breakfast, Iris invited them into the living room. She began squeezing her hands together, and asked, "Well, what are your feelings about Tim?" Iris looked back and forth expectantly.

Trish nodded for Peter to start. Peter took a deep breath and said, "To begin with, I was impressed with Tim in several ways. He's a very handsome fellow. He also had wonderful manners, dealing with all of us very respectfully. He's well spoken, actually quite gifted in his speaking. I was most impressed with the passion he has for his work. He really seems to have a vision for how the church can help underprivileged people. Ah, that's enough from me for now. Why don't you say what you feel about him, Trish?"

Trish combed her fingers through her auburn hair as though that would help her sort out her thoughts. "Yeah, I agree with Peter, that he really has a heart for his work and the mission projects of his church. I also agree that he's a charming guy. It's hard not to like him. Still, there was something about his attitude about service that reminded me of my Catholic church in Regina. I don't know if I can put my figure on it exactly, but it's the idea that giving loving service is the whole thing, the whole purpose of our life here on earth."

The room was quiet for a minute, like there wasn't an appropriate response to such a thought. Trish continued. "I think I was once in that space in my thinking. Then I met Jesus—and that made all the difference. I wonder if he has met Jesus like we have."

"I see what you mean, Trish," Peter said, shifting in his chair. "Still, it's hard to believe he could have such a compassion for underprivileged people if he were not a true Christian." Peter turned and gazed for a moment into his daughter's eyes. "Iris, you haven't said anything about what he said this weekend. What's your take?"

Iris smiled almost nervously and made a helpless gesture with her hands. "I admit I too have had similar feelings, but I don't know how to truly evaluate him. It's too bad Ralph couldn't have been here. He could've asked more questions that would better sort out his theological thinking."

Peter pulled his legs up, sat up straighter, slapped his jeans and began laughing. "Well, it sounds as if he'll get his chance if he goes through with his plan to visit Tim's forum."

✦ ✦ ✦

Milton hoped he had understood Iris correctly when she gave him directions to her home. According to his calculations, he should be around fifteen minutes from Badger Creek and then it would be only another ten or fifteen minutes to the Marten home. He felt honoured to have been invited to see Iris's parents. She was such a talented person. She was a woman of principle and integrity. As her image floated into Milton's mind, he realized afresh how beautiful she was, especially when she was telling him about something she was excited about. Most of all, she was a wonderful friend. He'd enjoy visiting with her parents, he was sure.

The road ahead abruptly darkened. Glancing up, he saw that large cumulus clouds had obscured the sun. *That's like life*, he thought. There were so many clouds of uncertainty, often bringing harsh and painful storms. He wondered if this time with Iris's parents might have some cloudy and stormy aspects embedded in it. He worried about their expectations. Would they think he was interested in wooing Iris? How was he going to answer questions in this regard? He hoped Iris would bail him out of embarrassing situations. He wondered if they'd want to talk about his being gay. He had no idea how he'd handle that. *Dear Lord, give me wisdom, understanding, and sensitivity with these people. Help me to remain true to you and to myself.*

When Milton drove up the Marten driveway, he was sure he was at the right place. It exactly matched Iris's description. He went up to the door and rang the bell. In seconds, the door opened wide and Iris's smile that was even wider than usual greeted him. Milton had the urge to hug her, but he hesitated, wondering if her parents were watching. Iris held her arms open and Milton took the cue and enveloped her in a big hug. He withdrew quickly and looked beyond her, spotting Peter and Trish. They came forward and shook his hand with warm words of welcome.

"Come in, Milton," Peter said. "We have lunch ready, but you might want to freshen up first after that long drive. Maybe you could bring in any bags you might have and then I'll show you to your room."

"Sure, I can do that." Milton was already feeling more settled with these hospitable people.

✦ ✦ ✦

As they began eating their lunch, Peter hoped he'd be up to the task of showing Milton acceptance, but also be able to fairly judge Milton's personality and character. He needed to do this for Iris's sake. Earlier that morning, he'd pleaded with God for both wisdom and discernment. He noticed that Milton was quite handsome, maybe not as much as Tim, but Milton's expression was very warm with intelligent and accepting brown eyes. Peter could also tell Milton wasn't as gifted with spontaneous speech. Peter observed with humour that Iris was more than making up for this deficit. She was much more spontaneous and chatty with Milton than she'd been with Tim. Iris was actually bubbly and obviously enjoying herself.

Peter was expecting that meal talk would be superficial. He was waiting for their after-meal coffee in the living room for more serious discussions. Iris, being so cheerful and accepting, was encouraging Milton to open up more than Peter expected.

"Milton, would you mind telling Dad and Trish what your plans are for this next year? Maybe tell them what events helped you to decide what to do, would you?"

Milton told them about his plans to work toward a specialty in paediatrics, and the experiences that had led him in that direction. "I especially remember that little baby with pyloric stenosis and the mother who was so scared. I felt so privileged to be able to be a part of the process that brought hope and joy back to that mother."

"That's what impresses me so much about Milt!" Iris said. "He not only has the intelligence to be a good paediatrician, but he has the sensitivity and caring that makes him a great one."

Milton blushed and laughed along with Peter and Trish, and he waved off the compliment. "Okay, let me tell you about your daughter." Milton proceeded to tell them about the boy with mononucleosis who was first thought to have leukemia. "Iris was brilliant there. And as far as sensitivity is concerned, she really connected emotionally with that mother. I'm confident she'll make an incredible haematologist."

Everyone laughed at the extravagant compliments. Peter dabbed at his mouth with a napkin and grinned. "My, you two must have formed a mutual admiration society. Before this gets out of control, may I suggest we get the dishes cleared away and then we can retire to the living room for our coffee?"

"Dad, so you think you can maintain better control in the living room?" Iris asked with sparkling eyes.

"Yes, that's my hope," Peter said with a chuckle.

✦ ✦ ✦

When all had settled in the living room with coffee, Peter asked Milton about his painting. "Iris told us you did some watercolour painting."

"Oh, I still do that when I need a break from medical stuff. I don't get nearly as much done as I'd like. There are too many other demands on my time, it seems."

"You mean your medical training?" Trish asked.

"Yes, that's most of it. I also go to my church's choir practice and a Friday evening home study group." Milton suspected he was going to end up talking about his faith and maybe the issue of homosexuality. He wasn't sure he was ready for all that. He breathed an inner prayer. *Dear God, help me to be honest and open and pleasing to you.*

To no one's surprise, Peter asked, "Milton, do you mind telling us about your church?"

Milton told the Martens about the main features and the basic mission of his church. Iris decided to keep quiet and let Milton say as much as he was comfortable.

"You spoke of a Friday evening home group. What's that like?" asked Peter.

"I suppose it's your typical home Bible study group, but it had been a godsend. The group has been very helpful to me. I've learned lots about the Bible and about Christianity."

"What do you value most about the group, Milton?" Peter asked. Iris breathed in sharply. Her dad was cutting to the quick. Milton noticed the reaction, and flushed around the neck.

Milton felt an inner knowing that this would come and that he had to be honest. "Ah, well, what has been the most important for me is the fellowship and interactions with the men of the group. As Iris has probably told you, I've been troubled with same-sex attractions. I guess you could say I'm gay."

Iris offered Milton an encouraging look. Milton went on. "What I found so helpful was being accepted and even being hugged by these heterosexual guys. At first I was very scared, but eventually, I could enjoy being involved with sports and building projects with these men. The more I do these things, the less I have unwanted same-sex desires and fantasies. The whole group is also encouraging me to trust God in healing me of homosexuality."

Everyone was silent for a few moments. Finally, Milton said, "I know this may seem like a stretch for you. I have no certainty that God will heal me. I'm just trying to go with whatever light he gives me."

Milton noticed Iris sitting a bit stiffly as she glanced back and forth at her parents.

Trish was the first to respond. "You know, that's all we can do. We have to listen for God's voice in our lives and follow it the best we can."

Milton felt some relief with those words, but could see that Iris's father was struggling to find the words he wanted. Finally, Peter spoke. "You are very fortunate to have such a supportive group, Milton. I have to admit to ignorance when it comes to how contact with heterosexual males helps you, but I'm happy for you and will pray for further success in this area."

"I really appreciate that, Mr. Marten. I know I can count on both of your prayers." After a moment, Milton took a deep breath. "Now that I've been under the microscope for a while, I'd like to ask you about your lives. Judging from the interesting person Iris is and what she has said about you,

I'd love to find out about you. For starters, I'd be interested in hearing how you two got together."

With lots of laughs and even tears, Peter and Trish told their story. They shared how Peter's first wife died of leukemia and Peter's subsequent dark period where he contemplated suicide. They told of Trish coming to Badger Creek as a librarian and helping Iris and Peter with their search for truth in science and Christianity. They also told Milton how their love blossomed.

Milton asked many questions, fascinated by what they shared. "I'm particularly interested in those Jesus meetings you used to have with Iris."

"At first we thought of them as meetings where Trish would come up to speed with Iris and me," Peter said. "But we soon realized that we all had a lot to learn."

"Yeah, I was really confused regarding my faith," Iris said. "In fact, I didn't really have much at all. I think all of us were caught off guard by how much we were learning about Jesus. As we read, talked, and prayed together, somehow my faith began to rise, and with it, I really fell in love with Jesus. Actually, I long to feel that way again. I suppose I've lost something in the past five or six years."

"That can change, Iris." Trish's eyes were sparkling with certainty. "Jesus' words to the Ephesian church were that they'd forsaken their first love. He was calling them to repent and go back to their first love. I'm sure Jesus is willing to do that for you, too."

Iris looked at the floor, nodding slowly for a few seconds. "You're right, Trish. I just don't know how to repent and find Jesus again. Feel free to pray for me. I know I need it." She looked up into the faces of Trish and then her dad.

"You know we will, Iris," Peter said with a bright smile. "In fact, we've never stopped doing that." Peter looked over to Milton, and Milton realized he was seeking his reaction. "As you can see, Milton, we tend to get kind of honest and self-effacing at times."

"Oh, I love this about all of you," Milton responded with glistening eyes. "I envy Iris for being able to go home to a family like yours. How blessed she is to have you." Milton gazed at Peter and then Trish.

"Stop it, Milton," Iris said, laughing. She swiped at some tears with her finger. "You'll have us all crying in a minute."

"What's so bad about that?" Milton said with a big grin. "Crying is usually a reflection of our being honest and transparent. And that's got to be good."

"Milton, would you mind telling us about your parents?" Peter asked. "We asked Iris one time and she told us to ask you when we had the chance. Do you mind?"

"No, not at all. They live in Calgary." Milton went on to tell them about his dad's real estate business. He also told them of his father's limited church involvement and his mother's atheism. He shared about his grandmother and the influence she had on his faith. "So, you see," Milton continued, "the only Christian influence I had as a child came from my grandmother."

Trish got up and refilled everyone's cup with coffee. While doing so, she asked, "So, did you become a Christian as a child under her influence?"

"No, but Grandma was a big factor in my being open to God. The other person who helped me to find Jesus was my biochemistry professor." Milton related with considerable excitement Dr. Sandoski's role in helping him come to belief in Christ. He went on to tell Peter and Trish how his involvement in the small group study helped in his growing faith.

✦ ✦ ✦

About four o'clock, Iris invited Milton to see Badger Creek and to show him the school she used to attend. Milton was a keen listener and asked many questions about her childhood. He was particularly interested in Iris's experiences in the Christian school. On the way back to the Marten home, Iris pointed out the place she was in a car accident because of tire stem valves having been loosened by some guys intending to scare her. Iris told him how, during her high school years, there had been a conspiracy in Badger Creek to get rid of the Marten family because of her father's beliefs and teaching in school about the age of the earth. They were just pulling into the Marten driveway when she finished all the sordid details of her experience.

After the evening meal, Iris asked Milton if he would like to go for a walk. "We could walk in the creek if you'd like."

"Oh, sure. Barefoot or with rubber boots?" Milton asked with raised eyebrows.

"Either. I'll just use runners. The creek is dry and has been so since the spring thaw." They both laughed and headed out.

On their walk, they talked mainly about the nature around them. Milton seemed to be much more aware of the beauties in nature than Tim had been. Milton pointed to the silvery leaves of the wolf willows that stood next to a clump of dogwoods with their maroon stems. He then pointed to a nearby large fieldstone partly covered with moss-green lichen. "How wonderfully God's nature displays their contrasting colors!"

Iris wondered if Milton's giftedness in painting was the reason for this. *Appreciation of nature is just one more thing we've in common,* she thought.

They reached a large sandstone outcropping and climbed up to better view the creek bed. Milton stared out in wonder, overwhelmed by the beauty of the creek bed, the trees, the rock outcroppings, and the puffy white cumulus clouds lazily drifting in the dazzling blue sky. Iris watched Milton's face more than the scenery. How incredibly handsome he was! Why couldn't he be hers forever? *Guard your heart,* she remembered reading in a poem once. That's surely true for me, she thought.

✦ ✦ ✦

Milton gladly joined the Martens as they headed for their Sunday morning church service in Peter's Chev. Iris noted that her dad seemed partial to used Chevs. The current one was just a newer model than the one he had been driving the last time she'd been home. Iris sat next to Milton in the back seat. She sensed he was a little tense about attending her parents' church. She smiled at him when she caught his eye. "You'll probably find this church not too different from yours, theologically. The difference will be in how the members relate to us. A small community church like this tends to be more curious and they'll all want to meet us. They'll be wondering if you're my steady boyfriend. It's hard to remain anonymous here."

"So, what do we say about ourselves—that you picked up a transient on the way to church?" Milton said with a crooked grin.

Iris giggled. "No, they wouldn't believe that. You look entirely too distinguished to be a transient."

"Well, thank you, Iris. You look marvelous yourself." They both laughed.

Peter glanced back with a grin. "Are you two trying to beef up each other's courage before facing the interrogation of our church members? Just say Milton is a medical classmate and a friend and leave it at that. They can think what they like."

When they walked into the church sanctuary, Iris and Milton could feel the curious eyes on them, but they tried to look as though they attended there regularly. A lady was playing hymns on a piano before the service started. The tunes were familiar to Iris and even Milton recognized most of them.

Once the regular service got started, a song leader rose and led the congregation in a rousing series of hymns. Milton and Iris shared a hymnbook. Iris sang alto and Milton sang tenor. Iris was surprised how good Milton's voice was. She felt a thrill go through her body as their voices blended beautifully. Wouldn't it be glorious to share her life with someone who sang like Milton? *We could bring up our children with music everywhere. Stop it,* Iris told herself. *Guard your heart.*

✦ ✦ ✦

Milton's senses were ratcheted up more than usual. He was trying to determine how this service was different from his own. Certainly the centrality of Jesus in the worship was similar. The service was more casual, with no concern about imperfections. There were more noises from small children than he was used to. No one seemed to mind.

Milton was also aware of how comfortable he felt with the Marten family. What he felt mostly was joy and warmth of sitting next to Iris. When his arm brushed against Iris's, he felt electric prickles arising where they had touched. He noticed Iris had let her hair grow longer. He liked it that way. She'd put on a blouse that showed off her feminine features better than the clothes she'd worn in the past year. He also noticed her perfume—delightful. When they sang the hymns, her voice was golden. What a pleasure it was to blend his voice with hers!

When the pastor got up to speak, Milton said to himself, *I can't let this wonderful girl distract me. I want to hear what this man is saying.*

The message was taken from the book of James and it involved praying with wrong motives. Milton felt himself agreeing with the pastor for most of the message. Then the pastor said, "We often can feel quite sure we're praying for what we truly need and so can expect God will answer and give us what we ask for. Sometimes God will withhold the answer our hearts so eagerly desire and we feel hurt and confused. We need to understand that what we're so sure we need may not be what God wants for our lives. We need to let God be sovereign and trust that He knows what is best for us."

An unsettling thought flashed through Milton's mind. Was he sure God wanted to heal him and transform him into a heterosexual man? Would he let God decide what was best for him? He remembered what God told the Apostle Paul when he asked for the 'thorn in the flesh' to be removed. God told him, "My grace is sufficient for you."

After the benediction was said and the service was over, Milton focused on the people around him. As Iris had predicted, many in the congregation wanted to meet and shake hands with Iris and Milton. He could see many questioning looks as if they were trying to understand their relationship. Taking Peter's advice, Iris and Milton were friendly and greeted everyone with big smiles.

Milton then spotted a friendly looking fellow and his wife walking toward them. The Marten family was obviously greeting longtime friends and there were both handshakes and hugs all around. Milton found Harold's hand grasp strong and sure. Iris said, "Harold, I'd like you to meet my co-worker and friend, Milton Saunders. Milt, meet Irma and Harold Shea."

"What a pleasure it is to see you again, Iris, and to also meet your friend. I take it you are a physician as well, Milton?"

"Yes, I am. I'm in the first year of the paediatric residency program in the University of Alberta Hospital."

"You'll have to forgive me, but I'm not one to beat about the bush," Harold began. "Iris, you introduced Milton as a friend. Is that it, or are you planning something more profound in terms of your relationship?"

Iris blushed and said with a laugh, "I warned Milton there'd be lots of curious people here. No, we are just friends. We got to know each other in school." Iris glanced at Milton for reassurance. He nodded to her to go on. "We tend to think much the same way about scientific and medical issues. Milton has become a Christian in the last few years and was interested in the family and church I came from."

"So, how did you find the family and the church, Milton?" Irma asked.

Now it was Milton's turn to blush. "You're expecting me to be truthful, standing with the family and in the church in question?"

"Yeah!" Irma chuckled. "I think the family and the church can survive your honest evaluation."

Milton gulped, and paused a moment. "Actually, I was deeply impressed with Iris's parents. I feel very comfortable with them. I found them so honest and self-effacing. Their faith in God comes across as very real and exciting. I know Iris should be and is very grateful to have such parents. I also know she deeply appreciates and loves them. Now as far as the church is concerned, I found the service more easygoing than our church, but otherwise the doctrinal and faith issues are much the same. The sermon was good and several points really impacted me."

"That was a pretty risky question you asked, honey," Harold said to his wife with mock seriousness. "You could've had us all in a lot of trouble."

"I had no worries," Irma said firmly. "Hey, why don't we join forces and have lunch somewhere here in town? I hear good things about that new café on Main Street." Everyone in the two families enthusiastically agreed.

Chapter Twenty

July 1962

Scattered cumulous clouds marched across an otherwise blue sky—a perfect day for some jogging. Tim had called his old friend Delmar to join him that Sunday afternoon in late July. Both were dressed in t-shirts and shorts. They left their cars in the parking lot next to the Saskatchewan River and walked toward the trail.

"Thanks for joining me on such short notice, Tim said. "When I saw the fantastic weather, I knew I had to be out in it."

"Thanks for asking me. Since I got married, I haven't done much jogging. Jane isn't much into that kind of thing. She prefers tennis, so I've gotten out of the jogging routine."

When they got to the trail, they both worked themselves up to a brisk trot and said little, other than to occasionally comment on the passing scenery. After about twenty minutes, they came to a nice lookout on the riverbank. They stopped at the same time as if both sensed their need of a rest.

"How are you enjoying married life?" Tim asked.

"It's been great. We've had our disagreements, but we've been able to keep talking and working out compromises."

"That's good to hear."

"What about your love life, Tim? Where's that going?"

"Well, if you hadn't come in to wreck my plans, I might be doing better," Tim commented with a crooked grin.

"You're referring to the time I passed on some gossip about Iris, I presume."

Tim nodded. "You got it."

"Now don't bring that up again," Delmar said while doing some leg stretches. "I gave you my apologies. I understand you're still seeing her in spite of my blunder."

"Not often enough. She's so busy with all her medical projects, she seems to have little time for me."

"Oh you poor thing," Delmar teased. "You've nearly got me in tears."

"Well, the truth is, she puts medicine and research ahead of marriage."

"Listen, Tim, how hard are you pursuing her? Does she know how devoted you are? I see you flirting with all kinds of women. Maybe she's heard that and doesn't think you're really serious."

They began walking down the trail when Tim turned to Delmar. "Sure I flirt. It's just part of my nature. I got that from Dad, I guess."

"How serious does it get with the women you flirt with, Tim?" Delmar asked as he tore some leaves off a bush he passed.

"Oh, I doubt it gets very serious at all, Tim chuckled. "I just enjoy the sexual buzz it gives me."

"Are you ever worried that the little tryst might turn into something more?"

"Yeah," said Tim. "Sometimes I feel guilty about the effect I'm having on these women."

"So you should feel guilty." Tim looked into Delmar's eyes and noticed they were quite serious.

They walked on in silence for a while. "So, my counselor friend," Tim said, "what's your counsel for me?"

By this time, they had reached the end of the trail and decided to retrace their steps. "Tim, I would advise you to decide once and for all if you want to marry Iris. If you do, then you should keep your focus on Iris and Iris alone. Pursue her with all your heart. Some women seem to need that approach. Either she'll agree to marry you or she'll declare herself not interested. And stop flirting with other women. That will only distract you from your main goal."

They'd stopped again. Tim gazed thoughtfully into Delmar's eyes.

"Thank you for being so honest and decisive with me. You've given me a lot to think about."

The two went back to jogging and said little until they were back at the parking lot.

⁎ ⁎ ⁎

Iris had been a little surprised that it took Tim this long to contact her since he'd visited her parents in Badger Creek. Well, he had contacted her yesterday, Friday evening, while she was trying to develop a new research plan. He had sounded upbeat, almost as if he'd planned his tone of voice. He invited her to go to the beach on Lake Wabamun with him. Now, that was different. She didn't even own a proper swimsuit; that's how long it had been since she'd gone swimming! She had been tempted to go to the Army and Navy to pick up some drab swimsuit, but then thought better of it. Somewhat against her plan to disdain nice clothes, she instead went to Eaton's. The clerk looked at her figure and immediately selected something a bit more daring than she had in mind. When she tried it on, though, it was perfect. It looked modest enough, but it emphasized all her curves quite pleasantly. A little to her chagrin, Iris still enjoyed looking nice.

On Saturday morning, Iris pulled on a large grey t-shirt and charcoal slacks. Tim would be used to these kinds of clothes. When Tim drove up to the apartment block, she was ready for him and immediately strode out the door and headed for his car. He was holding the passenger door open when she got there. She couldn't help but be impressed with his eagerness to please her. "Hi Tim. What a nice idea you had, and you picked a nice day for it, too." She threw her bag with the swimwear in the back and sat down in the passenger bucket seat.

When Tim got in, he looked at Iris with a broad smile. "Well, I'd two thoughts. One was that Saturday promised to be a hot day. The second was the thought of what would be a good way to cool off. The lake fit the bill."

The two chatted amiably on the way to the lake. Each caught the other up on their recent activities. Iris excitedly reported the progress with her research project and her hope to get it published soon.

When they arrived, they found a beach where there were washrooms and change rooms. Tim was ready first so he waited for Iris to emerge. When she did, he caught his breath and just stared. She looked gorgeous. "Iris, you, you… I thought you were dressing drab these days."

Iris laughed. "You can pop your eyeballs back in. I let an Eaton's clerk make a decision I should've made. Come on, let's walk along the water's edge awhile. I need to be careful with the sun. As you can see, my skin's as white as porcelain. As soon as I start getting pink, I need to run for shade."

Tim, who was carrying the food basket, pointed to a shaded picnic table and said, "I'm really hungry. Let's eat first and then we can stroll down the beach. Are you okay with that?"

"Sure. I just hope you like what I made. They're just buns and meat slices."

They chatted about the other people at the beach. Tim commented on the great number of children playing in the sand. "Those kids sure make a lot more noise than what would be necessary for reasonable communication."

"Who says kids are reasonable?" Iris laughed as she laid out the lunch.

After they'd eaten, Tim jogged back to his car to deposit the lunch basket. When he got back, they walked along the wet beach sand, noticing the antics of several water-skiers.

After a time, Tim said, "Do you find yourself leaning toward continuing on in research as a career? You seem so excited about doing this kind of work."

"No, as I told you before, I still think I'm best suited to do clinical work. Nothing changed in the last few months. I love to interact directly with people and deal with their medical needs on a personal basis. In the research lab, one is often quite remote from the people you're trying to help." Iris turned so that she could better see Tim's face. "Has anything changed in your work?"

Iris could tell from Tim's glances that he was being distracted by her swimsuit or, more likely, what it didn't cover. "Well, things have changed a bit. The head of our church met with me a month or so ago. He wondered if I could see basing myself here in Edmonton, but being willing to travel to the various places in the world to oversee mission programs. Also, he sees I have a vision for missions in third-world countries and he says I'd be the best person to develop the programs needed to bring the vision to reality."

Iris took Tim's hand and pulled both to a stop. "That sounds exciting, Tim. Do you think you'll do that?"

"I'm not sure yet. I'd miss living among the people I was trying to help in Africa, India, or wherever. Maybe the time spent with the people at the time of my trips would suffice.

"Hey, I'm way too hot," Tim said, switching topics. "How about some cooling off?" He tossed the bag of towels on the dry sand, picked Iris up and charged into the water until he was up to his knees. He tossed Iris headlong into the water. She let out a shriek of delight. They both swam until they were well above their heads when they tried to stand. After another ten minutes of swimming, testing their depth, and splashing water at one another, they headed for shore and more walking.

They chatted another twenty minutes about Tim's mission efforts. Then Iris stopped and looked at the skin of her shoulder, lifting a strap to see the differences in colour. "I'm heading for those aspens."

After settling on a towel in the shade of a large grove of aspens, Iris asked, "How're plans going for the Comparative Religion Forum in October?"

"Oh, we've all the participants lined up already. We still have much work to do on the program. There's a lot of sending preliminary plans out and getting feedback and then revising and sending the revisions out, et cetera, et cetera. It should be good, though. It starts at ten o'clock, October 21, and runs all day. Are you able to attend?"

"There *is* a problem with that time and date. I found out about the conflict in dates just last week. I have an all-day conference with Dr. Pinsky. It's a very important meeting, as we are strategizing the next phase of our research with the staff and aides. I'm sorry, Tim. You'll have to tell me all about the forum. Will you be speaking too?"

"Oh, yes. I have to give one of the Christian perspectives."

Iris felt she had to do a bit of acting. She was actually glad she couldn't make the meeting, since Ralph was planning to attend and find out what Tim really believed about Jesus. "So, you won't be giving the only Christian view at the forum?"

"No, there will be a Roman Catholic priest giving the Catholic slant on Christianity. I've been asked to give the Protestant view."

"That's a pretty tall order, to represent all the views of all the branches of Protestantism, isn't it?"

"Yes, of course. But each of these religions has many branches and we could never have each represented. I think everyone will realize we can only represent a very brief sampling."

"What other religions are being represented?" Iris asked as she lay on her back and traced the outline of the puffy white clouds with her eyes.

"Let's see, there's a speaker for Islam, another for Buddhism, and another for Hinduism. Then there're the two of us representing Christianity."

"Have you figured out what you're going to say?" Iris noticed Tim's broad, strong shoulders. He sure was a handsome brute.

"Not in detail. I've a general idea what I'll say in my main speech, but I'll have to wing it in the question and answer part led by a moderator. That could get quite interesting." Iris could see Tim's steady gaze as if he were trying to discern her true feelings.

Iris couldn't help anticipating Ralph sitting with notebook in hand in the back row. Would he even ask some of the questions? Probably he would, knowing him.

They continued chatting about the forum's format. Iris noticed the sun going behind a bank of quite dark clouds. "Looks like we have some bad weather heading in our direction. I suppose we should get changed and get back before those clouds decide to dump on us."

"Okay. I noticed it had gotten cooler, but I hadn't noticed that cloud coming up behind those trees."

Once they had gotten changed and into Tim's car, there already was a breeze coming from the west. They were soon cruising down the highway heading for Edmonton. As they drove, they could see that the rain clouds were veering off to the north.

Iris looked over to Tim. "Well, the beach time was a little shorter than expected, but I enjoyed our time together. Thank you for thinking of this splendid idea."

"It's not hard to think of things for us to do together. The hard part is finding something that fits with your busy schedule."

"I know," Iris said softly. "I wonder if that will ever change. That seems to be the nature of this beast called medicine."

Their conversation went on to the relative busyness of the various branches of medicine. When they were nearing Edmonton, Tim cleared his throat and said, "When we get back to your place, could we look at our schedules to see when we can get together? Maybe we could attempt having a get-together at least once a week. Would you be interested in that?"

Iris felt herself tensing up. She wasn't surprised that Tim brought up this subject, judging from the way he kept looking at her all afternoon. She felt she must make a difficult decision again. She wondered what was holding her back from marrying Tim. There always seemed to be some issue that needed resolving before she took that step. She thought again of Milton, the real roadblock that kept her from opening her heart to Tim. She needed to be rational about this whole mess in her love life. A happy married life with Milton seemed a million miles away. Tim was at her doorstep. Yes, she needed to get rational.

"I'm sorry for not answering right away, Tim. I was just trying to see how I could alter my schedule to accommodate your suggestion," Iris lied. "Sure, we'll go to my room and look over my schedule. Do you have yours with you?"

"Yeah, I do. I anticipated your asking this question, you know."

"I'm not surprised at that. You're so organized," Iris said with a sweet smile.

✦ ✦ ✦

Milton had received an unexpected phone call from his father. He'd shown uncharacteristic interest in what Milton had been doing and how his paediatric residency had been going. After having chatted for about five minutes, his father had finally said, "Your mom and I would like to make a trip to Edmonton to see some of the sights there, but mainly to have a visit with you. Would that be possible?"

"It would be a pleasure to host you and mom. I could show you around, and then we could eat out somewhere. I'd love to catch up with your lives, Dad."

They'd agreed on a Saturday when Milton wouldn't be on call. Now, they were due any minute and Milton was ready.

When they arrived, Milton showed them through the house where he was staying. He took them to the kitchen and introduced them to his landlady. She welcomed them and then said she'd be out in the garden if they needed her. Milton prepared some tea for his parents. He'd been given freedom to do that should guests come.

When they were all seated, Milton asked about their lives and what they'd been doing recently.

"Well, I'm still doing the artistic design business," his mother said. "I've several craft stores in Calgary who regularly buy my designs. It's a lot of work since I have to get the design just right, but I still enjoy it. Most people my age seem to be retired, but as long as I enjoy what I'm doing, I figure I should keep going."

"Yeah, that's wise, Mom. My plan is to work until someone kicks me out," Milton said with a grin. "Are you still playing the piano?"

"Not so much now," Gladys admitted. "Your dad used to sing along with my playing. Now he wants me to play hymns. He likes them better than the bar-room pieces I'm used to playing."

"Now that's a load of bunk, Gladys," Fred chided good-naturedly. "I never complain about what you're playing. You just don't like me humming the hymns I'm recalling. I never asked you to play a hymn and you know it."

"So, what's this about humming hymns, Dad? I've never heard you do that before." Milton looked at his father with surprise and excitement.

"He's been going to that Anglican Church near our place every Sunday," Gladys said. "He takes his mother along since she can't drive anymore."

"Why don't you go along, Mom?" Milton said with a wink.

"Fred wouldn't let me. I'd be too bad an influence on those pious church people," Gladys remarked with a crooked grin.

"Gladys, that's an outright lie. You'd always be welcome to join me. I've never asked you since you've always been so adamant about avoiding all things religious."

Milton was laughing so hard his face was red. "I love your kibitzing around like that." Milton looked at his father. "How's real estate business? Are you still so busy?"

"No, I've definitely slowed down. I've given a lot of my responsibilities to my junior partners. Since I've been attending church, I've realized that I've made my business a god. I've decided to spend more time understanding God and what he wants for me. I've even started joining with some of the men of the church in projects to help single-parent families and unemployed people. I've been a lot happier, and have a greater sense of purpose."

"I'm so excited by what you're saying. I'd no idea that you had changed so much." Milton's eyes had filled with tears and his face beamed with joy.

"Yeah, he's hard to live with, he's getting so religious on me. I fear we'll soon be in poverty, what with Fred working much less and his giving money to the church." Milton could see his mother wasn't being too serious.

"Now Gladys, have we had any financial trouble since I started going to church? As a matter of fact, I think we're in as good a financial state now as we ever were."

"That's probably because you aren't gambling anymore. I'm so thankful for that. Actually, Milton, since your father's been going to church, he's spent more time at home, allowing us to do lots of activities together. To tell you the truth, he has been a lot more fun to be with."

"Well, well, Gladys, maybe we should come to visit Milton more often so I can hear all those sweet words about me."

Everyone laughed and Milton caught the glances of affection passing between his parents. A deep feeling of thankfulness filled Milton's chest.

Milton joined his parents in their sedan and directed them through the traffic to various sites of interest, including the parliament buildings and several well-planned city parks. Following a light lunch at a café, they went to the art museum. Milton had spent many hours there studying various paintings, so he provided commentary. Gladys seemed to be more aware of some of the more famous artists, but Fred knew little of art—it was his first visit to an art museum in years. Fred tried his best, but soon was yawning as he trailed behind his wife and Milton. After about two hours, Milton knew he'd need to give his parents a break. They settled at a table in the museum coffee shop.

"Milton, I see that you really love art and, in particular, painting," Fred said.

"Sure, I've always loved the textures and colours found in nature. I find painting them very relaxing and fulfilling. Since I became a Christian, that interest has picked up a notch or so. I love to reflect on God's wonderful creation and reproduce it on canvas. Recently I've been trying to represent various emotions or moods. That's more challenging but also more fun."

Milton's mother commented on the various styles and expressions in modern art and wondered what style Milton liked. Fred remained quiet and thoughtful.

Fred then took a deep breath as though to fortify his courage. "Milton, I want to say a few things about my attitude and actions when you were growing up. I see now that I really missed seeing the talents emerging in you. I'd some preconceived ideal of what a boy should be and when you didn't fit that picture, I criticized and made fun of you. Now I see how wrong I was and I want to apologize to you about all my hurtful words. Would you forgive me, Milton?" Fred looked intently into his son's eyes.

Milton's mouth fell open in surprise and then his eyes filled with tears. He reached across the table and put his hand on his father's, unable to speak for a few moments. Then he said with a husky voice, "Dad, of course I forgive you. I can't get over how much you've changed. What you just said must have taken a great deal of courage. You'll never know how much your words mean to me."

Fred clasped Milton's hand and gave it a good squeeze. "I also want to say that I'm very proud of you for what you've achieved in medicine, as well as in art. I want to especially say how much your mother and I appreciate you as a son. Being gay doesn't change our loving you and being proud of you." By this time, all three were crying and Gladys also put her hand on Milton's.

After they all made good use of the tissue on the table, they headed back to Milton's boarding house. Milton warmly thanked his parents for coming. He hugged his mother and then went to his father. Fred shook Milton's hand, but Milton pulled his dad in for an embrace. Fred's arm slowly but surely tightened around Milton. That had never happened before.

"Good bye, Mom and Dad," Milton's said with deep emotion. "This has been one of the best days of my life." Both his parents had very happy faces as they walked out of the door.

✦ ✦ ✦

September 1, 1962

Once again, Iris was waiting for Dr. Pinsky to open his door and invite her in. She used to get very upset with his purposeful delay in seeing her, but now she just thought of it as a joke. If that made him feel more important, so be it. She wasn't going to worry about it.

Since July 1, Iris had poured herself into the research project on oral polio vaccine (OPV). When she had her first meeting with Dr. Pinsky in the first week of July, she set a goal of September 1 for completion of the first phase of her research. This phase involved determining the presence and mechanism of secondary immunization via the fecal/oral route. She hoped to show that children given oral polio vaccine would not only be protected from wild polio, but that OPV is readily passed out in their stool. Then, through contamination of their hands with that stool, OPV would contaminate food eaten by other children they encountered. The OPV thus ingested would then secondarily immunize other children so that they, too, would be protected.

Iris and her team traveled all over the city to identify those children receiving OPV immunization. Then they collected stool samples of not only those given the immunization, but of other family members who didn't receive the OPV. They also had to collect stool samples in families where no one received OPV, as a comparison. It was exacting, tiring, even boring work. The excitement came when they checked for OPV in the children's stool. As expected, there was a much higher incidence of OPV in stool from children in those families where OPV had been given to one child than in those families where no child was given OPV. That trend confirmed what Iris had previously found in animal studies. It meant that even if an immunization program weren't complete, all would eventually become immunized.

In the last two weeks, Iris had been busy writing up her report. Numerous revisions had been necessary as late results trickled in. Iris had asked for help from several lab workers and staff who had publishing experience. Three days ago, she felt the project was ready for submission to a publishing company and she'd placed the manuscript in the hands of Dr. Pinsky's secretary. She hoped that he'd agree to have the manuscript sent immediately to the publisher. She knew the results in her work hadn't been previously reported in any scientific journal. She had carefully checked that. Time was of the essence here.

If I can get this research published, she thought, *it could turn some heads in the academic world and I might be offered a good position somewhere.*

The door opened and a smiling Dr. Pinsky waved her in. "I see you've been working a lot harder in these summer months than many of my colleagues." His smile faded as he sat back in his swivel chair and tented his fingers. "I've done a once through on your report, Iris. It looks good so far, but I need to read it more carefully and have some of my staff go over the analysis."

"So you think it's still not ready for publication?" Iris felt disappointment sweep over her.

"You obviously haven't published before. We can't afford to blunder into publishing something that's flawed in any way. We need to check all the methodology, the statistical analysis, and the conclusions. We also need to make sure no one else has come up with the same findings. And, if so, we need to carefully credit them for their findings. Any miss-step could be disastrous."

Iris really felt frustrated and her face flushed. "But, I did carefully review the literature to see what other labs and scientists have done. This is new stuff."

"Calm down, Iris. You need to be a bit more patient. We'll get it published, but only when it's ready."

"But it's ready now!" Tears welled up in Iris's angry face. "If we don't move quickly on this, someone else will publish before us."

Dr. Pinsky's smile belied the deadly serious look of his eyes. "I'm the head of this department. You're a first-year research worker. You need to understand that. When we're finished with proper evaluations and revisions of this study, we'll move on to publication." At that, Dr. Pinsky stood, and Iris knew she needed to just quietly leave. Her legs felt like lead weights.

✦ ✦ ✦

Iris walked sluggishly back to her lab and her waiting co-workers. As much as she wished she could throw a tantrum, she knew she had to be very careful in what she said to her team. Maligning Dr. Pinsky publically could get her into a lot of trouble. She needed to calm down and show respect for her boss, even if she didn't agree with him just now.

"Iris, how'd our project fly with the boss? Did he hassle you about the report? You look unsettled."

"Oh, I was a bit naïve, I suppose. I thought he'd okay it and just send it on its way. Well, he said he'd have to study it some more and have his own people go through every detail. He said we have to be careful to do it right. So, yes, I'm disappointed." Iris was desperately trying to keep tears back, but her eyes were glistening.

"Aw, you had that report nailed, Iris, and you had good advice from excellent statisticians," another lab aid said. "I can't see what all this hesitation is about."

Iris took a deep breath and held up a hand. "Okay, let's just leave it at that and be patient like Dr. Pinsky says."

After a pause, another aid asked, "So what're you going to do now?"

"Oh, there are some other areas of research that could be done on OPV, like looking for side-effects of this form of immunization compared with the Salk vaccine," Iris said. "I'd have to spend some time developing an action plan. I'm sure Dr. Pinsky will have his own ideas. He'll likely call a conference of our team, recommend a project, and then decide who's going to do what. I'd sure like to keep most of you on our team. It's been so much fun working with all of you."

The team expressed their wholehearted agreement.

✦ ✦ ✦

When Iris dragged herself into her suite that evening, she didn't have the heart to do anything substantive like studying. She tried to read a novel, but her mind kept drifting back to that awful meeting with Dr. Pinsky. Eventually, she threw her novel down and walked over to the telephone. She needed to unload. Only one person came to mind—Milton. She prayed he was home.

"Hello. Dr. Saunders here."

"Dr. Saunders, are you on call?"

"Yes, Dr. Marten. What can I help you with? Have you got an ill child I need to see?"

"Yes, Dr. Saunders. It's the child in me that's been hurt. I could let her talk to you, and then you could see what you'd recommend."

"Well, Dr. Marten, that sounds like an unorthodox way of doing medicine, but I'll give it a try. Let her speak to me."

"Well it's like this." Iris pitched her voice about four tones up. "The adult Iris submitted her research paper to Dr. Pinsky, hoping he'd send it on for publication. He dragged out all kinds of excuses to delay publication, all kinds of things he had to do before it could be submitted. Adult Iris accepted this, but I didn't. I got mad as hell. I desperately wanted to have a full-blown tantrum, but adult Iris wouldn't let me. I feel put down and undervalued. I feel like sticking that report in a real painful place in his anatomy.

"So, what do you recommend?"

Milton was laughing so hard, he couldn't answer for some time. Finally, he said, "Okay Iris, the adult, please explain exactly what happened at that meeting."

Iris filled him in. "I just had to spill my guts. You're the only one I feel I can do that with."

"Thank you. I'll take that as a compliment."

"Okay, now that you've heard me out, how should I respond?"

Milton thought for a moment. "You know, all you can do is patiently wait and hold your tongue. From what you've told me about Dr. Pinsky, I can see him wanting to change the report enough to justify making it his, too. At worst, he may want to shoulder you out and take the lion's share of the credit. But I think that's being way too paranoid. I doubt he'd do that."

"Oh, I don't know. I need to be prepared. You know, I really don't trust that man."

"Okay, I'll pray you'll be able to relax and do the research work that's in front of you and leave God to deal with Dr. Pinsky."

"Thank you, Milt. You have a true gift of wisdom."

"I doubt that," Milton said. "I've just learned how to listen. Listening to you is always pure pleasure."

"Thank you, Dr. Saunders. Your medicine is just what this patient needed, and it was easy to take, as it came with just the right amount of sweetening. Goodnight."

"Goodnight, and may that inner child rest peacefully."

✦ ✦ ✦

Iris was getting increasingly anxious and annoyed. It was October, and there hadn't been any word from Dr. Pinsky. She'd tried to keep her focus on the next phase of her research. She'd been reading everything she could lay her hands on regarding the effectiveness and the untoward events and complications related to the two forms of immunization, the injectable Salk polio vaccine and OPV. She was also planning the research she and her team would be doing to best compare these two vaccines. She knew that the planning meeting with Dr. Pinsky and his staff later in the week would deal with these issues and she needed to be well prepared.

Ralph came to mind. It was his birthday. He'd be driving to Edmonton in a few days to attend Tim's Forum. She couldn't wait to hear his thoughts on Tim's beliefs.

Iris called Ralph's dorm around seven, hoping he'd be around. When she heard his voice, she said, "Ralph, it's good to hear your voice. Happy birthday, brother! You're twenty-two, if my math is correct."

"Hey, it's my favourite sister! Thank you. I'm twenty-two and beginning the slow physical decline destined for all mankind."

"Oh, how depressing. You're actually at the threshold of an exciting and fruitful vocational and spiritual life. That should give your flagging emotions a boost."

Ralph laughed. "You're right. I need to focus on the good in life. Speaking of good, how is research going?"

"To be honest, frustrating just now. I'm still waiting on Dr. Pinsky to submit my project for publication—well, it's *ours*, I suppose, but I feel I've done almost all of it. Now he's dragging his feet. I've a feeling he wants to doctor it up so he can say he was the main contributor. At least that's what my paranoid mind thinks. Meanwhile, I'm trying to come up with a good plan for our next research project."

"What's it going to be about?"

"It's going to be more about polio, but it will be comparing the two types of polio immunization now available for effectiveness and complications."

"I'm glad you're doing it and not me. I hardly know what you're talking about," Ralph mumbled. "Say, Iris, do you remember that I'm heading your way in another three days? I figure I'll need to leave here around 4:00 a.m. to get there in time. Maybe I should leave here the day before. What do you think?"

"You need to be fresh when you go to that forum. Why don't you leave the day after tomorrow, get here around nine, and stay on my couch for the night? Then you could stay again the night after. I want to have a good chance to visit with you, Ralph. Can you spare the time?"

"I suppose so. I've been really pushing my courses and assigned papers in the last few weeks so I'd be in good shape for this trip. I'm really looking forward to it."

Chapter Twenty-One

October 1962

Ralph had had little trouble finding Iris's apartment block and had experienced a delightful visit before Iris tossed him some sheets, a blanket, and a pillow for the couch. He had slept well and had enjoyed the toast, fried eggs, and coffee Iris made for breakfast. Now he was entering the meeting room in the Department of Education building for Tim's forum. There already were a few dozen people present. Many more were streaming in. He decided to take a seat near the front of the auditorium, since he was eager to catch everything.

When it was time to start, the room was nearly full. Obviously, the meeting had been well advertised. Ralph noticed a whole row of what looked like East Indians sitting near the front. He also saw several men with bushy black beards and, in the same row, several women dressed in hijabs.

The head of the Philosophy Department rose. He welcomed all present and then introduced the moderator, a professor of comparative religion. The moderator provided a brief overview of the planned events. "There will be six speakers, one for each of the Hindu, Buddhist, Islam, Jewish, Roman Catholic Christian, and the Protestant Christian faiths. Each speaker will get thirty minutes to outline the major branches of their religion and to give the main features of their belief system. Each speaker is also free to share with the audience any unique features of his or her personal beliefs. Following each presentation, there'll be a fifteen-minute question and answer period with questions coming from the audience or moderator. This morning, we'll start with the Hindu speaker. The speaker for the Buddhists will follow him. The speaker representing Islam will present before we break for lunch. The afternoon session will start at one-thirty and we'll begin with the speaker representing Judaism. After that, the speaker for Catholic Christianity will present. There'll then be a coffee break at three pm and, following this, the speaker for Protestant Christianity will speak. We hope to wrap up by four.

"Now, to speak on behalf of the Hindus, please let's welcome Gosine Maharaj." Loud applause accompanied Mr. Maharaj's approach to the stage. He was one of the East Indians Ralph had seen sitting near the front.

Ralph had taken a course dealing with the major religions of the world last year, so he was quite familiar with much of what Maharaj spoke about. Maharaj emphasized the fact that Hinduism was the oldest of the major religions. He went on to speak of the various branches and said that in Hinduism there was no common set of beliefs, but it had more to do with a spectrum of distinct intellectual and philosophical points of view. He mentioned many Hindu Scriptures, one of the more important ones being the *Vedas*. It is considered to be the eternal truth revealed to the ancient sages. The *Bhagavad Gita*, spoken by Krishna, is described as the essence of Vedas. Krishna, the speaker said, is one of the most popular gods and was the most important incarnation of Vishna, one of the major gods and preserver of the cosmos. Ralph had been taking notes, but gave up with the descriptions of the various gods. He heard Maharaj go on about the various beliefs of Hindus. He remembered the speaker saying that for Hindus, evil was an illusion where good and evil are fused in the one ultimate reality, Brahman. The speaker quoted Krishna saying that in Brahman, the distinction between good and evil breaks down. He also said that in the end, all life, all good, and all evil flow from God and back to Him or it. Maharaj also mentioned that reincarnation was central to Hinduism. Wrong living in the present life would have to be paid for in a future life, whether that would be human, animal, or plant.

Maharaj's speech ended before the thirty minutes were up, and they moved into question period. Ralph recalled somebody asking, "For the Hindu, is the life that we're experiencing now real?"

Ralph heard Maharaj reply, "Behind the world of the transitory or non-real lies what is ultimately real." There were further questions about this statement, but the speaker didn't make his answer any more clear, in Ralph's view.

The next speaker was introduced as Alfred Wong, who was to speak for Buddhism. Ralph noticed that he looked rather young, maybe in his thirties, and he was of Chinese extraction. Wong refreshed Ralph's memory of the origins of Buddhism. Ralph heard the speaker say that the Buddha spent much time trying to understand suffering, anxiety, and stress (dukkha). Apparently, through meditation, he was able to achieve enlightenment. This brought an understanding that everything in life was interdependent. This enlightenment also revealed to him that through the elimination of human desire, suffering could be eliminated, thus bringing to an end the endless necessity to be reborn in an endless series of lives. Arriving at this peaceful state was to him *nirvana*. Ralph heard him speak of the various branches of Buddhism in the world. He also heard the speaker say that Buddhism was not strictly a religion, because the basic philosophies in Buddhism were more about ways of thinking and understanding life than about worshiping gods, as was the case with Hinduism, out of which Buddhism arose. Wong concluded his discussion by enumerating the various values that should be developed in followers of Buddha, including right attitudes and conduct.

Ralph thought Wong had done a good job and was surprised there was only one question put to him after his speech. It was asked by a student. "As mentioned in the lecture on Hinduism, there is the thought that behind the world of the nonreal lies what is ultimately real. Do the Buddhists take that view as well?"

Ralph guessed this student had done a lot of reading on these religions in the past. Mr. Wong replied, "Well, in Buddhism, this is just reversed. Buddhists say that behind the real world is actually impermanence. The reason we have cravings is because we think there is permanence in life. Once we know there is nothing permanent, we stop craving. Self is thus extinguished and all desire is gone, and when that happens, suffering also disappears."

All was quiet in the auditorium after that. It seemed everyone was trying to digest what had just been said. Ralph felt Christianity had a much better take on the reality of the physical world, as well as human desire and suffering. Ralph felt himself drooping and he was glad there was a coffee break.

As people were getting up and heading for the coffee urns, Ralph looked around the room, recognizing no one. He saw several people chatting to the speakers and wondered which one might be Tim. Well, he would find out soon enough, he thought as he waited in line. With coffee in hand, Ralph wandered over to the display tables and noted the various books and paraphernalia featured with each religion. He wasn't very interested in them. He was more focused on sizing up Tim. He knew he needed to take notes on what Tim said. Fortunately, Ralph was a fast writer thanks to a shorthand course he'd taken.

The Muslim speaker was introduced as Badru Kathir and Ralph noted that he was one of two men he had seen before the meeting had gotten started. He was a short man with a black bushy beard, receding hairline, and glasses. Ralph heard Kathir review the different branches of Islam and then go on to the life of Mohammed around AD 600. There was nothing new in what he was saying, as far as Ralph was concerned. Ralph found him a little amusing, as he seemed to be trying to show how similar Islam was to Judaism and Christianity. They were all monotheistic and they all respected the Torah and other Hebrew writings like the Psalms. Ralph heard Kathir say that Muslims respected many of the books written about Jesus. Ralph heard Kathir say Jesus was considered the greatest prophet the world had seen before the Prophet Mohammed. Apparently, the Muslims even believed in the virgin birth of Jesus. They believe that Jesus performed miracles and that Jesus was translated into heaven, although he was never crucified. "Jesus will return to this earth one day. He will return as a Muslim, having been enlightened by the great Prophet Mohammed."

In the question period, there were a few questions related to their diet, prayers, and attitude about gaining converts by military might. Kathir tried to placate his audience saying the Koran urged the faithful to seek the way of peace. Ralph knew that was only partly true, since the Koran also talked of using military force if there was resistance to Islam.

Ralph knew he would need to ask questions of Tim later on. He thought he might as well get used to the process now. He raised his hand and when invited, asked, "Does a good Muslim know he's going to heaven when he dies?"

Kathir looked at Ralph. "Actually, the answer to that is no. A good Muslim will be careful to follow all the requirements of the Koran, like praying five times a day, giving alms regularly, and being kind and helpful to the community of believers. The good you do will be weighed against the wrongful things you've done. Allah will judge whether you deserve to go to heaven or hell."

Ralph thought how different the Christian view was. In Christianity, being eligible for heaven had only to do with believing in and accepting God's gift of perfect righteousness won by Jesus when he died for mankind's sins—no matter how bad they were. For Christians, thought Ralph, doing good and right things to please God were done out of thankfulness for that gift—not to make them more eligible for heaven.

A break for lunch was announced and Ralph was glad he'd paid the full fee for the forum. This meant he'd be getting a lunch. He was starving.

✦ ✦ ✦

After enjoying a delicious thick salmon and sprout sandwich and a glass of pure orange juice, Ralph went out for a brisk walk. He needed to keep alert for the afternoon session. It's what he came for. The weather was cool but calm, perfect for walking and thinking. When he returned to his seat, the next speaker was already being introduced. He was Rabbi Fitzner from one of the synagogues in Edmonton. He seemed to be in his late thirties and had a bald head.

Fitzner's speech wasn't as satisfying as Ralph had hoped. He was quite sketchy about the roots of Judaism. He didn't seem to respect the authority of the Old Testament as Ralph had learned to appreciate it. He focused on modern Judaism with an emphasis on being a good citizen, upholding justice, and placing a high value on maintaining the peace in society. He also emphasized keeping up the pride of being Jewish in spite of ridicule and persecution.

The questions dealt mostly with diets and special days in the Jewish calendar. Ralph stuck up his hand, thinking he'd better ask a thorny question to bring a little life into the session that had become somewhat boring. "Rabbi Fitzner, what do you make of the suffering servant prophecy in Isaiah fifty-three?" Everyone in the room tusrned to look at Ralph. Many of the looks seemed irritable, some even hostile.

Rabbi Fitzner grinned with a patronizing expression. "Yes, I'm aware that many Christians have misinterpreted that passage to support their misguided views about their Messiah they call Jesus. Actually, Isaiah here is seeing the suffering servant as a metaphor for the nation of Israel. He was saying that Israel had to shoulder suffering without retaliation in order to bring peace to the other nations."

Ralph was going to ask more questions, but the moderator pointed to another person. The question was on an entirely different topic. There was no other opportunity for Ralph to follow up.

The next speaker was a Catholic priest, Father Allen Blake from the Edmonton diocese. He was blond with glasses and dressed in his clerical collar under a black suit coat. *He's a good communicator,* thought Ralph. Father Blake quickly reviewed the various orders in the church and Ralph thought he alluded to the Eastern Orthodox Church as if that were the only other kind of Christian church that counted. To his credit, Ralph thought, Father Blake pointed out that the earthly life and the crucifixion of Jesus for the sins of the world was the central issue of the church. He went on to say that the church consisted of faithful Catholics who had been baptized into the faith. He also spoke at length about the other sacraments of the church.

When it was time for questions, one surprised Ralph. "Does the Vatican officially approve of the actions of the popes that encouraged the Crusades?"

Father Blake paused as if he knew the question was loaded. "Well, we Catholics realize that all of us are capable of missing the mark sometimes; that includes popes. We also need to consider that those times were very different. We need to be careful how we judge people in that time. We don't know all the issues they were facing."

Ralph was more interested in hearing what the Father had to say about basic beliefs. He raised his hand and when he was acknowledged, asked, "What does the Catholic Church believe are the basic requirements for a person to be a child of God and to be able to go to heaven when he dies?" He noticed many looking over toward him, some shaking their heads and grimacing.

Father Blake looked squarely at Ralph and said, "The Catholic Church takes the view that anyone who is willingly baptized into the Holy Catholic Church of Christ in the name of the Father, the Son, and the Holy Spirit becomes a member of the Church and is a child of God. That person will enter heaven when he or she dies. In the case of infants and children, the Church believes that children baptized before the age of accountability are also children of God."

Ralph had his hand up the moment Father Blake finished and since no one else had a question, the moderator nodded again. "The Apostle Paul stated, 'Believe in the Lord Jesus Christ and you shall be saved.' Do you believe that, Father Blake?"

Ralph could see many who seemed to be annoyed with his questions, but there were a few nodding.

Father Blake took a deep breath, looked up to the ceiling a moment and said, "Luther and other protestants have championed the idea that only belief in Jesus is necessary to become a child of God. The Catholic Church takes the view that true personal salvation requires not only a belief in Jesus and his sacrificial death for our sins, but also that one needs to become a true participating member of the Holy Catholic Church."

Ralph stuck up his hand again to ask the priest if he believed that all Protestant Christians were lost. The moderator stopped him, saying there wasn't time for more questions. He wanted to give time for the last speaker.

During the coffee break that followed, Ralph looked around trying to guess who Tim was. He hoped he hadn't offended the moderator to the point that he wouldn't be able to ask questions of Tim, whoever he was.

When the moderator called everyone to attention, he said, "There is still one more speaker to present and that is Tim Branton, who will speak on behalf of Protestant Christianity." He went on to tell of Tim's education and current work in his church. "Let's welcome our last speaker." There was light applause.

Ralph saw a tall, young, handsome man with blond hair walk to the podium. So this was Iris's guy. *She knows how to pick them,* he thought. As Tim went through the introductions and outlined the various branches of Protestant Christianity, Ralph noticed that he spoke with eloquence. His voice was nice to listen to. Ralph heard him say that we could divide the church up not only by denominations but also by their conservative or liberal views. Tim went on to say what beliefs he felt were more or less common to all Protestant Christian churches. He mentioned such things as following the teachings of Jesus and the church fathers, celebrating communion, and participating in acts of caring, love, and mercy for those in need, both within the fellowship of believers and outside that group.

Tim then pointed to the Bible as the most important of the Christian scriptures. "There is a wide spectrum of belief among the different Christian denominations as to how to view these scriptures. Some take the entire Bible in a very literal way. Others look for overarching truths and inspiration in the writings without being committed to literalism. I'd see the church I attend more in the latter part of the spectrum."

Ralph was scribbling rapidly in shorthand. *I think I know where he's going.*

Tim spelled out what he called "the work of Christ" within the community of believers as well as to the poor, needy, anxious, and curious in the broader society. He sketched out the work being done among the poor in Edmonton as well as in the third world. Ralph was impressed with how skillfully Tim spoke about the humanitarian work of his church. Obviously, he was passionate about this endeavor.

When he finished, the moderator thanked Tim and led the applause of appreciation for his speech. He then opened for questions. Ralph had marked spots in his scribbling where he wanted to question Tim. Now, while others were asking questions, he jotted down what he wanted to ask. Most of the questions, Ralph noted, were to do with Tim's humanitarian work, but then a student asked him, "Do you believe in the virgin birth of Jesus like the Roman Catholic Church?"

Ralph could see Tim's head droop a bit as though he wasn't too pleased to get that question. Tim paused, as if to formulate his response. "I know that what I'll say will alienate me from some Christians. I think that the essential message of Jesus is not diminished by his being born as a natural person—that is, not divine."

Ralph heard a few gasps in the audience.

The girl who'd asked the question shouted out, "So, you're saying Jesus was born illegitimately?"

"Yes," Tim said softly, and Ralph could see that his neck was quite flushed. "I think that God chose to use the messiness of humans to convey his great truths to the world."

The moderator cut in and asked if there were other questions. Ralph shot up his hand. "We have heard other religions speak of coming to ultimate truth or coming to God in and after this life. What is your view about Jesus being the only way to God? You'll recall that Luke wrote, in Acts 4:12, about the words of the Apostle Peter, 'There is no other name under heaven given among men by which we must be saved'?"

Ralph could see Tim's eyes widen in alarm, but then he quickly composed himself. "I've no doubt that that view was Peter's and Luke's understanding of Jesus. They were seeing truth in life from the Jewish perspective. We now have a much larger perspective, as we can view the truly great religions of the world. We must now see that the way to God is going to be different for the Buddhist, the Hindu, the Muslim, or the Jew. I see a picture of humans coming to God like the spokes of a wheel, where each spoke is a religion with God as the hub. I see God expecting every human to be faithful to the light he has been given. For me, as a Christian, my duty is to follow the way of Jesus. For my Muslim friends, their way is Allah, and so on."

Ralph felt his stomach sinking and the back of his neck tingling. *That's horrible—pure heresy*, he thought. He knew he had to keep his wits about him, since he wanted to ask at least one more question. The moderator asked for any further questions and Ralph again raised his hand. The moderator grimaced and said Ralph should wait to see if there were questions from those who hadn't asked one yet. After a moment with no one else responding, the moderator pointed to Ralph. "Okay."

Ralph asked, "What do you believe about the essential story of Easter, that Jesus rose from the dead?"

Tim grinned at Ralph. "I can see that you really intend to pin me to the wall." There was general laughter that served to reduce the tension that had built up.

Ralph saw that Tim's face was blotchy. He clearly was nervous. Ralph saw him take a deep breath. "First of all, let me say that the majority of Protestant Christians still accept the traditional view that Jesus miraculously came back to life after being dead for three days. In this modern scientific world, some of us Christians have found this view difficult to believe and have searched for more plausible explanations." Tim looked around, avoiding Ralph's penetrating gaze. "We must understand that in the first hundred years of Christianity, there was no written record and, during this period, the church was under great pressure to see themselves as being unique and more powerful than the Roman Caesars, who saw themselves as divine. What better way to do this than to see Jesus as a god who had power to rise from the dead! By the time the oral stories of Jesus' life were written down, the idea of Jesus being God was well entrenched. The later the writing, the stronger the Jesus-God idea became. An example is the Gospel of John, the last historical book of the New Testament.

"You may ask what these more liberal thinkers really believe about Jesus. Well, a lot, as it turns out. They still believe he was a most amazing prophet with wisdom and a philosophy of life like no other. His deep love and self-sacrifice eclipsed anything the world had ever seen. For Christians, Jesus' life and death has been a huge inspiration to also live a self-sacrificing and loving life devoted to others." Tim had a pious glow about his face as he finished.

"So, what do *you* personally believe about that, Mr. Branton?" Ralph shouted out without raising his hand.

The moderator jumped up and said that Mr. Branton didn't need to answer that question if he chose not to.

Ralph could see Tim's face grow a little pale around his mouth. "No, I'll answer that. I do believe that Jesus' body is still in the grave somewhere. But his spirit is within us as Christians."

The moderator looked a bit flustered, but soon recovered, made appropriate concluding statements and closed the forum.

Ralph didn't need to scribble down any more notes. He wasn't likely to forget any of the controversial words Tim spoke. He glanced at Tim and saw that he was staring back at Ralph. *I don't think he likes me. Maybe he even sees the resemblance between Iris and me.* Ralph turned about, collected his jacket and notebook, and headed for the exit.

✦ ✦ ✦

Driving back to Iris's suite, Ralph noticed the blue sky beyond the street full of condominiums and apartment buildings. Many of the trees had been stripped naked of leaves, but there were still some glorious mountain ash with their clusters of scarlet berries and their bronze and yellow leaves. How pleasant and restful it was to dwell on the beauties of nature after the grind through all those conflicting religious philosophies.

Now, he would have to report to Iris. That part wasn't going to be hard. What really scared him was what he should advise about her relationship with Tim. She was bound to ask him. What should he say? *Help me, Lord, to speak only your words,* Ralph prayed. He knew that his natural instincts were to just be brutally honest and let the chips fall where they may; however, he knew he needed to act with sensitivity and wisdom.

Don't give any advice, Ralph. I can do that.

Ralph recognized the thought as from God. *Okay, I hear you, Lord.*

Ralph almost missed Iris's street. He couldn't seem to pray, think, and drive at the same time. Despite his lack of coordination, he felt light and peaceful inside. *Thank you for taking the fear and anxiety away, Lord.*

✦ ✦ ✦

The meal Iris had prepared was simple—just an omelet, toast, and some fresh fruit. She had just come home from her lengthy meeting with Dr. Pinsky and her co-workers. Iris and Ralph ate in relative silence. Then Ralph asked about her meeting with Dr. Pinsky.

"It was actually quite useful." Iris wiped her mouth with a napkin. "Dr. Pinsky included reports from groups doing other projects. He has the idea that better learning and planning can be done when there's input from many other scientists and their aides."

"So, are you clear on just what you'll be researching now, Iris?" Ralph asked as he munched on his toast.

"Yeah, pretty well." Iris got up and set a bowl of plums and apples on the table, then continued. "Some other scientists suggested more background reading that needs to be done. Then we can start collecting data from the health units and other immunization clinics so we can start comparing the two types of polio immunization."

As Iris cut her apple into manageable slices, she looked at Ralph and said, "Well, you've been remarkably restrained so far. Are you planning to tell me what happened at the forum? Was it so ugly that you're afraid it will damage my emotional health?"

Ralph laughed. "You can sure read my body language!" After a pause to organize his thoughts, he said, "The forum was interesting from an academic point of view, although there weren't too many surprises. As you know, I took a course on the great religions of the world last year at Briercrest."

"I really want to know about Tim's talk. What did you learn?" Iris asked.

Ralph didn't say anything. He rose and left the room. A moment later, he returned with his notebook and sat across from Iris. "I made a lot of notes so I could accurately report back. I knew you'd insist on that."

Ralph took great care to report practically all Tim had said without any editorializing. He was determined to leave that to Iris. He reported all the questions asked of Tim and his answers. Ralph was careful to say how passionate Tim seemed in telling how Jesus' life had inspired his life and his work.

Ralph noticed that Iris was sitting back in her chair with her shoulders slumped. Her face looked somewhat pale and her usual bright eyes seemed sad. "Thank you, Ralph, for doing this. I know you did it because you care for me."

Both were silent for a few seconds and Ralph saw tears form in Iris's eyes. "Ralph, I can't say I'm too surprised. I guess I was still holding on to a silly hope that he might admit to a more genuine and orthodox faith in Christ."

"It's interesting that you say that. I found the Catholic priest expressing more truth about the Gospel than Tim," Ralph said, looking over the rim of his cup.

"Yeah, I can believe that. Trish often said Catholics have a very good hold on the essentials of the Gospel."

Iris got up and began clearing the table. Ralph helped wash the dishes. They spoke little.

When they had settled on the couch, Iris blew her nose, as she was still holding back tears. She looked Ralph in the eyes. "Okay, brother, let me know your thoughts on my relationship with Tim. What do you think I should do about it? Can we make a successful marriage?"

Ralph stalled for time. He looked out through the living room window at the trees, trying to think of an appropriate answer. Finally, he said, "Iris, my sister, the answer lies in your theology. If you find yourself agreeing with him, then a successful relationship is quite possible."

"Oh, well, that was a nice psychologist's answer. Now, what would Ralph the Christian theologian say about my question?"

Ralph drew in a sharp breath in preparation to answer, but stopped for a moment before resuming. "As much as I'm tempted to shoot off an impulsive answer, I'm not going to do that. I think God will give you the answer, and it'll be a lot better than mine. It certainly will be much better received by you."

"Oh, you're a lot of help!" Iris threw up her hands in mock despair. "Actually, I can guess what you really think about Tim and me."

"That may be, sister, but you need to hear from God."

Iris slumped deeper into the couch and stared out the window. She knew Ralph was right. When had he matured so much? *Oh God, show me your way in this mess.*

Chapter Twenty-Two

Iris had just finished a breakfast of a boiled egg and toast. She looked at her calendar where she had all her appointments and to-do items listed. It was November 1, and she had a meeting with her research group in an hour. She was just about to wash the dishes when the phone rang. It was Myra.

"Good morning, Iris. Or is it good?"

"What do you mean, Myra?"

"Oh, you mustn't have read your CMAJ yet."

"No. It's still in the pile of unopened mail. What's in it?"

"Have a look at it and then, if you want to, give me a call."

Iris hung up the phone. She felt a chill wash through her. Myra sounded upset. Iris found the journal, tore off the wrapper and looked at the titles of the various articles. There it was—the article on oral polio transmission authored by Dr. Pinsky. No other names! Quickly she found the article. The title had been altered slightly. The preamble was not hers. In the original, she had acknowledged Dr. Pinsky and the other people on her team. This preamble said nothing about her or the team. Otherwise, it was essentially her words. She scanned the rest of the article, her hands now trembling. She saw only slight changes here and there. The conclusion had been reworded, but the meaning was exactly the same as in her article. *Well, the bastard changed just enough to make it his and his alone!* She could feel the rage exploding within her.

Iris fired the journal across the room. It struck a tumbler, knocking it into the sink where it smashed to pieces. She paced about the kitchen screaming obscenities at the walls. She'd fight this thing. She would get her revenge. She needed to report him to the dean. Iris felt her stomach tighten and writhe and then she knew she was going to vomit. She rushed to the sink and her breakfast shot into it, vomitus drenching the dishes and the broken glass. She felt her heart pounding. Iris needed to settle down or she'd have a stroke. She found another tumbler and drank some water to clear her mouth. Collapsing into a chair, she told herself she needed to think rationally. She knew she was far too upset to go to the planned meeting. The meeting should be cancelled because she wasn't well. Then she needed to take a walk to calm herself down. Maybe she'd talk to Myra. She'd be wondering how Iris had taken Pinsky's dirty trick.

Iris phoned her team's secretary to cancel the meeting. When she dumped on Myra, all Myra said was that she wasn't surprised Iris would respond that way. Iris quickly changed into her walking clothes and charged out onto the street with blood and thunder written on her face. If it were just an issue of her not getting proper recognition, she might be able to live with that. But what Pinsky had done was scuttle her chances of using her research success to gain a good academic position. Her career opportunities were damaged. Waves of fury washed through her as she replayed the injustice of Dr. Pinsky's action. After twenty minutes of brisk walking, she found herself heading toward the river valley. She took a deep breath, and slowed her pace as she took in the beautiful sight of the Saskatchewan River valley. The thought of God wafted through her mind. What did he think about this? She suspected he knew about human injustices! How would he want her to act? She knew then that she needed to confront Dr. Pinsky. She was sure it wouldn't be wise to do it in a rage. She'd have to calm down so she could speak to him rationally. That might take a while.

◆ ◆ ◆

Once again, Iris was sitting and waiting for his majesty to open his bloody door to one of his humble servants. She knew she was still angry, although it had been four days since she'd read that awful journal. She realized now that she needed to be careful if she wanted to keep her job. She needed to keep her cool.

Finally, the door opened and Dr. Pinsky appeared. He smiled at her, but she could see the smile was far from genuine. "Come in, Iris."

She walked into his office. He pointed to a chair across from his desk. When he settled in his chair, he asked, "You wanted to see me, Iris? What have you got on your mind?"

Iris felt like she would love to let loose the deluge of hatred she had for this man. She instead directed her inner self to a discipline she surely didn't feel. "Dr. Pinsky, I think you know what this is about. I'll try to let you know how I feel." Iris paused and Dr. Pinsky stayed quiet, acting mystified by what she was getting at. "When I gave you my research manuscript on OPV transmission, I felt I'd done a good job and that the article would be submitted for publication pretty much as it was. When I read the CMAJ publication four days ago, I was surprised and disappointed that the article was altered without my knowledge. Even more disappointing was the fact that there was no acknowledgement of my team or me." Iris's face was blotchy and her eyes were glistening.

Iris could see Dr. Pinsky was nervous and agitated. There was pallor around his mouth. He fixed a smile on his face and said, "Iris, you need to be aware of what's acceptable in publishing. The publisher knows his readers demand that the article to be published has the authority of the director of the research project. That's me. The director's job is to select the area of research, plan the research, inspire his team, and marshal the research through all the difficulties and pitfalls that are bound to occur. He then has to judge the value and integrity of the research and submit it in a proper format for publication. That takes a lot of work and experience."

Iris felt herself becoming very angry. She had to fight for emotional control. "Okay, Dr. Pinsky, but I saw only minor changes made in the published article from the manuscript I gave you. With all respect, I don't see that a lot of work and experience was required before you submitted the article for publication."

Dr. Pinsky leaned back in his chair and steepled with his fingers. "I know you are angry that you didn't get the recognition you desired after all the work you have put into the project. Once you are in practice and have gained a lot more experience, as well as a good reputation, you'll find your name displayed prominently behind your published work. You just need to have patience."

Iris found the situation ironic in that the one losing patience was Dr. Pinsky. She could see it in his face. Iris knew she needed to quit asking more questions or she was going to lose her job. With tears now running down her cheeks, she said, "Dr. Pinsky, I have to admit I felt hurt by what you did. But I'll try to understand this from your point of view. I still love the work I'm doing. I hope you will still allow me to continue." She found a hanky and blew her nose. "Thanks for listening to me."

Dr. Pinsky nodded as Iris got up to leave. He said nothing more.

✦ ✦ ✦

Iris choked down some food at the cafeteria, but when she was about halfway through her plate, she shoved it away, gulped down some water, and got up. She was calmer now, but still very angry. She needed to talk to someone to reduce some of the pressure she felt inside and get an outsider's view of her situation. Maybe she wasn't seeing something here. Of course, she thought of Milton.

When she got to her suite, she put a call through to Milton. "He's still busy with a case, Dr. Marten. He said to tell you he'll phone you back as soon as he has a chance," a secretary told her.

For another twenty minutes, she paced around the room to clear her thoughts, but she found herself getting more worked up.

The phone rang. It was Milton.

"Sorry, Milt, I'd just hoped to have a word with you." Iris marshaled all her resources to remain calm and rational.

"Of course, Iris. I'm always delighted to hear what you've got to say. I'm free now for a while, at least."

"Could I meet you in the medical lounge?"

"Sure. How about in ten minutes?"

Iris quickly primped herself up. She was always anxious to look good for Milton. When she got to the lounge, Milton was already there, in a corner where there was relative privacy.

"Thanks for coming, Milt. I always value your opinion when I get into trouble."

"Trouble? What's happening, Iris? You look very upset."

Iris brought Milton up to date with Dr. Pinsky's CMAJ article. She pulled her copy of the journal from her purse and showed it to him.

After a quick perusal of the article, Milton looked up. "Oh Iris, this so unfair! It's only got Pinsky's name on it."

"He made no mention of my part in the work at all! He doctored it up just enough to make it seem he was the only researcher involved. He didn't even give credit to the staff that worked with me. He's being highly deceptive, dishonest, and blatantly selfish." Iris's voice was escalating in volume and intensity. Her eyes were flashing and her face was flushed.

"I can see why you'd be upset, Iris. In fact, I'm shocked at the injustice of all this. What are you intending to do?"

"I'd like to report him to the dean. I know that's risky because I could get myself canned. I have to understand if this is considered normal procedure in research publication."

"Yeah, the fertilizer could hit the fan with the dean involved. You'd need to couch your words very carefully."

"You know, I'm so angry, I'd like to sue the daylights out of that bastard. Nobody should be able to get away with this."

Milton noticed Iris's face had become quite flushed. . She was really worked up. "I'm not going to advise whether you should or shouldn't do these things, but I would say you should take your time. You need to cool off a bit so your approach is as rational as possible. In the meantime, I'll pray for wisdom for you."

Iris looked up, her eyes blazing. "You do that, Milton. In the meantime, I'll do what I have to do." Iris was breathing heavily.

Milton knew now was not the time to say more.

After a few seconds, Iris's eyes filled with tears. "I'm sorry, Milt. You've been so generous with me and now I'm lashing out at you."

Milton looked into her face and said, "I'm sorry, Iris. You needed me to just listen and here I'm trying to give you advice."

They got up from the table and bid each other goodbye, both feeling quite unsettled.

✦ ✦ ✦

The Dean of Medicine's office was the picture of excellent décor. Iris had heard that the dean was very interested in how he and his office were viewed by his colleagues, as well as the whole medical staff. She'd had to wait three days for this appointment. Maybe this wait was also a ploy to demonstrate her subservient state, just like with Dr. Pinsky.

Iris was glancing at her notes when the dean's secretary told her to go in.

Dean Jorgansen got up and reached a hand out to Iris. "Dr. Marten? Do sit down." When they had settled into chairs, Dr. Jorgansen asked, "You had a concern about Dr. Pinsky? Do you want to tell me about it?"

Iris looked down at her notes. She saw her hands trembling. "Dr. Jorgansen, I just wanted to understand what the expected procedures are in relation to publication of research done in this hospital."

Dr. Jorgansen nodded to continue.

Iris detailed all the work she and her staff had done in obtaining and gathering the research material. Then she outlined the work she'd done to research the literature and document her findings. Finally, she told him about the process of writing up the article and presenting it to Dr. Pinsky. "I heard nothing more of the article until it appeared in the CMAJ with only Dr. Pinsky's name on it. There had been no substantial alteration in the article, aside from removing credit for my co-workers and me. I just want to know if this is within the accepted limits of standard procedure for publication within a research department."

Dr. Jorgansen just stared at Iris for a few seconds, obviously gathering his thoughts. "Dr. Marten, is this the first time you published anything?"

Iris looked annoyed. "Yes it is, but why is that important?"

"Well, sometimes those publishing for the first time can make the assumption that they should get all the recognition. In any research project, the researchers are under the authority of the department head. The department head has a big responsibility and deserves to be recognized."

Iris could see the argument going down the same track as with Dr. Pinsky. She was convinced Dr. Jorgansen had been in conversation with Dr. Pinsky about her concern. She tried briefly to justify her position, but soon realized she was only getting the dean angry.

"Dr. Marten," the dean said, leaning forward, "would you consider suing Dr. Pinsky over this?"

Now Iris felt herself edging toward a precipice. "Well," she stuttered, "I'd thought of that, I must admit."

Dr. Jorgansen leaned back in his chair with a grimace, shaking his head slowly. "Dr. Marten, if you tried that, you would get yourself in a lot of trouble. The chances of you winning aren't too great. I respect Dr. Pinsky. He's a fine researcher and department head. He's respected among his colleagues. You'd find yourself all alone in a legal battle."

Iris felt her sense of justice being violated. "So you feel it's okay to disregard the heavy work of researchers and give the scientific world the false impression that someone else, like the department head, did all the work? Isn't that being dishonest and unfair?"

Dr. Jorgansen gave a dry chuckle. "Oh, I suppose, it would've been nice for Dr. Pinsky to dish out due credits, but he acted within the norms of in-hospital publishing." With that, the dean got up, signaling the end of the conversation.

As Iris passed through the office door, Dr. Jorgansen said, "Suing or causing any more trouble would be a mistake, Dr. Marten."

Iris just glared back at the dean and then marched out of the office. *You're not going to scare me into complying with the wishes of your neat old boy's club,* she thought.

✦ ✦ ✦

The mirror, that Monday morning, told Iris she was stressed. She saw thin lines around her eyes she had never seen before. She had lost about five pounds since the fateful CMAJ article had come out. She knew she'd eaten poorly and had wakened more often during the night. Though she had made a determined effort to stay fully engaged in the current research, her thoughts dwelled on whether to sue Dr. Pinsky. One big problem was that she didn't have the money to pay a lawyer. She would need a good lawyer. The thought struck her that she could ask her dad for a loan, which she could repay when she began her clinical practice.

When Peter answered, Iris said, "Dad, I have a special request of you." She went on to tell him briefly the background of her problem. Then she asked, "Dad, would you consider loaning me a couple thousand dollars for a good lawyer? I could pay you back once I'm in clinical practice."

"Sure, honey," Peter said somewhat tentatively, "I guess I could do that, but why is it so important to sue this guy? I can see he's inconsiderate and selfish, but aren't a lot of people we deal with like that?"

"Oh, Dad, you're just as bad as Milton. Can't you see the gross injustice of this guy? He needs to be brought to task. It isn't just me. He's short-changed all my co-workers as well."

The two went back and forth for a while and then Peter said, "Iris, I trust your judgment. I'll wire you the money tomorrow. Trish and I'll be praying for wisdom for you."

"Thanks, Dad. Write this debt on your ledger to keep me accountable."

After hanging the phone up, Iris mumbled, "'I'll be praying for wisdom for you.' Wasn't that what Milton said?"

Chapter Twenty-Three

Milton had finished setting up his watercolour display at the small art gallery on Whyte Avenue. Now he had an hour to wait until people would come. He opened the wrap on the sandwich he'd picked up at a near-by kiosk. While chewing on his beef sandwich, he reflected on his life. His paediatric residency program was going well. He loved the clinical work, especially meeting the parents and discussing medical treatment options and translating complicated medical knowledge into simpler terminology.

As far as his social life was concerned, he continued to value the weekly meetings of his small group. He especially was thankful for the godly men in the group that accepted and befriended him.

He continued to meet with Bill Street from time to time. Milton liked the guy, but Bill hadn't been too much of an encouragement for Milton. Bill's values were mostly opposite from his. He knew he should maintain this friendship for whatever reason. Maybe God had a plan for Bill, who knew.

Then there was Iris. Not an hour would go by without thinking about that wonderful woman. His friendship with her was changing into something entirely more emotional, he realized. Milton had continued to communicate with Iris, mainly by sending small notes to her mailbox or via phone calls. Recently, there had been a lull in this communication, largely due, he thought, to the last sticky conversation they'd had about her wanting to sue Dr. Pinsky. Something about the whole idea of Iris seeking justice didn't ring true for him. She seemed constantly agitated and unsettled. Expressions of anger played around the edges of many of her activities in the last few weeks. In spite of Iris's dismissive comments when he offered to pray for her, he decided to pray for her more than ever.

He looked up to see several people coming into the gallery, look at his advertising sign, and then slowly walk past his art. He realized he didn't want to sell some of his favourite pieces, as they represented so much of who he was. He kept looking at the door, hoping Iris would come. He'd invited her a few days ago. She'd been noncommittal. Something about crucial meetings with her research team.

Milton slowly strolled toward two ladies looking at his art. When they noticed him, they engaged him in conversation about the pieces. Milton liked this interaction, because he loved to talk about his inspirations.

The two ladies were just telling him they wanted to see works of other artists as well when he saw a familiar face slipping through the door. Iris. Their eyes met and Iris rewarded him with a warm smile. Her dark blond hair was longer now, and curled. He could see a pretty blouse underneath her dark coat. She looked gorgeous. He could feel his pulse speed as she hurried over.

"Oh, Milton, are all these paintings yours? I had no idea your collection was so extensive. When do you get time to do all this?" Iris's eyes were wide with wonder.

"Well, this represents about five years of work. I do this when I need to relax. I suppose most people watch television to relax. I find painting works better for me."

Iris slowly walked around, halting before each of Milton's watercolours. Milton was silent, allowing Iris the freedom to take as much time as she desired. Then Iris walked back to one of his paintings and stood still for about five minutes. It was a painting of a happy family playing in a park, but there was a man watching them from a nearby grove of trees. His posture and face spoke of longing to be part of the family. Iris turned toward Milton. "Milton, please tell me about this painting."

Milton could see tears glistening in Iris's eyes. "You tell me what you see, Iris."

"Well, I see this guy looking as though he were envious of the family and wanting to be a part of something he had no right to be. Is that close?"

Milton nodded, too overcome with emotion to speak. Iris had nailed the meaning exactly.

Then Iris's eyes widened and her mouth fell open. "The guy is you, isn't it?"

"Yeah, I suppose it could be," Milton said with a gravelly voice.

"And the happy family with the kids is a family you know?" Iris said with a quizzical look.

"Oh nothing that specific, Iris."

"Oh, I see. The family represents the kind of life you yearn for but think is out of reach."

Milton nodded again. This time Iris saw his eyes wet with unshed tears.

Iris pulled a hanky out of her coat pocket and blew her nose. "Now you've got me crying and I've only been here twenty minutes. Milton, you've a wonderful talent to express your feelings in your paintings. But I'm not crying because of that. I'm so sad that you have those feelings."

"Well, painting helps me to deal with some of the hard things in life," Milton said, snuffling his nose.

"I can understand that. Playing my oboe does the same thing for me."

Iris noticed there were others looking at Milton's art pieces. "You'd better talk to those people. I'll look at everything else in the gallery while you're doing your promotion. How about I treat you to a coffee when you're finished? You certainly deserve it."

"That sounds wonderful. See you then."

✦ ✦ ✦

Tim had just finished a pastoral call at the University of Alberta Hospital with someone from his congregation who had come in with pneumonia. Now he was heading toward the second floor cafeteria. Earlier in the morning, he'd called Iris to see if he might join her for lunch. She seemed pleased to be invited. He was keeping up with Delmar's plan to keep after Iris. He hadn't actually met her for a few weeks because she was so busy. He had phoned her about twice a week. He was looking forward to having a comfortable chat with her again.

When he walked into the cafeteria, he soon spotted Iris sitting at a table by herself. She hadn't seen him yet. He was just going to head her way when he spotted a smiling young man approach her with a tray of food. He sat close to her and they began an animated discussion. Tim just watched them for a while. He noticed the man was smiling very warmly and Iris was responding in an equally warm manner, much to Tim's chagrin. He was quite sure the guy was that homosexual guy, Milton. The way they looked at each other was unnerving. Well, he was going to break up their happy little discussion.

"Hi, Iris. Thanks for waiting for me," Tim said in his deep, commanding voice.

Iris jumped up and looked like a naughty child who'd been apprehended by a teacher. "Oh, Tim! I didn't see you coming."

"So I see. Were you busy here?" Tim asked with raised eyebrows.

Iris's neck flushed as she tried to regain control of the situation. "Tim, I'd like you to meet Milton, a paediatric resident. We were in the same medical class."

Milton rose from his chair and extended his hand. "Tim, I'm glad to meet you. Iris has mentioned you a number of times." They shook hands, both men smiled politely.

"Milton, Tim asked me to join him for lunch, since he had to come to the hospital for a pastoral call," Iris said, looking mainly at Tim.

Milton grabbed his tray of food. "Excuse me, Tim and Iris. I'll leave you to your lunch engagement."

Iris noted a fleeting look in Milton's face that appeared altogether like jealousy. He quickly recovered and smiled graciously at both Iris and Tim before hurrying to another table on the other side of the cafeteria.

✦ ✦ ✦

Ever since that fiasco with Tim and Milt in the cafeteria yesterday, Iris had felt unsettled. She had to do some thinking again. She decided to take a walk. After her evening meal, she changed into her jogging clothes and runners and was off to the river and the valley trails.

There was no doubt in her mind that both Tim and Milton had shown their jealousy yesterday. This was all her fault. She had strung both of these guys along, not making a clear choice. She knew she was in love with Milton. She also knew that he really liked her. How utterly insane! She should have been refusing to see or talk to Milton so this ridiculous infatuation could die down. He was gay, for heaven's sake! She should be telling Tim she was okay with marrying him, especially now that he was going to be staying mainly in Edmonton. So, what was her hesitation? Her fickle heart was betraying her. Well, she needed to be decisive with herself.

During most of the walk, Iris railed at her own stupidity. She needed to take sensible steps to put her life back on track. She finally decided she needed to make another supreme effort at weaning off Milton and encouraging

Tim. She was beginning to feel more settled inside. As she headed back to her apartment block, she saw some movement next to her bedroom window. It was a man, by the way he was dressed. She was too far away to see who it was. When she drew near to the front door of the building, she saw the person look at her and then quickly duck behind a bush. A cold chill went up her spine. What was he doing there next to her bedroom? She headed for the caretaker's door and knocked. When he appeared at the door, Iris told him what she'd seen. He promised to check right away and then let her know. When he knocked on her door a few minutes later, the caretaker told Iris he couldn't find anything unusual.

Iris had trouble falling asleep that night.

Chapter Twenty-Four

Mid-November 1962

TRY AS HE MIGHT, MILTON COULD NOT GET HIS MIND ON AN ARTICLE in one of his medical journals. He'd decided to read the review article on kidney function, yet all he could do was relive the brief encounter with Tim at the cafeteria four days ago. Milton had to admit his emotions had been jostled with that encounter. He'd even experienced jealousy. Somehow, he'd begun to feel Iris would always be there for him. Now he had to face the fact that he might well lose her. What else could he expect, after all? As far as she was concerned, he was still gay. How was he to convince her he wasn't anymore? He was still having a hard time convincing himself that he'd become heterosexual. Sure, there had been changes within him. He'd stopped having fantasies about men. These changes were encouraging, but he couldn't be sure that the old fantasies and attractions would not reassert themselves in the future.

Milton thought back to last February, when he talked at length with Kent, one of his small group friends. Kent had been excited about claiming the good things God would give us if we only really believed. Milton remembered how he'd talked himself into believing that concept of prayer. He could believe for his complete healing from homosexuality, he had told himself.

Recently, he had come across some roadblocks to that understanding of faith. The series of sermons on the book of Job preached by his pastor made him realize God is unpredictable and must be viewed as sovereign in our world and our individual lives. God wasn't some genie Christians could make do their bidding if they prayed the right way and performed the right actions. Christians couldn't expect to always get what they wanted.

Then, just last evening in his regular Bible reading, he once again came to the statement by the Apostle Paul in his letter to the Corinthian church. Paul said he'd been given a thorn in the flesh—some physical ailment, Milton supposed. Paul said he pleaded repeatedly to God to heal him, but Paul heard the Lord say to him, "My grace is sufficient for you, for my power is made perfect in weakness." So even the Apostle Paul didn't always get what he wanted.

Milton realized he had been trying to bargain with God. His recent thinking was that if he faithfully prayed and lived a good life, God would have to come across with what he desired. Now he realized he needed to let God be God. Milton's job was to find out what God wanted and then pray for that to happen. He had no idea if his becoming heterosexual was in God's plans. Maybe God wanted him to live with his problem just like the Apostle Paul was told to do. Milton knew that if God wanted him to remain a homosexual, then God would give him the grace to do that, but that would be so hard to accept.

The worst part was that he'd lose Iris. Soon, he'd have to tell her their special relationship was finished. He wouldn't be fair to her to maintain a relationship that was blocking her from finding someone she could live with in a proper marriage.

As Milton thought about all this, he could feel his spirits sink into a cold, dark abyss. How could he live without Iris? Life would seem so meaningless without her. Regardless of how awful he felt, he knew he needed to talk to Iris, and soon.

✦ ✦ ✦

Iris heard her page while in the hospital medical library. She was reading journals dealing with the clinical experience with Salk vaccine. She wondered if it might be a notification of another polio patient admission. When she picked up the phone, it was Milton's voice. She'd hoped he'd never call again.

"Iris, it's Milton. Would you have time to meet me briefly before you leave the hospital? I promise it will only take a few minutes."

"Sure, Milton." She needed to keep with her plan and not let her emotions deal with this encounter. "I could meet you in the doctors' lounge in ten minutes?"

"Okay, that's fine." Milton hung up.

As Iris walked toward the lounge, she wondered what he had in mind. He seemed a bit curt and stressed. When she saw him, she could see she was right. He looked very serious, even a bit pale.

"Hi, Milt. What's up?"

"Thanks for seeing me so quickly. I wanted to clear the air with you." Milton licked his dry lips. "Ah, it's about our relationship. I guess I've let it happen without trying to see where it's going. Iris, I have to be honest with you. As much as I hope and pray that I'll become heterosexual, I know that I can't assure you, or me, that I'll always be free from being gay. You need to connect with someone who has more than hopes for being a proper husband. As much as this hurts me, I have to say that we need to stop seeing each other and even stop communicating. We need to let our feelings for each other fade away so you can have a better chance of finding a good mate—like Tim—and build a good relationship with him.

"Well, that's all I have to say." Milton looked down at his hands.

Iris could feel tears streaming down her face. She had been thinking that this was exactly what she had determined to do. The thought of losing Milton from her life, however, was quite intolerable. Yet, they both were doing the logical thing for their lives. Why was it so hard?

Iris managed to speak through her tears. "Okay, I'll try to do as you say. But it's going to be very hard. Obviously, we have to talk with each other once in a while in our medical duties, but I'll do my best to stay clear of you." With that, Iris openly cried and she had to find a hanky to stifle the flow of tears.

Milton made a supreme effort to keep from taking her in his arms and comforting her. He knew he had to just leave her.

"Good bye, Iris." Milton turned and walked away.

✦ ✦ ✦

There was little sleep for Iris the night of her break-up with Milton. She struggled out of bed still feeling tired and achy. How could a person as nice as Milton not be right for her? Life was so cruel sometimes. How could there be a loving God when life was so chaotic and uncertain. Well, she couldn't just mope and pity herself. She had to take charge of her life and get on with it. She threw her blankets off and marched resolutely to the bathroom.

As she did her usual washing and brushing of her hair, she again thought of Dr. Pinsky. *I've got to get on with that suit. I'll never be settled until I do.* When she'd last seen her lawyer, he'd told her to think about the process of litigation, and let him know if he should go ahead with the suit. As she ate some cold cereal for breakfast, she planned what she'd instruct her lawyer to do. She and her lawyer thought they had a case regarding giving appropriate credit for work done in research. The careers of co-workers and herself had also been damaged by not being given credit for their research work. If appropriate credit had been given her, she could've been widely recognized and so possibly secured an appointment in a prestigious medical school.

The lawyer's secretary transferred Iris's call to Mr. Lansdowne, her lawyer.

"Mr. Lansdowne, I've decided to go ahead with that suit against Dr. Pinsky."

"You have?" There was a pause as if he was surprised and maybe a little disappointed. "Okay, Iris, you have to realize that there'll arise some undesirable publicity, no matter how it all turns out."

"What do you mean, undesirable for Dr. Pinsky or myself?" Iris could feel herself getting angry.

"For both of you. Sure, some people will see you as a heroine, taking on the old boys club at the university, but there'll be a bad taste in some people's mouths for the action you've taken."

"Well, I don't really care. I'm going for justice here."

"Just so you know, there's going to be costs, Iris."

"Mr. Lansdowne, I would like you to proceed."

"Okay, Dr. Marten. I'll get things moving on a preliminary hearing and will deliver a subpoena to Dr. Pinsky in the next week."

After she hung up the phone, she felt angry and agitated. She had to settle down before she met with her research team. As she walked around the kitchen table, her anger was replaced by an empty, unsettled feeling. Was she doing the wrong thing? What about her faith? Would Jesus do what she was doing? Somehow she doubted it. On the other hand, Christians should stand up for what was right, not be walked all over. She wasn't sure where in Scripture that concept was mentioned, but it seemed right.

* * *

That evening, Iris was walking back from the grocery store, bags in hand. Her day had gone poorly. She knew she had been short with some of her team and she regretted her behaviour. Of course, she knew why. Her inner life was in turmoil, partly because of the suit she launched, but more because of her separation with Milton.

As Iris turned to head up her street, she felt she was being watched. She turned and saw a man staring at her. He dodged and headed away, down the street. He wasn't very big, quite slim. She wondered if he might be the same guy she'd seen near her bedroom window the other day.

* * *

Two days had gone by since his agonizing meeting with Iris. Milton remained deeply troubled. In fact, he realized, he was depressed. He was sitting in the medical library trying to read a journal, but totally failing to concentrate. He was having trouble thinking clearly about medicine or about his life in general. One thing was clear to him. He was losing hope in being permanently healed of homosexuality. He wondered where this uncertainty was coming from. Maybe some of it came from Iris. She always seemed so doubtful that he could be healed.

The other big reason for his being depressed was the fact that he was losing Iris. Sure, he could've tried to beat out Tim and win her affections. He knew that wasn't fair to Iris. His first allegiance was to God. Milton had determined to always stay true to God and his life principles. So, what was he getting from all this devotion to God? It was causing him to lose Iris!

Milton knew he had to do something quickly if he was to avoid a crippling depression. Even though it was mid-afternoon and Patrick would be busy at work in his plumbing and heating business, he was going to see if he could make an appointment to see him.

Patrick's secretary quickly found him and Patrick was glad to see Milton that evening at his place for coffee. That would work for Milton.

After their initial greetings, Patrick invited Milton to the living room where he and his wife Linda sat across from Milton.

Patrick looked closely at Milton for a moment. "I suspect you came here because you're troubled and want to talk to someone you trust."

Milton nodded. "Yes, you're dead on. I needed your thoughts about my situation. I'm digging myself into an emotional pit and can't think clearly."

"Okay, tell us what's troubling you. As you know, we will keep what you say between us."

Milton already felt better. What a blessing it was to have such caring and gentle friends! Milton told them about the progress in his moving away from homosexuality. He told them about Kent's teaching on healing and how Milton had grabbed onto the concept of getting whatever one asked in faith. He thus had developed high hopes of achieving the healing he so desperately desired. Milton then told them about what he now understood about God's dealing with Job in the Old Testament. He also cited the Apostle Paul's submission to God's no when he requested healing from the thorn in the flesh. Milton admitted what he'd recently been reading in the Bible had been discouraging. He finished by telling them about his decision to break things off with Iris because of the uncertainty of his ever being a good husband for her.

"Oh, Milton, I feel so sad for you," Linda said with tears glistening in her eyes. "Was Iris okay with that?"

"She looked a bit shocked when I told her, but I noticed she didn't try to talk me out of not seeing her anymore."

Patrick fixed Milton with a steady gaze. "So, I presume the real issue here is whether you, Milton, will be a good husband and a healthy sex partner for Iris."

"Sure, that's it," Milton said with a nervous repositioning of his legs. "There's no doubt about our friendship. That's always been special. I guess my main trouble is that I'm losing confidence that I'm going to become permanently heterosexual. I think Iris would only accept me if I could assure her of that."

"Well, Milton, I'd first of all like to say that life is always full of unknowns. Even seasoned Christians have to live with many surprising twists and turns. In fact, maturity in the faith usually comes as we live a life of confidence in God's love and care, in the face of life's many uncertainties. What I'm saying is that you may never get a definite word from God that you're going to get the healing you're praying for."

"That's all good and well for you to say. I'm not hoping to marry you! I was thinking about marrying Iris and she may not have the faith you have," Milton said, grinning, but with tears in his eyes.

The Bensons laughed and then Patrick said, "I feel badly that you got caught up in that spiritual rabbit trail after talking to Kent. I've been trying to show him that his faith ideas don't line up with Scripture. The bottom line, as far as I can understand Scripture, is that God is sovereign and he always does what's ultimately good for us. God is always good and he always loves us. Sometimes, what we so desperately cry out to him for is ultimately not good for us. In his great wisdom, he can see the whole picture and will work out things for the good of you and those you love. You need to trust him in that."

Milton was silent for a time. "Yes, I can see that, but I'm scared of the pain if he says that healing's not good for me ultimately."

"Even if he said that to you, he'll give you the strength that's needed and your life will eventually find joy and fulfillment, I'm certain."

"So you think I should stop asking God for healing?" The pain in Milton's face was obvious.

"Yes, maybe that's just as well, Milton. Perhaps it would be best if you just told God every day that you know he loves you and will work out what is best for you and Iris. That may well be very hard at first, but you'll find he gives you strength to live and grow in that faith."

Milton was quiet again and then looked up with a tearful smile. "I'll try."

Linda had been carefully following the discussion. "Milton, there's another fact you need to know. Iris will not necessarily demand certainty about you being forever free from homosexual impulses. Those are just *your* pessimistic thoughts."

Milton nodded and smiled weakly. "Maybe you're right. You, being a woman, will be a better judge than I can be."

The three spent a few minutes in prayer. They expressed their confidence that God loved them all and would work out what was best for their lives as they trusted in him.

Just before Milton turned to go, Patrick said, "Milton, I'm concerned that you might have some bad feelings for Kent. Maybe it might be a good idea for you to have coffee with him sometime soon. I think you'll find he's come around to a much more sensible approach to prayer."

"Sure, Patrick. I can do that."

Chapter Twenty-Five

Late November 1962

MILTON WAITED FOR KENT IN A CAFÉ NEAR THE UNIVERSITY. KENT WAS a young man in his early 30s. He was married and had two preschool children. He worked as a salesman for a car company. He had become a Christian in the last year or so. Milton recalled him as being quite opinionated. He was always looking for principles in the Scripture that he tenaciously defended. The thing Milton found admirable was Kent's willingness to listen to another opinion and even change his views if the argument was sound. Milton hoped Patrick was right about Kent's views on prayer.

When Kent strolled into the café, Milton rose to greet him with a big smile. They chatted amiably while they ate their muffins. As Milton sat back to drink his coffee, he said, "Well, Kent, as you know, Patrick suggested we meet to talk about faith and prayer."

"Yeah, Patrick talked to me about that not too long ago. I hope I didn't screw up your theology, Milton."

"I have to say I was somewhat vulnerable at that time and I swallowed what you said hook, line, and sinker." Milton took another sip of his coffee. "You see, I really wanted God to do a miracle in my life—you know, make me heterosexual. Well, I began seeing that God won't be manipulated that way. I read some Scripture that clearly told me that I first needed to find out what God wants and then pray for that."

Kent nodded. "Yeah, I know what you mean. I had that view, too—at least until Patrick showed me lots of instances in the Bible where even great Christians like the Apostle Paul didn't get what they asked. I'm afraid that you might go to the other extreme now and have no trust in God for helping you with the really important things in your life. Do you feel that's happened now?"

"Yes," Milton said with a grimace, "I did feel that way, but now I'm trying to rest in the knowledge that God loves me and wants the best for my life. I don't know yet what that will be, but I'm willing to let him tell me what to pray and trust for."

"Good. I'm so glad you've come to that opinion." Kent's eyes were sparkling with excitement. "Milton, I'll pray daily that God will show you his will."

They chatted about their group for another few minutes and then Milton said, "I appreciate you coming down to meet me, Kent, but I need to do some homework before tomorrow's clinic, so I'd better be going."

As they got up to leave, Kent hugged Milton, just as he often did at their group meetings. Milton noticed that someone in the next booth was staring at them. She looked somewhat familiar but he couldn't quite place her. Milton hoped he and Kent hadn't left a wrong impression.

✦ ✦ ✦

It was their ensemble practice night again. Before they started practicing, Iris told Myra and Sandra that the ensemble had been invited to attend the theology department Christmas banquet on December 1.

"Are you interested?" Myra asked, settling on the piano seat. "I'm never sure where you are with Tim, who likely invited us."

Iris laughed lightly. "Sure, I'd like to go. I think it would be fun to actually perform again."

"Ah, they'd just want us for background music," Sandra said while lifting her violin from its case. "If they have enough to drink, they'll never notice our imperfections and we wouldn't have to break our necks practicing."

"That's true," admitted Iris. "Maybe they'll ask us to play one piece as part of the program."

Most of the pieces they practiced were classical, mainly baroque. They also practiced a few carols and other seasonal tunes.

When they had finished, Myra offered to take Iris home. She'd walked to the Education building where they had practiced.

Once Myra began driving, she asked, "How are things with Milton? Is he still a part of your love life?"

Iris looked down and thought for a moment. "I think things have ground to a halt as far as the two of us are concerned. From my part, I've been thinking that I've become way too emotional about our relationship, especially in view of his being gay. Before I had a chance to tell him we should stop seeing each other, Milton approached me and told me he would not be able to assure me that he'd be a proper husband. He advised me to marry Tim or some other guy, and suggested we no longer see or communicate with each other. So that's it, I guess." Myra glanced at Iris and saw that she looked very sad.

"I feel so sorry for both of you," Myra said with concern in her eyes. "Milton is such a prince of a guy."

"You don't have to remind me of that."

"You know, I give him credit for having the courage and wisdom for stopping the relationship now, before you both really get hurt."

"Yeah, I know he did the right thing, but oh, it hurts."

"You *do* really love him, don't you?"

"Of course I do, I'm ashamed to say. He's such a wonderful, caring and interesting guy. He thinks just like I do. I couldn't help but fall for him. Now I have to somehow dig myself out of this hole." Iris had tears filling her eyes.

"I wouldn't be surprised that Milton is grieving the separation as much as you are," Myra said as she pulled up to Iris's apartment.

Iris opened the door, snuffed her nose and said, "Thanks for the ride, and thanks for listening to me spill my guts. You're such a great friend."

✦ ✦ ✦

Iris's was reliving the conversation with Myra as she walked toward her apartment block. Her eye caught some motion in the bushes. She stepped behind a lilac bush next to the sidewalk and peeked around to see if anything or anybody came in view. Then she saw someone step away from a row of spruce trees and head toward the building. She guessed him to be male. He had the same slight body build as the other sightings she had of him. Just as Iris guessed, he went to her ground floor bedroom window. Was he trying to break in? Horror filled her. Then she noticed him paste a piece of paper on her window and then quickly walk away, disappearing down the street. She tried to follow him for a bit but without success. Actually, she wasn't too eager to succeed, as she didn't know what she'd do if she caught up to him. So, trembling all over, she went to her suite and then into her bedroom. When she switched on the light, the note was stuck to the window and the writing was very clear. A cold chill crept up her spine as she read the note: *"Drop the suit if you value your health."*

Now what should she do? Should she call the police? She had thought of doing that before. This was the third time she'd seen this guy. She was quite sure the same person was responsible. The first time was six days ago when he'd been seen next to her bedroom window just after she had gone on a walk. A couple of days later, while walking home from a shopping trip, she'd felt someone was following her. When she had looked around she could catch a brief glimpse of him. He had quickly turned the other direction when she looked at him. As it had been after seven, the light had been too poor for her to get a good look. She had noticed he was male and that he was slight in build. Now, she was sure they all were the same person. She was not going to settle to sleep unless she called the police. She went to the telephone and did just that.

When an officer knocked on her door an hour later, she introduced herself as Officer Bates. "Dr. Marten, I hear you've been stalked. Could you tell me about it?" She pulled out a book to take notes.

Iris told her what she had experienced and observed on the three occasions. Then she showed her the note stuck onto the bedroom window.

After Officer Bates made careful notes, she said, "Dr. Marten, may I ask you a few questions?"

"Yes. Please, sit down." Iris pointed to a living room chair.

Once they were settled, Officer Bates asked, "Do you have any suspicions as to who this man might be?"

"No, none at all."

"Do you have some idea what this 'suit' is about?"

"Oh, sure," Iris responded quickly. "I've begun litigation against my boss." Iris went on to tell the police officer the details of her research and publishing efforts, and Dr. Pinsky's actions.

"When, do you think, Dr. Pinsky became aware of your litigation?"

"He may have become aware that I might sue him when I reported him to the dean of medicine. Let me think. That was over two weeks ago. Yeah, I think it was seventeen days ago. Then, he likely got a subpoena for a hearing two days ago." Iris felt quite nervous and her mouth was dry.

"Okay, Dr. Marten, it would seem someone takes exception to your wanting to sue Dr. Pinsky and wants to scare you out of going ahead with it." Bates put her pencil down and looked at Iris. "Do you have any idea who might be behind trying to scare you?"

Iris shook her head.

"Do you know if Dr. Pinsky has any staff members or any workers in his office that would fit the description?" When Iris again shook her head, Bates went on. "What about his family? Does he have children?"

"I don't know about his family. All I know is that he is married and has school-aged children. I've never seen his wife or his children."

Officer Bates made some more notations, closed her book and smiled for the first time. "Thank you for reporting this and for the very concise statement you made. I'd like to remove that note and take it to the detachment for evaluation, including fingerprinting. We'll probably have to ask Dr. Pinsky some questions."

With that, she left.

Iris was still shaking, not only from the implications of the threatening note, but the police interview. "Pinsky is going to be furious with police involvement, especially as it's due to my instigation," Iris mumbled to herself. She wondered if the stalker was someone Pinsky knew. Certainly it wasn't Pinsky himself. The stalker had a very different build. Maybe the stalker was someone trying to do Pinsky a favour?

After another hour of ruminating on the whole ugly issue, Iris felt settled enough to attempt sleep. Eventually she did fall asleep, but wild dreams awakened her frequently.

Chapter Twenty-Six

Early December 1962

The Theology Department Christmas party was tonight. Iris felt ready for it. She'd just practiced her own parts of the pieces the ensemble would be using at the party. Tim had phoned her about a week ago to make sure they were ready to do the background music. Iris had asked if they could play a piece as part of the program and he had readily agreed.

Iris had about an hour to wait until Myra and Sandra would pick her up. She paced about her suite, pondering her busy, chaotic life. It had been nearly three weeks since Officer Bates had interviewed her about the stalker. Bates had called her back after a couple of weeks to say they weren't having much luck finding the stalker. They'd found no fingerprints on the note. Whoever left it had obviously been quite careful. The questioning of Dr. Pinsky came up empty. Pinsky had seemed quite surprised by the story of the stalker. The officer said his children seemed too young to be considered suspects. The oldest son was thirteen, but nothing suspicious had come out of interrogating him or his younger brother.

Iris felt a little unsettled by the police coming up empty. Still, she hadn't seen any sign of the stalker since the threatening note had been left. Maybe the police investigation had spooked the stalker.

Iris's mind turned to Tim. He'd probably arrange a private time with her, either at the party or soon after. With Milton out of the picture, but not from her heart, would she be open to Tim should he pop the question of marriage? She felt a flutter of anxiety in her stomach. There were so many issues in her life. She needed to see the chaos settle a bit before she could give herself to the question of marriage. First, there was the lawsuit. She still wondered if she'd done the right thing. Then she was still grieving over the breakup with Milton. Finally, there was Tim's theology. Ralph's espionage had revealed some disturbing features of Tim's belief system. She'd always known he was a bit liberal, but now she understood that he was thoroughly liberal, a bit more than she was comfortable with. Could she live with someone who held such different religious views? She knew others had been able to—even Trish and her dad lived comfortably with somewhat different views of Christian worship.

What about her own faith? She felt it was in tatters. She was just playing the religious game. She knew her faith was just a jumble of ideas rather than something that really governed her life. In recent years, her faith in Jesus had had little impact in making the decisions required in her life. She knew she'd become more self-centered, making decisions using only her own brain. There was no real hearing from God or trusting in him to guide her life. She yearned for the faith she'd had before she started university. Even Milton's faith was far deeper than hers.

The doorbell rang and Iris knew she had to shake out of her depressing thoughts. She needed to be cheerful, or at least act like it.

✦ ✦ ✦

There hadn't been any surprises so far. As she heard the boring speech by one of the alumni, Iris reflected back on how the theolog party had gone. The background music was a bit disappointing—few paid them any attention, more intent on impressing someone else with their exciting lives. Alcohol likely caused this effect. The special piece, a Schubert, they'd done just before the speech went well, judging from the applause.

The speech concluded the formal program. The bar reopened and there was an announcement about dancing in an area next to the stage. Iris could see Tim coming toward her. *Well, here we go,* she thought. *Be on your guard, Iris. Don't put him off, but don't commit to more than what you're comfortable with.*

"Hey, Iris. That was fabulous, especially that special you did in the program." Tim had a wide, appreciative grin.

"Thank you, Tim."

Myra and Sandra, sitting beside Iris, thanked Tim with big smiles.

Tim hesitated a moment and then asked, "Are all of you going home right away?"

Myra looked at Iris with a twinkle in her eyes and then back at Tim. "Well, I think Sandra and I need to be heading back, but I don't know about Iris."

Iris gave Myra a little nod and a slight grin of thanks. She looked back at Tim. "Oh I think I could stick around for a bit. What did you have in mind?"

"I presume you could handle a drink of your choice, and a snack, maybe?" Tim smiled hopefully. "Come, let's get something to eat and sit by the window."

Iris followed Tim to the refreshment table. She saw some wine, beer, and punch. When Tim asked what she preferred, she chose a glass of wine. Tim followed suit and then picked up a small plate of snack foods.

When they were seated, she gazed into Tim's face for a few seconds as though trying to read his thoughts. He was so handsome, especially when he blushed, as he did just then. "How are you, Tim?"

The way Iris held his gaze, he knew she wanted more than a superficial comment. "Okay, Iris. I've been kept quite busy with administrative work and planning new mission initiatives in India. And how are you?"

Iris filled him in on her polio research, and the lawsuit. She had kept him informed about it in previous phone conversations. Iris took another sip of wine and then continued, "Life seems so hectic right now, much of it being my own doing."

Tim popped an olive into his mouth and said, as he chewed, "Iris, it's just in your nature to be busy. I think you like it that way."

Iris laughed. "Yeah, I guess you're right. I can't seem to simplify my life. I probably need someone around me to keep me organized."

"Oh, I think I've a solution for that. You could marry an organization freak like me," Tim said with a laugh.

"So you still want to marry me, Tim? You're sure persistent, I'll give you that. I'm just surprised you haven't gotten tired of chasing me."

"I have to admit you've often frustrated me with your delaying tactics." Tim was smiling, but Iris could see his eyes remaining quite serious.

"I'm sorry I am as I am," Iris admitted with a grimace. "I often wish I were different and could easily make up my mind. I envy people like that." Iris's face had turned serious and a little sad. She wondered if now was the time to make up her mind. Perhaps she should just give Tim the nod toward marriage and get this prevaricating over with. Her mind flitted to the issue of his liberal theology. Well, she'd just have to accept their differences in that area. She had to admit she was a lot more liberal than she used to be. Perhaps a reasonable compromise could be worked out.

"Iris, sometimes I wonder if your hesitancy about marriage is because you still have feelings for Milton."

Iris jerked her head up. She had thought this might come up, but it was still a shock to hear the words. She opened her mouth, hesitated, then closed it and looked down at her glass. "Tim, I have to admit I *do* have feelings for him, but I know it is foolish of me. There seems to be no future with him. I'm hoping that once I get away from working in the same hospital, these feelings will subside." Iris was still looking quite sad, and tears started forming in her eyes.

"I do hope you can see the folly in these feelings, Iris." Tim's eyes were looking darker and Iris could see flickers of irritation in his face. "Although I don't have proof, I've been told that Milton has a male partner now. Apparently, he keeps him under wraps, as it were."

"Who told you that?" Iris's eyes were blazing. "I suppose it was your friend Delmar again."

"No, it wasn't. It was a nurse who attends our church. I won't say who she is without getting her permission. She told me she saw Milton with another guy in a café. She noticed they were looking at each other with overly friendly eyes and when they got up to leave, they had the gall to hug each other. I know that doesn't prove anything, but, at least to her, it looked suspicious."

"Well, I'm not impressed with the evidence. Guys hugging is quite common in some circles and it doesn't necessarily mean they're gay."

"Oh, to be sure. It's just a little strange for normal guys, don't you think?"

"Yeah, a bit uncommon in public like that, I suppose." Iris wanted to wave this revelation off, but it made her feel unsettled. She felt she wanted to defend Milton. Why was that? She should be happy that he'd found someone. She needed to get him out of her mind so she could focus on Tim. Yet, she felt anger toward Tim for going after Iris's relationship with Milton.

"Tim, I'm getting tired and I need to get to bed if I'm going to be any good tomorrow at work."

"Okay. I was hoping for some breakthrough in our relation. But I can see it's not going to be tonight. I can see you're tired." Tim put on a smile but Iris could see the disappointment in his eyes.

"I'm not trying to put you off. I'm still interested in searching for a way to bring our lives together. Give me a couple of weeks when, I think, I'll be less busy. Maybe we could go for a Saturday morning walk when both of us would be rested. Would that work?"

Tim's eyes lit up with some hope. "Sure, that sounds good to me."

✦ ✦ ✦

Medical rounds had just finished, and Iris was heading for the exit. She heard her name and when she looked, there was Myra. "Oh, Myra, I'm impressed that you psychiatry types have time to join us at rounds."

"I might not if I didn't have to pass qualifying exams," Myra said with a laugh. "They want us to know just as much as internists, it seems. Hey, why don't we have coffee together? I want to catch up with your life."

They headed for the cafeteria. When they settled at a table, they could hear carols softly playing over the ceiling speakers. They also noticed a few decorations tastefully attached to the walls and serving tables. Myra looked up after taking a sip of coffee and asked, "How have you been doing, Iris? You look kind of washed out, if you don't mind my being blunt."

"Yeah, I've been off work for the past few days," Iris said. "I must've gotten a gut virus from one of my patients. I was sticking pretty close to the toilet the first few days. In fact, for a while my vomiting and diarrhea was so bad, I didn't know with which end to face the porcelain. I was scared I'd need to go to the emergency department for IVs. I managed to avoid that by drinking frequent small quantities of pop and water."

The two chatted for a few minutes about how easily infectious diseases could be transmitted in a hospital. Then Myra asked, "How did things go with Tim after we left the Christmas party? I don't want to pry, but did you enjoy your time with him?"

"You'll make a good psychiatrist, Myra. Your questions always get right to the point." Iris chuckled, and took another sip of coffee. "It went okay at first, but then he brought up Milton. He wanted to know if I still had feelings."

"Hey, I think *Tim* would make a fine psychiatrist with questions like that," Myra cut in with a hearty laugh.

Iris laughed with Myra, but quickly sobered. "I admitted that I still did have some inappropriate feelings for Milton. Then Tim said Milton was seen having a quite intimate conversation with a guy in a café. He was even seen hugging this guy, right in public. Apparently, the person who witnessed this thought their behaviour quite odd and wondered if they might be homosexual. Of course, she passed it on to her church friend Tim and he told me."

"So you believed this report?"

"I don't know. The conclusions Tim and this girl came to may be suspect, I suppose."

"I'd not put too much stock in that gossip. Gay people aren't the only ones to do same-sex hugging, you know. The other thing is that I've never heard of Milton having any encounters with gay guys and I consider the gay grapevine quite reliable. I'm sure you realize that anything that puts Milton in a bad light favours Tim and his friends. I think he's jealous."

"That's probably true, but his passing on this bit of gossip made me angry. That finished the evening for me." Iris finished her coffee.

"Iris, if you would allow me another observation," Myra said with raised eyebrows and a smirk, "I think your angry response to Tim is revealing. It shows you're still in love with Milton and you've a deep desire to defend him."

"Should I pay you now for this insight or do I wait until you qualify?" Iris grinned. "You're right, but that fact brings me no nearer to a solution to my problems."

"The psychiatrist's job isn't to advise solutions, but to help the patient discover their own. I have confidence in your ability to do just that," Myra pronounced with an air of authority.

"Well, thanks a lot, Dr. Sometka. If you won't give me any solutions, I'll have to seek divine assistance. I'm flat out of any ideas."

"You know, if I believed in God, I'd be at his doorstep to help me see the right road ahead," Myra said with a seriousness that surprised Iris.

Iris stared at the inside of her mug, noticing the way the coffee had dried at the bottom. "You can be sure I'll be doing just that."

Chapter Twenty-Seven

Mid-December 1962

The morning progressed much as usual. Iris was heading toward one of the medical wards to check on new case of suspected polio. She wanted to include all new cases in her study. As she walked, she became aware that her feet and ankles didn't feel right.

When she stepped off the elevator, her foot caught on the rails for the doors and she almost fell. That seemed odd. Through the morning, she became increasingly aware of weakness in her ankles and feet. By the afternoon, she was stumbling from time to time and had to be very careful not to fall. She decided to get to bed early and hoped a good night's sleep would fix the problem.

The next morning, she awoke as usual with her alarm clock's insistent jangling. She swung her legs out to head for the bathroom, but fell headlong onto the floor. Fortunately, she was able to brace her fall with her arms. She realized her legs weren't working. Slowly she tried to stand again. With great effort, she hobbled to the bathroom. She also noticed pain in her leg muscles. What was wrong with her legs? A cold chill went through her whole body.

Polio.

She'd tried to use all the safety techniques in working with polio victims and their excretions, but maybe that hadn't been good enough.

Iris quickly formulated a plan. She needed to get herself to the emergency department. Slowly and with great effort, she got herself ready and even had a bite to eat. She got into her car, wondering if she had the strength to push down the break and clutch. She did manage to get herself to the hospital. There, a nurse she knew saw her stumbling along and promptly helped her to get to the emergency department.

Iris's plight caused quite a stir, as they all knew her. The emergency physician evaluating her was very thorough, and very curious about her research. He wondered if she'd had recent contact with new cases. She said she often visited new polio patients to enter them in her immunization study. That seemed to worry the emergency doctor. He also wanted to know if she had any recent illnesses. She told him about the episode of gastroenteritis that she'd had the week before. He didn't seem to know if that had any bearing on the diagnosis. When he felt the muscles of her feet and calves, she felt soreness. He tested her ankle and knee reflexes and found them weak. He then ordered some blood and urine tests. When these came back, the emergency doctor told Iris he was going to have a neurologist see her. Several neurology residents saw her before the staff neurologist came in. His evaluation took less time than any of the others. He ordered a spinal tap that Iris endured with great difficulty. She realized it hurt considerably more than she'd ever envisioned when she'd performed them on patients.

The hours of waiting for tests to be done allowed Iris to build up frightening scenarios of her future. *This has got to be polio,* she thought. Her career was now in jeopardy. In fact, her whole life would be changed. Radically.

Finally, the neurologist, Dr. Miller, and his team of residents trouped into her room. The neurologist said in his nasal voice, "There are still some tests that might have to be done, but at this point we are quite sure you have polio."

Iris's mouth was very dry as she murmured, "How much worse is it going to get?"

"Well, we can't tell for at least another two or three days. All we can do is admit you and closely monitor you for any progression of paralysis or weakness."

The neurologist was about to leave when Iris asked, "Do you think I got it from the patients I was doing research on?"

"Oh, you could have gotten it anywhere these days. There is so much of it around. Sure, your work with polio patients greatly increased your risk." With that, the neurologist and his gaggle of house staff swept out of the room, leaving Iris alone. Fear gradually enveloped her until she was in a state of terror.

A nurse came in to check her vitals. Iris asked her, "Could you please page Dr. Saunders and let him know Dr. Marten is in the emergency department as a patient?"

"Sure, Dr. Marten." She quickly left.

Iris heard his page and suspected he would be shocked by what the nurse would tell him. She knew they had formally broken up, but she also knew he'd very much want to know about this calamity.

In about five minutes, Milton walked in looking worried. "Iris, what's happening?"

Iris told him about worsening pain and weakness in her legs. She also told him what the neurologist said her diagnosis was and also about plans to watch her in the hospital. Milton looked stunned for a moment, and then asked for more details. He then nodded. "Well, it does look like polio. What did the spinal tap show?"

"They didn't tell me and I didn't ask. I guess I was too devastated to think like a doctor."

Milton placed a hand on her shoulder. "Iris, I feel a bit overwhelmed myself, but I'd like to pray for you. Is that okay?"

"Yes, of course. I'd like that."

Milton placed a trembling cool hand on Iris's forearm, and prayed softly into Iris's ear. "Dear God, bring your light into this dark time of our lives. We pray for your peace and courage." Both Iris and Milton had tears in their eyes when they opened them.

"I suspect they'll admit you to a medical ward where you'll be isolated," Milton said. "I was in the middle of taking a history, so I need to get right back. I'll keep in close touch with you and the doctors looking after you." Milton gently squeezed her shoulder and left.

✦ ✦ ✦

The night was a blur for Iris. She'd been given some sedative to help her sleep, but the hours passed slowly with a parade of wild dreams and a jumble of terrifying waking thoughts. Her life was coming apart. She felt like she'd fallen off a cliff and was spiraling down into an abyss. By morning, her mind was further assaulted by the realization that she could no longer move her toes or ankles and was barely able to draw her knees up. She also felt deep pain in her legs. She had been warned that she might experience muscle pain, a common feature of early polio.

Someone brought her breakfast, but she couldn't stand the thought of eating. She managed a few sips of juice. A parade of house staff filed through over the next few hours. All of them were gowned and masked, so she could see little of them. She tried to be civil as they questioned her. She knew all too well what it was like to have a non-co-operative patient. Milton came in later in the morning. She hated not seeing his face, but was pleased that his caring eyes were still visible.

Milton inquired about any progression of symptoms. He got her to lift up her knees with all her strength. "Not much there," Iris moaned.

"No. That has certainly changed from yesterday," Milton said softly. He then pressed down on her thigh and asked, "Does that hurt?"

Iris yelped. "Yes, it does."

A nurse came in to turn her to prevent pressure sores. Milton excused himself, but before he left, he squeezed her forearm and said he hadn't stop praying for her.

That afternoon, Peter and Trish arrived. Iris couldn't see their faces, but their eyes looked very worried.

"Oh, thanks for coming," Iris said, trying to sound at least a little cheerful. "How was the trip?"

"It snowed a bit last night, so there was snow on the shoulders of the road. Iris, we were told that they think you have polio. Is that what you think?"

"Well, I don't know what else it could be. I probably got it from one of the patients in the polio study."

"Where is it affecting you?" Trish asked with a quivering voice.

Iris told them about the progression of weakness and the muscle pain she was experiencing. "It could still get worse in my legs and involve other areas in the next day or so. Usually after the first few days, no further paralysis or weakness is supposed to occur."

Peter took Iris's hand and asked in an uneven voice, "Has anyone given you any prediction about long-term deficits?"

"It's too early to do that. You can be sure there'll be some—maybe a lot. I need to prepare myself for that." Her last words came out in a broken voice as tears filled her eyes.

"How is your spiritual life doing, Iris?" Trish asked as she took her other hand.

"Not so great. I'm just so confused and terrified. I try to pray, but I don't feel much coming back."

"Well, I'm not surprised. When we are full of anxiety, we often don't hear God's voice too well," Trish said. "He'll speak to you, Iris, I'm sure."

"This morning as I was driving in," Peter said, "I was asking God what Scripture to give you. The verses in the fourth chapter of Philippians came to mind. It says something like, 'Have no anxiety about anything, but in everything by prayer and supplication with thanksgiving let your requests be made known to God. And the peace of God, which passes all understanding, will keep your hearts and your minds in Christ Jesus.' I know it's hard not to be anxious about your situation, Iris, but God can do great things even in our hour of greatest weakness and need. But we do need to ask. Do you mind if I pray for you now?"

"Of course not, Dad. I certainly feel weak and in need. So I qualify," Iris said with a little smile.

Peter reached for Trish's hand and prayed a short, emotional prayer for wisdom and skill for the medical team and for healing for Iris. Mostly, he prayed Iris would experience the presence of Jesus in this very difficult time.

Trish looked up and said, "Iris, I see the nurse motioning to us to leave. They have things to do, I guess."

"We'll drop in again after supper, Iris," Peter said, his eyes glistening.

✦ ✦ ✦

The next two days went by much as the first. Iris was praying and desperately trying to bring her growing fears in check. Weakness was steadily progressing. She couldn't move her legs and pelvis any longer. This morning was December 24, a day to anticipate Christmas, but today would be only another day leading her into the long night of frightening unknowns. She couldn't sit up and wasn't able to hold a spoon. She had extensive weakness and pain in both arms.

The various nurses and house staff had moved in and out of her room, saying little. They'd been trying to look cheerful, but she could read their eyes and careful words. She'd seen that they looked worried. Her parents had been staying in Edmonton and had visited briefly twice a day. Tim had even come in, also briefly. He had seemed shaken and had said very little. Milton continued his daily visits. He'd made very careful inquiries regarding her symptoms and always smiled encouragingly, promising he was keeping up with his prayers.

When Milton came in this morning, Iris could tell he was struggling to keep cheerful. He carefully reviewed her areas of paralysis and weakness and then asked, "Do you still have a lot of muscle pain?"

"Yes, but it's not so bad, now. In the last day, I've felt this weird sensation in my legs when the nurses change the sheets. It's like a burning sensation on my legs and trunk."

Milton slowly shook his head. "That doesn't make too much sense to me. Let me see if you still have muscle tenderness." He began palpating and squeezing her thighs.

"Yeah, that hurts."

"That's odd for polio, at least in the cases I've seen," Milton said slowly.

"That's what I was thinking," Iris said with a rare sparkle in her eyes. "I've never noticed much muscle tenderness in patients. My life is never simple and straightforward."

Milton laughed a little. "Yes, I've always found you most unpredictable."

✦ ✦ ✦

When Iris awoke from a drug-induced sleep, it was Christmas morning. She noticed she couldn't raise the sheets up with her knees—not even an inch. She also noticed she could only shrug her shoulders a half an inch and her hands moved very sluggishly. Even more troubling, she had difficulty taking a deep breath. She reported this new finding to the first nurse who came around.

"I'll let Dr. Pedersen, the neurology resident, know." She briskly headed for the nursing desk.

When Dr. Pedersen came, he quickly reviewed her level of muscle strength throughout her body and then had her take deep breaths into a spirometer that recorded her maximum ability to breathe deeply. He looked concerned and said he'd be measuring her breathing every four hours. When Dr. Pedersen noticed her short, rapid breathing and dilated pupils, he asked, "Iris, do you feel very anxious?"

"Of course I do." She took a couple of short breaths. "Do you think I'm going to die?"

"No, Iris. We have many things we can do to help you. Your colour is still good, but you're very anxious. We'll give you something to settle your nerves. We'll also watch you very carefully. If you need help to breathe, we'll get you on the iron lung."

"You don't have to tell me about that. I've talked to many patients in that machine." Iris took another few gasps. "Many never get out of them and live." Iris's eyes filled with tears.

"Iris, you've a good chance that the paralysis won't get any worse now. You may just need a few days on the lung, if at all." At that, Dr. Pedersen walked back to the nursing desk. Iris thought he was showing optimism to keep her spirits up. She wished she wasn't so experienced medically; maybe then she'd more easily be cheered up.

✦ ✦ ✦

Early in the morning of the twenty-sixth, Iris's nurse became concerned with Iris's restlessness and slightly blue colour of her lips. Her last spirometer reading had been marginal. When Iris was jostled awake, her nurse took another spirometer reading and it was definitely lower than the limit Dr. Pedersen had given them. She phoned Dr. Pedersen and in a few minutes, he came rushing onto the ward. After quickly assessing Iris's situation, he ordered her to be placed in an iron lung.

Within fifteen minutes, she was inside the huge contraption. The electric motor was started, driving a big piston back and forth, rhythmically producing periods of vacuum around her chest that would draw air into her lungs and simulate breathing. Iris's colour soon improved, she settled down, and, with the aid of an intravenous sedative drug, slipped into a restful sleep.

Later that morning, Dr. Pedersen told Milton about Iris's situation. "She's sleeping in the lung. You might be able to talk to her this afternoon. Be prepared for her to be able to only speak between vacuum cycles."

"From a medical point of view, her outlook is a bit grim just now, isn't it?" Milton looked deeply concerned.

"What other point of view could there be, Milt?"

"I guess you're right. I've been praying for her," Milton said with a weak smile.

"Okay, you keep it up. She'll need all the help she can get." Dr. Pedersen smiled and put his hand on Milton's shoulder. "I know she means a lot to you. You can count on my doing everything I can do for Iris."

That afternoon, Milton gowned, masked, washed his hands, and walked into the iron lung room, where there were four lungs in action. He talked to Iris's nurse who told him Iris had woken and spoken to several of the staff. Milton walked to her machine. His breath caught as he saw his dear, beautiful friend at the mercy of an iron monster. He steeled himself. "Hi, Iris. I see you're awake and you're looking good."

Iris smiled weakly and, between machine puffs, told him how she was feeling. "Besides still living, I feel like I'm a worm, trapped in an iron cocoon, totally helpless."

Milton noticed something odd about Iris's facial features. "Iris, could you smile again? You know, smile as broadly as you can."

"Do you need cheering up, Milt?" Iris said with her weak smile.

"Yes, but just do as I say," Milton said with a broad smile of his own.

"I'll give it my best." But her smile was still weak.

"It's quite weak. And it's symmetrical. That's odd. Polio usually produces asymmetrical muscle weakness."

"Now you're saying I'm odd. Did you just come here to insult me?"

Milton shook his head and chuckled. "Iris, you haven't lost any of your wit."

✦ ✦ ✦

Dr. Pinsky trudged up the path to his house that evening, his mind on Iris. Ever since he'd received the subpoena, his mind seemed never far from her and the lawsuit. He knew his work as a department head was suffering. It didn't help that he'd been sleeping poorly in the past few weeks. Things were deteriorating at home also, with tensions often at breaking points. He had tried to shelter his wife Nancy from the details of the suit and the reasons underlying Iris's action, but he could see she'd taken an emotional hit almost as much as he.

As he opened the front door, the fragrance of the evening meal met him. He should have been pleased with that smell, but he had little appetite and was almost repulsed by it.

"George, is that you? Supper's almost ready. Call the boys down from their rooms, would you?"

As had been the case recently, little was said at the meal. About five minutes after they began eating, Mrs. Pinsky looked toward her husband. "Have you heard anything more about Dr. Marten? I heard that polio has been confirmed. How much paralysis has she got?"

"Dr. Logan told me she's been put into an iron lung today. Apparently she wasn't able to breathe enough on her own."

"That sounds serious, George. Do you think she might die?"

Dr. Pinsky shook his head. "Logan said her doctors were thinking she'd likely make it and that this would just be a temporary thing to tide her over until her diaphragm took over again."

"What's an iron lung?" Sydney, the ten-year-old son asked.

"It's a big barrel where they put the patient with just their heads sticking out," Gordon, the Pinsky's thirteen-year-old, stated as if everyone should have known that.

"How's stuffing her in a barrel going to help her breathe?" Sydney asked.

"They pump air in and out of the barrel, silly," Gordon said with a sneer.

"Quit jumping on Sydney like that," Dr. Pinsky said angrily. "How should he know that?"

"How did you find out about that, Gordon?" Mrs. Pinsky asked.

"You always take me for a dummy. I can read, you know." Gordon got up to leave the table.

"Sit down, Gordon, and don't sass your mother," Dr. Pinsky yelled. "When we're all finished, you can go to your room and get your homework done for a change. You could try to get a decent mark for once in your tests. So far this year, your marks have been a shame to the Pinsky name."

Gordon angrily slumped back in his chair.

When everyone got up to leave the table, Mrs. Pinsky said, "Sydney, you remember it's your day to do the dishes. Maybe everyone could stack the dishes to help Sydney get started." She caught Dr. Pinsky's eye and nodded for him to come closer. "Could we talk in the den?" she said softly.

When the Pinskys walked through the living room toward the den, they noticed Gordon on the sofa reading a book. "Is that electronics book part of your homework assignment?" Dr. Pinsky asked with sarcasm.

"No. I'm just keeping myself informed."

"Or, just wasting your time."

When the Pinskys settled into their chairs in the den, Dr. Pinsky asked, "What were you wanting to talk about?"

Mrs. Pinsky glanced at Gordon through the door and said in a soft voice, "George, I'm really worried about you. You're so irritable of late and you've been so hard on the rest of us, especially Gordon. And I think you're getting quite depressed."

Dr. Pinsky sighed. "Yeah, I admit I've not been very good to live with. Nancy, it's that damn lawsuit that's getting to me."

"I thought that was the problem. You've been tossing and turning every night. How much sleep are you getting?"

"Not much. I keep imagining sitting in a courtroom trying to defend myself."

"I don't get it, George. Why are you so worried? You'll almost certainly win the case. You're not doing anything other heads of research departments do. And even if you lose, you have lots of support among your colleagues and your malpractice insurance will cover all your costs. So, what's your worry, George?"

Dr. Pinsky combed his fingers through his greying hair. "Okay, I haven't wanted to trouble you with all the sordid details of this situation, but I guess I'd better tell you what the issues are. First, the consequences of this case, whether I win or lose, are greater than you may think. Last spring, the chancellor approached me and asked about progress in our research endeavors. He noted that we hadn't published much of consequence in the last couple of years. He also stated that there is a review process on each of the department heads and when our department came up for consideration, his attention was drawn to a young talented virologist in St. Paul, Minnesota, that was looking to return to Canada. The chancellor said he still wanted to keep me, but he hoped to see some good work published soon. You see, Nancy, the attitude out there is 'publish or perish.'"

"So, you felt threatened by this young virologist and you felt you needed to get your name on Dr. Marten's publication."

"Yeah, I was so focused on making myself look good in the publication I made it look as though the research breakthrough was mainly my doing." By this time, Dr. Pinsky's voice was no more than a low growl.

"But lots of research projects are published under the names of department heads, since these heads are always supervising the research. Isn't that the way it's done?" Nancy shifted to better look into Dr. Pinsky's sad eyes.

"Yes, that's often the case, but I can't afford to look selfish and unfair. This will stir up controversy and division. That's the last thing the university wants to see in a department. But, Nancy, the thing that bothers me the most is that I could have been more generous and given credit to Dr. Marten and her staff and I didn't. I was just too focused on getting university recognition. All my waking hours have me imagining Iris's attorney asking me why I didn't do it. And I have no answer. How much I would give to have another chance to do it right."

Mrs. Pinsky put a finger to her lips and nodded toward the door and Gordon who, she noted, hadn't turned any pages recently. Dr. Pinsky went to the door and closed it.

✦ ✦ ✦

Three days had passed since Iris was placed in the iron lung. Nothing much had changed regarding her medical status. There'd been no further weakening of her muscles, but she was still very much dependent on the iron lung. Iris was allowed to see visitors, but this was mainly family and those working on her polio projects. Tim had also been allowed to come, on Iris's request. He'd just made one previous visit, but this day, Iris was told a Mister Branton wanted to see her.

"Invite him to come in," Iris told the nurse. She wondered if he'd have more to say than during the last visit.

Tim had looked so shocked then. She couldn't blame him. What was she going to say to him? Well, she should be honest and open, to be sure.

"Hello, Iris. The nurse tried to prepare me, but you look so helpless in that contraption." Tim spoke with his head close to Iris so they could hear each other above the noise of Iris's and the three other iron lungs. The noise of the machines afforded them reasonable privacy.

"You're right. I feel totally helpless. The only thing I can still do is to think, listen, and talk in spurts." Even that sentence took several cycles of her iron friend.

They spent the next ten minutes briefly catching up on each other since he saw her last. Then Tim asked, "What are the doctors saying about the outlook for your recovery, Iris?"

"Very little, Tim. They don't have to. I know just as much as they do what to expect."

"And what's that?"

Ponderously, Iris tried to explain through the many interruptions by her machine. She ended by saying, "Tim, let's face it, I may not live 'til next year, maybe not 'til next week. Even if I get out of the hospital alive, I'd almost certainly be in rehab for years. Considering even the best chances, I'd very likely be severely handicapped and would have to be in a wheelchair the rest of my life."

Tim was quiet for several minutes, as he seemed to be trying to come to terms with this stark presentation of the truth.

Finally, Iris went on. "Tim, I don't want your sympathy. I only want you to accept things as they are. I know we had some plans for marrying, but now I want you to think long and hard about the wisdom of seeking such a thing. In fact, I would advise you to think of me as a nice friend you once had and then get on with your life. You must find someone else to marry—someone who can fit in better with your chosen vocation."

By the time Iris had finished, she was sweaty and pale. Her nurse slowly walked to them and remarked that maybe Iris needed a rest.

Tim looked blankly at the nurse and then back at Iris. "I'll give what you said a lot of thought. I feel such a sense of loss for you, and us, and what we might've had together."

"Thanks for coming and giving me a chance to say these things to you," Iris said with her weak smile.

Tim had tears in his eyes—the first Iris had seen, in her recollection. He nodded and slowly walked out of the room. Iris wondered if Tim was also walking out of her life, forever. A deep sadness enveloped her.

Chapter Twenty-Eight

December 29, 1962

IRIS FOUND HERSELF FULLY AWAKE IN THE MIDDLE OF THE NIGHT. SHE could tell it was 2:15 a.m. from her luminescent clock next to her head. Waking at night wasn't unusual since going into the iron lung three days ago. She'd insisted on only very light sedation, so she was only sleeping three or four hours at a time during the night. She looked about the room, but could see only the dark forms of other iron lungs. The familiar steady hums of motors and the rhythmical sounds of the pistons could be heard. No nurses were in sight. They were all in the nursing station next to the iron lung room and she could hear their low voices. She'd been told that if one of the machines malfunctioned, an alarm would go off at the desk. That was reassuring.

Iris was startled by what seemed like movement to the right of her. She looked as best as she could and saw a form move. It looked like a man, but she couldn't see his face or see what he was dressed like. She did notice that he seemed quite slim. She wondered if he was an electrician checking on the machines, as the electrical cords feeding the machines entered the wall where he was standing. Just then, a nurse came in with a flashlight and began talking to another patient who she found awake. All movement near the wall ceased.

When the nurse came to her machine, Iris asked the nurse, "Is there a workman checking the machines? I thought I just saw someone near the wall to the right of me."

The nurse swept her flashlight around the room. "I don't see anyone and I'm not aware that any technician was called in."

"Well, maybe I'm suffering from hallucinations from that sedative I've been getting." Iris's explanation seemed to satisfy the nurse, who resumed checking her patients. Iris remained somewhat unsettled. She stayed awake for about two hours, but then drifted off to sleep.

✦ ✦ ✦

Next night, Iris once again awoke, this time just after 1:00 a.m. The room was in semi-darkness, usual for the night. It was quiet except for the monotonous chugging of the machines. Iris was a little surprised she'd awakened so early. There were no nurses in the iron lung room, but she could hear voices through the open door to the nurse's desk.

But something wasn't right.

She looked toward the wall where her machine's electrical cord was plugged in. Nothing. She wondered if she'd been awakened by some unusual sound, but she couldn't remember what that might've been. Then she thought she heard a sound close to her machine, but wasn't sure. She tried to look in all directions to catch any movement, but as she was doing that, her machine abruptly stopped. She quickly looked toward the right wall and saw movement. It was a vague shadow of a person—too dark to make anything out. A jolt of panic hit her. She then recalled that there was an alarm that would sound at the nurse's desk. They'd soon arrive. She waited, but nothing happened. Her heart was loudly pounding in her ears. She tried to cry out, but nothing came out. Then panic really settled in. Someone was trying to kill her and no one was going to help her. Well, God was near and could hear her inner cry. *Dear God, help me now. Send someone to help me.* Gradually, the panic subsided as she became drowsy. The machine began to fade. Soon she felt herself drifting along what seemed a long tunnel.

✦ ✦ ✦

Milton was on call and had been summoned to see a feverish baby in the emergency department around midnight. Since the baby was less than three months old with significant fever, he knew he had to admit him and carry out a complete investigation. This would entail obtaining blood, urine, and spinal fluid cultures and then placing him on intravenous antibiotics.

Anything less could lead to disaster. Milton worked steadily to complete all that was necessary and had just finished writing the orders.

Milton stood, stretched his muscles, and walked slowly down the hall leading to the doctor's lounge. He wanted to wait there to get the latest results from the laboratory before going home. The lounge was empty. He sat down and his mind went to Iris. That wasn't unusual. He always seemed to be thinking of her, especially now that she was so sick.'

Milton recalled his last conversation with Iris just the day before. Iris had told him not to bother coming so often. She'd said he needed to get on with his life and find new relationships. He'd told her their relationship was the most important one he had. He'd never leave her as long as she lived.

Tears came to his eyes as he relived that visit. How tragic to see such a beautiful and brilliant life slowly fading away. Milton prayed again—for something, anything, he could do to help her. He tried to imagine what she would be doing just then—probably sleeping. Maybe she was awake, feeling depressed. Milton then began to feel anxious as if something was wrong. Maybe it was the baby he'd just seen. He phoned the ward and was reassured all seemed well. He hung up, but the anxiety grew. Something was wrong. Could it be with Iris? Well, there was one way to find out. He jumped up and headed for the iron lung room.

The nurses at the desk in the isolation ward looked up in surprise when Milton arrived. Nothing seemed out of order, judging from their relaxed demeanor.

"How's Iris?" Milton quietly asked. "Is she sleeping?"

The head nurse shrugged. "Nothing's changed. She was sleeping when I last saw her about thirty minutes ago."

"Do you mind if I see her briefly? I have to be sure she isn't awake and worrying or something." Milton's mouth was dry and he could feel his heart racing.

The head nurse frowned, but then raised her eyebrows. "For you, Dr. Saunders, we'll do anything. Go on in and check her out."

Milton headed quickly for Iris's iron lung. He stopped cold when he realized her machine was not operating and that Iris looked like death. A wave of prickles went up his spine. He pinched her ear, but no response. Even in the dim light, he could see that her lips were blue.

Milton's nervous system exploded. Instinctively, he grabbed her jaw, lifted it forward and placed his mouth on Iris's and blew into her lungs. He noticed that her lips were quite warm, so she hadn't been without respiratory support for long. He kept breathing for Iris for about thirty seconds. When he stopped for a second to see how she was doing, he could see her lips were pink and her eyes were fluttering open. Then Iris looked at Milton and mouthed his name. Great relief filled Milton. He yelled loudly to the nurse's desk to come and help him. As soon as he saw a nurse rushing through the door, he turned to Iris. "Iris, I'm going to keep on doing mouth-to-mouth until they get this machine working. Just relax and let me breath for you."

Milton gently positioned Iris's jaw forward again and placed his mouth over hers. He blew into her lungs rhythmically to simulate normal breathing. The nurses quickly put on all of the lights and tried to find out what the problem was. They soon discovered the machine wasn't operating and then, to their horror, found the machine's electrical cord pulled out of the outlet.

"Who could have done this?" the head nurse yelled. "I'll plug it back in."

Soon Iris's machine was performing smoothly and Iris's breathing was back to normal. Her colour remained good after Milton ceased his mouth-to mouth support.

Another nurse asked, "Why didn't the alarm go off? It must have malfunctioned."

The head nurse shook her head. "We just checked them all last Thursday. It was working fine then."

"Hey, the sensor here seems to have been tampered with. I'm sure it wasn't like that when it came from the manufacturer."

Milton looked closely at it and agreed. "I think we should call the electrician to get it fixed and to see what he makes of it in case he thinks someone tampered with it."

"I think we need to call the police as well," the head nurse said. "I'll first call my supervisor and she'll do it, I'm sure."

"You'd better call Dr. Pedersen," Milton suggested to the head nurse. "He should be aware since he's the chief resident."

One of the nurses observed that all the other iron lung patients had been awakened with the disturbance. She told the charge nurse, "I'd better settle down the other patients here."

"Sure," the charge nurse nodded. "Just tell them there was an electrical malfunction in that one iron lung and that it's okay now."

Milton realized the nurses were quickly and efficiently doing what needed to be done. He'd let them do their work. He felt his whole body quivering from adrenalin. Milton felt he urgently needed to talk to Iris, so he pulled up a chair next to her. "This must be very unsettling for you. How are you doing?"

Iris slowly turned her head toward Milton and gave him a weak smile. Between her inspirations, she said, "Milton, I want to thank you for saving my life. I asked God to send someone to save me and you were God's answer." Tears filled her eyes.

Milton responded in a quavering voice, "I'd just stopped in the medical lounge after seeing a patient. I began to feel very unsettled and wondered if it had something to do with you. Now I realize it was God's Spirit making me feel that way. So just thank him. God nudged me to see you just then. He loves and cares for you, Iris."

"I know he does. He told me."

"What do you mean, *he told you?*"

"I went down a long tunnel and then I came into a place of wonderful, soft light. Then I saw a man with the most loving and caring eyes I've ever seen. I knew it was Jesus. He said he loved me more than I could ever understand. He said not to worry about theology and human relationships. He'd take care of that. He asked me to listen carefully for his voice. Then he said, 'Now go back to the work I called you to do.' Then I felt myself sliding back into this machine again. When I did, I saw you looking at me very concerned. So, I'm okay."

Milton was stunned. He could see in Iris's eyes that something like this had happened to her. "Well that's amazing. You look so peaceful I can hardly believe you just about died. I think you really did see him. You look different."

Iris just smiled and rested her eyes calmly on Milton.

✦ ✦ ✦

When Milton returned to the nurse's desk, the nurses wanted to know how he found Iris. Milton told them about the vision she had of Jesus. The nurses looked perplexed and one asked, "Did Jesus tell her who pulled the plug?"

"No, he didn't. I guess he didn't think that was as important as the other stuff he said to her."

Milton was just going to tell the nurses more when they heard brisk steps. Two police approached the desk. The police introduced themselves and then asked about the incident. The nurses briefly told them the story.

"Could we interview each of you separately and then we'd like to interview the electrician when he comes in to look at the machine. If any of the patients in this room were awake and noticed anything before Dr. Saunders called for help, they should also be interviewed. Finally, we'd like to interview the patient, Dr. Marten, if that's feasible?" The head nurse and Milton agreed.

The nurses found a visitor's room for the interviews. Milton was first. He told the police about his feeling that something wasn't right with Iris and when he checked, he'd found her not breathing and the machine not operating.

"Did you notice anything unusual about the iron lung—anything that would have stopped it working?" one officer asked.

"Yes, we noticed that the electrical cord had been pulled out of the outlet. We also noticed that the sensor looked as if it had been tampered with. The sensor is there to let the nursing station know if the machine stopped for some reason."

The other officer asked, "Dr. Saunders, do you have any idea who might have done this?"

"No, I haven't any idea." Milton lifted his upraised palms.

"Can you think of anyone who might like to do Iris harm if they got the chance?" asked the first officer.

"Not really, unless it has something to do with the lawsuit Iris launched against Dr. Pinsky." Milton explained the conflict between Iris and her boss. After the interview, Milton went home to try to get a few hours of sleep before his work on the paediatric ward would resume.

The police carefully interviewed each nurse separately. When they'd finished, the sleepy-eyed electrician had just completed his evaluation of the iron lung's electrical system, including the sensor. The police asked the electrician, "What did you find? Was there evidence of tampering?"

"There sure was," the electrician said. "The sensor had been pulled away from the iron lung so the inner workings were exposed. A small sliver of wood had been placed between two points to prevent a magnet from closing a circuit when the current was interrupted. It was done quite cleverly so the alarm wouldn't go off at the nurse's desk."

"So you think this person had to know something about electronics to have pulled this off?" asked the first officer.

"Yeah, it would seem so. I couldn't have done it better if I had the mind to do it," laughed the electrician.

The nurse who talked to the other iron lung patients found all had been asleep until Dr. Saunders's call for help, so the officers decided not to interview them.

The officers then wanted to interview Iris. The nurses found Iris quite willing. The officers were told to speak softly close to Iris's ear so the other iron lung patients wouldn't overhear. When they started, one officer asked Iris if she'd seen anything suspicious. She told them of the two times she had seen something move in the room, near the outlets. She told them what she could about her sense that the moving form looked like a slim person.

"Have you ever seen or experienced anybody threatening you recently?" one officer asked.

Iris told them about the stalker and Officer Bates.

"Ah, yes," one of the officers said. "I remember being told about those incidents. Do you remember the body shape of the person you saw previously?"

"I remember the person appeared to be male and had a slim build. I've a feeling it's the same person who did this to me."

"Dr. Marten, do you have any knowledge of anyone who'd want to harm you for any reason?" an officer asked.

Iris told him about the suit she had launched against Dr. Pinsky.

"So, do you think it might be possible that someone who'd want to support Dr. Pinsky or be in the good books with him might have done this?"

"Yes, I think that's possible, but I've no idea just who that might be."

The police asked a few more questions and then said they would do their best to apprehend the person and keep her informed about their progress. Iris thanked them and they left.

◆ ◆ ◆

The next morning, Iris reviewed the shocking events of the previous day. Someone had made an attempt on her life. Maybe she'd have been better off if he'd been successful, she thought ruefully. She speculated on what the police were going to do. Likely, they'd interview Dr. Pinsky and some of his staff. She could imagine how angry this would make Dr. Pinsky. She'd be his enemy for life. Somehow, some of the bitter hatred she had for him had dissolved since her encounter with Jesus.

Iris's thoughts turned to Tim. She doubted he'd visit any more. She wondered what she would say if he did come. She asked herself what the main reason for her hesitancy about marrying him was. She thought about his loyalty. Would he still flirt with other women? She could perhaps live with that if he kept to certain limits. She supposed she could adjust to his vocation, as long as he stayed in Canada, but then there was the issue of his theology. Before the vision of Jesus, she was prepared to adjust to that, too. Since that encounter, she saw things differently. She knew now that she would always be faithful to Jesus. He was the most important person in her life. The awful truth of the matter of Tim's theology was that he saw a very different Jesus than she did. He could never share with her the most important person in her life.

Then she thought of marriage, sex, and having children. For her, these experiences would never be realized, even if she survived the acute stages of this disease. She would be lucky to even be able to follow her career to some extent. Finally, she remembered what Jesus said about that. *Now go back to the work I called you to do.*

So, that sounds like he plans to help me into my career in haematology. That is reassuring.

Milton came to mind. Why was it that his life was continually intertwined with hers? As often as she tried to push him away, events conspired to bring him right back again. She realized that these chance encounters were driven by his love for her. How could someone with homosexual orientation have this kind of deep love for her? She couldn't understand him. He once told her that he was trusting God that he'd be healed of this condition. Could the Jesus she saw do that? She supposed he could. But how many miracles had she witnessed in her life? Not many. Then she thought about what Jesus had told her. *Don't worry about your relationships. I'll look after that.* A deep peace flooded Iris as she imagined herself lifting her relationship with Milton and placing it squarely on Jesus' powerful and loving shoulders.

◆ ◆ ◆

Peter and Trish came to visit Iris. They had been briefed beforehand on the attempt on Iris's life. They were very concerned that Iris would be quite disturbed by the incident and would need counseling.

A nurse brought in an extra chair so both parents could sit next to Iris's head.

Trish began, "Iris, it's so good to see you looking so well. Your smile seems fuller than when we saw you last. Tell us, are you troubled or anxious about the guy who tried to hurt you?"

Iris smiled. "No, I'm not disturbed about that. Sure, I hope the police bring the guy to justice, but I'm not worrying about it."

Her parents seemed surprised by Iris's lack of concern. "Why's that?" Peter asked.

"Well, I saw Jesus while I was dying. He's changed a lot of things in me. I know both of you've had a vision of Jesus. Now I've caught up with you guys."

Peter and Trish looked at each other with their mouths open. "Tell us what happened," Peter said excitedly.

Iris recounted her vision of Jesus. Peter and Trish were so ecstatic they jumped up and hugged each other with joy and tears on their faces. Iris filled them in on the details of her dying experience and told them how her view of theology had changed to being Jesus-centered.

Peter moved closer to Iris. "I believe that what's happened may have been meant to hurt you, but in reality, it has transformed you for the good. As hard as your illness is for all of us, I can see God at work, so we need to take courage."

Peter and Trish sat with Iris for a while, not speaking, just sitting in the hope of Jesus. Iris offered her weak smile, and then drifted to sleep. They kissed their daughter goodbye and walked out of the iron lung room with lightness in their step that hadn't been there when they walked in.

Chapter Twenty-Nine

Mid-January 1963

MILTON WAS SITTING AT HIS APARTMENT DESK WITH SOME PAEDIATRIC journals, trying his best to read the important articles and at least skim through the summaries of the less important ones. He needed to keep doing this if he were to keep up with current scientific thinking in the area of childhood diseases. It seemed he could only focus on Iris. In the last few weeks, he had been obsessed with the tragedy of what had happened to her. He'd been pleading with God to have mercy and heal her—or, at least, help her recover some muscular function. Somehow, he felt he needed to quit whining to God and just do practical things to help make her life more meaningful, but what could he do?

Milton looked at the clock on his desk and saw it was nearly 10:00 p.m. While he changed into his pajamas, he breathed a final prayer. "Dear God, help me to see what I could do to help Iris. I have to admit I love her a lot. I know you do, too. Please tell me what I can do that would help her and please you." Milton flopped into bed and a few minutes later, sleep claimed him.

At 5:45 am, Milton awoke with the end of a dream still playing in his mind. It was about him trying to resuscitate Iris and not being too successful. He was relieved the dream wasn't real life. Then he recalled an earlier part of the dream, where someone had been asking him something while he gave mouth-to mouth to Iris. It was a woman, asking if the reason Iris wasn't responding might be because she had something other than polio. He'd stopped resuscitating long enough to tell her she was wrong.

Milton began turning over, in his mind, the features of her polio when she was admitted to hospital. He began to realize some things didn't fit polio.

For one, her muscle paralysis and weakness was quite symmetrical. This was unusual in polio. She'd also developed unusual and distorted sensations in her limbs and trunk, with tender muscles. Again, unusual. Her face was mask-like with a weak, symmetrical smile. He hadn't heard of that in any polio patients. He wondered if her doctor had noticed these aspects of Iris's condition. No one had been spending as much time with Iris as Milton.

Charged with a jolt of adrenalin, Milton rushed through his dressing and shaving, planning how he was going to use the day. He had to find time to do some serious reading about polio, particularly about the various ways polio might present in its early stages. Just before going down for breakfast, he made a list of objectives. First, he was going to read Nelson's Textbook of Paediatrics on polio and look over any review articles he could find on the subject in medical journals. Second, he was going to carefully read Iris's medical chart, especially looking at all the lab tests. Finally, he was going to see Iris. He'd go through her history as if he was seeing her for the first time. Then he'd do a neurological examination. He hoped she'd co-operate and he wouldn't get any flak from the nurses.

Later in the day, he got a chance to slip into the medical library. He first read through Nelson's description of polio. His suspicions were right. There were features that just didn't fit. One thing was that Iris's development of weakness was not only symmetrical, but it progressed well after the first two or three days. That wasn't usual for polio. In fact, her facial weakness appeared about a week after her ankles became weak—much too long for polio.

Milton then searched the literature for any articles on polio in the last few years. This was helpful in giving him ideas about some unusual ways the disease could present. Apparently, there were instances of what was called a Landry progression. With it, paralysis occurred later than usual in the upper spine and face. That, however, had been very rare and the weakness was asymmetrical.

Then he came across a review article on polio where the clinician was urged to consider alternative diagnoses. The alternatives given were mostly unknown conditions, as far as Milton was concerned. One got his attention. It was Guillain-Barre Syndrome. He'd heard of it, but wasn't sure he could remember its main features. He turned back to Nelson's Paediatric Text and read about GBS. As he read, his pulse began speeding up. The description fit Iris perfectly. He made a chart with all the features of polio on one side and on the other he listed the features of GBS. The next step was to review Iris's medical chart.

✦ ✦ ✦

Milton was off after five that day and decided to slip up to Iris's ward to look at the chart. He wondered if the nurses would object, since he was not consulting on her case. Furthermore, the nurses would've guessed that Milton had more than an academic interest in her case. When he got to the ward, all the nurses were busy helping the patients with their meals.

Milton nonchalantly pulled out her chart from the rack and sat down at a desk in the nursing station. His eyes swept through the admitting history. There was nothing there he didn't already know. The consultation report from the neurology resident, Dr. Pedersen, was quite detailed. On the physical examination part, Milton noticed that Len noted that both legs were about equally weak and he added a note indicating that finding was a bit unusual for polio. He made no other comments regarding any other diagnosis that should be considered. He was probably quite influenced by the neurologist, Dr. Miller. When he looked over Dr. Miller's consultation, the writing was hard to read and quite brief. Dr. Miller had noted that Iris was exposed to many children with acute polio and that she'd been incompletely immunized. He just scribbled "polio" on the bottom of his note and said she needed "careful observation for the next 24–48 hours," especially for diaphragmatic weakness.

Milton flipped over to the lab reports. The urine and blood counts were unremarkable. Then he found the spinal fluid reports; that would be the most telling, he thought. The spinal fluid glucose and the cultures were normal, not surprising. The spinal fluid cell count was well within normal limits. He had read that occasionally in mild cases of polio, spinal fluid counts could be normal in early stages, but in most cases of polio, the counts were significantly elevated. In Guillain-Barre Syndrome, the counts were nearly always normal. He looked at the spinal fluid protein and found that it was over twice the upper limit of normal, the typical finding in G-B Syndrome! In polio, the spinal fluid protein was nearly always normal or only slightly elevated in the early stages.

Milton could feel his heart pounding with excitement. He couldn't wait to go to the next part of his plan, to visit Iris. When he stood up and looked into the iron lung room, he could see that Iris was being fed by one of the nurses. That was always a slow and painstaking process, so he didn't want to interrupt them. He would have to be patient and find time with Iris tomorrow. He knew the nurses would wonder why it was necessary for him to examine Iris, but he was sure they would cooperate.

✦ ✦ ✦

The next afternoon, Milton walked over to the isolation ward. He thought the direct approach was the best in getting the nurses' co-operation. When he got there, he interrupted the head nurse in her chatting with another nurse. "Could I ask for permission to take a complete history on Dr. Marten and do a brief neurological examination on her?"

"Well, that's a bit unusual isn't it? You should know her story, judging from the many times you've been to visit her, Dr. Saunders."

Milton quickly thought of a reasonable excuse. "Well, I'm thinking of presenting her case at rounds and I need to be very sure about some things in her history and physical."

The head nurse smiled. "I'll ask her if that's okay." She got up and headed toward Iris. When she returned, she said, "Dr. Marten said it would be okay only if you smiled and were nice."

Milton placed the palm of his hand over his chest. "I hereby pledge to do just that."

When Milton strolled in, Iris smiled at his beaming face. "So now, you just have to be nice," Iris said between puffs.

"With you, that'll be so easy. I promise I'll be patient and careful not to hurt you."

"Okay, Milt, get on with it."

"To save time, I'll go over the history as I understand it and you can correct any errors." Milton reviewed the history from the chart.

Iris nodded. "That's pretty well it."

"What about before you noticed any weakness. Were you well?"

"I had a bout of vomiting and diarrhea about ten days before."

Milton made careful note of this part of the history. "Did you see any newly discovered polio cases in the last few weeks?"

"Yes, I'm sure I did. It would've been about two weeks ago. That's still within the incubation period, so I could have gotten it from the boy I saw."

"I understand you had only one shot of the Salk polio vaccine when you were a teenager. Why was that?"

"I had a bad reaction with a rash over a large part of my body, so I was considered too high a risk for more shots."

Milton stopped writing on his pad and looked up. "Now, besides weakness, what other symptoms did you notice?"

Iris took a moment for the machine to breathe for her. "I can remember I had muscle pain," she said, and then it was time to breathe again. "When I pressed into my calves or thighs, they were tender." Another breath. "That's about all I can think of."

Milton knew he'd have to limit his questions, as her speaking would be very tiring. "Tell me, exactly where the weakness started and how it progressed."

Iris carefully reviewed her story, labouring between the iron lung's mechanical interruptions.

"Are you saying the muscle weakness progressed slowly, starting in the feet and then upward to the calves, the thighs, the pelvis, the trunk, the arms, the swallowing weakness and finally, the breathing weakness?"

"Yeah, that's mostly it. The swallowing and diaphragmatic weakness occurred about the same time."

Milton made another note. "Was the weakness symmetrical?"

"There were slight differences, but mostly, it felt the same on both sides."

Milton rose. "Now it's time for a brief neurological exam, if I can find enough of your anatomy within this iron monster."

"Now, promise not to embarrass me, Dr. Saunders," Iris said with a smirk.

"I promise." Milton laughed. "I need to test your strength and your sensation. I will be discrete."

Milton put his hands through two portholes and took great care in testing her strength, comparing the two sides. He found the weakness quite symmetrical. Sensation was mostly okay, but he found her muscles tender. Sensation over her trunk and thighs was a bit distorted. Then he tested her tendon reflexes. They were absent, as would be expected in both GBS and polio. He did the Babinski test, a stroking of the sole of her foot. Her big toes went up and all of her toes splayed out. That was typical in GBS but not in polio, where there would be no response in the affected limb.

"It fits," Milton whispered excitedly.

"What did you say?"

"Oh, I'm just mumbling." Milton had made up his mind he wouldn't tell Iris his suspicions until he was absolutely sure. He wanted to run his findings past his friend, Len Pedersen, and maybe the heads of the Medical and Paediatric departments before talking to anyone else. He didn't want Iris to have her hopes built up only to have them dashed again.

Chapter Thirty

Mid-January 1963

MILTON WAS ON CALL THE NEXT DAY, SO HE HAD NO OPPORTUNITY TO see Len. He'd paged him and they'd made plans to discuss Iris's case today in the medical lounge. Milton had found keeping his focus on his work on the children's ward difficult. In his mind, he'd been formulating all kinds of arguments favouring GBS over polio. The implications were huge. If Iris had GBS, she'd most likely make a complete recovery in time. It might take months, but at least she'd have hope to sustain her. He couldn't wait to tell her. *Be patient,* he told himself. He wondered what was holding up Len. Perhaps he'd received an urgent call and couldn't come. He thought he was going to explode if he couldn't tell someone about Iris.

Just then, Len hurried into the room. "I'm sorry, Milt. I got caught having to explain my actions in a case to Dr. Miller. I'll get a cup of coffee and then we can talk."

Coffee in hand, they moved to a table away from some of the other doctors who were carrying on a vigorous conversation.

"So, Milton, you look excited about something. Let's have it."

Milton quickly reviewed the story and the physical finding of Iris, just in case Len had forgotten some of the details. Then Milton said, "You remember you made a comment in your history that you were surprised at how symmetrical Iris's weakness was?"

"Yeah, I remember that. Usually the paralysis in polio is all over the place, very asymmetrical."

"So, does that bother you?"

"Well, sure. What are you getting at? Do you think we should consider some other diagnosis?"

"That's exactly what we should do. There are just too many features of Iris's condition that don't match with polio."

"Okay, so tell me what you've got. I'm all ears," Len said, leaning forward.

Milton pulled out a sheet of paper comparing physical and lab findings in typical cases of polio and Guillain-Barre Syndrome.

Dr. Pedersen carefully studied the paper for several minutes, nodding periodically and stroking his blond curly hair. Milton waited patiently, admiring his friend's willingness to reconsider one of his own cases. Finally, Len looked up. "You know, you've made a good case here for GBS. If you don't mind, I would like to review Iris's medical chart and re-examine her. Then I'd like to do my own research on GBS."

"I can understand," Milton said after drinking the last of his cup of coffee. "In fact, I hope you do, to make sure I'm not missing something. Maybe you could look into something in her history that still mystifies me. She says she'd a bad bout of vomiting and diarrhea about ten days before her weakness began. See if you can find any significance in that fact."

"You bet I'll do that. Hey, this is getting exciting, Milt."

✦ ✦ ✦

A day later, Milton was writing up a history of a new admission when he noticed Len approaching the nursing station.

"Hey, there you are. I just want to tell you what I found so far." Dr. Pedersen excitedly took a seat next to Milton. "Do you have some time?"

"I always have time for this, Len. What have you got?" Milton laid aside the chart he was working on.

"Well, I agree with your neurological findings on Iris. Her sensory disturbances and her pattern of weakness fit GBS—not polio. The positive Babinski also fits."

Milton nodded.

"Then I did a pretty detailed search of the literature on recent reports of Guillain-Barre Syndrome and I found something really exciting. Several reports of GBS indicated that some viral-type infection had occurred around ten days before the onset of weakness. The infection was usually gastrointestinal. If that isn't exciting, I don't know what is!"

Milton became so excited he jumped up. "Do you think we could present Iris's case at grand rounds on Friday?"

Len looked up at the ceiling for a moment and then said, slowly, "You know, I think we could postpone the case we had planned and present Iris's instead. This can't wait. Oh, this will be sweet."

"I hope it doesn't make Dr. Miller look too bad. We have to be careful of that," Milton cautioned.

"Oh, I think he'll come up with a good argument for his diagnosis and if he can't, he'll figure out a good excuse. Don't worry about him. We need to be sure the heads of all medical and even surgical departments come. We have to come out of those rounds with a clear-cut diagnosis, for Iris's sake."

"Okay, who is going to do what? I'm happy with you doing the main presenting, Len," Milton suggested. "Is there anything I can do?"

"Yeah. Help me make transparencies for the overhead projector. Make up a table comparing the two conditions. That should be impressive. Maybe you can get a picture of her before and after the illness started. That will have to do in lieu of not being able to get Iris into the auditorium. I would want you to say why you first came to this conclusion. People need to know you were the one to first think of GBS."

"I don't think that's necessary at all. The only thing I want out of these rounds is an agreement on the diagnosis," Milton said.

"Sure, I understand, but I will ask you some questions about her, so be prepared to answer."

Milton nodded. "Okay, have it your way. We have our work cut out for the next few days."

Dr. Pedersen began walking out of the station as he called over his shoulder, "I'll give you a call at home tomorrow night to see how things are coming together."

Milton went back to the chart he was working on, but he was too excited to think properly.

✦ ✦ ✦

It was 10:50 a.m. and Milton headed for the auditorium for the grand rounds. Len and he had carefully prepared for this session. All the transparencies had been made to best show the presenting features of Iris's illness, the progression of her physical changes, as well as the laboratory findings. Great care was made to not give away the ultimate direction the rounds would take. Photographs would also be included. Milton had needed Iris's consent regarding the presentation of her case. That was not hard. Iris was so committed to medical education she could not refuse. She had wondered why her case merited grand rounds, though. Milton told her it was because her presenting features were a little unusual for polio and because she'd been only partially immunized. He knew this was a white lie, but he hoped she would understand later.

Getting permission to get photographs of her was more difficult. He had, for some time, had a photo of her on his night table. He'd obtained it when he'd visited the Martens in Badger Creek. Milton had shown her the photo and told her about asking a photographer employed by the hospital to prepare it so it could be presented at rounds. He also had asked if the photographer could take one of her in the iron lung. Iris had thought for some time, and then had looked to Milton's excited face. "Milt, I don't know what you've up your sleeve. You look like a small boy peeking under the Christmas tree. So how can I refuse? Just tell the nurse to brush my hair before that photographer comes."

Milton had made a summary of the literature search he and Len had done. He'd made a table of all the physical and laboratory findings on both polio and Guillain-Barre Syndrome to better show the comparison.

Both Len and he had advertised the meeting more than for most grand rounds. Each had personally contacted all the department heads, as well as other clinicians. They especially focused on the staff doctors who loved a good controversy at rounds. They were calling it, "An Unusual Presentation of Polio?" The question mark was Len's idea.

When Milton entered the auditorium, Len was already there, making sure all the equipment was working. Quite a few medical students and some staff physicians were already present. Milton saw a contingent of medical students and even some staff from the Royal Alexandra Hospital. That was thanks to getting flyers placed in the Alex. As 11:00 a.m. approached, people streamed into the auditorium. Soon there was not a seat left and extra chairs were brought in.

Milton sat next to Len in the front row and tried to calm himself. He hadn't been so excited in a long time. "Well, Len, I hope we haven't laid a big egg. We might get shot down, you know."

"That doesn't matter. We've done our best in this case. If some don't agree with us, it doesn't matter. The truth will come out over the next few weeks."

"You mean in terms of Iris's progress?" Milton said with a dry mouth.

"Yeah, Milton. You're just too pessimistic about this whole thing. I've a feeling this round is going to be a lot of fun."

The head of the department of medicine, Dr. Erlinger, stepped up to the podium and brought the meeting to order. He made a few housekeeping announcements and then announced the first case to be discussed. It concerned an unusual rash and was presented by the dermatological department. Many attendees filed up to the front of the auditorium to view the patient more closely. A dermatology resident gave a short discussion of the case, with further comments by a staff dermatologist. Milton's pulse began accelerating as Iris's case presentation was approaching.

The next and last case was then introduced and Len stepped up to the podium while Milton went to the overhead projector. Len briefly introduced the case, saying that most would recognize the patient. Len nodded to Milton and he put on the first picture of Iris. It was a lovely one of her sitting on some wooden rails in front of the Marten home. She had a wonderful teasing smile. There were many chuckles and murmurs throughout the auditorium. When the next picture was shown of her in the iron lung, there were a few sympathetic groans.

Len gave a precise account of all the presenting features and laboratory results. Len was careful to tell the truth, but not emphasize the findings that would bring the diagnosis of polio in doubt. He went on to say that the Neurology service was consulted and Dr. Miller also saw her. He pointed out that the admitting diagnosis was acute paralytic poliomyelitis.

"We were aware that she had only been given one polio shot as a teenager because she developed a rash," Len said. "We were also aware that she'd been exposed to a number of new cases of polio in the last month. You may know that Dr. Marten has been involved with polio vaccine research in this hospital in the last six months."

Len then looked over to Milton and nodded. "Now I'd like to turn the meeting over to Dr. Saunders, who began to notice some unusual features about the patient." Len stepped away from the podium and took his place at the projector.

Heart pounding and face flushed, Milton stepped up to the podium and looked over the attentive but silent audience. "A few days ago, I read Dr. Marten's chart for the first time and noticed Dr. Pedersen's comment about how unusual it was to see such a symmetrical pattern of paralysis in polio. It was that and a few other features of her physical findings, as well as her lab results, that made me wonder if the diagnosis of polio was right."

Milton discussed the results of his medical literature research. He pointed out that Dr. Pedersen had helped in this project with his own research and important observations. Milton said that the main alternative diagnosis that should be considered was Guillain-Barre syndrome. Milton then pointed out the distinctive features that differentiated between polio and Guillain-Barre Syndrome. Len put up a transparency of Milton's carefully prepared comparison chart.

Milton paused. "Dr. Pedersen and I have come to the conclusion that Dr. Marten has Guillain-Barre Syndrome, not polio." Milton looked over to the head of the department of medicine, who had been chairing the proceedings. "I'll now turn the meeting back to Dr. Erlinger."

Dr. Erlinger walked to the podium and said, "Well, well. That was a heart-thumper of a case. I'm sure there'll be questions and comments. Who wants to be first?"

There were many questions asked. Milton and Len fielded them without difficulty. Then Dr. Miller stood and walked toward the front of the room. Dr. Erlinger motioned him to the microphone. He cleared his throat and said, "I think we need to be careful that we don't make a mistake in our gleeful rush to a fancier diagnosis. There are some things to remember. First of all, some new cases of polio present with no increase in CSF cells. Secondly, CSF protein can be a little elevated in new cases of polio. Finally, there are cases of polio, well reported, that can show an unusually late progression of paralysis into the facial area. This is known as the Landry progression. In all due respect to the good work done by our keen residents, I think we should move carefully. We don't want to give our patient too much hope before we are more certain of the diagnosis." Dr. Miller didn't wait for questions. He turned from the podium and walked back to his seat.

Several of the younger physicians waved their hands for attention. Dr. Erlinger pointed to a resident in internal medicine, who said loudly, "I believe the case for GBS has been made very well here. I've seen a case recently and the picture was virtually identical with that of Dr. Marten."

The other physician, a paediatrician who had just qualified in the last year, said, "The sensory distortions, the muscle tenderness, and positive Babinski signs are never found in polio. Furthermore, the CSF protein, being over twice the upper limits of normal, is conclusive in my mind. Dr. Marten has GBS, plain and simple."

There was considerable chatter at that point, with most comments in favour of GBS. Dr. Erlinger tapped on the microphone to get everyone's attention and then began his closing remarks.

Dr. Miller raised his hand. "Would you mind if I made a few additional comments?"

"Of course, Dr. Miller. Do come up to the podium."

Dr. Miller slowly approached the podium as if he were trying to formulate what he was going to say. When he got there, he looked over the audience and then said, "I need to make an apology and give credit where it is due." He paused a few seconds. "I made my diagnosis of polio on the basis of my findings on the day of the patient's admission. I admit that I didn't carefully follow her case thereafter so I could see the progression of her paralysis." Dr. Miller looked over to Len and Milton. "These young residents have done their job well. They've made careful observations and were thinking and doing the work that's needed in the high level of medical care we look for in this hospital. I want to commend both Dr. Pedersen and Dr. Saunders for their excellent work. I'm now convinced that Dr. Marten does have Guillain-Barre Syndrome." With that, he walked back to his seat and the auditorium erupted in loud applause and even some cheering.

Dr. Erlinger waited until the applause subsided to say, "Well, I think we've been treated to very exciting and informative rounds today. And I want to add my congratulations to Drs. Pedersen and Saunders for organizing these rounds and showing us all the obvious fact that they will make great specialists in their chosen areas in the future. Thank you all for coming." With that, the grand rounds concluded.

As everyone got up to leave, several physicians crowded around Milton and Len. Among them was Dr. Miller. He said to Milton, "Dr. Saunders, we need to tell Dr. Marten about this new diagnosis. I think you should be the one to do it, in view of all the work you've done to establish the diagnosis. The rest of us can meet her in the coming days to confirm what you tell her." The doctors readily agreed with that suggestion.

As they walked out of the auditorium, Len said to Milton, "You did well, Milt. Now go talk to Iris. I'll go around later this evening and confirm what you say, as if that were necessary."

"Thanks, Len. You've been such a help to me in all this. I really appreciate you."

Milton headed for the iron lung room with his mind in a whirl. How should he present Iris this news? He recalled that he'd once prayed that Iris would be healed, but in recent days, he'd forgotten that prayer. As he walked, he sent up a prayer of deep thanks to God.

The ward was quiet and the nurses were all doing charts. He smiled at the in-charge nurse and asked, "Is it okay to see Dr. Marten?"

The charge nurse looked up. "Well, she might be sleeping, but you can go in and see."

When Milton got to Iris's machine, he could see she was indeed sleeping. He sat down on a chair and reached through the portholes, placing a hand gently on her forearm. Her eyelids fluttered open. She looked at Milton a moment. She then gave him a big smile and sleepily asked, "How did the rounds go?"

"Good," Milton said without giving anything away. "We all agreed that you look very beautiful."

"Oh, Milton, you're an incurable liar. The picture of me in this machine would have been quite pathetic, I'm sure. Now tell me what they thought of your presentation."

"Well, they told us that Len and I did a good job."

"So did anything new come up? Were the other doctors in agreement with the management of my care?"

Milton was so excited he felt he could burst. "Iris, I've come to tell you what Len and I've been thinking for a few days now, and what the conclusion of the rounds was. We think you've been given the wrong diagnosis. Instead of polio, we think you have Guillain-Barre Syndrome."

"What?" Iris's eyes were wide and her pupils dilated. "I'm not sure I remember what that disease is."

Milton briefly told her about GBS and the fact that the prognosis for complete or near-complete recovery was excellent.

"Milton, you aren't fooling me, are you?"

Milton was grinning and very flushed. "You need to trust me. The other doctors, including Dr. Miller, wanted me to tell you first. Some of the others will talk to you later and confirm what I'm saying."

Milton filled Iris in on his early suspicions, his and Len's research, and the discussion at rounds. "Iris, the picture is now quite clear. You have a condition that'll resolve in time, hopefully completely. It may take time, like two to six months, but you'll get well."

For the first time, a glimmer of hope shone in her eyes and she gave Milton a big smile. "You always seem to play an important role in my life. Why is that?"

"I'm not sure. It may have something to do with how much I care for you. By the way, I think your smile is more complete in the last few days."

"Well, today's smile is stronger because I'm so happy. Thank you for all the work you've done to come to this diagnosis and thank you, God, for giving me hope again."

Milton looked at Iris's happy face. He noticed her lips and thought, wouldn't it be nice to touch them again with his—not to try to save her life, but to kiss them.

"Milton, could you please phone my parents and tell them the news?"

"That would be a pleasure, Iris."

"Now, Dr. Saunders, you must have some lunch before they close the cafeteria."

Milton smiled inside and out at the return of Iris's banter. "Thank you for being aware of my needs, Dr. Marten. Yes, I need to move it if I'm to find some food. I'll see you tomorrow sometime. Goodbye."

Iris smiled again in reply. For sure, her smile was stronger.

✦ ✦ ✦

As soon as Milton got back to his residence that evening, he called the Marten family. When he got both of them on the line, he said, "Iris wanted me to give you a message. It's about her diagnosis."

"What do you mean? Does she have a worse form of polio than they initially thought?" Peter's voice sounded quite anxious.

"No, not at all. You see, a few days ago several of us residents began to think she might not have polio at all. Now we think she has a condition known as Guillain-Barre Syndrome. Other doctors agree with us."

"What's that?" Trish asked.

"It's a condition that can follow an infection like gastroenteritis. Ten days after an infection, one may develop a progressive weakening and paralysis of one's muscles, starting from the feet and slowly progressing upwards to even affect their breathing and facial muscles."

"So, is there anything that can be done to help people like that?" Peter asked.

"Actually, the only thing that can be done is to support the patients until they start recovering. That might involve supporting their breathing, as in Iris's case. The recovery is a slow process with recovery of strength in the opposite direction—from the face to the feet. That might take two to six weeks, or even longer. In most cases, recovery is complete. Some residual weakness occasionally is seen."

"Oh, Milton! That's a much better outlook than with polio," Trish said with obvious relief. "At what point can she be discharged from the hospital?"

"I'm not in charge. I'd think that when she can breathe, swallow, and eat on her own, she could be discharged. She'll need someone who can help her with her bathroom needs and can help her with her mobility."

"How and when do you think we can help, Milton?" Peter asked.

"That all depends on what you are prepared to do. It might involve quite a bit of work, at least initially."

"Well, I can do lots of things if I am shown how," Trish said with conviction. "I could spend a few days at the hospital prior to discharge and learn from the nurses ways to help Iris. I'd have to take a leave of absence from my work at the library. Milton, we've been so worried. We'd do a lot better if we could do practical things to help her."

"Yeah, I'd hoped you'd be prepared to do that. I'm sure Iris would do better recuperating at your place than anywhere else."

"Thanks so much for all your care for our daughter," Peter said. "You seem like family, Milton. We think so highly of you."

"Thank you for being such wonderful parents for Iris—and for me. I feel you are parents to me, too."

"Okay," said Peter shakily. "We'll wait to hear from you about her future progress, Milton."

Chapter Thirty-One

End of January, 1963

THE NURSES WORKING IN THE IRON LUNG ROOM WERE ECSTATIC ABOUT Iris's improvements. She had full facial movement and her swallowing reflexes were strong now. She was also showing some good shoulder movements. As the nurses were excitedly reviewing Iris's latest accomplishments, a police officer came to the desk and asked if he might see Dr. Marten for a few minutes.

"Is it an update about the guy who tried to hurt her?" the charge nurse asked.

"Yes. I wanted to bring her up to date on our investigation as we promised her."

The charge nurse escorted the police officer to Iris and set out a chair for him. The nurse reintroduced the officer to Iris and left.

"Dr. Marten, we promised to keep you appraised of our investigation."

"Thank you for coming," Iris said in her usual halting manner. "I've wondered how things were progressing in your department."

"Well, our progress is slow, I'm afraid to tell you. No fingerprints were found. He was certainly a careful fellow. We know he had a good understanding of electronics. We've interviewed a lot of people and haven't come up with much from that effort. I can say that we interviewed Dr. Pinsky and he seems to know nothing of this. He denies any knowledge of anyone who might want to gain his favour by trying to harm you. We're sure he isn't the person we're looking for."

"Well. I guess not," Iris interrupted. "Dr. Pinsky is pudgy in build. This guy was rather small and slim."

"Yes, that's what we thought," the officer said. "We interviewed Dr. Pinsky's wife and his children and little came of that. He has two sons, one aged ten and another aged thirteen. The thirteen-year-old guy wouldn't say much, but what he did say indicated that he took little interest in what his parents are doing. The ten-year-old boy was very talkative and said his older brother was a loser. The parents said their oldest son could be very good in school if he tried. They said he was very bright but difficult to manage, whereas their youngest was a breeze. We also interviewed all of Dr. Pinsky's staff and really came up empty."

"That doesn't sound very hopeful."

"We haven't given up by any means, Dr. Marten, but right now we don't have any good leads."

As the officer left, he said, "We'll keep you posted, Dr. Marten."

"Thanks," Iris offered, feeling a little unsettled. Would she be harassed again?

✦ ✦ ✦

By February 15, Iris was able to breathe on her own for about ten minutes at a time. She could handle food items with her hands and bring them to her mouth. All of her facial weakness had disappeared and she could speak much better when off the iron lung. She worked very hard to be as independent as possible.

Iris spent much time thinking about her relationship with Jesus. Many times each day, she'd recall his image from the vision. He seemed to be calling her to a more intimate relationship with him. She wanted this, of course, but she couldn't read and few wanted to read a Bible to her other than Trish and her dad when they visited. She thought about Tim and his church. She realized she'd taken on a much more liberal view of Scripture since being involved with that church. In the last few weeks, she'd been praying to God that he would help her understand how to take the Scriptures.

On this day, she'd had another brief dream about Jesus while snoozing after her meal of ground-up solids and juice. In the dream, she remembered asking Jesus for guidance on the Bible. She didn't get an answer in her dream, but after awakening, a thought came to her quite forcefully. *God made mankind capable of communicating with him and reflecting philosophically on life. Surely, God would be faithful to mankind to provide a reliable revelation of the truth about God, mankind, and life in general.* That revelation was the Scriptures of the Old and New Testaments. She knew she had to decide what she was going to do with the truth of those Scriptures. Well, she decided she was going to believe what Jesus and the apostles said in the Scripture. After that, she felt much more settled about that issue.

✦ ✦ ✦

Milton had finished breakfast in his boarding house and gone back up to his bedroom. It was Saturday morning. He wasn't on call. In the last few weeks, he'd been pushing his studies a lot, preparing for resident tutorials. He was determined to keep up his plan to thoroughly research each clinical case he saw on the ward. Today, he wanted a break from that. He wanted to relax and think about his life—where he was headed. He decided to take a walk along the river valley. The weather had been relatively mild and the walking paths were clear and dry. He would head out to Saskatchewan Drive, find a place to park and walk from there.

He pulled on his runners and jacket, and soon was driving to his destination. What a lovely day! The sun was warm. The trees, shrubs, and snow-covered lawns seemed to be anticipating spring. After parking, he headed down the path. He decided on a modest jog so he could think about his life, not his aching muscles.

Milton's thoughts drifted to his church. He remembered chatting with Dr. Sandoski and his wife after the morning church service. Dr. Sandoski looked older than when he had been his professor, but was still as bright and cheerful as ever. His sense of humour was always so wholesome, never demeaning. He and Patrick were his role models for life.

Patrick had been a father and a pastor to him. The whole group reflected the love and caring the Bensons had within them. He knew he needed the group's fellowship more than food or sleep. He rarely missed the weekly meetings; the only exceptions were when he was on call.

Milton stopped jogging and just gazed at the parliament buildings and wondered for a moment what the legislators were up to. He had no time for politics in his hectic life. He looked back at the trail and walked briskly. *Just keep in the path the Lord is laying out for me,* he thought.

The question of his homosexuality once again invaded his brain, as it often did. He'd learned to relax about that, at least for the time being. He just kept giving any anxious thoughts to God, trusting him to guide his thoughts to please God. He realized he still found it easier to relate to women than to men, but he had taken Patrick's advice to talk to and inquire into the lives of heterosexual men. He'd found that though he'd be initially nervous, the conversations would go better than he'd anticipated. He also used every opportunity to shake hands with and, if that seemed appropriate, even hug other men. He found that men related with each other a great amount via sports. He was never very interested in sports as a teenager and, until he started attending the small group, he avoided sports as an adult. Recently, he decided to try playing sports with other guys no matter how this frightened him. He was amazed how athletic he was proving to be. He even had begun challenging other men to play racquetball. Mostly, he lost these games, but he didn't care as long as they were having fun. He intuitively felt that all this effort to relate to heterosexual males in a non-sexual way was paying off. Just how much, he wasn't sure. He decided to give that judgment over to God and let him worry about it!

He was excited about some changes he'd noticed inside him. Just the day before, while making ward rounds with nurses, his mind flipped to the appearance of the nurse telling him of her patient observations. His eyes had drifted down from her attractive face to her neckline, where he could see the upper gentle swell of her breasts. He caught himself being excited by the prospect of touching her breasts and feeling them against his body. He'd quickly yanked his thoughts back to the patient the nurse was addressing. As he reflected on this event, he was a little embarrassed, but also delighted that it had happened. It was the first time a woman, other than Iris, had affected him this way.

Not surprisingly, he once again thought of Iris. Would she ever fade from his life? He doubted it. Her lovely face filled the sensitive screen of his mind. And those lips he'd touched with his own now fired his imagination. He was replaying the mouth-to-mouth resuscitation scene over and over in his mind, even in his dreams. He imagined touching them again, this time when she was brimming with the health she'd regain in time. He shook his head to reset his imagination. He couldn't allow this kind of thinking to go on. He had little idea how relations were between her and Tim. Even if that relationship had ended, could Iris and Milton ever build something between them? Only God knew. What would Iris think of their lives being lived together? He knew Iris had feelings for him, but she was a rational woman who would not let her feelings make her decisions. Would she be willing to experiment in them getting married? She'd probably think that there'd be too much risk, no matter how much he would claim to have changed.

Milton determined to get on with what he knew he should do, and that was become a paediatrician. With that thought, he broke into a brisk jog again.

◆ ◆ ◆

Spring had arrived, at least by the calendar. Iris had shown great determination to free herself from the iron lung through the month of March. By mid-March, she made up her mind she no longer needed the services of the iron monster. A nurse had been assigned to watch over her during sleep to make sure her colour remained good. By March 21, she was pushing herself around in a wheelchair. Leg movements were coming along, but her legs were still too weak to bear her weight. Iris had been transferred to a regular medical ward.

One of the nurses stepped into her room and announced, "You have a visitor, Dr. Marten."

Myra walked in with a big smile.

"Myra, what a pleasant surprise. A visit is far overdue. I'll get into the wheelchair and we can go to the cafeteria to have an old-time chit-chat."

"Oh, really?" Myra looked very surprised. "I thought you were still bedridden."

"Just watch me!" Iris said with a sparkle of excitement in her eyes. "Give me a hand with getting the wheelchair next to the bed so I can transfer."

Soon, Iris had herself in the wheelchair. She was dressed in jogging clothes to facilitate these transfers. She pushed herself out into the hallway and then to the nurse's desk to tell them where she'd be. "You can push this device if you think we're going too slow for your liking. You're always in such a hurry."

"I'll do that," Myra said. "I don't want you so tired you can't visit when we get there."

After getting their coffee and snack, they found an empty table and settled in for a visit. They chatted about events in each of their lives from when they had last met.

With their snacks eaten and their coffee cups empty, Myra asked, "So when are you going to be discharged?"

"My goal is to be out of here by the end of March. They want me to be able to manage walking a little on crutches before I go. I think that's achievable. Even the physiotherapists think so."

"I love your determination and optimism. Where are you going to recuperate?"

"I'll go to my parents' in Badger Creek. They've got everything ready for me."

"What happens the first of July? Are you going to try to start haematology?"

"No, I won't only try. I *will* start haematology July first," Iris said with fire in her eyes.

"Okay, okay. I get your point," Myra said, facing up her palms toward Iris as if holding up a stop sign. "Hey, I'm really excited for you and your future. You've lost nothing because of your illness. I suppose you're going to pursue your suit as well then."

"Yeah, I guess I will. Since I nearly died and had some visions of the afterlife, I've had a little change in motivation regarding the suit."

"How so?"

"Well, I now see that I'm carrying on with it more for the others who worked with me. They deserved better recognition for their work. They're looking to me to help them through this suit."

"Oh, so you're now selflessly working for the good of others," Myra said, grinning crookedly.

"Yeah, I suppose," Iris said with her face quite serious.

"Would you tell me about these visions of the afterlife, please? I might have to make a referral to one of my staff psychiatrists if you don't explain yourself better than that." Myra's grin had turned wicked.

"I'm not scared of you or your mental gurus," Iris came back with a grin of her own. "I'll tell you just the way things went for me and you can think whatever you like."

Iris told Myra what happened after someone unplugged her iron lung. She held nothing back even though she knew Myra would try to explain the whole experience via the grid of her psychiatric training.

When Iris finished, Myra sat with her mouth hanging open. Finally, she said, "Iris, I don't know what to make of all that. I've heard of something like that happening to people who've been brought back from the brink of death. They call it a near death experience. I suppose that's what you had. Did this Jesus look like any paintings of Jesus that you might have seen?"

"Actually, no. He didn't look like anyone I've ever seen before."

"What do you make of the idea that this Jesus would look after the theology issue?"

"I think it means that he'll help me straighten out my thinking about my view of Jesus. You see I'd gotten quite liberal in my thinking, going to Tim's church. I think Jesus wants me to take what he said in the Bible more literally."

Myra raised her eyebrows. "Iris, you aren't going to go fundamental on me, are you?"

"I really don't know and I don't care. Whatever I am, I am. I've just made up my mind to listen to Jesus as best as I can. That's not going to change our relationship, Myra. You can be sure of that."

"That's reassuring," Myra said with her hand over her heart. Iris didn't know if Myra was being completely serious or not. "You did say this Jesus said he'd help with your relationships. Did he say anything about Milton?"

"No, nothing. Jesus just told me not to worry about my relationships. I'm trying, but it's not easy. I've long tried to discourage Milton and I being together, but he keeps intersecting with my life. It's not that he's pushing this at all. Life just seems to be developing that way, like when he resuscitated me. I keep pushing him away, but I don't think I could live without him." Iris had tears shining in her eyes.

"Now that's an inner conflict that could use some professional therapy, don't you think?" Myra was trying to use a bit of humour to deal with the emotional tension. Myra remained quiet for a moment and then said, "I really don't have any words of advice for you. I doubt you were looking for that from me. I want to tell you I really care about our relationship. I've so valued our friendship. I'll always be your friend as long as you let me."

"Myra, you've always been so open and transparent with me, and I know you really care for me. I respect you so much. How could I ever not be your friend?"

Myra got up, came next to the wheel chair, and hugged Iris. Both had tears in their eyes.

✦ ✦ ✦

It was the last day in March and Iris was going to be discharged, just as she'd planned. The physiotherapists had been working relentlessly with Iris to coax her weakened thigh and leg muscles into action. Every day, they'd been noting improvements. In the last two days, Iris had been working with crutches with minimal success, until this morning. With intense determination, she was able to walk about six feet. She'd met the goal set by the physiotherapists. She was able to transfer herself between chairs and bed, and on and off the toilet.

Trish had traveled to Edmonton by bus and arrived the day before discharge to learn the routine and get advice from the physiotherapists. She'd stayed all day and had been an enthusiastic learner. The physiotherapists felt Trish was doing so well, she should consider doing that as a profession!

Peter had driven from Badger Creek and walked into Iris's room just as she was eating her last meal in the hospital. Teary-eyed hugs followed, and the three chatted cheerfully for the next twenty minutes.

"Well, I see you're ready to go, Iris," observed Peter. "Do you have other stuff from your apartment to take along?"

"Yes, I'd like you and Trish to help me pack a few things."

"Okay, we can do that after we leave the hospital. When we go to your apartment, you can use the wheelchair I brought."

"Sure," said Iris. "There is just one thing I need to do before we leave here. I want to page Milton to see if he wants to say goodbye. He asked me to do that before I left the hospital."

Iris pressed the buzzer to alert a nurse and soon had Milton paged. In five minutes, Milton walked into the room. Cheerful greetings with the Martens followed.

"You mustn't have been too occupied with patients if you were able to come so quickly," Peter said.

Milton laughed. "I was making my own rounds to the patients I'd admitted during the last week, but this takes priority."

Trish and Peter wanted to know more about Milton's responsibilities on the paediatric ward, so they chatted for a bit.

Peter then got up and said, "I think we need to be going if we're going to get back before dark."

Milton went over to Iris and took her hands in his. "Iris, I don't want you to overdo it with your aggressive physio. The strength will return just as well with a modest approach. I'll keep in touch with you. I know your phone number and you know mine. The postal service is still operating, last I heard. Listen, if I don't hear from you, I'll have to drive out to see how you're doing."

"Oh, then I won't write you at all." Iris and everyone laughed.

Still holding her hands, Milton said, "Goodbye, Iris." He let go, briefly grasped Peter and Trish's hands in turn, and quickly walked out. Both Peter and Trish noticed tears in Milton's eyes as he left.

Only Trish spoke. "That man really has feelings for you, Iris."

Chapter Thirty-Two

Mid-April, 1963

IRIS AWOKE WITH THE RECOLLECTION THAT IT WAS HER BIRTHDAY. SHE was twenty-seven. That made her happy but also a little sad. Would she become a spinster like many other female medical people? She'd always loved children and had hoped to have some of her own. Maybe God had other plans for her. She tried to think more positively by thinking of the many women she knew who lived what seemed like happy and fulfilled single lives.

She reached for her crutches and quickly moved to the bathroom. She'd made good improvement in her mobility since moving back home. She was even able to move slowly across a room with only a cane. As she washed her face and did her other "usuals," she thought again of Milton. She recalled the deep and searching look he'd given her when they'd last met in her hospital room. She couldn't get those warm, sensitive brown eyes out of her mind. *Yes, he does have feelings for me,* she thought, recalling Trish's words. That thought warmed her insides and put a smile on her face, at least until she chided herself for such foolishness.

Iris hobbled down stairs and there, on the kitchen table, was a huge flowering plant and a set of candles. She also saw a nicely decorated wrapped gift next to her breakfast plate. Then Trish and Peter walked in and sang a vigorous round of *Happy Birthday.*

Iris threw her crutches down and hugged her parents with teary eyes. "You didn't forget."

They all enjoyed a pleasant breakfast with lots of reminiscing of previous birthdays. Iris opened her gift and found a book, probably from her dad, as he often gave her his favourite books to read. It was *Mere Christianity* by C.S. Lewis. The other gift was a lovely necklace, obviously from Trish. Iris rose again and hugged them both.

The three chatted amiably for the next few hours. Peter had decided he needed to celebrate Iris's birthday, so he'd taken time off his principal's job. Trish had also taken the day off from her work at the library.

Late that morning, there was a knock on the door. When Peter answered, a special delivery man handed him a package. When Peter returned, he handed the package to Iris. "It's for you."

Iris looked at the return address and blushed. With a smile she tried to suppress, she said, "It's from Milton."

"Do you have the courage to open it up in front of us?" Peter said with a laugh.

"Oh, sure. I've nothing to hide." Iris quickly opened the package and out came a blouse and skirt. Iris was at first shocked and flustered and couldn't say anything.

"Hold them up against yourself, Iris," suggested Trish.

Iris did so and Trish made a whistling sound. "I love the colours. They fit your complexion. Why don't you try them on and see if they fit. I imagine Milton will have kept the receipts so you could exchange them."

Iris picked up all her gifts in one hand and one crutch with the other and somehow managed the stairs to her room. She took off her tracksuit and tried on the blouse and skirt. She looked in the mirror and tears immediately filled her eyes. The clothes were a perfect fit. They showed off her curves wonderfully, bordering on sexy. Then she had an idea. She put the necklace on from Trish as well. Perfect! She grabbed her crutch and quickly hobbled down and stood in front of Peter and Trish with a huge smile.

Both Peter and Trish gasped and then hooted in delight. "Those clothes and the necklace were just made for you, Iris," Trish said.

"I love these clothes," Iris said with a sparkle in her eyes. "I just don't know on what occasions I'd wear them. They're kind of risqué, aren't they?"

"Well, if I might comment, being a male, they are slightly evocative alright." Peter tilted his head with a grin and raised eyebrows. "The thing I find curious is who did this. How Milton knew what would fit you so perfectly and why he sent these kinds of clothes is a good question. Would you care to comment on that, daughter?"

"Dad, why do you need to know? Can't you accept them from a nice, caring fellow resident?" Iris was blushing again, trying not to give her tumultuous emotions away.

"Okay, I don't want to pressure you to express your feelings if you don't want to. This action shouts for an explanation. I just thought you might be happy to provide that for us. You don't need to say anything more if you'd prefer." Peter waved his hands to signify the subject closed.

"I'm happy to tell both of you how I feel." Iris wiped at a tear making its way down her cheek. "Maybe you can help me know what I should do about that. I find myself being filled with great joy about how Milton cares so much for me, but I'm also terribly conflicted about our relationship."

Trish stepped close and put her hands on Iris's shoulders. "You really love him, don't you, Iris?"

"Of course I do." At this, Iris started openly sobbing. "He's such a nice guy and I know he cares for me. But I don't know just *how* he does. Do you know what I mean?" Trish leaned down to hug Iris. She sobbed some more, and then found a handful of tissue to blot away her tears and blow her nose.

"Well, I'm puzzled by how deeply he obviously cares about you, Iris," Peter said. "Sending these clothes suggests he'd love to see you dress that way. What does that say about him?"

Iris just shook her head. Her eyelids and cheeks had red blotches on them. "I really don't know, Dad."

"Has he told you any more about his homosexual inclinations and whether he feels he's being healed?" asked Peter.

"No, nothing recently. I think he's trying to trust God that he is helping him to become heterosexual. I really don't know more than that."

"You know, I think Milton has it right," Trish said. "We all need to just relax and trust God that he'll help all of us do what pleases him. Why don't we pray right now? The apostle Paul said in the letter to the Philippians, 'Have no anxiety about anything, but in everything by prayer and supplication with thanksgiving let your requests be made known to God. And the peace of God, which passes all understanding, will keep your hearts and your minds in Christ Jesus.'"

Peter nodded. "That's a great advice, Trish. I'm amazed you can recall those verses like that."

"Normally, I wouldn't be able to, but I read them yesterday morning and decided I needed to memorize them for myself. So, let's pray."

Peter and Trish gathered around Iris's chair and they all held hands. Peter prayed a short prayer along the lines of the verses Trish had shared.

Trish looked at the clock. "Hey, we need to make some lunch. Peter needs to get going to work in an hour."

✦ ✦ ✦

That evening, Iris phoned Milton. She hoped he wasn't on call. She had to thank him, but she had no idea what she was going to say.

When she heard his voice, a thrill went through her. "Dr. Saunders?"

"Yes, can I help you?"

"You did something you promised not to do and I want to lodge a complaint."

"My humble apologies, Dr. Marten. Is there anything I can do to right the wrong?"

"You've taken advantage of my fragile emotions with those seductive clothes and now I can't seem to make a rational decision about you anymore. You promised you wouldn't bring up the topic of sex or our relationship, didn't you? Now you've gone and spoiled it all." Iris made her voice angry and accusatory.

"I didn't say a thing. I just sent you a birthday gift to try to cheer you up."

"Oh Milton, I want to thank you so much for your gift." Iris's voice had suddenly become warm and serious. "They're the most lovely clothes I've ever had. They fit perfectly. How in the world did you get the colours and the size right?"

"Well, I don't have much trouble visualizing your complexion and your body shape and size. I've got that vividly in my memory bank, I guess."

"You make me feel very loved and cared for, Milton. I'm happy for that, and then I'm scared. You must think I'm crazy. Do you understand what I'm saying?" Iris was nearly crying again. She needed to keep her emotions in check.

"I understand all too well. When the impulse to give you that gift came, I fought it, but then I gave in and just did what I deeply wanted to do. I care for you a lot and it's hard not to act on powerful feelings." Milton paused. "Listen Iris, I'll try to do better in keeping our agreement. Now I want to wish you a happy birthday. Sleep well."

"Thanks again, Milt."

Chapter Thirty-Three

May 1963

The first of May had come to Badger Creek and the snow had pretty well disappeared. A few dusty banks were still visible on the north side of tree groves in the dry riverbed. Most of the songbirds had found their way back to their nesting sites. Iris had been walking with the aid of a cane for a week now. Today, she planned to walk without any aids. She continued to see steady progress in her lower limbs. For that, she was very grateful. Her goal was to be jogging before the first of July, when she'd be returning to Edmonton and starting her haematology residency.

In the last month, she'd spent a steadily increasing time reading about haematology, thanks to subscriptions to several medical magazines. She had also purchased the latest haematology textbooks. She planned to hit the road running, as the saying went. Once she got back to Edmonton, Iris also planned to get back to regular oboe lessons. She knew music helped keep her emotionally healthy. She could only read so much each day in the Marten home, and playing her oboe had brought a welcome change.

Iris had the house to herself, as her dad was at the school and Trish was working at the library. She finished cleaning up after breakfast and then put on her runners and a jacket. As she slipped out of the house, she noticed the sun was already high in the sky. There was a soft cool breeze, but she figured she'd be okay, since the path was mainly in the sunshine. She needed to walk slowly and with care so as not to stumble.

She looked up to the poplars on the escarpment opposite her path. The trees had large buds and soon would be bursting into life with their gloriously aromatic leaves. The path led into a stand of spruce and she smelled the faint aroma of their sap. A red squirrel began chattering at her about her right to invade its territory. She thought it best to just accept its reprimand and move on.

Iris's mind drifted to the lawsuit. She'd been informed by her lawyer that Dr. Pinsky would be defended by the university legal team. A preliminary hearing date was soon to be set. She'd been in touch with her research coworkers and they'd informed her that they were getting cold stares from other research staff who weren't working under Iris. Some had even given them advice to find work on a different team. So far, Iris was glad she had the solid support of her own coworkers.

Iris's thoughts turned to Dr. Pinsky himself. Was he feeling the effects of her suit? Was he bothered by the police investigation? She wondered if he and his family were suffering pain from all the trouble she'd caused him. Then she thought she shouldn't have to worry about that, considering all the pain he'd caused her. As soon as that thought crossed her mind, she felt some kind of inner check as if that thought was selfish. She felt an urge to pray for him. The next thought was that he was not worth praying for. Finally, she stopped and looked up to the empty sky and said to the heavens, "Oh God, help me to see things your way. I feel confused in what my attitude should be." There was no response. Well, she hardly expected an audible voice.

She resumed her walk and Tim came to mind. He'd phoned her about two weeks ago and told her how pleased he was about her improving health. She found him polite, but there seemed little urgency to resume their relationship. She wondered why. Perhaps he'd finally given up on her. Or, better, he'd found a new relationship more suited to him.

Then she recalled Milton's request for communication. They'd exchanged phone calls and even a few letters, but Milton was careful to keep their feelings for each other out of them. This made these communications seem empty and she found herself longing for some intimacy in their conversations. *Please, Lord, work out your purposes through our relationship. Help us not to get hurt.*

A crow cawed quite near her and made her realize she'd better quit daydreaming and get back to the house. Her legs had held up well, but she could feel some fatigue setting in.

* * *

Ralph had come home after his second year at Briercrest Seminary. He was due to spend his summer at a church in Saskatoon, but that wouldn't start until July first. Iris enjoyed getting to know Ralph as a fully mature adult. He'd taken his studies seriously. She loved to hear his thoughts on a variety of theological issues. Much of their visiting occurred while walking together along the dry creek bed path.

Now that they were in the last week of June, Iris had, true to her plan, begun to jog. That had gone well and Iris felt she was nearly back to where she'd been before GBS struck her down.

The day before, she'd packed in preparation of her trip back to Edmonton. She wanted to get there a few days before she began the haematology residency. She had asked Ralph to drive her to Edmonton in his car, as both Trish and Peter would be at work. On the night before her trip, Iris had made sure she had a quiet visit with her family.

The Marten family had an earlier than usual breakfast followed by tearful goodbyes. Peter took Iris's hands in his and said, "Tough things come into our lives, but God has a way to bring good out of them, especially when we are yielding our lives to him. I see this disease you're recovering from is one of those times. At least one good thing that I've seen is getting to know you better these last three months, Iris."

"Another important outcome is you coming into a new level of maturity in your faith, Iris," put in Trish. "I see you so much more at peace now."

Iris hugged Trish and her dad once more, but couldn't trust her voice to say anything more.

Soon Ralph and Iris were on the highway leading westward to Edmonton. For a while, little was said. Iris needed time to digest all the events that had taken place in the last three months at home.

Finally, Iris turned to Ralph and asked, "So, what are your plans once you're finished getting your degree in theology?"

Ralph looked ahead for a few moments. "I've thought about that a lot. I've also prayed for guidance. One thing I've found is that I like to teach. I guess I inherited that from Dad. I like presenting material in such a way as to inform and inspire others. I love seeing them get it. I find that so fulfilling."

"You're a teacher, Ralph," remarked Iris forcefully. "You need to be doing that for a life's profession. Would you see going to university and taking education to teach in the school system like Dad?"

"No, that would be a second choice for me. I'm in love with theology and the Bible. I'd want to teach biblical stuff."

"Well, that leaves you to teach in a Bible college or even in a seminary. Does that interest you?"

"Yes, it does. I'm not seeing into the future far enough to know just what form that'll take. I need to go for my degree and trust God that he'll light the path in front of me for the next stage of my life."

"That's so exciting, Ralph. I'll pray for the direction you'll need."

"Thank you. I rely so much on the prayers of my family." Ralph paused since he needed to concentrate on getting the right turn onto another highway. "I'd like to know how things are between you and Tim. Are you still seeing him?"

"Things have come to an end between Tim and me, I think. We've had our relations grind down before and somehow it revived again. This time, I think it has truly ended. Largely, that's because Tim has finally given up on me, especially when he realized I'd be permanently crippled. You know, the event that ended it for me was my vision of Jesus. I knew then I could never live with a man who didn't share my passion for the truth of the Scriptures. With what I've learned about Tim's beliefs about Jesus and the authority of Scripture, I knew I couldn't be happy sharing my life with such a person."

"Tim will soon discover that Iris, his old girlfriend, is well again and will come calling again."

Iris shook her head. "We talked on the telephone a few weeks ago. He'd heard of the change in my diagnosis and he congratulated me on my improvement. He didn't seem eager to resume our relationship, and I didn't encourage him."

"So, are you saying you're never going to marry?" Ralph said, glancing briefly at Iris.

"You know, since I've had my near-death experience, I've lost any sense of urgency to find a mate. When I got started in medicine, I had no concerns about marrying. I just wanted to focus on becoming the best doctor I could, and figured I'd worry about romance later. Somehow I got caught up in relationships anyway. I'm much more relaxed about that, now. In fact, I'm quite at peace about that. If God wants to show me someone he wants me to marry, I'll be glad to cooperate."

Nothing was said for twenty minutes as they contemplated their own thoughts. Finally, Ralph braked and signaled to turn off the highway. "There's a small café. Let's get a coffee. I also need to stretch my legs."

They got their coffee and light snack and decided to sit at a table. At the next table were a mother and two preschoolers. Iris couldn't help but smile at them and soon was chatting with the mother about her children. Iris asked them questions about their lives. Soon the children were chatting amiably with Iris. Ralph observed this interaction with interest.

When they were again settled in Ralph's car, Ralph remarked about the ease Iris had in engaging the two children in conversation. "You have a way with children that's quite amazing. You love children, don't you? You'd love to have your own, I bet."

"Of course I would." Iris suddenly found herself choking up as tears flooded her eyes. "Maybe God will give me a chance of serving children in my chosen profession. That'll have to be enough."

Once Ralph had gotten the car cruising at speed limit, he said, "I'll be praying that he gives you a godly husband to give you a chance to have your own family. I know God would be delighted to see you care lovingly for your own children."

They were silent for a time and then Ralph asked, "You haven't said much about Milton since I've been home. What do you hear from him? Is he still trying to break free from his homosexuality?"

Iris caught Ralph up on her various encounters with Milton, especially after he resuscitated her. "I have to be truthful, I care for him a great deal. He's such a kind, considerate, and selfless person. I know he cares for me. I don't know where he is in terms of his being gay. I know he's trying to trust God to awaken true heterosexual feelings that he thinks God would want for him. Beyond that, I don't know. I've been trying not to worry about that anymore—just leaving it to God to work out."

The rest of the trip went by quickly as both continued sharing about their lives. Iris and Ralph felt a deep gratitude for the close relationship that had developed between them.

Chapter Thirty-Four

July 1, 1963

IRIS WALKED BRISKLY ONTO THE MEDICAL WARD WHERE MOST OF THE haematology cases were being treated. She was ready for action and keen to see her first cases. She was also keen to meet her new boss, Dr. Conner, Chief of the Department of Haematology. She'd heard he was very popular and highly respected. She'd also heard he was a Christian through and through.

The head nurse approached Iris. "Dr. Marten, I'd like you to meet your fellow residents." She nodded to three other residents standing around the desk and mentioned each of their names. "We're waiting for Dr. Conner, who should've been here by now."

At that moment, an energetic, slim man in his forties, with slightly greying hair walked rapidly toward the group. "Ah, my troops, I presume."

The head nurse introduced each of the four residents to Dr. Conner. He waved to the group to follow him to the charting room where they all took a seat. "I'm so glad to meet all of you. I hope to get to know each of you and your families in time. I want you to know I care very much about each of you, and will do all I can to help you achieve all that you hoped for in this residency program. I'm very approachable and will be glad to answer all your questions to the best of my abilities.

"I'm a patient man, but I don't have patience for anyone who is lazy or puts their own ambitions ahead of those of the patients we're here to serve. We always want to make the patients and their family members feel that we really care for them as valuable human beings. We need to assure them that we'll make every effort to make their stay here as comfortable as possible. We'll fail at times, and that includes me. When we do, we need to frankly apologize and determine to do better. For me, that means I ask God to forgive me, to repair the damage where I can, and to help me do better next time." Dr. Conner got up, paced around a moment, and then leaned against the wall behind him and smiled.

"Now, I'd like to start to get to know each of you. Perhaps each of you in turn could say where you come from, what kind of family you were raised in, where you did your schooling and medical training. More importantly, I'd like to know the vision you have for your future service in the medical field." With that, he sat down. "Well, who wants to start off?"

Iris immediately said, "I'd be glad to be first. I tend to get too nervous if I have to wait for others to finish." Iris shared where she had come from and what her schooling and pre-med and medical training had been. Then she said, "My vision for myself is to be a haematology specialist anywhere I can get a job. I'd hope that would be in Alberta or Saskatchewan, as I wouldn't want to practice too far from the wonderful home I came from. I'm looking forward to this residency program, where I hope to become a well-educated and skillful clinician, but also where I can learn to be a compassionate and loving human being in my work as a doctor." Iris sat down and glanced toward Dr. Conner. She was surprised to see his eyes glistening with unshed tears.

The other three also gave brief sketches of their lives and their dreams. After that, a senior resident came in and gave each a copy of their daytime schedule for the next month. Their on-call schedules for nights and weekends were also provided. Finally, each was given several names of hospital patients that were the responsibility of the haematology department. Iris was only too eager to see her patients and develop a plan of investigation and treatment for each of them.

✦ ✦ ✦

It was Friday and Milton was three days into his second year of paediatric residency. So far, he hadn't met Iris since she'd returned. A picture of Iris filled his mind. He imagined his eyes tracing her lovely face and then the smooth curves of her body. He felt himself yearning to touch her body and gently stroke her with his hands. Things were indeed changing inside him. He longed for a good visit with her. He finally paged her around 4:00 p.m. and when she answered, he said, "Dr. Marten, I've a patient with a strange blood disorder where red cells change shape and become dumbbells whenever the patient feels separation from his or her love object. It's been dubbed 'separation disease.' Would you think we could meet for coffee in the cafeteria and I will fill you in on this patient?"

"Sure, Dr. Saunders," Iris tried her best to keep from laughing. "Perhaps you could bring your patient along to the cafeteria and we can discuss management strategy and begin therapy."

"I'll ask him." Milton paused. "He says he'd love that. He even says he feels a lot better already."

"Is your patient's name Milton by any chance?"

"Why, yes. How did you guess that?"

"I'll be able to meet both of you in about ten minutes, Dr. Saunders."

"Great."

✦ ✦ ✦

Milton was already standing by the entrance of the cafeteria when Iris strolled in. "Hey, you're doing great, Iris. You seem to have gained most of your strength back."

"Yeah, I feel nearly back to normal."

They soon had their coffee and found an empty table. "How have you found haematology so far?" Milton would have loved to talk about much more intimate matters, but he felt he needed to respect Iris's emotional space.

Iris told Milton about her very positive impressions of Dr. Conner.

"What I've heard about Tom Conner is all good," Milton said. "You're very fortunate to have such a principled man as a mentor. He seems to be a great ambassador of true Christianity here in the medical community. He reminds me of Dr. Sandoski in many ways."

Iris closed her hands around her cup as though to absorb its warmth as she organized her thoughts. "You know, sometimes I think God places people like that in our lives to encourage us. You do that for me too, Milt. I just hope my life encourages others in the faith."

"I love to hear you speak like that. Your faith seems so alive recently. I've no doubt that many patients as well as your colleagues will be inspired by your faith."

"I hope so," Iris said, looking steadily into Milton's eyes. "Tell me how you are finding your second year?"

"I like it better than last year, since I'm given more responsibility and more one-on-one with the chief and other staff."

"What's the plan for you next year? Will the department be arranging a third year for you?"

"No, that's not going to happen. Eventually there'll be a complete paediatric program here, but not yet. If I want to go on, I'll have to take my last two years in some other hospital. Right now, I'm thinking of doing that in the Hospital for Sick Children in Toronto."

Iris's spirits plummeted. "Oh Milton, that's so sad. I think *I'm* starting to feel the symptoms of separation disease coming on. The UAH now has a complete four-year program in haematology. I've been planning to do my whole specialty training here."

"Well, two years isn't forever, Iris. I'm sure I'll come back to Alberta and probably to Edmonton to do my last year while preparing for my fellowship exams."

"Ah yes, but two years is a long time." Iris felt she wanted to say she desperately needed Milton, but she couldn't say that. She had to rein in her emotions. They were in turmoil.

✦ ✦ ✦

A day later, Iris was sitting in the charting room, writing up a case she'd just seen. She heard a familiar voice of greeting.

"You look deeply engrossed in your task, Iris. How are things going?"

"It's been hectic, Milt. We've had a real run on anemia cases. What brings you here?"

"A fifteen-year-old I saw on paediatrics last year was admitted this morning on this medical ward, since ours was overflowing. I wanted to follow up on him. So I'm here." Milton paused a few seconds. "When we were talking yesterday, I forgot to ask you about your lawsuit. How is it coming?"

"Well, Dr. Pinsky has been subpoenaed to a preliminary court hearing set for September third."

"So, you're going through with it, are you?" Milton slumped down in a chair near Iris, looked down, and studied the wood grains on the table.

"Why, of course. I'm not the type to back down under pressure."

"I admire your tenaciousness. I just wanted to ask what you hope to gain from this suit. Are you asking for a monetary compensation for damages?"

"Well, sure. It's not much as suits go. We're only asking for twenty thousand for all of us who were damaged."

"Will that help to correct the injustice?"

"Maybe to some extent. It's not just a way to get some money from a guy who can easily afford it. It's about serving notice to him and anyone who'd be tempted to do likewise that those in positions of responsibility and power can't run roughshod over those working for them. It's about giving those who've laboured diligently a sense that they are worthy of respect and honour in our university and medical departments."

"Will Dr. Pinsky want to work in the future with anyone who has anything to do with this suit?"

"I suppose not," Iris conceded. She felt herself becoming defensive. She could read Milton's face and body language. "Milton, you seem to have some problems with my doing this. Am I right?"

"Iris, I'm trying not to judge you in this situation. I just wanted to explore your motives."

"So, you think I should've been passive and allowed Pinsky to get away with treating his workers like dirt and not stood up for the rights of my co-workers?" Iris was getting quite angry and felt a rising sense of not being understood and being unfairly judged.

Milton raised his hands, palms forward. "Please don't misunderstand me here. I'm not saying you're wrong for suing Dr. Pinsky. I just wanted to ask if you had considered the option of not suing. I sure didn't want to start a fight with you." Milton's neck was flushed, and his forehead veins bulged as he tried to explain himself.

Iris's whole face was flushed with anger. "Milton, you're just a pleaser. You're scared to stand up for your rights and the rights of others. You just want to keep the peace at all costs, don't you?"

Milton said nothing. He couldn't believe Iris had reacted so drastically to his inquiry. He finally said, "I'm sorry how my questions came across. I need to go now." He quietly left. Iris remained sitting stiffly at her desk, her jaw pushed forward.

✦ ✦ ✦

It was mid-July and, true to his word, Dr. Tom Conner had begun to invite the haematology residents and their spouses, if they had any, to his home to meet him and his wife for a comfortable visit over a meal. Iris had been told how much one of the residents and his wife had enjoyed their time with the Conners. Iris was the next to be invited. She went home after seeing all the haematology consults assigned to her. She showered and spent more time than usual making her face up and primping her hair. She put on a modest but smart dress and looked in the mirror. She wasn't trying to outshine anyone else. She just wanted to honour the Conners by dressing nicely.

When she knocked on their door, a slightly built woman of about forty-five greeted her. Mrs. Conner smiled broadly and stuck out her hand for a brief handshake. "Dr. Iris Marten, I'm Cheryl Conner. Do come in. My husband Tom is outside barbequing." Mrs. Conner motioned Iris to take a seat in the living room. Mrs. Conner sat in a nearby chair. "May I ask you how you like doing straight haematology so far?"

"I love it. I'm too busy to worry about other areas of health care." Iris then told her roughly what her duties and responsibilities were and also what her reading and study program entailed.

Soon Dr. Conner entered with a plate containing three generous steaks. "Dr. Marten, I hope you like semi-rare steak. Will that do? If you like yours more well done, I'll be glad to pass it over the flames again."

"Semi-rare is perfect, Dr. Conner," Iris said with an appreciative smile.

"Listen," Dr. Conner said after setting the dish on the table. "Why don't we agree to call each other by our first names? Is it okay with you if we call you Iris?"

"Yes, that would be just fine with me."

They took a seat at the table and Tom said a short blessing that included a request that God bless Iris in her medical work and in her life in general. Soon all three were enjoying their tasty steaks and chatting about where each had been born and raised.

Not surprisingly, they soon were chatting about many issues related to the University Hospital and the type of patients that came for investigation and treatment. Tom cleared his mouth and said, "The politics of the hospital sometimes become frustrating. I try not to let that bother me too much. I try to keep focused on my patients as well as the people and responsibilities I've under my charge. My greatest obligation is to see that the patients my staff and I see are treated with care and respect, and that they receive the best medical service we are capable of. To do that, I have to rely on God helping me with wisdom and love that come only from him. I don't know if you appreciate what I am saying, but that's the way I function here."

"I do understand what you're saying, and I also am trusting God for those same virtues, Tom."

"So you're a Christian, Iris?" Cheryl asked.

"Yes, I am." Iris told the Conners about her early history that included her faith journey. The Conners took great interest in Iris's story.

The conversation moved on to Iris's research project on poliovirus transmission. Tom took a drink of water and then remarked, "I heard that someone is suing the head of the virology department in our hospital. Do you know anything of that, Iris?"

Iris almost choked on a chunk of steak she was chewing. She quickly swallowed some water and turned to Tom, her neck turning red. "I have to say that it's I who am suing him."

Both the Conners' eyes widened. "What's the reason, Iris?" Tom asked.

Iris briefly told them about the publication of their research work and Iris's part in it. She told them what Dr. Pinsky had done, not recognizing her or her co-workers as he clearly should have.

The Conners listened carefully and asked clarifying questions. Finally, Tom asked, "Iris, why are you pursuing litigation? What benefit do you see in doing that?"

Iris gave them the same reasons she had given Milton. "I feel I need to do this to correct an obvious injustice. If no one does anything to stop guys like that, injustice just keeps rolling on in our educational institutions."

"I understand what you're saying. I can see how much you and your co-workers would've been hurt by this. Not only was it unfair, but you also potentially lost academic esteem and even opportunities to obtain appointments in prestigious institutions."

"Exactly," Iris said, feeling she'd finally been heard.

Tom sipped some tea and stretched back in his chair. "Iris, do you think the overall harmony of our hospital medical staff will be helped by this suit?"

Iris felt a wave of discomfort. "Well, maybe not in the short term. It might help other department heads and others in positions of responsibility to be more fair and respectful." She set her utensils on her empty plate.

"Do you think this suit could have a negative impact on the relationship between medical clinicians and house staff?" Tom persisted.

"Yes, I guess, for a while it could."

"Do you think patient care might suffer with the increased tension in the staff?"

Iris began to feel quite defensive and this did not go unnoticed by Tom. "Iris, I don't want you to feel that I'm criticizing what you are doing. I just want to make sure you've thought about all the implications of your action. I really care for you and I don't want you to get hurt."

Iris felt like telling Tom she could look after herself, thank you! But she said, "Thank you for caring about me this way. I'll think about what you've said."

Cheryl steered the conversation into less troublesome waters. "Our son, who is taking engineering, got into trouble with one of his professors a few months ago when he criticized one of his research projects for being an environmental hazard. He nearly got himself kicked out of his program. He backtracked enough to stay in, but he still has some issues to work out with the professor. The road of wisdom is often hard to identify when the issues are so complex. I agree with Tom that our source of wisdom is always God."

After looking at her empty cup and letting her eyes follow the design on the outside, Iris said, "Yeah, you're right. I need to let God direct my way, whatever that is. I'd be happy for your prayers for me in this regard." Iris looked up at the Conners with glistening eyes.

"We'll do that, Iris. You can count on us."

Tom suggested they move to the living room. Iris got up and began clearing some dishes. Cheryl told her that she didn't need to help, but Iris insisted and soon all the dishes were stacked on the counter.

The three then moved to the living room where an animated discussion arose over ideal medical education and where teaching could improve in the university hospital.

✦ ✦ ✦

Milton was on call the evening a ten-year-old girl was admitted onto the paediatric floor. He'd seen her briefly in the emergency department. A pathologist had already read the peripheral smear of her blood and the results had been phoned to the referring paediatrician. The diagnosis was acute lymphatic leukemia (ALL). Admission was automatic.

The patient was pale, with scattered small bleeding spots over her arms and neck. Otherwise, she didn't seem too sick. Milton saw that her face was very serious, mostly reflecting the fear she saw in her parents who were hovering over her. Milton tried to be supportive and gentle as he went about gathering the relevant medical history and doing the physical. He noticed a slight enlargement of her spleen and more small bleeding spots (petechia) over other parts of her body and in her mouth. Little else could be found. He told the parents he'd get her assessed by the haematology department and then they'd talk to them about the treatment program. He wished he could pass on some glimmer of hope, but he could think of nothing to quell the raging fear and grieving he saw in their eyes.

Milton found that Iris was on call for the haematology department. As he called her, he thought he needed to stay clear of personal issues.

"Hello, Dr. Marten. I've a sad situation for you to see. This time I'm telling you the truth." Milton went on to describe the case.

"Okay, I'll be there in about ten. Are the parents there to give a history?"

"Yes, I told them you'd be coming. They've been told the diagnosis by the referring paediatrician. Bring a good supply of tissue along to soak up the tears."

"I understand."

As Iris came onto the ward, she was glad Milton was back to being communicative, not allowing their recent blow-up to influence their professional relationship.

After Iris had gone through the same routine as Milton and had written her findings and recommendations on a consult sheet, she turned to Milton, who was doing some charting on another patient. "So, what do you think? Is the game up for this girl?"

"Well, her chances are slim. I've read about a few cases of ALL that survive, but all we can usually offer is a temporary period of improvement, maybe weeks or months at best."

"Unfortunately, that's about it. We'll start prednisone tonight and vigorously treat with antibiotics at the first sign of an infection. I'll need to contact our chief resident and the staff physician. I'll also let Dr. Conner know, as I'm sure he'll be asked to see her."

Milton took a deep breath as if trying to relieve the tension inside him. "What can we do for these parents, Iris? They are hurting so much."

Iris could read the pain in Milton's eyes. He was so sensitive. That was one of the characteristics she loved in him. "I don't know, other than offer to answer any questions they may have as well as to allow them to express their grief."

Milton nodded. "You're so good at that, Iris. That's why God put you in this role."

"Right now I don't feel too talented in that regard. I need God's wisdom and love, as Tom Conner often says."

Milton nodded again. "We'll both be needing those virtues."

✦ ✦ ✦

Milton was off the following evening. He was weary, but he'd been thinking of Bill Street several times that day. It had been over a year since he'd last seen him. They'd had three short phone conversations in the last year. Milton had found out that, true to his predictions, Bill had hooked up with several guys. These were short-term affairs, according to Bill. He was still looking for the elusive long-term relationship.

Milton wasn't ready to abandon his friendship with Bill. Perhaps, someday, Bill might be ready to seriously talk about what Milton had found in Christianity and in his small group support. Milton wanted to be available should that happen.

Milton heard Bill's familiar voice answering the phone. "Hi, Bill. I wondered how you're doing. I haven't heard from you for a few months."

"Good to hear your voice again, Milton. I was watching an old movie on TV. I've seen it before so I know how it goes. Are you still flat out busy as usual?"

"Yes, as usual, but I'm off tonight. Are you free for a short visit?"

"Sure. I've even got a few beers handy. See you in a bit."

Milton looked up to the bright evening sky as he walked from his truck toward Bill's apartment. The sun was still high, as it was nearly the longest day in the year. As he walked, he breathed a prayer: *Help me be sensitive to Bill's true needs.*

The door flew open before he knocked. "Milton, you old sock, you haven't changed a bit. Come on in."

As Milton found a comfortable seat in the living room, Bill yelled from the kitchen, "You still drink beer, Milt? You haven't gone so religious you've given up the pleasures of a beer, have you?"

"No, Bill. God's still working on more important failures in my life. He hasn't taken time to deal with my beer drinking yet."

"Well, I sure don't want to stand in the way of your becoming a priest. You have an aptitude for that line of work, you know."

Bill placed a bottle of beer and a glass in front of Milton. "Thank you, Bill. How's your work at the plant? Are you still doing quality assurance?"

"Yeah. The work is increasing in volume of late," Bill said as he slumped down in his favourite chair with a bottle of beer. "With more government regulation, there are more time consuming checks needed. Soon I'll be needing some help if the company wants to keep up the quality."

Bill enquired about Milton's training program. Milton filled him in on the kinds of patients he'd seen as well as his efforts to study each patient's particular disease.

Milton then asked, "Do you have any partners currently, Bill?"

"Oh, sure, but most are still short-term. There's one guy I'm keeping my eye on. He's just coming out of another relationship and is still grieving, I think. When he gets over that, I'm going to show up and see if he's interested."

Milton took a sip of his beer, put the glass down and looked steadily at his friend. "Bill, are you satisfied with this sort of life?"

"What do you mean, 'this sort of life'? You mean my encounters with other gays?"

"Yeah. Is this way of life okay with you for the rest of your life?"

"Well, as you know, I'd prefer a long-term relationship. What else is there for me? I know I have to have a sexual fix with a guy from time to time. The pressure builds up so much, I just have to have it, even if it's just a one night thing. I've tried being celibate like you. That didn't last long. We're all made differently, I guess. In your case, you got religion to prop yourself up. Maybe I need that?"

"You said you weren't interested the last time I talked with you."

"Well, times change. The other night, I woke up and remembered a dream I'd had. In my dream, I saw a man who told me he had something other than sex to give me when I was ready. I didn't make much of it at the time, but I keep remembering the dream. Maybe it has some religious connotations. What do you think?"

"Bill, I'd take it seriously. I've heard of Jesus or an angel speaking to people in their dreams. You might remember the Christmas story where Joseph was told in a dream that he should take Mary for his wife even though she was pregnant. The angel told him the child in her womb was put there by the Holy Spirit."

"Yeah, I remember that story. In my case, the message was a little less dramatic." Bill raised his bushy eyebrows and laughed heartily.

Milton remained serious. "Maybe no less real, though."

Bill slowly sobered as he thought about what Milton was saying. "Tell me what you found in religion and how it works for you."

Milton couldn't believe the conversation had turned this way. He needed to share what having Jesus in his life meant for him. Very simply, Milton explained about his troubled early life and how he'd been attracted to the story of Jesus through his grandmother and his biochemistry professor. "I saw something different in these people's lives. They were connected in a very vital way to the creator. I could see their lives had substance and meaning, as well as power to overcome their failures."

"Yeah, that's what I see in you, Milton. You seem to have a strength that I don't."

"It's not a strength that I've built up. It's a strength given to me by God." Milton wondered if he was explaining the gospel in the right way, but he decided to go on. "You see, Bill, I'd nothing in me to offer God in any relationship we might have. In fact, I knew that I was so full of sins and failures that I could never make myself right before a perfect God. The biochem professor helped me to understand God's plan to deal with mankind's dilemma. You see, if someone that was perfect, like God himself, would die as a human, in the place of all mankind, then mankind could be completely forgiven. In fact, a perfect relationship with God could be established forever. Jesus was such a person. But this only works if you believe what Jesus did for you."

"What if I decided not to go with the plan?"

"God would respect your wish, Bill. If you didn't want to go with God's plan, any relationship with God would be impossible. It's your choice. God is determined to give us a free will to decide for or against him."

Bill shook his head. "I'm not sure I can take all this spirit stuff in. When you can't see what you're talking about, it's hard to believe that it's real."

"I understand, Bill. We, in the twentieth century, are so used to dealing only with what our five senses tell us. I can tell you, I experimented with the spirit world where Jesus resides, and I can say that it's very real. I've felt his words, his ideas, and his power in my life. That shouldn't be surprising—Jesus said to his followers before he left them for heaven, 'And lo, I am with you always, to the close of the age.'"

"Thanks for being so open about your life. My brain is in overload mode just now. I need to think about what you said. You quoted from the Bible. Do you have a Bible you could lend me? I'd like to read it."

"Sure, I could get you one. I'll drop it by sometime in the next week. Could I make a suggestion? Start reading in the New Testament. Read the Gospel of John first and then the other gospels. Then read the rest of the New Testament. It would make more sense that way."

"Thank you so much, Milton. Maybe you could put a note in the Bible where I need to start."

As Milton prepared to leave, he said, "I'll leave the Bible in your mailbox if you're not home, okay?"

As Milton drove back to his suite, he felt great joy. He'd listened to God's nudge to visit Bill. Even though Bill wasn't quite getting the truth of the gospel yet, Milton was able to give him something of God in his own life for Bill to think about. That was all God expected him to do, at least for now.

✦ ✦ ✦

Iris found herself becoming ever more deeply involved with the girl with leukemia and her parents. She could see the girl gradually losing ground. The prednisone seemed to help for the first week, but then she developed a lung infection. In spite of intravenous antibiotics, she'd remained feverish. In the last few days, her breathing became more labored. She still showed lots of immature cells (blasts) in her blood smears. Her platelets were still low and she was in danger of bleeding into vital organs.

Iris had met with the parents frequently to offer what hope she could give, which seemed meager at best. Milton had visited several times each day, partly to encourage the parents and to show them he cared, but mostly, he came to support Iris. He sensed she was taking this case very hard and was in danger of being overwhelmed emotionally. He asked simple questions to get her to express her feelings. He urged her to keep track of her other patients and spend less time with the girl. He even offered to spend time with the family so that she could get some rest and do other things. Iris did take Milton's advice and took more rest and spent more time with her other patients, but her thoughts were never far from this grieving family.

After the girl had been in the hospital for only two weeks, she quietly let go of her struggle to live. The parents were devastated. They gave full vent to their immense grief. Milton wept inside for them. He also struggled with anger that there wasn't more modern medical science could've done to avert this horrible tragedy.

Milton's attention was drawn to Iris, who was sitting next to the parents who were still holding the hands of their deceased daughter. Milton became aware that Iris was crying as much as the parents. The intense grief he observed in her face startled him. She was falling apart. He went and laid his hands on her heaving shoulders. He could do nothing more than just pray inwardly to give him wisdom to deal with Iris's fragile emotions. Out of the corner of his eye, he noticed someone drawing near to the parents. It was the mother's sister, whom he had seen before.

After a few moments, Milton whispered into Iris's ear, "Come away for a little while. Let her aunt comfort the parents."

Iris blotted away some tears, took in a ragged breath, and nodded. She got up, squeezed the mother's hand and walked away with Milton. As they were walking toward the nursing desk, Milton had a thought. "Iris, have you talked recently with Dr. Conner?"

"No, not for a few days. Why?"

"Why don't you phone him and tell him about our patient?"

"Well, it would be more appropriate to call the staff paediatrician than Dr. Conner."

"Iris, just do it for me. I think I need his words for us at this time."

"Sure, I guess I could." The deep sadness in Iris's eyes tore at Milton's heart.

Iris picked up the phone and soon had Dr. Conner on the line. "I just wanted to tell you, our girl with leukemia died."

"I'm not surprised." Dr. Conner paused a moment and then asked, "Iris, how are *you* doing?"

Iris attempted to answer, but then sobbed before saying, "I guess not too well just now."

"Listen, I'll be there in twenty minutes."

Iris tried to object, but Dr. Conner assured her he was on his way.

When Dr. Conner came in, the ward was silent as though everyone were grieving what had just happened. He went to the girl's room and gently squeezed the arms of both parents and said, "When these things happen, we medical people feel so utterly helpless. We struggle with a sense of failure, but I can assure you that the staff here did whatever they could for your precious child. The staff were aware how much you loved and cared for your daughter. My prayer is that both of you will grieve well and support and love each other while you do that."

The parents expressed their sincere thanks for the work the staff had done and for the care and love shown to them.

Dr. Conner then walked into the charting room where Iris and Milton were waiting. Dr. Conner took in the scene of grief and said, "Come on, both of you. Let's go to the 'quiet room' next door." They followed Dr. Conner into the room and he shut the door. "Let's sit down and talk about this case—not about the disease, but about our dealing with tragedy. First of all, I'd like to know how each of you is feeling right now."

Milton spoke up first. "Well, I feel sad and a bit helpless. I feel medical science failed this girl and her family. I know we did everything we knew to do. It just wasn't good enough. I feel especially bad for the parents and the incredible loss they must be feeling now. I know I can only offer my simple words of caring, but that won't do much to help them."

"Don't underestimate those few words you say to them, Milton. As long as you're sincere, they will see that in you and be comforted that others really care."

Dr. Conner turned to Iris, who was still quietly trying to control her sobbing and blowing her nose with a fistful of tissue. "Okay, Iris, it's your turn. How are you coping with this girl's death?"

Iris took a moment to compose herself. "I don't know, really, why I'm taking this so hard. It's caught me by surprise." She paused to blow her nose again. "I was just so torn up by the grief I saw in the parents. I guess I identified so much with them."

"I know you have a very compassionate heart and that's a great asset in medicine, but I'm wondering if you have any idea why this case was particularly hard for you."

After a pause and a shaky deep breath, Iris said, "I really don't know. I'm afraid this is going to be a problem for me in the future."

Milton looked up sharply with an idea. "Maybe, Iris, this case reminded you of your mother. She died of leukemia too, didn't she?"

"Yes, she did. I can see now that there were some similarities to this case."

Dr. Conner nodded. "Well, I can see that you could've been identifying with these grieving parents in a much deeper way because you were once again grieving for your mother. That makes sense."

Everyone sat quietly as they processed these thoughts. Then Dr. Conner sat forward and said, "As much as I admire the compassion both of you showed in this case, I've some observations and some suggestions to make. They come from lessons I've learned along the way. I see that there are often three ways clinical people like us deal with medical tragedies like this girl dying. One is to become detached emotionally. That is to just use the medical science and tools available to give the best care we know how without investing anything emotionally. The second way is to deeply identify with the patient or their family's suffering. So much so, that we feel drained and become impaired in our ability to further help the patient, or his family, or even serve other patients. The third way is to serve as Jesus did. He could serve huge numbers of very needy people with compassion every day, and yet always seemed ready and available to help more. He said he only did what his father told him to do. So, when we serve, we should do the same. Meet problems head on with the confidence that we're serving in the name of Jesus and with his strength. Then pray inwardly, or even outwardly when the patient seems receptive, praying that God will use your medical service and comfort for the patient's good. Then leave the burden of responsibility to heal in God's hands. This leaves you free to serve others, including your own family, with the energy they deserve. To transfer the burden of healing onto God's broad shoulders is an act of faith, but what a relief it is!"

Dr. Conner stopped talking and just waited. Finally, Iris squeaked a tearful but sincere thank you. "You said what I needed to hear, Dr. Conner. I can see I need to carry out my practice of medicine in Jesus' name and in his strength. I've been trying to do it in my own strength far too much." Iris looked over to Milton and gazed a moment at his concerned face. "Milton, I want to thank you, too. You recognized that I've been grieving my mother's death through this girl dying."

Milton nodded and smiled briefly.

The three got up and prepared to head in their separate ways, but they all felt a sense of inner relief and peace.

✦ ✦ ✦

Three days had gone by since her patient died, and Iris could feel a steady improvement in her emotional health. She thought daily about Dr. Conner's wise advice. She planned to follow that advice. She was just finishing the supper dishes in her apartment when the telephone rang. When she answered, she was surprised to hear the voice of Vera, a friend she'd made while doing research for Dr. Pinsky. Vera had taken a year after her residency program to do research in muscle diseases. She was specializing in internal medicine. Iris got to know her from meetings both had attended in medical research. Vera had since successfully finished her exams and qualified as an internist. Iris had heard Vera had gotten a very good job at the Toronto General Hospital.

"Hey, it's good to hear your voice, Iris. I have been thinking of you recently, mostly about your suit against Pinsky. I heard about it just before I left Edmonton to take up my appointment in TGH. How is it going?"

"Well, it's slowly proceeding. We're coming up to a preliminary hearing soon. After that, it depends when my lawyer can slot our case in."

"Oh, I'm so proud of you, Iris. I wish I'd the courage you have to stand up for my rights."

"Thanks, Vera. I'm not sure how much good it'll do for my career, though."

"Maybe the popularity of the case will get the ears of the people who make decisions in your favour."

"What do you mean, Vera?"

"Well, having done research looks very good in your curriculum vitae. That's what did it for me. I've since talked to a member of the selection committee that interviewed me. He confided that it was the year of research that made the difference between me and the next most successful candidate."

Iris's felt a renewed sense of injustice done to her. "Well, yeah. That's partly why I originally decided to sue him."

"You need to make sure your lawyer stresses that you may potentially lose out on a good academic appointment because you weren't given the recognition you deserved."

"Yes, I agree. I've mentioned that to my lawyer already, but I'll tell him about your situation."

The two talked for another few minutes about Iris's training program and about Vera's new job. Iris had a hard time concentrating on what Vera was saying. Her mind kept flitting back to what Vera said about Pinsky's injustice.

✦ ✦ ✦

That night, Iris couldn't sleep. Her mind was in turmoil. She was pitching about in bed as if in a storm-tossed sea. She felt she was in the midst of a battle. Vera had stirred up her sense of injustice at what Dr. Pinsky had done to her and her colleagues. She felt she had an obligation to root out the evil in the Virology Department. She justified her feelings by thinking that the university and her hospital would benefit from the attention the court case would have in focusing on giving of proper respect to employees and research workers. Lots of people would thank her. Then she thought about the disarming questions Milton and Tom Conner had asked. Even her dad and Trish had little enthusiasm for the suit. Clearly, they all were disturbed by her pursuing litigation.

Her mind went to the life of Jesus. His face materialized in her imagination, just like in her vision. Somehow, she had a hard time imagining Jesus dealing with injustice this way. She felt Jesus might just accept the injustice after telling the perpetrator the truth of how it affected his life. The picture of Jesus advising us to 'heap coals of fire' on the heads of those mistreating us came to mind. Obviously, Jesus was asking us to treat those hurting us with kindness.

By three o'clock, she threw the blankets off her sweaty body and stood up in the middle of the bedroom. She held her hands up and cried out, "Dear Jesus, please help me make sense of the mess in my head. I want to do what pleases you. Please show me your way."

She then quietly crawled back into her bed, carefully covered herself up, and soon was asleep.

The next morning she awoke at her usual time. At first she felt calm, but, in a few minutes, all the issues she'd struggled with before she fell asleep again assaulted her brain. Soon she was so stressed she couldn't think about eating. What should she do? She had to talk to someone, but who would be around now? It was Sunday morning—not a good time to talk to people, especially church-going people. She paced around the kitchen area and then thought, *Milton's a good listener.* She wasn't sure she wanted to hear his solutions to her problems, but she needed to talk to someone who was really willing to listen to her. She now felt herself willing to hear what Jesus would want her to do. Maybe Milton would have some insight about that.

Iris went to the phone and, as she dialed, she prayed God would give Milton and her wisdom. Milton answered sleepily.

"Milton, I'm so sorry for waking you up."

"You don't have to be. I should be up and going by this time. What have you got on your mind, my friend?"

"Would you be willing to discuss the whole issue of the suit I launched?"

"Oh, I thought you didn't want another word about that from me. What's changed?"

"Well, several things. I need someone who will listen to all the voices shouting their various opinions in my head."

"Iris, if you're hearing voices, you should be talking to your friend Myra. I'm just a humble paediatric type."

"Funny! You know that was just a literary expression. So, would you be willing?"

"Of course I'm willing. When would it suit you?"

"How about now? Oh yeah, you go to church this morning, don't you?"

"A meeting with you takes precedence, in my books. You name the time and the place."

Iris suggested a familiar café on Whyte Avenue at ten o'clock.

Both pulled into the parking lot about the same time.

"You're looking good for having had a lousy sleep, Iris," Milton said as they got out of their cars.

"I'll take that as a compliment." Both laughed.

They walked into the café, the usual smells of fried onions and toast tempting their appetites. "How about eggs, ham, and some strong coffee, Iris. I know I could use something like that."

"Sounds wonderful." Somehow, she felt so at home and safe with Milton. *Yeah, he's what I need just now. Just now? Wouldn't it be lovely if it were forever? Stop it, Iris.*

Soon they were munching on their food, tossing out inconsequential remarks. When they had finished all but their coffee, Milton studied Iris's face and smiled. "Okay, I'm listening."

"You don't know how much I appreciate you being willing to listen to me, especially after being so rude to you when you were trying to bring some sense to my thinking. Thank you, Milton."

"Iris, you know our friendship supersedes any argument we might hold. To listen to you on any subject is a joy to me. You know that!"

Iris smiled and repeated her thanks. "I'd like to tell you what I was thinking last night. I need your help to make sense of it and also to help me find a path that pleases Jesus."

"Sure, take all the time you want. I'm in no hurry."

Iris told Milton the various points of view she had struggled with. "Do you think Pinsky wronged me and my fellow workers?"

"Certainly, you and your helpers were treated unfairly."

"Do we not have an obligation as good citizens to stand up against unfair treatment of workers in a public institution?"

"Yes, I think you have an obligation to bring to the attention of authorities wrongs that you see committed, especially if it is hurting others," Milton said.

"Just if it's hurting others?"

"I think it's often a good idea to go to the one who hurt us and honestly say how it has hurt us and also admit how we might have contributed to the hurtful words or action being done."

"Well, I *did* tell Pinsky how he hurt me. He didn't do anything to correct the situation. He didn't even apologize."

"I know, Iris. He didn't respond positively to your speaking to him about your hurt like he should've. You even brought the issue to the attention of the dean, with no results. What we're to do as Christians, when we are wronged by a non-Christian or, at least, someone outside of our own church community, is a challenging problem. The only two areas in the Bible that impressed me on this issue are in Matthew and 1 Corinthians. In Matthew 5:11, Jesus says, 'Blessed are you when men revile you and persecute you and utter all kinds of evil against you falsely on my account.' Then in the same sermon, he says, 'But I say to you, love your enemies and pray for those who persecute you.'"

"But those verses don't say anything about seeking justice in court."

"True, but I just wanted to try and understand Jesus' attitude he was advocating for those who did him wrong. I thought Paul also had something to say regarding this issue. In 1 Corinthians, he says, 'To have lawsuits at all with one another is defeat for you. Why not rather suffer wrong?' Here, the writer is speaking to Christians, but I can't help but feel Paul would have the same advice when the adversary was outside the church community."

"Milton, you're asking me to do a very hard thing. You seem to be saying that I'm to stand by passively while evil is allowed to flourish. That man needs to be punished."

"I can understand very well that way of thinking, but I can't get out of my head the words of Jesus: 'But I say to you, love your enemies and pray for those who persecute you.' I'm wondering how much we love Dr. Pinsky. I would imagine that if we loved him, we might try to understand his current situation. For instance, how much he's suffering because of this suit and how much he's suffering because of the police interrogation of his family, and how much guilt he's feeling for having not recognized you and your fellow workers."

"You know how to lay a guilt trip on people, don't you?"

"I don't like being in this role. Actually, I hate it. I had to say what my understanding is of the Scriptural teaching in this regard. I can understand that I may be seeing only one side of the situation. And that some theologian might do a better job." Milton turned his palms up in front of him, indicating he had no more to say.

Iris was quiet for a few moments and then she sighed and said, "Well, I'll think about the Scripture. That's all I can say on the subject for now." She looked into Milton's face and added, "I want to thank you for caring about me and being willing to risk rejection by giving me your honest opinion."

They looked at each other quietly for a few moments and then, as if each sensed it was time to go, both got up and headed for their cars.

Chapter Thirty-Five

End of July 1963

When Iris returned from her brunch with Milton, she found her Bible and looked up the verses he'd given her. Before reading, she prayed God would give her some light and wisdom to do the right thing. She re-read Paul's question to the Corinthian church: *"Why not rather suffer wrong?"* The Apostle Paul was challenging the Corinthian church to suffer injustice rather than going to court with the offender. Iris began rationalizing that her taking Pinsky to court wasn't just about herself. She was thinking of the others not given due recognition. She asked herself, would she have been willing to go to court had Pinsky recognized her but not her co-workers? She doubted it. So, whom was she kidding? She was really doing it mostly for herself.

Iris turned to the fifth chapter of Matthew, the Beatitudes. She read Jesus' sermon. The verse Milton mentioned jumped out at her: *"But I say to you, love your enemies and pray for those who persecute you."* Milton had told her to imagine how Dr. Pinsky might be suffering. He said that was a way to love Dr. Pinsky. She shuddered. How could she love that man? She got up and looked out the window, seeing the clouds in the sky. A thunderhead was forming in the west. *Imagine Pinsky's suffering. Help me see that, Lord.* She shut her eyes and the image of Jesus' kind face formed behind her eyelids. Then his face morphed into the face of Dr. Pinsky. She was startled at how full of pain it was, with deep lines, especially around his eyes. She found herself feeling sorry for Dr. Pinsky. She even felt she wanted to comfort him. She wondered about his wife. Although she'd never seen his wife, an image of a woman about his age came to her mind's screen. She not only looked sad, but she was crying. Iris wondered what Pinsky's two boys were feeling. She imagined seeing his thirteen-year-old boy and saw a sullen but hopeless look on his face.

Iris shook her head and looked at the clouds again. Even they looked sad. She found herself deeply troubled. After a few more moments, she began to feel deep compassion for the Pinsky family. They were hurting, no doubt. And she was the cause. Iris had once been told that when a patient sued a physician, the physician usually experienced painful emotional turmoil and often became depressed. These responses had nothing to do with money, she'd been told. The pain came with the discrediting of their sense of worth as a physician. So, were the Pinskys being affected in this way?

Iris tore herself away from the window and stormed around her small kitchen, knocking chairs roughly out of her way. Where was her backbone? Why was she shrinking back from what she needed to do? She should go ahead with her plan and let the chips fall where they may.

She stopped and then slowly walked back to the west window. Yes, the clouds were forming into a large cumulonimbus formation. It would make for a good thunderhead. Jesus' image formed in the towering white clouds. "Pray for those who persecute you." *Okay, Lord, help Dr. Pinsky feel better and take the sorrow away from Mrs. Pinsky. Forgive the thirteen-year-old for any evil he has done, even if it was to try to kill me.* Iris wondered why she prayed that about the boy. She admitted she'd briefly thought about him being the one trying to hurt her.

Tears flowed unabated down Iris's cheeks. *Forgive Dr. Pinsky, Iris.* "How can I?" she screamed aloud. "This is so hard!" She again started pacing about the room.

Who said living for me was easy?

"Okay, I'll do it!" she yelled. She hoped no one heard her. They'd be phoning the psychiatric emergency line.

Iris slowly and deliberately walked back to the window. The sky was darkening. Her eye caught the brief glow of lightning in the nimbus of the cloud. "No matter how much of a fool I'll make of myself, I'll do it! I'll do it for you, Jesus."

Iris paced around the living room, wondering what she should write in a letter to Dr. Pinsky. For the next thirty minutes, she struggled with how she'd explain her actions, not only in the letter, but also to her colleagues. She walked back to the window and noticed the wind picking up, now coming from the west, whereas before it was coming from the east. A bright flash of lightning and a crash of thunder followed immediately.

She needed to start writing. She found a writing pad, sat, and began.

Dear Dr. Pinsky,

As you know, I've launched a suit against you for taking sole credit for the polio research work done mostly by myself and my co-workers. I acknowledge that I felt hurt and damaged by your action. After much reflection and thought, I now realize I was wrong in trying to sue you. This change of mind has mostly to do with a consideration of my faith in God and my desire to be more like Jesus. You may not understand this, but it's the reason for this change. I want to sincerely apologize for the hurt and stress this has caused you and your family. Let me assure you that I am dropping the suit and I am holding nothing against you. I forgive you.

My hope is that we'll eventually become friends again. I'll be instructing my legal counsel regarding this change and you'll be receiving a letter from him regarding the same.

Sincerely,
Dr. Iris Marten.

Iris looked out the window and saw a few large drops of rain hurtle toward the window. She quickly folded up the letter, addressed an envelope, and found a stamp in her purse. She pulled on a raincoat and resolutely marched out of her apartment and to the mailbox on the street. She wrenched open the door of the box and fired the letter in. She looked up to the threatening sky and, laughing with tears streaming down her cheeks, said, "It's done!"

Rain began to fall. By the time she ran into the apartment block door, rain was cascading down in sheets. Iris ran up the stairs and into her room. Then she stood at the window, watching the rain pour down on the pavement. A deep sense of relief, peace, and joy began to well up within her. She saw the rain wash all the dust and bits of garbage away. The same process was happening inside her.

Chapter Thirty-Six

Since Iris had returned to Edmonton, she, Sandra, and Myra had resumed practicing their ensemble every Thursday evening. Their plan was to become good enough to do a mini-concert in the University of Alberta Hospital meeting room where grand rounds were held. It would be mainly for their friends and other music lovers on staff. They'd been practicing three pieces. Sandra also wanted to play a violin solo piece she'd been working on for some time. She needed Myra to accompany her on the piano. Myra had long had one of Chopin's etudes down perfectly, and wanted to play that as well. Iris was okay with that, as she had enough trouble bringing her oboe playing up to standard for the three trio pieces. She knew she couldn't handle any more, given commitments as a resident.

They planned the concert for August 10. Sandra had made invitation cards to hand out, about a hundred. Iris made sure Milton got an invitation because she knew he loved the music they'd be playing. It was mostly classical, but they threw in one Celtic piece, to add a bit of colour and excitement.

The three decided they would dress formally. They'd also have tea served in a formal way, using a nice table covered with a white linen tablecloth. They even ordered an attractive floral arrangement for the table. Iris didn't have a dress that would work, so she had to shop for one. She was quite pleased with her purchase. She'd have to have her hair done the afternoon of the concert.

On the night of the concert, the three met in a small room next to the meeting auditorium just before the start of the concert.

"I peeked in the meeting room and there are at least eighty people there already and they're still pouring in," Sandra said nervously. "I hope we don't disappoint them."

"Oh, you'll knock them out with that Bruch piece," Iris said. "I love the way you play that. Your fiddling in the Celtic number is so authentic, it will raise the roof."

"Thanks, I needed that, Iris. I get so nervous before performing. Once I'm playing, I tend to settle down, so I guess we'll do okay."

"I'm sure we will," put in Myra. "Our last practice went quite well and my experience is that we tend to kick it up a notch once we're playing before an audience. Ah, I see it's just after eight. Time to go."

The three walked into the meeting room. As they walked to the stage, the audience welcomed them with polite applause. Myra stood next to the piano while Sandra and Iris, instruments in hand, took their places in the centre of the stage. Iris then walked to a microphone at one end of the stage and welcomed everyone. Before she spoke, she spotted Milton in the front row. He gave her his brightest smile. Warmth filled Iris's chest. She'd play for him, just as if he were the only one there. She refocused on her audience. "We welcome all of you and are so pleased you have come. The three of us felt that, since there is often so much tension in the hospital, we'd like to do something about that. So we've chosen some pieces that we hope will relax you. Please enjoy!"

All three felt a bit nervous in the first piece, a Schubert, but each player seemed to feed off the others and soon all were quite relaxed. Iris kept on glancing at Milton, thinking, *I'm playing this for you*. The next piece was by Mendelssohn. It was rather fast, but Myra was really into it and that spurred the other two on, it seemed. The ending went perfectly and there was a huge response with clapping and cheering. Intermission followed that piece.

Milton rushed up to the three. "That was fabulous. That should have been recorded."

"Why, thank you. We're so pleased you liked it," Sandra said.

"Would you like to be our advertising agent, Milton?" Iris asked with a mischievous grin. "We could hit the road and make a lot of money. Then we could quit all this medical stuff and find our true place in life."

"That sounds like escapism, Iris. Aren't you concerned with that emotional aberration in your oboe player, Myra?" Milton looked at Myra with mock concern.

"I've learned to put up with all kinds of weird behaviour in this ensemble," Myra said. "We just have to accept ourselves as we are."

✦ ✦ ✦

Many other admirers pushed their way in to compliment the musicians.

After the intermission, Myra and Sandra did their pieces. They felt good about how they had performed.

They still had the Celtic piece to play—their finale. All of them had to really shift gears mentally, as this tune would be very different. Iris announced the piece. "This piece may cause you to want to tap your toes. There's no room for dancing, though, unless you want to go out into the hall." Iris laughed lightly and resumed her position in the middle of the stage.

All three played together for the slow part. The mood was nostalgic. Milton kept his eyes fixed on Iris, and from time to time their eyes met. For Milton, the music fit his mood. Then, the music switched to the fast part and both Sandra and Iris moved their bodies gently with the music. Milton kept his gaze on Iris. He felt his own body responding with the rhythm of her movements that he realized were quite proper, but nonetheless, evocative—at least for him. Sandra took the next slow section on her violin. Iris continued her gentle swaying motion with a little smile. Milton loved it! Iris then did the third slow section and Milton felt his insides turning to butter. They ended with an animated fast part and the audience went wild with cheering and yelling their delight. Milton was so excited he stood, clapping vigorously, and soon the whole audience stood with prolonged applause.

The three performers looked at each other as though not sure what to do for an encore. Then Myra began playing *Danny boy*. Iris and Sandra quickly slid into their parts. They'd rehearsed the song a bit, just in case they needed an encore, so they were quite comfortable with it. After that, there was another round of applause by the delighted audience.

The tea after the concert was a great success. At least half of the audience stayed for it. The three performers met as many people as they could and chatted with each one briefly. Milton knew many that stayed for the tea and enjoyed chatting with them. He found he was now much more comfortable talking with males than he'd been several years before.

As many of the audience were leaving, Milton looked for a chance to visit briefly with Iris. When he spotted her free for the first time, he quickly walked toward her. "Iris, all of you did so well this evening. You sure hit a home run with that Celtic piece! You seemed to be enjoying it."

"Oh, yeah. We all found that the most fun to play." Iris was laughing, but then she sobered and looked into Milton's handsome face. "Milton, I'm so glad you came. You seemed to be enjoying the concert. I kept looking at you, watching your face to see if you were liking what you heard."

"I loved it—mostly because you were playing."

Iris flushed a bit, and changed the subject. "I wanted to tell you that I wrote Dr. Pinsky a letter."

"You did? What did you say?" Milton's face rapidly changed to one of concern.

"I told him I was dropping the suit and I apologized for trying to sue him. I forgave him for hurting me. I have to admit I didn't feel like doing it, but I did it because I knew God wanted me to."

Milton's face was alive with relief and joy. "Oh, Iris, you'll not regret what you've done. That took a lot of courage, I'm sure. Do you still feel okay with what you've done?"

"I feel as free as a bird in the spring. I'm not worrying about how Pinsky takes my letter. I just know I did the right thing."

Milton had the greatest urge to take her into his arms for a long hug. "You need to get some rest after all that work and excitement. I'll see you on the ward soon, in all likelihood. I have to present a case at Paediatric Rounds next Friday. If you're free, come along."

"Yeah, I'll do my best to get there."

Iris picked up her oboe and waved him goodbye with a bright smile on her face.

✦ ✦ ✦

Iris had just returned to her suite after the concert when her telephone rang. Who could be phoning her at such a late hour when she wasn't on call?

"Hello?"

"Ah, I've been trying to get hold of you all evening."

"Who is this?"

"Oh, it's Gordon. I wonder if I could talk to you?"

"Gordon who? Do I know you?" Iris felt the hair on her neck rising.

"Yeah. Well maybe not. I'm Gordon Pinsky."

Iris paused as she tried to think quickly. This must be Pinsky's oldest son, since his voice sounded adolescent. "Hi, Gordon," Iris said tentatively. "What can I do for you?"

"Well, ah, I was the one who disconnected the iron lung on you. I just wanted to apologize."

Wild impulses raced through her whole body. What should she do? Should she tell him she'd report him to the police? He sounded so emotional and sincere. Suddenly, she had a desire to meet with him, face to face. "Gordon, would you be willing to meet with me—someplace private so no one else knows about our conversation?"

"Yeah, yeah. That'd be good."

"How about in that Safeway store on 109th Street near Whyte Avenue. I'll meet you tomorrow at 7:30 p.m. in the back. There's a coffee dispenser and some chairs. If they're filled, we can just stand and talk.

"Yeah, I've often been there. I'll see you then."

✦ ✦ ✦

The next evening, Iris entered the Safeway and looked around. She didn't know who she was looking for, since she'd never seen Gordon before. All she could do was stand at the location she'd suggested and hope Gordon would identify himself. She went to the back of the store and stood by the coffee dispenser. The chairs were empty, thankfully.

"Hi." Iris recognized the voice. She turned and saw a young man with a slight build with blond straight hair coming towards her. *This must be Gordon,* she thought.

"Gordon?"

"Yeah. You Dr. Marten?"

"Yes," Iris smiled and stuck out her hand. He took it after a moment's hesitation. "Why don't we have a cup of coffee and sit down. If you don't like coffee, I see there's some water here too."

They both filled their cups half full and sat down.

"Okay, Gordon, you said you disconnected the iron lung." Iris could see Gordon was very nervous and distraught.

"Yeah."

"And you jimmied the electronic sensor on the iron lung so the nurses wouldn't be warned that the machine stopped."

"Yeah."

"Would you mind telling me how you managed to get by the nurses, alter the sensor, and disconnect the iron lung without being caught?" Iris hoped Gordon would go beyond his monosyllabic responses to her questions.

"Okay, I found out through Dad that you were admitted to the hospital with polio and that you were in the iron lung." Gordon fidgeted with his cup. "Ah, I know a girl who is a junior volunteer, a candy striper. She's about my size. So I borrowed her uniform and found a bob-cut wig and used Mom's lipstick and posed as a candy striper. I bought a cheap bouquet of flowers and went to your ward's nursing station. Making my voice higher, I said that I was a new candy striper and needed to deliver those flowers to Dr. Marten. They pointed me to you and I put the flowers next to you, telling you they were from an anonymous admirer. I quickly looked over the electronics of the machine and noticed the sensor. Before I left the ward, I asked the nurses how they'd know if the machine stopped working, since there were no nurses in the room where the iron lungs were. They pointed to an alarm that would be triggered if the machine stopped working. 'There's a sensor on the iron lung that will notify us here,' they said."

"So you left the hospital then?" asked Iris.

"Yeah. The next day, I again came as a candy striper, but this time in the evening. I'd brought along some tools that I packaged with a wrapping paper and a bow. I told the nurse I needed to give it to one of the iron lung patients and they let me through. I then hid behind some big equipment and waited until the lights were turned down. I looked over the electrical part of the iron lung and carefully opened up the sensor. I had a good idea of how it worked. I've been very interested in electronics since I was a small kid. I carefully stuck in a sliver of wood to insulate the trigger so it would malfunction. Then I simply unhooked the main power cord and hid near the door. When everyone rushed in to resuscitate you, I snuck out the door and made my escape."

Iris found her heart pounding. "So, I assume you were also the one stalking me and also left the threatening note on my window."

"Yeah."

"Gordon, I sense that you enjoy pulling stunts like the one on me."

"Yeah." He was back in the monosyllabic mode.

"Why."

"Oh, I've always been interested in electronics and I like to contrive electronic devices to play tricks on people."

"So you enjoy hurting and threatening people, even at the risk of their lives?"

"No, no. It's not like that." Gordon's face puckered up as if he were going to cry. In a wobbly voice, he said, "I was trying to help out Dad. I knew he was torn up about the suit and it was wrecking our family. I was really mad at you for doing this to my family. I really wanted to hurt you. I thought I could help Dad out because he was so depressed. You see, Dad always favoured my younger brother and I was always looking for a way to make him proud of me. Well, when these ideas came to me about how I could do some damage to you, I just got carried away. I wasn't thinking about what the outcomes might be."

"You didn't think about the fact that you could have killed me?" Iris felt a surge of anger.

"Not really. I just thought I'd give you a good scare. I thought the nurses would easily find you before it was too late. I wasn't thinking right." Gordon sobbed openly and Iris found a napkin on the table and gave it to him.

When he was more composed, Iris asked, "Gordon, would you tell me what made you decide to come to me and apologize like this?"

"Dad showed us the letter you sent him. When I read it, I was very relieved that Dad wouldn't have to go to court. When I thought about it, I couldn't get over the fact that you forgave him and even wanted to be friends with him. Then I began feeling terrible about what I'd done to you. It got so bad I couldn't sleep anymore. I thought I'd go crazy. I finally decided to go to the police and turn myself in. Then I thought that if I did that, they'd probably throw me in jail and I wouldn't get a chance to tell you I was sorry. So, that's why I came to you first. Now you can tell the police about me. At least now I know that you know the real story and I've been able to say how sorry I am that I did those things to you."

By this time, Iris was all choked up with tears flooding her eyes. She wiped her eyes and blew her nose. "Gordon, I know I should tell the police what you just told me, because the things you did are definitely criminal deserving a jail term. Maybe, because of your being a minor, you might get off more lightly. I can see that you are really remorseful and have a good chance of never doing such a thing again. I am going to trust you in this." Iris could see Gordon's face was puckering up again. "Gordon, I'm going to forgive you and I am not going to report you to the police. I'll tell my parents and Dr. Saunders about what you said, but I will tell nobody else and I know my parents and Dr. Saunders will keep what you said secret."

Gordon broke into renewed sobbing. When he finally controlled himself and wiped his nose, both stood up and Gordon looked into Iris's face. "You must be some kind of angel. You'll never know how you have changed my family and me. I want to thank you, Dr. Marten."

Chapter Thirty-Seven

THE NIGHT OF THE CONCERT, MILTON HAD GONE TO BED, HIS imagination charged with Iris and her wonderful gift of music. Though she was so forthright and assertive, she was also humble and quite willing to see her mistakes. As he rolled over in bed and tried to fall asleep, he had a hard time getting Iris's lovely image out of his head. Eventually, however, sleep claimed him.

A few hours later, he awoke with his heart pumping furiously. He had another dream of him resuscitating Iris. After blowing into her mouth, he felt her responding with breathing on her own. He drew back and saw her looking at him sweetly, smiling. Her lips were beautifully pink. He again put his lips on hers as if it were the most natural thing to do and felt the lush contact. An explosion of wonderful sensations spread down his body. He awoke and felt himself sexually aroused. At first, he just wanted to get back to the dream! Of course he couldn't. He then thought about his prayer to God about his sexuality and a huge sense of thankfulness overwhelmed him.

✦ ✦ ✦

The first patient to be presented at paediatric rounds involved a case of fever of unknown origin in a three-year-old boy. Milton tried to concentrate on the case, but his mind kept going to his own presentation due next. Iris was sitting in on the rounds and Milton felt a bit more nervous since he wanted to do a good job for her.

When his turn came, he signaled to a nurse and she went out and soon came in with a five-month-old girl and her mother. Milton introduced the mother to the audience that consisted mainly of paediatricians from the

UAH and other Edmonton hospitals. Milton handed the mother a microphone. He talked into another microphone.

"Mrs. Larsen, could you tell the audience when you noticed that something was wrong with your baby?"

The mother nervously responded, "Well, I didn't notice anything wrong until I took her to the health unit and the nurse asked me if I thought she looked pale. I told her I hadn't noticed anything. The nurse suggested the lab get a blood count done on my baby. To do that, I needed to see a doctor. So I went to the emergency department. There, they did a blood count and found it was very low. That's when the doctor asked you to see her."

"Thank you for telling us what happened, Mrs. Larsen." Milton smiled appreciatively. "Would you tell the audience how your daughter has acted, fed, and slept at home?"

"She seemed fine. Maybe she slept more than some other babies, I've been told. She ate well and she pooped and peed at regular times."

"Mrs. Larsen, could you tell us how the feedings went? Did you breastfeed?"

"I tried breastfeeding, but after a few weeks, my milk didn't come anymore. She was always hungry. So I started feeding her cow's milk, using a formula the health nurse advised me to use."

"And what was that?" Milton asked.

"Well, I was told to add a certain amount of sugar and water to homogenized milk and then I was told to bring the formula to the boiling point but not actually boil the milk."

"How much of this formula was usually taken by your baby, Mrs. Larsen?"

"Usually about five bottles a day."

"How much in each bottle?"

"Eight ounces." Mrs. Larsen seemed quite proud that her daughter was feeding so well.

"Did you give any supplements, like vitamins or iron?"

"Only three vitamins: A, C, and D."

Milton looked at the audience and said that the Larsen baby was taking about forty ounces of the formula per day, with the average being about thirty ounces. Milton paused and then asked, "Are there any more questions for the mother from anyone in the audience?"

"Are the baby's stools a normal yellow-brown, or are they dark, black, or even red?" This came from Iris.

"Good question," Milton said with a nod. He addressed the mother and asked, "Would you tell us what the poops look like, Mrs. Larsen?"

"They are usually yellow, sometimes a bit greenish. They are never dark or black. I never saw red like blood in the stool."

"Now, Mrs. Larsen, would you mind if some of the doctors and nurses came down and had a closer look at your baby?" Milton asked with a little smile.

"Yeah, that's okay."

Over half of the audience lined up to have a closer look, many raising their eyebrows and rounding their lips in surprise. When all had returned to their seats, Milton thanked the mother for bringing her child and for being willing to answer the questions. The nurse led the mother and the baby out of the room.

Milton then addressed the audience. "I can assure you that we found no liver or spleen enlargement, nor any lymph node enlargement."

Milton slipped a transparency on the viewer, showing all the lab results. The most astounding result was the extremely low hemoglobin level. "You'll notice the hemoglobin is less than one quarter of what it should be. The white blood cells are normal. The platelets are slightly elevated. The mean red cell size is quite small. The blood smear shows a remarkable pallor of the red blood cells. They look small and often misshapen."

Milton looked over the audience. "We still have some tests we've ordered, but the reports aren't back yet. I'd like to ask some of the house staff what further tests you'd like to be done?"

One paediatric resident from another hospital stuck up his hand. "I'd like to see a reticulocyte count."

Milton asked, "What would you be looking for?"

"I'd like to see if the baby had an anemia where the red blood cells were breaking down too rapidly—hemolytic anemia."

"Would anyone else of the house-staff be willing to comment on that?"

Iris stuck up her hand and said, "Hemolytic anemia is unlikely, since she looks so well. The severity of her anemia, her blood smear, and red blood cell size favour iron deficiency anemia."

"You're right, Dr. Marten. What further test would you like to see done?" Milton nodded to Iris.

"A stool test for blood would be helpful to see if she is slowly losing blood through her bowel."

"Good, Dr. Marten. We ordered that and serum iron levels, but those tests are not yet reported." Milton looked around the room and asked, "What do you think the cause of this very severe anemia is? Anyone?"

A recently qualified paediatrician stuck up his hand. "There have been some impressive reports coming out of Pittsburg that suggest that cow's milk diet in infants in the first year can sometimes induce a slow blood loss from the gut. Eventually, severe iron-deficiency anemia can occur."

"Thank you, Dr. Ladd. I ran across the same article. A paediatrician's comment in that same journal was that this form of anemia isn't found in breastfed babies, nor in babies given canned formulas that are heated a lot more than pasteurized milk."

There followed a flurry of questions and comments, many stating that they'd had parents use similarly prepared formulas without running into trouble.

Milton then moved the discussion to treatment. Several paediatricians raised their hands. Milton asked each of them for their suggestions regarding management.

Milton let that discussion go on for a while and then drew attention back to himself. "I've heard a comment in reference to this case that the mother should be investigated for negligence because she let her child get so anemic. What do you think?"

A vigorous discussion followed, with many voices speaking for and against the mother. Milton let the discussion go on for a few minutes before he made closing remarks.

✦ ✦ ✦

Iris watched this interaction with vague interest. What fascinated her more was Milton. He was doing such a good job of involving everyone in the audience and maintaining everyone's interest. He was a natural teacher. She doubted he was aware of that. She also loved his ability to keep the house staff involved in the discussion. She was so proud of how competent and in charge he was, but never focusing attention on himself. He was so handsome. She found herself desiring this man for herself—forever. She was shocked at the passion she felt for him.

Iris heard Milton's closing remarks. They involved giving his opinion of the mother. He said, "Actually, I've found this mother to be very loving and capable. I believe the anemia developed so slowly that she didn't notice the subtle changes occurring day by day. It took someone else to notice the difference between her child and other normal infants of that age." Milton thanked everyone for participating in such a lively discussion. "That's what makes these rounds so much fun," he concluded and walked from the stage.

Chapter Thirty-Eight

End of August 1963

Iris couldn't get Milton out of her mind. Now she'd just gotten back to her suite after eating supper at the cafeteria. She had to do some serious thinking. Outdoors was the best place to do that, she decided. The August sun was still high in the sky and the day was nice except for a light breeze and a few nonthreatening clouds. Iris pulled on her runners and a light windbreaker. She jogged for a couple of blocks, enjoying the late summer yards. Edmonton gardens seemed so lush compared to those in many other cities she'd seen. She slowed her pace and then began walking.

Why did I have that sudden outburst of passion for Milton? I should've been concentrating on the anemia case. After all, that's my business. I can't seem to get him out of my mind. I can no longer just treat him as a friend. If I'm going to get him out of my mind and heart, I need to never see him again. But I can't live without him.

Iris picked up her walking pace as she fought her inner war. *I know he cares for me. In fact, he cares for me more than he would for a friend. I can see it in his eyes. He says that God has changed a lot of stuff inside him. Should I take a chance on him? Oh, God, I love him so much. Help me to know what to do.*

Tears were streaming down her cheeks. She hoped other people hadn't noticed her. She blew her nose into a tissue, turned around, and headed for her suite. She looked up to the puffy white clouds slowly drifting eastward. She felt that the clouds were whispering to her to relax in God's care and plan for her life. He wouldn't fail her. He'd work out all things for the good of both Milton and her.

By the time Iris walked back into her suite, she was almost surprised at how peaceful she felt.

✦ ✦ ✦

Patrick Benson had once again led the group in a thought-provoking study of the Apostle Paul's letter to the Ephesians. Discussion had been good with most of the group contributing. Milton, however, couldn't seem to get his mind fully engaged that evening. His thoughts and emotions were still trying to digest the meaning of his highly charged dream of Iris. He wanted to discuss the implications with Patrick.

After the session closed and the group broke up for a snack, Milton went over to Patrick and asked if he could talk with him privately sometime. Patrick agreed to see him after all the other members left for home.

When all the rest had said their goodbyes, Patrick said to Milton, "Please have a seat, Milton. Is it okay if Linda's in on the discussion?"

"Oh, that'd make me happy if she could be part of it." Milton smiled at Linda.

"What's on your mind, Milton?" Patrick asked.

"Well, it's about my relationship with Dr. Marten—Iris. I've told you about it before, but now I've some more questions."

"Okay, I know about Iris. I believe you've always seen her as a special friend."

"Yes, we have become quite close. For several years now, we've both felt that a romance and marriage was out of the question because of my being gay. As you know, I'd give anything to become heterosexual. This isn't just so I could convince Iris to marry me, but because I deeply desire to be heterosexual. As you also know, I've prayed many times to God to help me change. This small group has helped me a great deal toward changing. I no longer have any desires or even any fantasies about men."

Patrick had been nodding his understanding. "Milton, we all have been praying for you daily that God would bring you out of homosexuality and would give you heterosexual desires. We've all seen changes in you that suggest these prayers are being answered."

"I am so grateful for your encouragement and your prayers. Now, I want to report some things that have been happening to me." Milton shared that he was developing a sexual attraction to Iris. "I've even had two dreams of kissing her and since then, I've been fantasizing having intimate encounters with her."

Linda couldn't help but squeal in delight. "Milt, I believe God's healing you."

"That would seem to be so, Milton." Patrick nodded. "Those are very good signs of change. Tell me, have you experienced any change in the way you see other women?"

"Yes, to a lesser extent than with Iris, of course. I, um, notice women more than I used to. Does that mean I'm becoming depraved?" asked Milton with a slight grin.

"No. You're just becoming like the rest of us men." Patrick paused a moment and then said, "You probably want to ask me if you should openly pursue a relationship with Iris with a view to marriage. Am I right?"

"Right on," Milton admitted. "I want both of your opinions and then your prayers if I should do that."

Patrick was quiet for a long moment. He glanced at Linda for support and then said, "You know, I don't feel I should tell you what I think, because this is such an important decision and you want to be sure God is speaking to you about what he wants in both of your lives. Why don't we pray right now?"

They bowed their heads and were silent for a while. Then Linda prayed, "Dear God, you made us and you made our emotions and our sexuality. We are sure that you want the best for us so we can honour you with our lives. Milton has asked you for the gift of heterosexuality so he can be happy and fulfilled in his life. We thank you for helping Milton grow so much in his spiritual life with you. We also thank you for the changes you brought about in his sexual desires. Now, we ask that you give him wisdom about his budding relationship with Iris. Please speak to him about how he should proceed in this relationship. Thank you, Jesus."

"Thank you, Jesus," Patrick echoed.

Patrick looked up and fixed his gaze on Milton's teary eyes. "I believe God will speak his wisdom to you. You need to hear from God because the implications are so great, not only for you, but for Iris as well."

Milton nodded and got up to go. Patrick and Linda arose and both hugged Milton. "We'll pray fervently in the next few days, Milton," Linda said with tears in her eyes.

"You've both been such a support to me, and tonight you've given me renewed hope. Thank you so much."

◆ ◆ ◆

Two days had gone by since Milton had talked with the Bensons. He'd been very busy on the ward and, the night before, he'd been on call. He'd been called to emergency in the late evening to admit a child. He'd also had to go to the children's ward twice in the middle of the night to start intravenous lines.

This evening, he ate supper at the cafeteria and then went to his room for a short nap. After twenty minutes, his alarm rang and he tried to read a journal, but soon gave up. His emotions were still in turmoil. In fact, the only reason he could concentrate on anything other than Iris was if the problem at hand was very severe, requiring all his attention.

The weather was cool and cloudy with a stiff west breeze and even light rain. However, he had to think and pray and he needed to walk. He pulled on a sweater and a raincoat and went out. The streets were empty, all the better to concentrate.

Milton guessed that Iris still thought he was gay, although he'd told her he'd stopped fantasizing about men and that he was praying God would change him. He'd heard that someone had spread a rumour that he had a gay partner. He doubted Iris believed the rumour, but rumours had their power to build suspicions and doubts.

He wondered whether Tim had contacted Iris since her recovery. He wouldn't be surprised if he had. What would Iris's response be? She had mentioned nothing about him since her illness, but she might not have said anything for fear of hurting Milton.

Milton thought of his dilemma. If he told Iris about the dreams and his feelings for her, he'd really be asking to date her with a view to marriage. Would that be fair, unless he could be absolutely sure that he'd permanently become heterosexual? Could he say that? *Oh God, where are you? I need to hear your voice in my life. I need your direction.* Milton heard only the sound of his feet trudging along the lonely street.

Milton's thoughts turned to his dream of Iris. How radiant she had appeared. There seemed to be no hesitancy or doubt in her eyes. Yes, he remembered that he saw only deep trusting love. If only that dream were true! Milton stumbled along, tears now running down his cheeks.

I gave you that dream, Milton. Now act on it.

Milton took in a sharp breath. Was that God? Those words didn't seem to be his own thoughts. He then looked up into the sodden sky and said aloud, "Dear God, I'm taking those words as your words to me." He walked on for a few blocks tossing over in his mind the implications of the words he'd just heard in his head. Finally, he said to whoever wanted to hear, "Okay, God, I'll do it."

✦ ✦ ✦

Three days after his walk in the rain, Milton felt the need to settle himself down inside. He decided some painting was a good way to accomplish this. He'd helped his landlady with the evening meal dishes and his evening was free. He quickly set up his watercolour equipment in his bedroom. After flipping through scenery photos he'd taken, he selected one that showed potential for inspiring him. He liked using a photo only to point him in the general direction his painting would take. The picture was a typical Saskatchewan scene featuring a salt flat next to a field of canola.

Milton laid down a light blue wash for the sky, light toward the horizon, but leaving patches for clouds. He needed to allow the paint to thoroughly dry before proceeding. As he waited, his mind drifted to Iris's lawsuit against Dr. Pinsky. He was so pleased she had told him that she had forgiven him for hurting her. He knew she was listening to the voice of Jesus as he had advised. No matter what Dr. Pinsky would do with her letter, Iris was freed from the weight of guilt and anger that often accompanied litigation. He was so proud of her.

Next, Milton made some quick brush strokes with light ultramarine on the patches left for clouds and dabbed darker colour nearby before the lighter colour dried. Ah, those clouds looked like they could rain. He recalled the University Hospital music concert and Iris playing oboe. She and the other girls had done such an excellent job. That first piece suited the plaintive sound of the oboe. The sadness, even sorrow, had come through so well. He wondered if the piece was chosen because of the way Iris felt about their relationship. He was quite sure it was.

Milton defined the horizon with a light moss green to show light shining on distant fields. His dream about resuscitating Iris came to mind again. How good those lips felt. He still recalled the electricity spreading delightfully right into his stomach and down into his toes. Was the dream really a gift from God? Yes, he now was sure it was. One thing it showed him—he was alive to heterosexual feelings. That was good. Very good!

After mixing a light sandy colour, Milton created a salt flat, allowing crests of white to show through. He knew he possibly still had homosexual issues, but he was so amazed and thankful that God had changed him so much. He began to feel a little more confident that he could actually be a good husband to someone. Could he be so lucky as to think that someone could be Iris?

Using a soft yellow, he painted the fields with a brighter shade for the closer fields of canola. Would Iris be too fearful of future reversals in his sexual healing? He'd read of other marriages where, in spite of having children, one of the spouses was homosexual and the relationship eventually fell apart. What a tragedy if that were to happen to Iris and him. She'd be safer with a guy like Tim.

Using a stiff bristled brush with darker moss green and deep brown, he created tufts of grass circumscribing the salt flat. "Lord, you told me you gave me the dreams and you said to act on them. That means doing some things in keeping with those dreams." He grew still and waited. A thought drifted through his mind. Ask *her to join you for a walk this Sunday afternoon. You both have it off.* Well, wouldn't that be nice if that were God saying that! *Why couldn't that have been God?* Milton tossed his paintbrush into a jar of water, jumped up, and headed to the phone in the hallway. He would call Iris before some other voice came to advise him not to—like it had happened so many times before.

"Hi, Iris. Are you able to talk for a minute?"

"Sure, Milt. You're always my first priority."

"That's comforting. How has it been in haematology these last few days?"

"I couldn't be happier in this department. The work is challenging, but Tom Conner is such a wonderful teacher and friend. He's almost like a father to me."

"That's wonderful. The head of Paeds isn't quite like Conner, but I'm enjoying the program—that is, when I'm not falling over with fatigue. I'm seeing lots of very exciting patients like that girl with iron deficiency anemia."

"You did such a good job with that presentation."

"Thank you. I enjoyed doing it. Hey, listen. Are you busy this Sunday afternoon?"

"That depends. What are you planning?"

"I'd enjoy a walk with you, perhaps along the river valley. Are your legs strong enough for that?"

"That sounds like fun. My legs are as strong as they ever were. If I know you, you have some agenda in mind. What's perking in that wonderful brain of yours?"

"Well, you guessed it. I do have something to discuss. First I need to ask you if it's okay if we break both parts of our agreement to not talk about religion or our relationship?"

Milton could hear her take a sharp breath. "I don't know if I should be scared or happy."

"Well, I really don't know how it'll affect you. I've just got to get something off my chest, Iris. I'd love it if you could patiently hear me out on something."

"Is two o'clock at our usual place at the trail head okay, Milt?"

"Perfect."

Milton walked back to his room and picked up the now dry painting. "Yeah, it's okay, just a bit bleak." *That's what my life is like. It just needs some life in it, like Iris.*

Chapter Thirty-Nine

September 1, 1963

IRIS WAS OFF FOR THE WEEKEND AND SHE FOUND HERSELF GETTING VERY excited about the meeting with Milton. She hoped he wouldn't say something negative—maybe even say he'd decided to become a celibate or, even worse, live a gay lifestyle. No, she was pretty certain Milton wouldn't do that. She wasn't going to go to their meeting with a spirit of defeat. Regardless of what Milton might say, she wanted to impress Milton with her upbeat attitude and a pleasing appearance. So, on Saturday she went to a beauty parlor. Her hairdresser pulled off a miracle with her hair. She decided to wear some nice slacks and the same blouse Milton had given to her. She'd also wear a bright scarf and some earrings. On Sunday afternoon, she looked into the mirror, smiled and said to the mirror, "Well, I think I'm ready for him."

✦ ✦ ✦

Milton had arrived at their meeting place a bit early. He parked his old truck in the little parking lot and looked over the valley. What a restful sight. He needed to calm his jangled nerves. His emotions were doing summersaults. There seemed to be so many things against a deeper relationship with Iris. For all he knew, Iris was still seeing Tim. Marrying Tim would be a safer choice for her. He was so virile, so male, so athletic, and so handsome. He'd certainly give her the children she so much desired. Tim had so many features Milton didn't possess. Yet Milton loved Iris more than he could bear. He breathed a prayer. "Oh, God of my life, help me to face whatever happens today. Give me the grace to do the things that are best for Iris. You know what they are."

He heard her car before he saw it. It was a greenish Volkswagen. He raised his hand and she drove up next to his truck. As she emerged from the car, Milton's breath caught. She looked stunningly beautiful. He didn't deserve her. *Oh God, let me just be me today.* He wanted to compliment her but he was speechless.

✦ ✦ ✦

"Hello, Milt. Are you okay?" *Oh God, I shouldn't have dressed up. I've embarrassed him.*

"Yeah, sure, Iris. You look so wonderful I'm speechless."

"I wanted to please you."

"Oh, you've done that—more than you could imagine."

Iris responded with a radiant, hopeful smile. With a nod down the path she said, "Come on. Let's walk. It's a glorious day."

With that, they strolled along the walking path descending toward the river. As they came into view of the river, they saw a flotilla of about ten geese—two parents and their offspring. Milton and Iris stopped and stared. Iris breathed, "Beautiful." She longed to be like them—husband and wife with a bunch of children. Could that ever be her lot in life? Then she thought, *Would I be able to live with Milton even if he remained homosexual?*

As they moved on without saying anything, she thought that maybe she could. They had such a close friendship. She supposed it might actually work if both chose to remain celibate. She'd decided to be celibate herself, after all.

"You look very thoughtful, Iris. Care to share in what you are thinking?"

No. She couldn't say what she was actually thinking! "Oh, I was just thinking about geese mating for life," she lied. "I think I once heard that they did."

For another twenty minutes, they talked about a variety of subjects ranging from nature that they saw along the riverbank to their busy call schedules. Then they came to a bench and decided to sit for a while. Iris looked over to Milton and saw his handsome face looking thoughtfully out across the river. Wouldn't it be wonderful to be sitting together in a living room of their own house, drinking coffee, chatting away about their experiences in medicine, and sharing their difficult medical cases? No one was more fun than Milton to chat about things like that. That would require that they'd be married. *Oh, God help us.*

"You're going to drown in that ocean of thoughts, Iris."

Iris realized Milton had stopped surveying the river and was looking right at her. How long had she been lost in thought? "Sorry, Milton. Come on, let's walk again."

✦ ✦ ✦

They walked on in silence for a while. Milton's mind was a jumble of thoughts. He was convinced Iris deserved to have a husband that could fulfill all of her sexual needs. Could he give that to her? He wasn't certain, even though God had changed a lot of things inside him. How could he be sure? Here would be a good case for a trial of sex before marriage. No, that wasn't God's way, he was sure. He'd just have to trust God. That was so hard.

Who said trusting me would always be easy?

Where did that come from? If that's you, God, I'll trust you to do things your way.

Iris reached out and yanked at Milton's arm. "Milt, now you're the one lost in your thoughts. I'm sure you came here with a very specific issue you wanted to discuss. Why is it so hard to tell me about it?"

Milton stopped and looked at Iris's hand on his forearm. It felt good, and reassuring. He had to get this out, now. His mouth felt dry. He licked his lips, took a deep breath and said, "Well, here goes. First of all, please tell me how things are going between you and Tim?"

Iris pulled Milton to resume walking. "That's finished. I told him we could never agree on the most important things in life. Yeah, it's all over with Tim and me."

"And what, for you, are the most important things in life that separate you from Tim?"

"Our view of Jesus is very different. Also, the way we view Scriptural authority is very different. There are other differences, too, but not as major."

"Iris, I'm so pleased to hear that. I know your faith had been very important to you when you first came to university. Have you gone back to that?"

"Yes, I have. Only now my faith seems more mature, somehow. You know, Milt, you've helped me get there. I don't know that I would've been strong enough without you."

"Thank you, but I can't take much credit there. God cleared the way for that to happen. I just followed God's nudging."

"So, is that what you wanted to ask me?" Iris skipped ahead so she could better see Milton's face.

"Yeah, but that's not the only thing I wanted to say." They stopped walking and faced each other. "Iris, I think God has done something inside me, like about my sexual situation." Milton could see Iris's mouth drop open. "As I told you before, I stopped having homosexual fantasies quite a while ago. It's been months, and they haven't returned."

"What do you attribute that to?"

"You know, I think it really started getting better when I started attending my church and especially after I began going to our small group. First of all, they accepted me as I was, even with my homosexual inclinations. Most important, I'm sure, was the action of the leader, Patrick, who touched me and hugged me non-sexually. It was as if he affirmed my maleness through his maleness. The other men in the group completely accepted me just as I was. Ever since, I could feel God healing me. Do you understand what I'm saying?"

"I told you, I would have thought any male-to-male contact like that would worsen the homosexual condition. That took real courage for Patrick to do what he did. Is that some kind of new treatment?"

"I don't really know. He said he just got the impression from God that that is what I needed. He's very sensitive that way. Anyway, as I said, I've noticed these changes and I've become quite hopeful."

"That's so wonderful. How has that changed your feelings toward people of the opposite sex?"

Milt reached over and took Iris's hands in his. Touching her soft fingers sent electric impulses shooting through his whole system. "Iris, I don't know when it started, but for the last few years, I've cared more and more about you. I used to think it was just a developing friendship, but something more is happening." Tears filled Milton's eyes, but he kept going. "I find you very attractive. Oh, I've always thought that about you. In the past year or two, I've found you attractive as a woman—your sexuality. That's why I wanted to buy you those sexy clothes." Both giggled.

Milton snuffed his nose a bit and carried on. "I think it really started when you had Guillain-Barrie Syndrome and I gave you mouth-to-mouth resuscitation. I couldn't forget about your lips. I kept fantasizing about them.

I even dreamed about that resuscitation twice. I kept wanting to resuscitate you so I could touch those lovely lips again."

By this time, Iris's face was all puckered up and tears were streaming down her cheeks. With a soft voice, Iris asked, "What else did you want to do with me, Milt?"

At this, Milton let out a good laugh. "Oh, lots more, but I need to keep this clean. The squirrels might be listening."

"Oh, but they won't mind it if I need resuscitation again." Iris sobered her face in mock seriousness. "I don't think I can breathe, Milton. Do you think you could help me?" Iris's eyes were sparkling in delight.

"I've wanted to do this for so long." Milton took Iris in his arms and gently touched her lips with his. He pulled away and then kissed her again, this time passionately. When they finally pulled apart, Milt muttered, "Wow, that was far better than my dreams."

Iris jerked loose, threw her arms in the air and yelled a loud "Whoopee!" Then she ran back to Milton, threw her arms around him, and planted another firm kiss on his lips. For a good while, they just stood holding each other, without a care for anyone who might have passed by.

"I can only offer you what I am now, Iris," Milton said. "There are still many uncertainties in my future. I don't know if you can live with that."

Iris gently smoothed out the lines of concern on Milton's face. "I'm prepared to live with those uncertainties. I don't want you to worry about them on account of me. I know your heart, Milt, and I trust you. I also trust God who rules both of our lives."

"Oh, Iris, you'll never know how much that means to me." Milton kissed her again.

Eventually the two lovers slowly strolled back to the trailhead, their arms around each other. They seemed to be floating in a surreal world where they could scarcely believe that what they were doing was real. But it was. They couldn't stop their outbursts of joyous giggling. The nature that surrounded them seemed to be laughing with them. When they got near the trailhead, Milton stopped and said, "You know, we need to give God our thanks and praise. He answered our prayers."

"Agreed. I'll start." Iris held Milton's hands and thanked God for his loving care and his ingenious way of bringing them together. Milton thanked God for healing his thinking and emotions. He ended, "Please Lord, be our guide for whatever future you have planned for us."

Iris smiled as she looked into Milton's brown eyes and said in a low voice, "And what do you think that future holds, Milt?"

"That all depends," Milton said with raised eyebrows.

"On what?"

"On what your answer is."

"What's the question?"

"Iris, will you marry me?"

"On the one condition that you never stop being the person you really are."

"Well, I need God's help for that."

"We'll always need God's help in our marriage."

"Do I take that as a yes?"

"Yes, Milton, you can take that as a passionate yes." Iris's face beamed and Milton pulled her in for another long kiss.

Chapter Forty

Iris and Milton were eager to make wedding plans, but they'd had to put it off to mid-September when they'd both be free of ward obligations. They'd finally found an evening that worked for both of them. They met at their favourite coffee shop on Whyte Avenue. Each brought their wall calendar and a notebook.

Milton took a sip of his coffee and asked, "So, what date have you in mind, Iris?"

Iris smiled. "Sometime soon, before the weather becomes a factor, don't you think?"

"Sure, that suits me. We might need to keep the wedding fairly simple then."

"That's okay with me. I don't like elaborate, showy weddings."

"My sentiments exactly." Milton smiled.

"Let me see," said Iris as she looked at her calendar. "What about November the first? Could you be free that day and a few days after?"

Milton flipped to November in his calendar. "That day is okay, but I'd have to make some trades for night calls for a few days beyond the wedding day. I'm sure I could get the other residents' co-operation."

"Good, now let's look at where to have the wedding," Iris put her pencil down and sipped some of coffee.

"Usually, the wedding occurs at the bride's family's church. That would be in Badger Creek."

"You know, Milt, that would work fine for my family, but then the guests would have to do a lot of traveling. I'm wondering if it would be better to have it in Edmonton, maybe at your church. My parents wouldn't mind driving in. Would your church be willing?"

"They'd be honoured to host it. My pastor would be delighted to officiate, I'm sure."

"Well then, that's decided. What kind of ceremony would you want, Milt?"

"I've always liked a simple ceremony; maybe just a bridesmaid and a best man, with your father giving away the bride. Simple standard vows are okay with me."

"You're easy to please. Yeah, I'm happy with that. If I were to choose, I'd like to ask Myra if she'd agree to be my bridesmaid."

"No problem with her. She's a real dear," observed Milton. "So far as best man is concerned, I could choose any one of many good friends, but I feel I wouldn't want to ask anyone from my home group because it would suggest I had a favourite. I don't have favourites in my group or my church. I've been thinking I'd like to invite Bill Street. He's not a Christian and he's a practicing gay. I hope you wouldn't object to him being my best man, would you?"

"Ah, that's precious! I love that, Milton. Myra's in the same category, you know."

"I think by inviting known gay and lesbian people to our wedding, we'd send a message to the gay community that we still respect and care for them."

"I couldn't agree more. Before we finalize the date with the church, I need to make sure I can come up with a wedding dress, unless you want me in the outfit you bought for me," Iris said looking mischievously at Milton.

"That would certainly create a sensation! No, I think you need to buy a dress or have one made. So once you find out how long it will take to secure a wedding dress, we can contact my church and arrange a date."

"For special music during the ceremony, I'd like to ask Sandra to play her violin with Myra accompanying her. Would you be okay with that?"

"I'd love that. It would have to be a more modest piece than that Celtic number you played at your concert."

"I agree. She'll find something nice."

"Now, if that more or less takes care of the ceremony, we need to decide where we'll have the reception. I'd suggest we have it in our church's basement. There's a large dining area there."

"Sure, that's okay with me. We could go potluck on the meal if we wanted to save money," Iris said quite seriously.

"I like that idea. We haven't got much money to spare and we'll be a while until we're able to make decent salaries. Besides, it'd give a chance for our guests to feel they were contributing toward the wedding."

"Perhaps we'd need to feel out some of our guests as to what they would think about that idea."

"Good thought, Iris. So that would need to be done as soon as we agree on whom to invite. You know, I'd like to invite a group of musicians I've heard play on campus. They play my favourite baroque music. I don't think they'd be asking too much of a fee. They could play a few pieces at the reception as background music while we're eating."

"Sounds good to me, Milt. Ask them."

"Now about whom to invite," Milton said, "I'd like to invite my parents, my brother and his wife, and then all my home group and also the Sandoskis from our church. What about you, Iris?"

"Well, my parents, of course, and Ralph and his girlfriend if he has one. I'd like to invite my research colleagues and also Dr. Tom Conner and his wife."

"Yeah, that sounds good. I'd be very happy to see both the Conners and the Sandoskis there."

"There're two other people I'd like to invite, but I don't know if you'd agree. I'd like to invite the Pinskys."

"You would?" Milton exclaimed with excited surprise. "That's so generous, forgiving, and loving of you. I'd love to see them invited, but I don't know if they'd come."

"I know they likely wouldn't, but I'd like to ask them." Iris was pleased Milton agreed to this.

Iris drank the rest of her coffee and then looked into Milton's face, smiled and said, "I've one more person I'd like to invite. If you nix my request, I don't mind. I'd like to invite Tim. I don't know, but somehow it seems right—maybe for both of us to finish processing a failed relationship."

"I'm good with that, Iris. It would help to bring closure to that relationship."

"Thank you, Milton."

The waiter refilled their coffee cups a third time as the two continued working on their invitation list. They were feeling great about how easily their plans were coming together.

◆ ◆ ◆

Iris was sitting in the beauty parlor with a dryer over her head. Her mind wandered to the responses to their wedding invitations. Her dad and Trish were beyond excitement. They'd been informed the day after Milton's proposal, but their excitement about attending the wedding eclipsed the initial announcement. Ralph also was elated and promised to come. Nearly all of her research colleagues were also planning to attend. Myra had always been a little skeptical about the success of a marriage involving a gay person. She'd become more accepting of the idea and was very honoured to be asked to be bridesmaid and to accompany Sandra on the piano. Sandra was happy to come and had phoned back in a few days to say what she was going to play. She asked if she could bring her boyfriend along and Iris had been happy for her to do that.

More amazing, however, was a note from the Pinskys that they'd be glad to come. When she received the reply, she'd cried with joy and thankfulness. Tim also replied and said he'd like to attend. Then he asked if it would be okay if he brought his fiancée, Katie, along. Iris had been a little shocked at first, but then happy that Tim was getting on with his life. She'd replied that he should certainly do so, adding her congratulations to the couple.

As Iris reflected on the upcoming wedding, she felt that the guests were just as important as she and Milton making their public marriage vows.

◆ ◆ ◆

Milton was in his room setting out his clothes for the wedding. He had plenty of time to dress and get to the church, so he had time to reflect on the day ahead. He thought about all the people that would be coming. Right after he and Iris had agreed to marry, he'd called his parents. They'd been stunned by the news. He hadn't given them any warning, so they were speechless for a few moments. Finally they began talking. His mother seemed apprehensive about the success of the marriage since Milton was gay. His father became quite excited and had said, "Milton, I believe God will give you what's needed to make the marriage successful in every way."

His mother had said, "Son, I'm just hoping that you have made a wise decision. We're definitely coming to your wedding."

His father had asked, "Could you use a little help with the expenses in any way?" Milton had told him there weren't any big expenses, but his father had asked him if he was going to wear a tuxedo. Milton had told him he was going to wear the best suit he had in the closet. His father had responded, "You buy the suit you'd like and I'll pay for it."

His mother had said, "See, Milton, he used to be a tightwad, but now he thinks he's Santa Claus." Milton chuckled again as he thought of them. He couldn't get over how much his father had changed. Milton had called his brother in North Vancouver, but he declined, as he and his wife would be vacationing in Mexico.

Milton's entire small group had promised to come. Patrick had said he was very honoured for him and Linda to be asked to attend and would be glad to be the emcee at the reception. The Sandoskis had told him wild horses couldn't keep them from coming.

When Milton had asked Bill Street to be his best man, Bill had been overwhelmed. He'd finally asked, "Why would you ask me, a practicing homosexual and a sinner, to stand up for you, especially when you're trying to shake off the stigma of homosexuality? I just don't get it."

Milton had told him, "You continuing to live actively in a gay lifestyle and you not becoming a Christian doesn't change our relationship. We're still good friends and it'll stay that way." Bill had seemed dumbfounded by Milton's attitude, but finally had agreed to be his best man.

Yes, this was going to be an interesting wedding where most if not all knew about Milton's homosexual past. Yet, he was quite confident no one would bring the topic up at the wedding or reception—not that it would matter if someone did.

✦ ✦ ✦

Iris was standing with her father in the church foyer. It was exactly 2:00 p.m. The time had finally come and she was brimming with excitement. She looked at her father who seemed equally excited and happy. He couldn't seem to stop smiling. She looked down at her wedding gown—glistening white satin. Out of the corners of her eyes, she saw that her shoulder-length veil was in place. The wedding gown as well as the bouquet she was carrying were paid for by her dad and Trish. She looked through the open door into the sanctuary and saw Milton and Bill standing primly in their assigned positions. She hadn't seen Milton's new suit. She was too far away to see the suit or Milton's face properly.

The chamber orchestra Milton had arranged had been playing while the guests arrived. They were on their last piece and they sounded so wonderful, she could cry. She had to restrain her tears or she would smudge her mascara. She shouldn't have worn any makeup and then she could cry all she wanted.

Her father nudged her. "Time to go, daughter."

"Could you carry me? My legs feel so week, I'm so excited."

"I'm in no better shape than you are. Let's hang on to each other."

As they slowly made their way up the aisle, Iris kept her eyes on Milton who looked very happy. As she got closer, she could hardly believe how handsome he was. His eyes seemed to be drawing her to him.

Just before the pastor began to speak, Peter whispered to Iris, "It's not too late. Do you want to make a run for it?"

Iris had to make a supreme effort to keep from bursting out in laughter. That broke the tension and she began to relax and enjoy the ceremony.

✦ ✦ ✦

As Iris was slowly walking down the aisle with her father, Milton was utterly amazed at how beautiful Iris was—just like the dream he had of her. She seemed so happy. How blessed he was to be having this gorgeous woman coming toward him to give her whole life in permanent union with him! A wave of deep thanks to God filled his being for bringing this moment about.

The ceremony went along simply, but with deep meaning. Milton's pastor then had the couple sit on decorated chairs after which he delivered a short sermon. He emphasized the importance of each giving their lives to God daily, even before giving their lives to each other. If they did that well, their marriage would stay healthy and enjoyable. He mentioned how Milton and Iris had allowed God to mould their lives in such a way to allow for this wonderful healthy and godly union to take place.

Sandra and Myra played well during the signing of the registry. Then Milton and Iris were being pronounced husband and wife. The chamber orchestra played a rousing Vivaldi piece for the recessional. Milton and Iris, along with Myra and Bill, greeted all the guests as they emerged from the sanctuary. Iris was excited to talk briefly to all the people that they'd invited. When Milton's parents came along, Iris could see how deeply the connection was between Milton and his father. That was a miracle, considering what life was like for Milton in his growing up years. She noticed that Milton had his mother's eyes.

Iris spotted the Pinskys and when they smiled at her, her eyes filled with tears. "I'm so glad you came," Iris said.

"We are so grateful you invited us," Dr. Pinsky said. "We'll see you later at the reception." Iris noticed the genuine smile on Mrs. Pinsky's face.

The potluck meal was a hit with everyone and when the tributes and all the thank-you speeches were done, Patrick announced that the bridal couple would be making their way around the room to greet and thank people for coming. Iris and Milton rose and their first stop was to talk to Milton's grandmother. She was wizened with age, but beaming with joy. "Oh, I'm so happy for you two. My prayers have been answered. Iris, you have married a wonderful man. I can't wait to get to know you better."

"We're planning a trip to Calgary to meet you and Milt's parents next summer, Mrs. Saunders," Iris said with a big smile. Both Milton and Iris hugged Rachel before moving on.

Iris quickly scanned the guests and spotted Tim. "Let's see Tim and his fiancée next," suggested Iris.

When they got to the table, Iris said to Tim, "I'm so glad you came, Tim, and I'm delighted to meet you, Katie. Now that you know how to do weddings properly, you can get on with it," Iris joked, feeling a little awkward, wondering where the conversation was going to go next.

"It was simple but beautiful and full of meaning," Tim said with a genuine smile. "I've told Katie all about my on-and-off relationship with you, Iris. As you told me, I need to find someone who can share my dream and vocation.' Well, I finally did. Katie is a teacher. We're planning to spend two or three months of each year in Africa or India working in our mission project, doing what we feel is our calling. Our heartfelt wishes are that both of you will have a happy and fulfilling marriage."

"We wish you the same," Milton said with a wide smile.

The couple wandered about to speak to many others. As they made their way back to their table, they came to Myra. She rose from her chair and said, "Iris, I want to say how much I think of you as a human being. You astound me by the quality of your character. You truly are living up to the life of this Jesus with your forgiving and loving nature. Milton, you've married a remarkable woman. I hope you realize that." Myra had tears in her eyes.

Milton nodded. "I couldn't agree with you more, Myra."

"You're so encouraging, Myra. Thank you for those kind and generous words," Iris said. "I hope I can live up to them." She chuckled but had tears in her eyes.

When Milton and Iris returned to their seats, Patrick announced an open microphone. Iris and Milton were a little nervous about doing that because of what some people might say. However, they had nothing to hide and they had prayed it would be a time for some good words of blessing and encouragement.

Dr. Sandoski slowly approached the microphone. Milton could see that he had aged. When he took hold of the microphone, he chuckled in his characteristic way and said, "When I first saw Milton, he looked like a scared rabbit. I soon discovered that he had a keen mind and a sensitive spirit. He was eager to discover the wonders of science. I was very pleased to find that he was also eager to discover the creator of science. I wish I knew Iris more than I do, but I can tell you her life will be vastly enriched by her newly acquired husband. Thank you for inviting my wife and me."

The next to speak was Fred, Milton's father. "My wife Gladys has always understood the great person Milton was and is, but I was slow in appreciating his fine qualities. I eventually caught on and now I'm so proud of his accomplishments and of him as a person. I confess that for many years of my life, I was only interested in making lots of money. I needed that to feed my gambling addiction. Then one day, Milton came home and told us he'd become a Christian. That didn't impress me much at first, but then the new life we saw in him ignited in me a desire to search for the same thing he had. Well, I thought I'd check out the nearby Anglican Church that my mother attended. I found the good news there and my life has never been the same. I say all this just to thank Milton for showing me the God that now guides my life." Milton stood up and, in front of everyone, hugged his father. When Milton returned, Iris saw tears in his eyes.

Then, to the shock of both Iris and Milton, Dr. Pinsky rose and went to the microphone. "Most of you won't know me. I'm a science professor in the virology department of the University of Alberta Hospital. I first met Iris when she was a medical student. She won a competition to work summers in our laboratory. She proved to be a valuable researcher in the area of poliovirus transmission. She was then given a job to continue this research. Since she made some pivotal discoveries, she was asked to prepare a paper that could be published. She did that job brilliantly. At that time, I have to admit, I was filled with the ambition of making a name for myself. I made a grievous error in not acknowledging her important work and the work of those working under her. She responded like any reasonable person would. A litigation process was launched against me for the damage my actions would cause her career.

"You could never know how much being sued depressed me, and my family. It got so bad, I could hardly work. I think the worst was the thought that I knew I was at fault. Then just before the preliminary hearings were to start, I received a letter from Iris. She stated that she was withdrawing the lawsuit. She also said she was forgiving me for any hurt or damage I had done to her. She even apologized for causing my family and me so much pain. She said she did all this because she felt God was asking her to do it." By this time, Dr. Pinsky was having trouble controlling his emotions. After a pause, he continued. "I want to take this opportunity to publicly apologize to Iris for the pain and damage I've inflicted on her. I know my wife and I have been thinking a lot about a God that can produce such a wonderful spirit in someone like Iris. She even expressed a wish that we could once again be friends. Well, I'd like that. Thank you for giving me a chance to say these words." Dr. Pinsky walked back to sit next to his wife who was wiping her eyes.

Iris and Milton were also wiping their eyes, and blowing their noses. Iris became aware that her mascara would be a mess, but she didn't care. Dr. Pinsky's words brought profound relief and joy deep inside her. Once again, she breathed a prayer of thanks for a God who could change her hard heart and produce this wonderful result.

A few others wanted to say a few words to encourage the couple. Before Patrick brought the program portion of the reception to a close, he gave his own tribute to Milton. He ended with, "Milton is an intelligent, sensitive and principled physician who has the admirable ability to allow God to develop the fruit of the Spirit in his life. Now, understanding Iris better after the extremely generous words by Dr. Pinsky, I can see that these two wonderful children of God will be a great force for good in God's kingdom. Thank you, Milton and Iris, for letting me be emcee."

Gradually, people got up and began mingling, but they all realized that they had experienced the most extraordinary wedding in their lives.

Epilogue

December 24, 1963

When Iris and Milton pulled up to the Marten home in Badger Creek country, they were once again impressed with the beautiful home and setting. The aspens with their white trunks stood proudly next to the dark green spruce, whose sturdy fronds were resolutely bearing the glistening clumps of snow. The spruce, aspens, and squat junipers snuggled against the house as if to keep it warm and cozy. Beyond the house, on the far escarpment across the dry creek, the distant boulders and leafless red cranberry bushes huddled against layer upon layer of lodge pole pines and willows. This winter scene was very familiar to Iris.

The door flew open and the red hair of Trish flashed into view. With a huge smile, she spread her arms and enveloped Iris and then Milton in a generous hug. Peter was right behind, hugging and patting them on their backs. Leaning against the doorpost was Ralph with a tentative smile. He seemed to be waiting until all the commotion died down before he greeted the newlyweds.

As Iris and Milton entered the house, the rich fragrance of a huge fresh pine tree stimulated their senses. It was proudly standing guard in the corner of the living room, next to the fireplace.

This was Christmas in Badger Creek country. How blessed she had been to be part of this home! Here she'd suffered the enormous pain of the loss of her mother. Here also was the family's struggle to redefine itself in a new way. Yes, that struggle had been fruitful in maturing her into adulthood and finding a new and fulfilling relationship in the form of a new mother, Trish. Here her father had grown immeasurably in emotional maturity and in spirit. As she sat comfortably on a couch beside Milton, the love of her life, Iris now realized that this home would also become Milton's second home—a place he could also come for nurturing of body and soul.

"Would you both like some tea?" asked Trish.

Iris looked toward Milton. He nodded. "Yes, Trish, that would be great."

While Trish disappeared into the kitchen, Ralph and Peter took seats in stuffed chairs opposite Milton and Iris. Peter inquired regarding the trip from Edmonton. The three discussed road and weather conditions until Trish brought in a tray of tea and cookies.

"You two didn't have much of a honeymoon, did you?" asked Trish as she poured the tea.

"No we didn't," Iris said. "We decided to go to the McDonald Hotel for three days. That allowed us to walk to nearby restaurants and the Citadel Theatre. That worked out really well. After that, we were back to the sweat shop."

"Where are you living now?" Ralph asked. "You weren't able to squirrel Milton into your small apartment, were you?"

"No, the owners wouldn't allow that even if we wanted to," said Iris, smiling. "We found a suite in another apartment block just east of the campus. It's a humble dwelling, but it will do until we have to move again."

After some discussion of Iris and Milton's work situations, Peter excused himself. "I need to make a trip into town to pick up a few items from the grocery store. I hope to be home well before supper."

"Just as long as you get back by six," Trish said. "Bring along a small container of whipping cream, Peter."

As Peter headed out, Trish said to Iris, "If you want to give me a hand with the potatoes and salad, Iris, I'll work on the roast and the other vegetables."

Iris sprang to her feet. "Of course, I'm glad to help out." She looked at Milton and then Ralph. "You two could get to know each other, just as long as you're not comparing your views of me since you both know me so well."

"We'll try to respect those limitations," Milton reassured.

Milton and Ralph discussed their training programs, and eventually talked about the families they had come from.

"It seems we are doing very different things now in our training programs, but we're both in the health field," Ralph said. "You're working with people's physical health and I'll be working with their spiritual wellbeing."

Milton laughed. "Yeah, I never thought of it that way before. I'd be hardpressed to say which would be considered more important in the grand scheme of things. I can say this, though. There are many illnesses, even in children, where there is a significant emotional or spiritual dimension. When patients or their parents have a true faith in God, they deal with illness much better, I've observed."

"That's fascinating. Do you remember some examples of that?" Ralph asked.

Milton told Ralph about the family's response to the man who was dying of a bowel cancer. "When patients and their families have a hope of a future life beyond the grave, their attitudes are so much better. When there is hope, I've found, their chances of surviving longer are improved."

"That makes sense," Ralph said. "I've observed a number of people who have made bad spiritual choices that resulted in emotional wreckage with physical spillover. Often, in these cases, erroneous assessments have been made when the only focus was on their physical problems with no recognition of root spiritual problems."

In the kitchen, Trish and Iris carried on an animated discussion of their own, while preparing supper. They both possessed the ability to multitask.

"So, are you still working full time at the town library, Trish?" asked Iris as she finished peeling a potato and tossed it into a pot.

"No, those days are gone. I'm still chief librarian, but I only work three days a week now. I've some good helpers who could easily take over if I ever quit. The town says they couldn't get on without me, but I think they're just flattering me," Trish said with a laugh.

"Oh, I imagine they are being honest. I remember very well the days I began to sneak into your library and how helpful and caring you were. You were and still are very special to me." Iris looked at Trish with glistening eyes.

"Those were exciting and wonderful times for me. I always felt so good when I could be of help to you or your dad."

They chatted on about old times, including when Iris had played her oboe with Trish accompanying her on the piano.

Around ten minutes to six o'clock, the front door opened to admit Peter.

"Just in time," shouted Trish. "I began to get worried as to what had become of you, darling."

"I'm sorry, I met my old friend Harold in the grocery and time slipped away," Peter said.

"You can wash your hands, Peter, and then we can all come to the table," Trish said loudly enough for all to hear.

After Peter prayed, the food was eagerly passed around. Once everyone had filled their plates and they had begun eating, Peter reflected on past Christmas celebrations, going right back to when Iris and Ralph were little children. Iris felt the dull ache of nostalgia as she thought of her loving mother preparing Christmas dinners. She saw that Ralph looked sad and was unusually quiet. She knew he was feeling the same pain she was.

Peter picked up on the change in mood and looked over to Milton. "Would you tell us what some of your Christmas celebrations were like?"

Milton cleared his mouth while slowly formulating his thoughts. "Well, when I was growing up, we didn't make a lot of Christmas, not in a spiritual way at least. I can remember receiving gifts that I thought came from Santa Claus. We always had a Christmas tree and had a few decorations around, like Santa's reindeer that we hung on the tree. I remember dad buying me things like skates and hockey equipment that I had little interest in. Dad never made much of Christmas. It was Mom who fussed about it. Neither of my parents said much about the true significance of Christmas, especially Mother who prided herself of being an atheist."

For the rest of the meal, Milton, Trish, and the Martens talked about each of the different ways they had enjoyed the Christmas season as children.

As was Peter's custom on these occasions, he suggested everyone help clear the table, put away the food, and wash the dishes. Then with freshly brewed coffee served, everyone could retire to the living room. Iris, Ralph, and Trish laughed, as they were only too aware that Peter had in mind to discuss some serious matters. The best way to accomplish that was to have everyone in the living room.

When all were settled, Trish said very seriously, "Well, Peter, parliament is in session. What matters of business do you want to bring forward?"

Peter laughed and his neck and cheeks flushed. "You're making fun of me, my love. I only wanted to ask more questions, maybe some that are a little more serious."

"Yeah, we guessed it, Dad." Ralph laughed heartily.

When the laughing settled, Peter looked at Iris and Milton and asked, "I'm interested in knowing both of your educational plans. Will both of you be able to do all your specialty training in Edmonton?"

"I could," Iris said, "but Milton can't." She looked over to Milton. "Do you want to answer that?"

"Iris is right. There's no training program in our paediatric department beyond the first two years. If I want to continue, I'll have to find another teaching hospital that has a four-year program. Toronto's Hospital for Sick Children has a well-recognized program. I've applied to start there next July."

Trish groaned. Everyone else was quiet trying to process this disheartening news. Eventually Peter asked, "Can you arrange a continuation of your haematology training in Toronto, Iris?"

"I'm quite sure I can. I've applied to nearby hospitals like Toronto General and Mount Sinai. I've been told my chances are good."

After a few more questions related to living in Toronto, Milton turned to Ralph and asked him what he had in mind to do once he obtained his Masters in Theology.

"I haven't planned that far. I suspect I could find a job as a pastor, but I really think my talents are more in the area of teaching. I'd like to eventually teach in a seminary somewhere. I've no idea where, though."

"While you're pursuing your theology dreams, Ralph, have you left any time to pursue a pretty damsel?" asked Iris with a hint of a smile.

"They're probably pursuing Ralph and he can't make up his mind," Trish offered.

"Okay, you romance speculators, can't you leave me to my plan? I need to get my MA degree and *then* I'll have a look around to see what's out there."

"Life doesn't always work that way, son," Peter said with a broad smile. "When the right girl comes along, you won't be able to wait two weeks to get married, let alone two years."

"To tell you the truth, I've been eyeing several real nice girls, but I haven't felt the go-ahead for any one girl. So you guys will have to exercise patience just as I have to," Ralph said with finality.

Everyone was quiet for a few moments and then Ralph turned slowly toward Milton and said, "So that I can better assess whether it's safe for me to seek marriage, I'd like to ask Milton and Iris how their marriage is going."

"It's going fine. We can recommend marriage as an institution for Ralph, can't we, Milt?" Iris had a mischievous grin.

"That's not very forthcoming," Ralph said. "Let me rephrase the question. How have your sexual expectations been fulfilled so far?"

Peter and Trish's mouths dropped open and their eyes nearly popped out. Peter gasped, "Ralph! That's not a fair question to ask out in the open like this." He looked at Iris and then to Milton. "You don't need to answer that."

"I highly suspect that this question has been uppermost on everyone's mind ever since the Saunders arrived today," Ralph argued.

Iris started laughing and Milton quickly held up a hand and said, "I'll be happy to answer that question." Iris looked at Milton with a knowing smile and nodded.

"Firstly," started Milton, flushing, "I want to be sure Ralph is aware of my having been homosexual."

"Yeah, I've been aware of that background, Milton." Ralph nodded.

"Good. Then let me preface my answer by saying that I've felt God has, with the aid of some wonderful people in my church, helped me move away from that state toward heterosexuality. This has taken years of hard slogging for me. I never was sure how far this process had occurred and that's why I was dragging my feet so long with Iris. Eventually, however, I felt God telling me to go ahead." Milton looked around as if to gain some courage. Trish smiled and nodded.

Milton, feeling free to proceed, said, "I admit to having had periods of anxiety about future intimate relations, but Iris continued to be very accepting and encouraging. I don't need to get too explicit here, except to say that our intimate times together have been delightful and fulfilling and we are full of hope for the future."

By this time, everyone in the room was crying, including Milton. He still managed to add, "For Iris and me, this long tough road toward our marriage has been an example of God's patience, his love, and his power to heal."

"God will use your story to help many others, I'm sure," Peter said after blowing his nose.

"Well, if it's going to be that much trouble to get married, maybe I'll do without," Ralph said, snuffling his nose and grinning. Ralph got up, went over to the couple, pulled them up and hugged each one. "I'm so proud of you both."

"So are we," agreed Trish and Peter.

Iris and Milton smiled at their family and then shared a knowing look, realizing they had a wonderful life ahead full of, and surrounded by, love.

Read More About the Marten Family in
Creation Wars by Victor J. Ratzlaff
978-1-77069-528-3

The principal's careful planning and ambition has powered a small prairie Christian school to become a bastion of 'true Scriptural science'. But Peter, the school's talented and popular science teacher, struggles with the school's belief about the age of the earth. When Peter is compelled to come clean, and his 16-year-old daughter, Iris, discloses her Darwinian beliefs right in class, shock waves hurtle through his Grade Eleven class and beyond.

When a resourceful and gifted new librarian comes to head the town library, Iris seeks her out to find answers not available in the school library. Peter, also seeking answers as he feels his faith crumbling, is drawn to this kind and attractive woman. However, she is Catholic.

As powerful 'Scriptural science' and anti-Catholic forces build in the community, will Peter and his family be crushed spiritually and forced to leave? Will the community be swallowed up in hate? Will Peter find love again after the tragic death of his wife?

CPSIA information can be obtained at www.ICGtesting.com
Printed in the USA
LVOW08s0106100914

403338LV00014BA/394/P

9 781486 60472